Plague

KARI NICHOLS

Plague

Copyright © 2018 by Kari Nichols

All rights reserved

First Edition

ISBN: 978-0-9906123-6-0   (MOBI)
ISBN: 978-0-9906123-8-4   (Paperback)

Edited by Melissa Harlow

Proofread by Traci Craft (http://www.craftreads.com)

Cover design by Kari Nichols

Author photograph by Cottonwood Studios (http://www.cottonwoodstudiosworldwide.com)

Signet design by Nadine Pau (http://nadinepau-stock.deviantart.com/)

Title font by Tomasz Skowronski

Name/Chapter font by K-Type

Handwriting font (First) by David Kerkhoff

Handwriting font (Second) by Colin Kahn

Handwriting font (Third) by Birdesign

For more information about Kari Nichols, please visit:

www.KariNichols.com

Dedicated to those who create.

Never stop dreaming. Never stop pushing the limits.

Keep filling the world with the art, literature, and music

that only you can make.

"DEATH MUST BE SO BEAUTIFUL.

TO LIE IN THE SOFT BROWN EARTH, WITH THE GRASSES WAVING
ABOVE ONE'S HEAD, AND LISTEN TO SILENCE.

TO HAVE NO YESTERDAY, AND NO TO-MORROW. TO FORGET TIME,
TO FORGET LIFE, TO BE AT PEACE."

—OSCAR WILDE, THE CANTERVILLE GHOST

ONE

AHUZZAN'S EYES popped open, and he tried to inhale a deep breath. But there was little air to be found. The darkness that surrounded him was blacker than night. Panic filled his mind.

Is this a tomb? Am I buried beneath the earth? This enclosure presses too closely. I do not remember being in such a place, he thought frantically, trying to push at the substance which restrained him from movement.

He had not been confined before in any fashion. For he was Ahuzzan—the great leader of soldiers. He could not be defeated—he won every battle of which he was leader. His reputation for swift and deadly retaliation kept his enemies at bay and his allies in the palm of his hand. *This cannot be imprisonment,* he decided. *None would risk my wrath. Where am I?* he wondered again as he tried to move his limbs more vigorously. He could not tell which direction was up and which was down. His body was in an immovable state.

He calmed his racing mind and pounding heart for a moment, pressing his eyes shut and focusing solely on his weight distribution. When he realized he was lying face down, his determination faltered. It would be more difficult to maneuver from his position if he first had to turn over.

He began to work his arms, legs and waist a little at a time, doing everything in his power to take short breaths. He would run out of air soon. Whatever he was surrounded by was clingy and soft—but there were also fragments of hard, staff-like objects mixed with the gooey matter. He kicked his feet forcefully away from his torso, and everything crumbled, dry and dusty, where they touched. He did not let his mind concentrate on the confusing blend of the surrounding elements. He only focused on a plan to escape his confinement.

The materials around him shifted as he kicked, allowing his arms a little movement. He did his best to clear the area around his face, but the weight of the objects pressing down on his back was substantial. He knew he must be buried deep in the earth. Every motion was labored, the ground crumbling around him wherever he made space. After a tiresome battle against the earth, his body was finally on its back. He needed to begin his climb to the surface. *How did I come to be here?* he worried, not understanding what led to a complete memory lapse of the events leading to a burial.

He pushed his legs upward hard, feeling the surrounding substances give way at his forceful movements. As the ground at his feet moved, he used his hands and torso to move the earth above his head into the area his feet had cleared. After several attempts, he was able to sit up. He coughed and a cloud of dust exploded from him. He squeezed his eyes shut more tightly, holding his breath until the dust settled a little. But his effort mattered little; with every breath he inhaled, more dust entered his lungs. He thrust his body upward, pulling his feet beneath him, and though it was painful to stand on… whatever he was standing on… he used the same earth-clearing technique to push the dirt around his body and pull himself closer to the surface—closer to the fresh air his lungs craved more and more every second. He moved one lump of material from over his head, and when he breathed in, his mind registered the stench that surrounded him. It smelled like the aftermath of a battle. It smelled like death.

Was I on the battlefield? Has someone thrown me in with the dead? His mind protested as his body worked tirelessly to free itself from what he now recognized as a trench dug for the bodies of the deceased.

The decaying flesh and entrails of the dead around him made up the tacky, soft earth he had pushed aside. The fragmented sticks were bones. He swallowed the bile that rose in his throat, threatening to add to the stench of his surroundings.

More forcefully, he commanded his tired limbs. They struggled urgently. His hands grabbed at the putrid flesh of the decaying bodies that kept him underground. Now that he understood what blocked his escape, he felt skin and muscle slide from the bones as he pushed against them with his shaking hands. The weight and effort lessened the farther he pushed upward.

He risked opening his eyes for a moment after he cleared a small space over his face. The faintest glow of light seeped through a space above, and it was enough to make him move with even more ferocity.

He shut his eyes tightly again and refused to think about the bodies around him. As he ascended higher, the bodies became less gooey. They felt more like the crumbling bark of a tree. He felt a glimmer of hope—he was close to the surface where the maggots and carrion-eaters had already picked the bodies clean. He felt like he could lose consciousness at any moment—he was starving for a bite food, and his mouth begged for just one drop of water.

He opened his eyes again and saw light coming in from multiple locations. He was almost there. Almost to the surface. He would emerge with just a few more pulls from his arms and pushes from his legs.

He could feel freedom in his grasp, but his breaths became more labored with each effort. The air around him was dusty with the cracking remains of the deceased. He coughed after each breath, which caused him to inhale more dust. Hope was slipping from his grasp as he felt his mind begin to darken once more.

He bent his knees as much as he could, and his feet searched to find purchase on anything solid. He thrust one last time with all his might, his hands plunging up toward the sun above.

Stay awake, he begged his failing mind. *Just for a few more seconds*, as he coughed too hard and sucked in too much dust. *Stay...*

Priest sat up in bed, his eyes searching for the light he always kept on beside his bed. He breathed in the fresh air greedily. He had dreamed that dream too many times. He had awoken in terror for far too long.

"Enough," he whispered wearily. "Please. I have had enough."

TWO

Castello San Romolo, Present Day

PRIEST LET his legs fall over the side of the bed. He didn't want to think about the previous week's events. He couldn't believe his beloved Elias was dead. Samuel's death had not bothered him so much—his youngest son had always been a thorn in his side. Samuel had almost given away the identity and secrets of the Family many times over. He was inept at finishing a task by himself—one of his brothers or nephews usually needed to step in to rescue him from imminent failure. And Samuel was the reason... *No!* Priest scolded himself. He could not allow ancient sentiment or resentment to creep in at a time like this. There were present, more pressing issues that needed dealing with.

He stood and stretched his stiff muscles. No matter how long he slept, he never felt fully rested. He could not remember the last time in his life when sleep came easily and he awoke feeling refreshed—or it might have been more accurate to say he didn't allow himself to think back that far. *It was a different life. A different place. And I felt joy and happiness for a fleeting moment. But that was long ago.* He felt his memories forcing their way into his thoughts once more as he walked mindlessly to open the large, east-facing window, allowing the cool autumn air to wash through the room. The sun was too high in the sky—his nightmares had lasted longer in the night than usual.

The time draws closer. I can feel it in my chest. I am almost finished, he thought as he breathed in the breeze that swept into the room. *Only a little longer until I am free.*

THREE

MATTIA LAY silently beside his fiancée as she slept. Lissie had taken the trauma of the previous week's events quite well considering she had watched her fiancé kill one of his uncles as another lay dying in front of her. She had been told Mattia was finally out of this kind of life, yet Priest had managed to find a way to bring him right back into the middle of his schemes.

Mattia, on the other hand, had not been handling the events so well. His dreams were wracked with nightmares of Samuel dying in his arms as Elias bled to death on the ground beside them. He woke several times a night to the memory of Lissie's scream. The blood that coursed through his veins beat so loudly that when he woke, he could not hear whether Lissie was breathing or not. Not wanting to wake her, he would gently place his fingers on her wrist to feel for her pulse, sighing in relief as he attempted to calm his pulse and fall back to sleep.

He had awoken four times this particular night, and when the sun began to crest over the rolling Tuscan hills, Mattia dressed and headed down the stairs quietly, hoping to grab some breakfast before the rest of the Family woke for the day. He wanted a moment to himself before the funeral that afternoon.

"Nice of you to join us, Mattia," he heard his father say as he stepped into the kitchen. Mattia stopped in his tracks and looked up. Standing around the room were his father Thomas, his brothers, Antonio and Marcus, and his Uncle Sergius, Uncle Felix, and Uncle Gregorius. Mattia froze in place when he saw Gregorius—it was Gregorius's twin brother, Elias, who had been killed by Mattia a week earlier. He had only seen Gregorius once in the past week since he and Lissie had returned to the Family castle—and that was to ask forgiveness for killing the twin brother. Mattia still didn't know how he felt about asking forgiveness for that kill—it was Elias who killed Samuel (and who was trying to kill Mattia and Lissie before Samuel's timely intervention). But Mattia kept telling himself that Elias was simply following orders. And the rest of the family had assured Mattia that Elias was a wreck before he left to obey the order. Mattia looked down at the floor, unsure of where else to look. The tension in the room felt like a rubber band pulled too tight.

"Did I miss the memo that there was a meeting this morning?" Mattia asked under his breath, glancing up at his father.

"No. I believe we were all experiencing the same restlessness in the night. Few of us have had a good night's sleep since…" Thomas's voice faded. Gregorius sucked in a sharp breath and let it out slowly. Sergius, who was standing closest to him, clasped Gregorius on the shoulder as the twin fought back tears. Mattia sensed only grief from Gregorius, and he felt his body relax slightly.

"We were discussing the funeral," Thomas began again, clearing the emotion from his throat. "Gregorius will speak for Elias—that was clear to us all—but we've gone back and forth on who should speak for Samuel. We think we've come to a satisfactory decision, but we still would like your vote."

Mattia leaned back against the door post, putting his left hand in his pocket and rubbing the back of his neck with his right. He had known all along that either his father or Uncle Sergius would speak for Samuel at the funeral, but he didn't want to have to cast a vote in either man's favor. *Please don't ask me whom I would prefer.*

"We want to make sure you approve of our choice," Sergius interjected. He had been acting as leader to the entire household for the past week, keeping his emotions hidden and his door open to any who might need something. He joked with Felix, sat quietly with Gregorius, and avoided eye contact with Mattia. Mattia had felt the pity in so many of the family's gazes, and it put his stomach ill at ease. Sergius cleared his throat to reclaim Mattia's attention. "Before we force you into doing something that will make you uncomfortable."

Mattia's hand dropped from the back of his neck.

"Obviously, we knew Samuel far longer than you, so Sergius or I would be the obvious choices to honor our little brother," Thomas began. Mattia felt sweat bead on his back and forehead as his father spoke. "But we think you might have known him the best. He was open and candid with you in a way that he never could be with the rest of us. I think you gave him the opportunity to excel where the rest of us expected him to fail," Thomas added with guilt thick in his voice.

"He found you by hacking into the car rental agency's server," Antonio said with his eyebrows raised. "We didn't even think he knew how to restart his cell phone."

Mattia choked down a moan of frustration while his brothers and uncles shared a short chuckle in a rare tension-easing moment. He was glad for his family to feel any break from their grief, but when it was at Samuel's expense, he found he couldn't bear the jokes. He felt a tear form in the corner of his eye and quickly wiped it away, unwilling to let the others see his emotions—there would be plenty of time for that at the funeral.

"If you truly believe I should speak for Samuel, I will do my best to honor his memory," Mattia agreed after a short pause. Everyone's shoulders seemed to relax at his agreement—apparently they all felt he should give the speech—and Mattia's nerves kicked into high gear.

"I'm going to grab some bread and get out of here. I guess I'm preparing a eulogy for this afternoon," he sighed, rummaging quickly through a basket of rolls his mother had prepared for the Family.

"Don't you think it's right that we should let him come to his sons' funeral?" Uncle Felix whispered to no one in particular, slowly shaking his head in disapproval of the decision to keep Priest away from the mourning rituals.

"The man responsible for their deaths?" Mattia turned, yelling at his shocked uncle. Everyone was stunned by the outburst. "I hardly think today is the day for our Family to interact with our esteemed psychopathic-killer of a leader. Let us deal with our grief as a family—and if anyone is unclear on my meaning, I mean to say that Priest is not, and should no longer be considered, a part of this Family. We can deal with him when it's time for his trial. Today is for grieving those dead by his hand."

He looked at each of the men in the room, but no one contradicted his outburst.

"If anyone sees Lissie when she wakes up, tell her I'm roaming the vineyards, preparing a eulogy," he muttered as left. When he woke up that morning, he had thought the day couldn't get more difficult to bear. He sighed. *I will honor you, Samuel. That much I can promise.*

FOUR

CATERINA METHODICALLY wove the ends of Thomas's tie together, arranging the perfect knot at just the right length on her first try. No matter how many times he tied one, Thomas still couldn't quite get it right without her help. She tried not to show any emotion to her grief-stricken husband. His eyes had been rimmed with red since that horrendous night—and were often glistening with moisture that his anger had somehow managed to hold at bay. But she knew once Samuel was laid in the ground, that anger would rain down upon the castle.

She had carefully concealed her emotions after the day of the phone call. Her tension had been so tightly wound before that call, everything came gushing out in one massive flow. As selfish as it sounded, relief had been her first instinct—Mattia and Lissie were alive. But in the next second, the realization of Samuel's and Elias's deaths had slammed into her like a horse galloping at full speed. She had cried that entire evening while the house waited for Mattia and Lissie to arrive from Cyprus with the bodies. Thankfully, Felix had maintained a reliable connection with a contact in Beirut who had offered to fly Mattia, Lissie and the two bodies from Cyprus to Florence in his private jet. From the moment of the incident until their arrival home, only twelve hours had elapsed—but those hours felt more like days or weeks than mere hours.

"Will you speak today?" Caterina asked Thomas as she stepped back and observed her olive-skinned husband with his wavy brown hair. She loved that it always looked slightly disheveled. Every time she looked at him, she still felt the same admiration for the man who had rescued her from her seclusion in Kutsamil. The man who had killed for her as they crossed the Atlantic Ocean. The man who still stole her breath and her heart each time they kissed. But she wondered if he would recover from the loss of his brothers. The look on his face was exhaustion and grief, and she hoped this funeral might provide a sliver of relief from the pain he had experienced.

"Saint will open and close, Gregorius will speak for Elias, and Mattia will speak for Samuel. We've decided to limit the speakers to just those three, but at the feast afterward, we'll all share our favorite memories," Thomas's voice faded to a choked whisper by his last word, and Caterina knew he would not be able to speak again until the funeral was over. She had seen the determined look in her husband's eyes many times over the course of their marriage—it warned her not to press him further. The explosion of emotions when he was pushed too hard often ended with her walking away with hurt feelings and him wrestling with guilt-ridden sleeplessness over his verbal tirade. Of course, Thomas never meant to erupt, but she had learned the signs long ago—she only pushed him past his boiling point if she wanted a fight.

Caterina wasn't surprised that Mattia had been chosen to speak for Samuel, but she worried about her youngest son. He had killed Elias in self-defense. He had held Samuel helplessly in his arms while the life drained from his veins. *How on earth will he come back from this?* She worried.

"I'm going to check on Lissie to see if she needs anything," Caterina said as Thomas nodded wordlessly.

Thomas was no fool. If he'd heard a single word she'd said, he would have known she was going to check on Mattia, but his thoughts were elsewhere. She shut the door quietly and walked down the hall to Mattia and Lissie's room. She knocked gently, hoping she wasn't disturbing them, and only waited a few seconds before Lissie answered the door. Lissie enveloped Caterina in a tight hug, holding her for a few moments before slipping into the hallway and shutting the door behind her.

"Do you need anything?" Caterina asked, squeezing her future daughter-in-law's hand. Lissie shook her head, but a few tears escaped her lovely blue eyes.

"Is Mattia ready?"

Lissie nodded with a tight, forced smile and furrowed brow.

"All right. Come get me if you need anything at all," Caterina spoke softly, turning back to her own room again.

Caterina had spent the week doing her best to care for the entire Family. She had grieved heavily in those first twelve hours, but as soon as she had seen her son's expression when he walked through the castle door, her motherly instincts had taken over. She had immediately pushed her emotions to the back of her mind to care for Mattia and Lissie—she knew she would have time to deal with her own emotions once everyone else was cared for. She and some of the other family members had cooked massive amounts of food to be reheated whenever someone decided they were hungry. Very few of the Family had dined together over the course of the week; others had not eaten at all. She thought Gregorius had lost between two and three kilos, maybe more. Others had practically lived in the kitchen, barely taking a moment to allow their food to digest before eating more. She snorted a laugh as she remembered the way Claudius had inhaled a stew she prepared which should have yielded eight servings. He had sat for three hours, alone at the table, staring at the grain of the wood on the ancient table, eating bite after bite. "That was delicious," he remarked with a look of contentment when he finally left the room. At least Claudius wasn't moping around sullenly or joking around as if nothing had happened. The emotions of the Family varied so wildly from man to man, it was a comfort to have a few people simply existing in the "emotional middle".

Caterina had arranged the catering for the post-funeral feast as well. The caterers had been instructed to meet her just before the funeral to hand off the food and immediately leave—no outsiders needed to witness the mass gathering of the immortal Family. The rest of her time was spent comforting her husband, brothers-in-law, sons and daughter-to-be in whatever way they each needed. She felt as if most of her attempts had been futile, but Lissie, at least, was receptive to her efforts.

Caterina passed the door to her room—Thomas didn't need her hovering over him—and headed to the dining hall to make sure everything was set up for the feast. The house was nearly silent—a rarity even when most of the Family were away from the castle. But with over one hundred individuals swarming the grounds for the occasion, Caterina could feel the heaviness that hung over the home like a drenched blanket.

Her phone rang, announcing the caterers had arrived... which meant the funeral would start in a few moments.

Holy mother, pray for this Family as we begin to mourn our losses. And that we will have the wisdom to decide the fate of the one responsible.

She opened the back door and let the caterers bring in their trays and dishes full of food. Once she thanked them and ushered them back to their vehicles, the chapel bell rang. She squeezed her eyes shut and breathed deeply. It was time for the funeral.

FIVE

PRIEST LISTENED to the bell ring. He stood to face the mirror on the wall in his study, his ancient eyes reflecting the pain he felt over the loss of Elias. The face staring back at him was only thirty-one years of age, despite the thousands of years his body had survived. But he knew the truth. His mind had taken a beating over time that had left him weary in a way his physical form would never reflect.

The funeral was about to begin, and he alone was omitted from the guest list. Rage swirled in his chest, begging to escape. *Elias, one of my favorite sons, is dead... and his brothers will not grant me the right to mourn him.* If all had gone according to plan, Mattia and Lissie would be dead—no one else. But as usual, Thomas and Samuel interfered where they ought not, and because of them, his obedient, brilliant boy was gone forever. Priest could not mourn Samuel's death. From the moment Samuel had entered the world, he had been a blight on Priest's life, and Samuel had stayed the course right up until his death.

Priest sat down in his armchair and rested his head against the high back. He had barely found slumber since Elias was killed. But in his delirious state, somewhere between conscious and dreaming, he allowed himself to remember his life—the life he had worked so hard to forget.

Priest had only twenty-two short years with the woman who made him whole—the one that had given him a moment of peace in his otherwise horrible life. She was the only person who had ever fully owned his heart, and with her death, his heart had died too. Once she was gone, he was incapable of truly loving another. Incapable of living a single day without feeling empty. Incapable of forgiving the one responsible for his loss.

Six

The Middle East, 1050 B.C.E.

AHUZZAN STUMBLED into the city, pressing onward despite his intense hunger and failing legs. Every few moments he paused to catch his breath, his lungs still heaving with the exertion of his climb through the sea of corpses.

The city was silent—far too quiet for the middle of the day. Ahuzzan peered around, a sense of panic rising in his chest.

"You! Murderer!" a woman's voice called from the doorway of a small home. "You did this. You killed my husband and children. And now you dare to haunt us? Leave this place!" she screamed.

Ahuzzan stared as the woman screeched furiously. He did not understand her bitter cries. *What could she mean?* he wondered. He continued farther into the city, noticing more terrified yet angry glares from eyes that tentatively peeked out from open windows and doors. Only a few people walked through the streets of the once-bustling city. A boy ran from him, pleading to the gods to save him from the demon.

Once Ahuzzan reached the center of the city, four men came out to meet him, their weapons drawn.

"What is the meaning of this?" Ahuzzan stood straight despite the protests from his feeble body. Even though he was dehydrated and malnourished, he did not want to appear weak to the soldiers.

"You may not stay here, demon. You brought sickness upon our homes. You killed thousands upon thousands with your actions. You lay dead, and we put you in the grave and covered you with mud and the bodies of those you murdered in order to contain your spirit. Three weeks we sacrificed our choicest fowl and beasts to the gods to keep you in the earth, but we now see that your madness cannot be contained. Be gone from here. Do not haunt us any longer.

The living want to mourn in peace. Leave!" the man yelled. Ahuzzan recognized the man as a second in command from one of the other battalions of soldiers.

"How dare you command me!" Ahuzzan rebutted, now angered by the audacity of the lower-ranked soldier.

"I am the chief commander of the army. Your actions killed all others who outranked me," the man sneered.

"You lie. I killed no one," Ahuzzan challenged.

"You may not have brought the sword to their throats, but your actions led to our city's destruction. You are not welcome here, spirit," the chief commander announced with finality.

Ahuzzan had no time for the foolish man's words. He turned down the lane and headed to his home, hoping to recover his strength in the company of his wife and children.

"Leave, spirit!" the man called after him.

"No," Ahuzzan spat vehemently. The soldiers exchanged glances with one another but didn't challenge him as he walked away. He felt their presence following from a distance, watching as he moved through the streets, but they didn't speak to him again.

When he reached his home, it was empty. He called to his family, searching all the familiar places he knew they frequented. He walked to the home of his mother and sister, praying to the gods his wife and children were there. But when he walked in, only his younger sister was home.

"Where is my wife? Where are my children?" he asked, running toward Fadila. She looked up at him in terror.

"You were dead. Everyone is dead," she choked out in a whisper.

"Fadila," he began, grasping her shoulders to shake her out of her delusions. "Where are my wife and children? Where is our mother? Where is our brother?"

"Everyone is dead," she answered more forcefully.

"No. You are mistaken," he refused to believe her.

"You have been dead for three weeks. I watched them throw your lifeless body into the bottom of the grave. And a few days later, people all over the city began falling ill. Your family were among the first to die. Mother took care of them for as long as she could, but she died soon after them—and our brother a few days later. I stayed far from them, and I never fell into sickness. But everyone said it was your fault. You brought this into our city. You angered the gods," she accused.

Ahuzzan fell to his knees, bracing himself with his hands to keep from collapsing to the floor. No, he reeled as the memory of his actions came rushing back. He finally recalled that which his sister spoke of. He thought it had been a nightmare. A horrible nightmare. *It was real. What they say is true. I brought this upon our city.* He vomited on the floor of the home while his sister backed away, frightened.

"Get out of this house," she hissed. "I did not survive the sickness only to be killed by the demon who created it."

He crawled away, unable to rise from his hands and knees, feeling the depths of the shame which he brought upon his household and his father's household. *Mother must have died ashamed to have me as a son,* he thought as another round of vomit poured out of his throat. There was nothing to throw up but spit and dust, but he heaved nonetheless.

He finally forced himself to his feet, making his way to the well closest to his parent's home. Only a few people were there. He could not remember a time when he had seen fewer than twenty people gathering at that particular well.

"I need water," he gasped, looking from one scared face to another. "Please," he begged, his body sagging from the lack of sustenance.

One woman threw a bucket at his feet and left. Everyone else quietly slipped away once Ahuzzan leaned down to pick up the bucket. *You did this,* he scolded himself. *You deserve death.* He gathered water for himself and drank deeply, feeling the pangs of hunger in his stomach diminish as it filled with the water he was so desperate for.

He searched the ground around the well for the edible plants he often ate on the battlefield—they were not exactly appetizing, but they would be sufficient in providing nourishment to his starving body. As his stomach filled with food and water, realization flooded his mind.

My wife and children are dead. My mother and brother are dead. My sister hates me. All because of my own actions. I am unwelcome in my own land. This entire nation will surely know what I have done. He sat in silence, wondering how to proceed. *You will be despised by all men,* he heard a voice echo in a distant memory. Chills ran up his spine—intense fear gripping his mind. He was bereft of options.

He looked around the well for a stone with a sharp edge and found one easily. He sank to his knees, squeezing the rock firmly as it cut into his palm. Without pondering over the matter for too long, he cut the skin on both of his wrists and slashed the tender part of his neck as blood began pouring from his body. Hot wind rushed around him, kicking up dust as he squinted to keep it from his eyes. But in the wind, he heard a faint voice whisper *"not yet."*

He searched for the person who spoke, but not a soul was nearby. The wind died down as quickly as it had stirred, and he hoped he would soon lose consciousness. But when he looked down, his skin was closed and no blood pooled around his knees where it had a moment before. He blinked, wondering if he was in shock. But when he reached up to feel his neck, there was not even a hint of the wound he had opened there before.

Not until the appointed time, he shivered at the memory. He screamed, kicking the dust on the ground and throwing whatever he could find to throw. The water bucket shattered against the side of the well, and the rock he had used to cut open his skin was flung as far as he could hurl it. After a few minutes of blind rage, the haze began to lift from his mind. He sat down against the well, facing the village where he had lived most of his life.

Bitterness welled inside him—at the death of his loved ones, at his inability to take his own life, and at the betrayal of his people. They were forcing him to leave his home—after a lifetime of service to his nation. *But,* he realized with a smirk, *my people are at war with many neighboring nations—and there is no longer a reason for me to stand beside my own.* He would travel to the surrounding tribes and help them defeat the people he had lived to protect. *I must go east,* he decided, hoping he might earn a living as a mercenary.

SEVEN

IN THE FOLLOWING YEAR, Ahuzzan was rejected by dozens of tribes. He was a foreigner whom most suspected was a spy, and more often than not, he had to fight his way out of a city and hide for a few days to avoid being attacked by those from whom he sought employment.

You will be despised by all men, he heard again as he was rejected by yet another tribe. Ahuzzan rubbed his temples roughly, trying to forget the words. *If I cannot wage war against my own people, I will go to Assyria. The empire with many cultures and a renowned army. The ever-expanding empire that wages countless wars on its neighbors. Surely they will find no fault with my nationality as long as I serve their king on the battlefield.*

He stole a horse from a stable in the city and rode in the direction of the Assyrian borders. It was not difficult for him to find an encampment of their army, and he was inducted quickly, and without much suspicion into their ranks. They were so varied in origin and homeland due to thousands of years of conquests, that it seemed normal for a foreigner to want to join the Assyrians. Ahuzzan was made a lowly soldier for his first two years of service, but his superiors took note of his abilities in battle, and he quickly rose to prominence as a commander. In only five years, he was the leader of one hundred Assyrian soldiers. He could not help feeling annoyed that it had taken him so long to secure a command post—in his own army, it had taken him far less time at a much younger age. But no matter how famous he became within the Assyrian ranks for both his skills as a fighter and his abilities as a leader, neither his men nor his peers wanted to spend time with him—the strange outsider. Ahuzzan had always maintained a level of camaraderie with his soldiers, but now, he could see his men respected his decisions for no other reason except he was their superior. He was utterly alone despite being surrounded by thousands of soldiers. A year earlier, he had felt like he might be able to thrive in the distance between himself and the rest of the world. But when he looked at the forever that stretched before him, he did not know how he could survive that way.

After twenty years at war, his commanding officer finally noted Ahuzzan's youthfulness. Ahuzzan did his best to age his face, but in the heat of battle, it was difficult to keep up appearances.

"We must exchange your post with that of another commander. The men will start to notice soon… if they haven't already," the commander said nonchalantly.

"You do not fear my… condition?" Ahuzzan asked, confused by the man's indifference.

"You are an excellent leader and strategist. You serve our king well. Nothing else matters," the man responded, barely glancing up from the map of the Assyrian territories. "I think we'll move you north. I'll send a courier to the commander there to give him notice of the change. And of your… youth."

"Thank you, sir," Ahuzzan mumbled, his head reeling from the conversation.

EIGHT

"YOU HAVE SERVED our nation well, Ahuzzan. You, our most notorious and fearsome warrior for nearly two centuries, will be honored with a position in my royal guard. I am having you removed from the battlefield to serve as a guardian in my palace alongside the Lamassu—with whom I am certain you are already acquainted," King Ashurnasirpal II said with a pointed look.

Ahuzzan did not respond in word or expression. No. He did not know of these Lamassu. Nor did he feel honored at being removed from the one place he felt useful in the world. The battlefield was his only home—the only place where men accepted and respected him. He felt like spitting, but the king was attempting to award him a great honor, so he remained silent, hoping his emotions were not visible to the king.

"I am certain *they* will be pleased to see *you*. And in an effort to lavish you with further glory, I have chosen a ceremonial name that will suit your new position. When you arrive at my court, you shall be known as Nirgali. My wisemen searched the stars for the answers to your past, and they assured me you must be the son of Nirgali. I will not push you for confirmation of our findings, but I must ask if the name is satisfactory to you," King Ashurnasirpal pressed.

Ahuzzan felt ill the moment he heard the name. This was surely punishment—a kick in his side to remind him of the destruction that followed his every step. He had studied the Assyrian religion in depth—though he refused to worship any form of deity. Nirgali was the Assyrian god of war and plague. Ahuzzan was grateful for the summer heat that scorched all the Assyrian lands. Without the heat, the perspiration that covered his entire body upon hearing his new name would have been too obvious. He swallowed hard.

"Your wisemen are very wise," Ahuzzan responded cryptically, accepting the new title with as much grace as he could muster. The king seemed thrilled that Ahuzzan had "admitted" his parentage.

"Once my palace is ready in our new capital, I will send for you."

Ahuzzan watched the king leave without knowing how to feel. *I will no longer be called by my given name? I suppose my time as Ahuzzan has lasted long enough, but how strange it will feel to be called Nirgali.* He cringed at the word. *The child of the god of war and plague.* He blew out a derisive snort. *Too fitting.*

NINE

Byblos, Phoenicia, 877 B.C.E.

SIX MONTHS PASSED before Ahuzzan heard from the king. The time sped by too quickly—he felt the pressure of the coming separation from the battlefield each day he waited, never knowing when the king's envoy would arrive to take him away from the place he felt most comfortable.

"Nirgali," the gaudily-adorned messenger stated with a reverent bow. "Our great king's palace is ready, and he requests the arrival of his newest protector," the man reported, avoiding eye contact with Ahuzzan.

Ahuzzan studied the messenger for a moment, trying to guess what might be in store for him at the king's new palace. The messenger wore fine silks of blues and greens trimmed with gold threads. His headpiece was adorned with gems, and his beard was curled into a distinct pattern that looked more like a painting than reality. Ahuzzan felt sweat bead on his forehead. Were he to be forced to wear such a horrible costume, he would flee the palace—hoping to be caught and killed. He sighed, knowing death would not come so conveniently.

He had tried to take his life on more than one occasion—a vial of poison, an opening given to an opponent on the battlefield, a dagger thrust into his side by his own hand. But no matter how he searched, death had remained hidden from him. And he quickly understood that his end would not come easily. Immortality was his curse, and death would not soon spread its arms to welcome him.

"If you will gather your belongings, I will wait here for you," the messenger's words shook Ahuzzan from his dark thoughts.

"I will only be a moment," he replied, retreating to his tent to gather his few belongings. The tent in which he had resided for the past month of his campaign had been rather comfortable by a soldier's standards. The fabric was sturdier than his previous tent's, and the flap had clips along the edges that allowed him to keep out the winter winds. The temperature was bearable until the wind blew—which was a bit too often for his liking. He looked around the tent. *Very little to speak of,* he thought. He tried always to leave his favorite belongings behind—unwilling to cling to any fond memories of his past. Ahuzzan rolled his bedding, grabbed a fur blanket from his chair, and systematically sheathed his sword and three daggers as he did each day before heading out into the world. He knew he would need little else once he arrived at the palace, and the messenger's guards would have saddles equipped with bread and wine for the journey.

As soon as they began, Ahuzzan was convinced the trip would *seem* far longer than it would actually take. The messenger sang and told "jokes," though the humor was lost on Ahuzzan. The guards spoke of the glory of their new capital as if it was the single greatest city in the history of all the world—a city that would never fall. Ahuzzan did his best to stay silent. He had seen the great cities of the Assyrians, the Phoenicians, and the Israelites. He had burned "unassailable" temples to the ground and razed entire cities to dust. *Nothing in this world can withstand the wrath of an ambitious ruler—except maybe for me.* He chuckled to himself.

"You dare to mock the great city of our lord?" one guard stopped abruptly, challenging Ahuzzan with a glare.

"I do not mock our king or his city, only your estimation of the glory of his new capital," Ahuzzan explained, riding slowly past the offended guard.

It was not until ten days later, as the group rode into the city of Kahlu, that Ahuzzan understood the guard's indignation at Ahuzzan's flippancy. The walls of the city spanned so far to the east and the west that Ahuzzan guessed it might take two days (at least) to walk around the exterior. The walls were so high, he did not think any earthly army could successfully lay siege to them. The city was built so that no homes lay outside of the walls—no villagers milled about beyond the protection of the city guards. It was as if the place was abandoned—

except he could hear the distinct sound of a bustling city beyond the reach of his eyes. There was a great river to the west of the wall—which the guards told him had been dug out to feed the city water from the Upper Zab.

It is a canal? Surely this is a lie. Ahuzzan had not seen a river so large dug by the hands of men. But then, he had never seen a city so large with walls so monstrous. He felt he was seeing something wondrous—something that few might ever behold in a lifetime.

"It is quite a vision," he whispered. Those in his party appeared pleased with his appraisal of the city.

As their horses rode through the gates, Ahuzzan's eyes widened in surprise. They had ridden for days through barren desert—only seeing patches of vegetation by the great rivers or small oases. But his eyes beheld lush green grasses and trees, small streams flowing here and there with beautiful bridges built to cross over them. The smallest homes of the poorest villagers on the outskirts of the city held a kind of charm that made even the homes of the wealthy in Byblos pale in comparison.

He looked up to the great mound in the center of the city. A wall of alabaster white surrounded the palace that would be Ahuzzan's residence for an undetermined span of his life. He felt uncomfortable simply looking upon the walls. He was not meant for riches and glory, comfort and peace. He was meant for war and filth and nights freezing in tents while fires died in the rushing desert winds.

They passed under a set of massive doors leading to the palace, only to see flowering vineyards, orchards, and stone carvings of Assyrian gods three or four times larger than the size of a normal man. The palace was a monument to the greatness of King Ashurnasirpal II and the whole of the Assyrian empire.

After the orchards and vineyards, they rode through a second entrance that put them in a second courtyard full of manicured gardens and fruit trees. More carvings—even larger than the previous—decorated the exterior walls, and Ahuzzan gulped to rid his throat of the surprise he felt upon seeing such a city.

He could see there was another entrance to a third courtyard, but the messenger stopped and dismounted before Ahuzzan could glimpse what lay beyond the next passageway.

"Follow me," the messenger commanded without turning around. Ahuzzan and the soldiers dismounted and fell into line, following the man through a different passage and into a massive courtyard filled with hundreds of people milling about. There did not seem to be any congruency amongst the mix of people in the courtyard. There were soldiers training with swords in one corner, rows of chariots in another, royalty and dignitaries standing near the fountain in the center, and groundskeepers working in each corner. With every step, the palace seemed larger and more complex. The whole city was unlike any Ahuzzan had seen.

Surely this city will stand for all time. This is a place I would die to protect, he sat straighter at the idea. Perhaps he *could* feel at home here. Perhaps this would be a place for him to find peace at last.

TEN

Kalhu, Assyria, 878 B.C.E.

AHUZZAN WAITED nervously for the king to arrive in the courtyard right outside the palace's main entry. The guards and messenger that had ridden with him from Byblos flanked him on every side—the messenger in front and the guards to his left, right and back. He despised the feeling of being surrounded, but he could tell the formality was simply routine for the others.

One small, cloaked man—perhaps a priest—came out from the palace and beckoned they follow him through a pair of gigantic doors that were made from beautifully carved wood planks with polished gold straps bracing them from top to bottom. Upon entering the room, Ahuzzan's eyes widened at the hand-painted designs along the center of the walls. Every wall in the room was split into thirds—the bottom third was overlaid with ornately-painted stone carvings depicting the story of the king's military campaigns, the middle third was covered with intricate designs of blue, gold, red, and white, and the top third and ceiling were a solid alabaster stone to reflect the light of the hundreds of large candles throughout the room.

At the end of the room was a throne of solid gold—one that, Ahuzzan noted, was missing the king whom he was supposed to be meeting. The group stopped short of the throne beside a doorway that was flanked by two stone carvings of giant winged creatures with the heads of men and the bodies of lions.

The messenger turned and gave Ahuzzan a quick nod of dismissal, and he and his soldiers left without any further conversation.

Bizarre, Ahuzzan thought. But he had never known palace customs… maybe that was normal.

"You smell like a long journey," the cloaked man grimaced. "We will prepare you now to see our king." Ahuzzan followed the man through two sets of doors and into a smaller, more private courtyard. This one was obviously reserved for the royal family and their personal guests. He received barely a glance from the women and children, but the guards protecting them regarded him carefully.

When at last they arrived in the bathing area, the cloaked man stripped off Ahuzzan's clothing without warning and tossed them to a waiting servant. "Burn those. He won't need them again." The man looked at Ahuzzan's knives in their leather holsters for a moment before commanding he remove them as well. Ahuzzan did not want to begin his new assignment with violence, but rage was starting to seep through his skin.

"Be at peace, Nirgali. I am having new ones made for you with better materials," the man said authoritatively. Ahuzzan blinked in surprise. *Surely he did not know my thoughts,* he hoped.

"There are many gifted beings here, Nirgali. Do not allow yourself to believe you are somehow special in this palace because you have lived longer than most," the man said in response to his thoughts.

"You can read my mind?" Ahuzzan asked. To test his theory he thought one thing only—*I am not Nirgali.*

"I can read *you.* And your name *is* Nirgali. It is unwise for you to appear affronted in every instance you hear your new title used."

Ahuzzan took a tiny step away from the man.

"You need not be afraid of me. I assure you—I am harmless. I simply have a knack for understanding what others are hiding. And you may call me Khza Eil. My name is not that which was given to me at birth either, but it is still my name," he elaborated as servants poured water over Ahuzzan's naked body and began scrubbing him vigorously. By the time Khza Eil was satisfied with "Nirgali's" cleaning, his skin was bright red, and his hair and beard had been cleaned, combed, and curled. He had *never* taken such care of himself, and he cringed when Khza Eil informed him that this process was a weekly ritual for the royal guard.

"You are finally prepared to see the king. You need only your new clothing before you can meet him," Khza Eil remarked, snapping his fingers. Two eunuchs ran in holding a thin white shirt and trousers, and a white robe with blue and gold trim around all the exposed edges of the garment. The shirt and trousers were quite comfortable, despite how flimsy they appeared. The robe shut with tiny hooks that ran along the entire front, and Ahuzzan decided he could not bear to look at his reflection in the water while adorned in such a ridiculous manner. He wanted to yank his hands through his beard to put it back into its disheveled normality. But one look from Khza Eil warned him against such behavior.

"Follow me," Khza Eil requested, leading him back to the throne room along the same path. Ahuzzan kept his eyes to the ground, worried that he might catch someone ogling at his appearance and be tempted to strike out at them in anger.

When they reached the throne room, King Ashurnasirpal was waiting, and Ahuzzan took notice of the amusement on the king's face when he saw his newest royal guardian.

"You have done well, Khza Eil. I did not think it possible for Nirgali to be presented in this way," the king smiled.

"I think Nirgali will surprise us all," Khza Eil said, glancing sideways at his creation.

Ahuzzan was trying to understand the dynamic in the palace, and so far, he understood nothing. He kept his head lowered to the king and remained silent, hoping it was appropriate.

"Dear Nirgali, you show proper decorum despite your years of battlefield living. How is it you came to understand proper behaviors in the presence of royalty?" the king asked.

Ahuzzan cleared his throat and answered, "I have no prior knowledge of how one should behave around royalty. I know only that I am lowly, and that you are a king. I suppose anyone with sense might come to the same conclusion."

The king let out a guffaw and nodded. "You are right. Though I believe there are too many in the world without any measure of sense. I am glad you are here in Kalhu and that you brought your good sense along with you. Now, Khza Eil, I believe the Lamassu are waiting for our new friend to visit. If you don't mind taking care of that for me, I have some matters to discuss with the head of the planning council about next week's celebration." The king turned to the waiting men, and Khza Eil motioned for Ahuzzan to follow him out of the throne room.

"You will be a good fit here I believe," Khza Eil said with an appraising gaze. "Not many have the ability to stay silent when is needed and respond without terror when they must speak. You do not fear the king, which can be useful for members of the royal guard. You do not fear death or battle or anything so far as I can tell. What is it that you *do* fear?"

Ahuzzan sagged a bit, knowing that Khza Eil was likely asking out of respect for his mental privacy rather than out of necessity. He surely already knew the answer, but Ahuzzan would say it aloud because Khza Eil had asked —and Ahuzzan found himself wanting the mysterious man to like him. He sighed and looked up at the eerie shadows the candles were casting on the ceiling of the room. It was true there was only one thing he truly feared. He breathed the terrifying word, barely louder than a whisper.

"Life."

ELEVEN

"YOU MUST DRINK this tonic before you speak with the Lamassu," Khza Eil insisted, handing a small glass filled with a cloudy liquid over to Ahuzzan.

He took the glass, eying it suspiciously before throwing his head back and swallowing the contents in one gulp.

"You will be a fine servant indeed," Khza Eil nodded. "Stay in this room and wait. Sit if you wish. The Lamassu will come to you when they are ready."

He left Ahuzzan alone in the room. Ahuzzan was not sure what to expect from the Lamassu, but the hair on the back of his neck prickled more and more the longer he waited for them to arrive. He would be on his best behavior, regardless of what happened next. It was possible the meeting with the Lamassu was some kind of test. He reached down to make sure his daggers were at the ready, grunting in frustration as he remembered he did not have them. He was defenseless aside from his fists and feet. His hand-to-hand combat skills were sufficient, but his ability to wield swords and daggers was what made him deadly on the battlefield. He sighed at his weaponless body and hoped the meeting would only be a conversation.

He stared at a flame for several minutes, watching the way it bent and whipped about under the slightest movement of air. He did not know how long he stood there—something in the tonic he drank had made him calm, more focused. He turned to look at the stone winged creatures that guarded either side of the doorway, but he blinked and rubbed his eyes when they seemed to move. He stared as they began to vibrate—almost as if they were breaking away from their stony cages. Ahuzzan stumbled backward and sat down in a chair by the wall farthest from them, certain he was succumbing to some hallucination from the tonic. The creatures twisted away from the doorway, leaving the carved stone exactly where it had been before. But the creatures were corporeal. They moved about on their four paws, stalking through the room in a gait reminiscent of a large, predatory cat. They flexed their wings open and shut, as if stretching muscles that had been still for too long; then the wings lay flat against their sides once more. The creatures had the faces of giant men—complete with beards curled just as Ahuzzan's was.

Ahuzzan was too stunned to speak. He had noticed that the light of the candles had flickered wildly as the creatures stretched their wings, and one candle was blown out completely. *But this is a hallucination,* Ahuzzan thought, his eyebrows high, never letting his gaze leave the two creatures that looked down upon him as though he were their prey. He wished now he had his daggers. A voice in the back of his mind cautioned him to remain still and silent.

"We are Lamassu," he heard one of the creatures speak, though neither of their mouths had opened. "We are the sons of Sahim. Some call us Elioud. But we are Lamassu—they that escaped Irkalla."

Suddenly Ahuzzan found his chair had been mysteriously transported to the middle of the room as the Lamassu circled him, their feet pounding the ground with each step their enormous bodies took. *This is most certainly a hallucination. I would remember being physically moved from the corner of the room to the center,* he assured himself.

"The young king's wisemen are not so wise, we think," the other Lamassu said in a mischievous tone. "For we have met Nirgali—he guards the land from whence we escaped—and you are most certainly not his son."

"I never claimed to be his son," Ahuzzan finally spoke, his voice sounding much stronger than he thought it would.

"He has not lied, his words are true," one of the creatures muttered to the other. "But then what is he?" They continued circling, sniffing at his hair like a curious beast might sniff at an unknown object.

"He is most certainly *man*. Though he is old. Much older than he should be. He does not smell of death, but his eyes contain the secrets and shadows of one who has returned from the land of the dead," they continued to speak to each other, and Ahuzzan listened to the words, fascinated that he heard their conversation even though the Lamassu's mouths did not move.

"What are you?" they asked simultaneously, their bodies turning to face him directly, their dark eyes boring into his soul.

"Cursed with life," he answered, not knowing from whence the words came. He had not thought before answering. It had been as if the creatures made him speak that which he did not consciously know.

"Will you die?" they pressed.

"Not until the appointed time," Ahuzzan replied, again not understanding how he knew the answer.

"Will you betray the Assyrians?" they asked, their eyes becoming slits.

"Never," he spoke of his own accord.

"Then you shall have no need to see us again," they hummed as they returned to the doorway, their bodies slowly hardening as they again became one with the stone carvings.

Ahuzzan felt air return to the room, though he hadn't realized it had ever left. He looked around; the candles were all lit—even the one that had been blown out before. But as he breathed a sigh of relief that the hallucination was finished, he noticed his chair was in the center of the room, and a single paw print remained on the dusty floor.

TWELVE

"I SEE YOUR MEETING with the Lamassu went well," Khza Eil smirked as he swept into the room and stood in front of the chair where Ahuzzan still sat.

"It did?" Ahuzzan asked, unsure of the man's meaning.

"Of course! You are alive... *and* conscious. Which means a great deal," Khza Eil added with raised eyebrows.

"The tonic did make me hallucinate, but I *am* pleased I remained conscious," Ahuzzan responded without admitting to his conversation with the Lamassu. He knew the two creatures *felt* real, but he was unwilling to openly admit that anything could be capable of emerging from a stone carving to move freely amongst the living.

"You are so certain? Then you must be correct." Khza Eil's tone had Ahuzzan doubting his resolve. "But it matters not. You are still here, and we can move you into your new quarters now."

Ahuzzan followed Khza Eil through room after room and courtyard after courtyard before coming to an area filled with guards dressed the same way as Ahuzzan. The first and largest room appeared to serve as a private dining and lounging area for the guards. To the left and right were small sleeping quarters, and in the center of the wing was another courtyard equipped for fighting and training. Ahuzzan felt a bit lighter upon seeing guards engaged in sword training. His eyes scanned each man quickly, and within a few seconds he knew there were twenty guards within striking distance. He thought three of them were built for the spear, eight would likely wield a sword most comfortably, and four were most assuredly archers. The other five looked, by Ahuzzan's estimation, to be the most well-rounded of the guards—equally comfortable with a sword and shield as they would be without any weapon at all. He had a knack for placing soldiers strategically on the battlefield based on his perception of their strengths. And ninety-nine times out of one hundred, his appraisals proved true.

"Nirgali?" Khza Eil called, tapping Ahuzzan on the shoulder. "I said this will be your personal area. This is your mat and this basket is for your personal belongings and your robes. I will have your new holsters sent over as soon as the tanner completes them. Your knives have been cleaned and sharpened," he held out a neatly-wrapped package.

"Thank you," Ahuzzan responded with a bow of his head. "You have been most gracious today."

"Think nothing of it. I will likely see you soon. Your duties will begin at first light." And without any decorum or introductions, Khza Eil left Ahuzzan alone in the guards' wing.

He knelt down on his mat and untied the package, pulling his knives out one by one to inspect them. He relaxed as he held his three oldest possessions in his hands, the only remnants of his time on the battlefield.

"Nirgali?" a man called from the courtyard.

Ahuzzan tucked his knives under his sleeping mat and went to the courtyard where a group of the royal guardians had gathered. As he approached, he checked the mood of each man who watched him. The emotions ranged from curiosity to aggression with nearly everything in between. One of the guards looked like a small child about to receive a gift. *That one looks like a madman... I must keep an eye out for him.* As soon as he came to a stop in front of the guards, the one in charge spoke.

"We were told that you have fought for the Assyrian army for some time. Tell us about your victories and losses," the man commanded.

Apparently there would be no introductions or pleasantries. Ahuzzan already liked them.

"I have served many kings of Assyria and won many battles for the glory of the kingdom. I came here from Byblos, and before that I was part of the conquest of the north for many years," he answered vaguely. He did not know how much he should share about his time on earth.

"We have heard of the victories in Byblos and the North. What of your losses?" the leader pressed.

"I have none to speak of," Ahuzzan quipped.

The men rolled their eyes and snorted their derision—clearly unable to believe his battle record was perfect. The only losses Ahuzzan had suffered were prior to joining the Assyrian army.

"Before my arrival here today, my name was Ahuzzan, commander in the North. Perhaps you have heard of me?" he narrowed his eyes, ready to receive the respect due him no matter what information he would have to divulge to receive it.

"That is simply not possible. The commander Ahuzzan fought for the armies of the kings of old," the man scoffed.

"I took back Sinabu and Tidu, fought against the lands of Aram and Babylon, and helped maintain our borders with the Elamites. Surely my years of service to the army have earned me the right to be respected by my fellow guard," Ahuzzan spoke without emotion.

"Impossible," he heard one guard whisper.

"If I must prove myself, I am more than willing to comply. You three—spear throwers—I will fight you at once," he said, pointing to the three surprised men. He was glad to know he had placed their skill sets accurately. He moved to the middle of the courtyard without a weapon as the others watched incredulously.

Ahuzzan closed his eyes and listened as feet shuffled to the edges of the courtyard. He heard three spears come off the rack in the southeast corner of the square. Three sets of footsteps circled him quietly, kicking up dirt as they moved. He heard the inhale of breath as one guard drew back his spear, ready to thrust it toward him. Ahuzzan opened his eyes and stepped to the left, successfully avoiding the tip of the spear. He spun, his right hand capturing the shaft of the spear, and as his body continued to rotate, he twisted it from the guard's hands, leaving the man weaponless. Ahuzzan positioned his now-armed body with the two armed guards to his front and the other to his back. He heard the pound of feet running at him from behind, and he ducked out of the way, knocking the unarmed guard to the ground and placing the tip of the spear at the man's throat. The two other guards simultaneously pressed toward him, and he parried their thrusts with the shaft of his spear. He landed a solid kick into the abdomen of the left guard, but the man quickly recovered and an intense three-way battle ensued. The two guards matched Ahuzzan blow for blow, and after ten minutes of combat, all three of them were dusty and bruised. One misstep from the taller of the two guards allowed Ahuzzan to sweep his feet under the man's legs and place the tip of his spear into his groin. The guard groaned in pain, though Ahuzzan was careful not to damage him. The remaining guard readied himself, searching for an entry through Ahuzzan's defenses and finding none. But Ahuzzan was equally confounded by the guard he now faced alone. This man was clearly the best of the three he had faced.

"Enough," the head guardian called, and the fighting stopped—though both were disappointed. "You have proven your skill with a spear. Should we begin your training with the sword and shield?"

Ahuzzan did not understand the question. "Why would I need training with a sword and shield?"

"Is not the spear your weapon of choice?" the commander asked with a furrowed brow.

"No. I have not used one since my youth. I fight with a sword—sometimes accompanied by a shield. I also use my daggers. I find the most successful way to defeat an enemy is to strike at him before he is aware I am in his midst. I could use some practice with a bow and arrow—though I doubt I'll have use of such frivolities guarding the royal wing of the palace." He thought through the layout he had observed as he arrived and decided he was correct.

The guards stared at him in disbelief. "We will spar with swords nonetheless. We were informed you are the best in the king's army, but we maintain a certain decorum in the admission of every guardian to the palace. I ask that you take no offense," the leader of the guard apologized.

"I would take offense if special allowances were made. I have commanded thousands; I understand the need to maintain order and routine," Ahuzzan stated with a nod.

By nightfall, Ahuzzan had proven his skills with every available weapon—and even taught a few techniques to his fellow guardians. He could see why the group of men had been chosen to guard the king's palace. They were the most gifted group of fighters he had seen in one place.

"In one week's time, guests will begin arriving for the new city's christening. Tens of thousands will attend, and it is our responsibility to choose soldiers from the army to aide in our duties. There are ninety permanent guardians quartered here in the palace. An additional two hundred live in barracks outside the palace to patrol the city and man the walls and gates to Kahlu. Nirgali—I wish for you and Shalmanisar to assist me in choosing the additional guards," Yomadan announced. That was the name of the head guardian—but Ahuzzan had learned throughout the course of the day that each guard assigned to the palace was given a name by the king's wisemen—just as he had been ceremonially named. He would need to do his best to accept his fate as Nirgali—even if it was a constant reminder of the death and destruction that followed him.

That night, he lay on his mat, attempting to fall asleep to the deafening sound of silence. There were no cries of wounded men, no animals howling into the night sky, no battle plans swirling in his mind, and no risk of being killed in his sleep. That night, within the walls of Kahlu, he had never felt more alone or more terrified. *How will I survive this life?* he wondered.

In the hope it would tire his mind, he began silently chanting, again and again: *Nirgali. I am Nirgali. Nirgali. I am Nirgali. Nirgali.*

THIRTEEN

"No! By the gods! No!" Shalmanisar yelled, walking away from Nirgali with his hands pressed to the sides of his head.

Nirgali opened and closed his fists, taking deep breaths to calm the pounding in his chest. *I am right! I have protected myself and others for long enough to know I am right.* Yomadan sat down in front of him and spoke calmly.

"We will discuss some potential scenarios—and you must tell me how a guardian should react," Yomadan worried with a crease in his brow. "You are guarding the queen in the palace, and someone you have never seen before begins to approach. It is a man wearing clothing not indicative of an Assyrian. How will you respond?"

"I would rush at him before he knew what was happening, grab him by the neck and throw him to the ground. If he survived the impact, I would interrogate him over his intentions," Nirgali answered with a proud nod.

"Umm. No," Yomadan groaned. "You would simply step between the man and the queen and ask his intentions. This situation is quite normal in the palace —many messengers travel from many foreign places to ask favors or bring tribute to the king and queen. Killing a messenger could result in an unwanted war."

"Is it not safer to know—without question—the messenger is not an assassin *before* he approaches the queen," Nirgali stated as if his answer were a certainty.

"It is best to ask the messenger's purpose without laying a hand on him. Simply position yourself between them and ask. This is the *only* acceptable response," Yomadan insisted sternly.

"A very skilled assassin can perfectly mimic a harmless messenger in attitude, clothing, and words," Nirgali began.

"They are never assassins. If someone is allowed into the innermost courtyard of the palace where the queen most often stays, that person has already been searched. It is simply your duty to protect—you will only kill if it is apparent a weapon is present and the queen is in danger," Yomadan cut him off loudly.

"I have personally carried out two assassinations using that exact technique, and I was successful because none suspected me," Nirgali calmly muttered.

Yomadan's eyes narrowed as he searched Nirgali's face for a sign of a joke. "Then you are the only assassin capable of such an act, and I am glad you are on our side.

"Another scenario," Yomadan moved on. "You are stationed at the entrance to the palace and five men approach you claiming to bring tribute to our king. They have livestock and linen, and they ask to be brought to the king to present him with their goods. What do you do?"

"I search each linen and make the men strip to check their bodies for weapons. I assume the livestock are harmless—as beasts can hardly be trained to kill a king, and once they are searched, I will send them into the king?" Nirgali answered more as a question than a statement. He was beginning to feel that he was unfit for this post.

"I suppose it would be all right to check the linens. You would not be able to make the men strip—but you could search their bodies and clothing for weapons while they remained clothed. Your response to the livestock is correct —I half expected you would want to slit each of the animals' throats in case there were daggers stored within their stomachs," Yomadan groaned.

That would be clever, Nirgali wondered at the idea, wishing he had thought of using the animals that way when he was still on the battlefield. *That could have been useful.*

"Your social skills within the confines of the palace are a bit barbaric, Nirgali. Perhaps we should keep you away from any interaction with the guests of the king and queen. If you watch from more of a distant viewpoint, you will still be able to alert the other guards to imminent danger while allowing the guests to live through their meeting with our king or queen. If an unscheduled visitor arrives and requests an audience with our king, it is common practice to send a servant to find Khza Eil. He arranges the king's schedule and will provide temporary quarters to guests if the king is otherwise engaged."

Nirgali spent the next three days with Yomadan and Shalmanisar, watching young soldiers fight one another in the training courtyard, each trying to prove himself more worthy than the others. The opportunity to guard the palace for the celebration could be beneficial for future placement as a permanent palace guardian if a position became available. Each man was giving his all, but Nirgali found he was much harsher on the soldiers' abilities than his fellow guardians. After the first day, the list of men he found suitable to the task was only twelve names long. Yomadan's listed forty-one. Shalmanisar had written down sixty-four names.

"We must have at least one hundred additional guards for the event. There will be too many guests for so few to keep an eye on—and we will be working in shifts all through the day and night. These events may continue for weeks, and I don't want any of us working under the influence of a sleepless night. A fatigued guardian is a careless guardian," Yomadan worried as he looked over the three lists side-by-side. Nirgali watched as Yomadan circled the twelve names he had written—they would be a part of the royal guard for the occasion, and Nirgali was pleased the head guardian took his names first. The man then compared his list with Shalmanisar's and circled another twenty-four names—the names both men had listed.

"These four were useless with a sword. They should never leave the wall," Nirgali muttered with disgust.

"I am aware, Nirgali. These men will be posted to the outer wall. A bow and arrow will be sufficient for them," Yomadan sighed in frustration.

After the next two days of watching young men attempt to prove their worth, Yomadan chose one hundred sixty-four in total to join them for the celebration. Nirgali felt only fifty-two were fit for the task, but his arguments only heightened Yomadan's stress and frustration, so he tried to stay silent. *Why did he ask me to assist if he chooses to ignore my advisements?*

Upon returning to the guard's quarters that night, Shalmanisar pulled Nirgali to the side. "He was testing you. He wanted to know for sure that your loyalties lie with the king. He has commanded men who are not as dedicated as they should be, and he will not allow them to guard the palace. These trials were his way of making sure you wanted the best for the guard. You surpassed his expectations," Shalmanisar reported, turning to his own mat and leaving Nirgali to his thoughts.

The rest of the week Yomadan's time was dedicated to organizing the guardians' schedules for the celebration, and Nirgali was grateful to be excluded from the planning—he knew the leader's inability to heed his counsel and caution would only frustrate him. He grew familiar with the various posts around the palace, and he shadowed different guardians each day to learn the specifics of every duty. When the first of the guests finally arrived for the festivities, Nirgali felt comfortable about facing his upcoming responsibilities.

FOURTEEN

"THAT ONE LOOKS suspicious. We should interrogate him," Nirgali narrowed his eyes at a man who seemed far too nervous and sweaty.

"No. He appears drunk, and likely drugged. He probably doesn't even know where he is right now," the other guard groaned with the roll of his eyes. "You must stop, Nirgali. This has continued for over a week, and no one has made an attempt on the king's life."

Nirgali crossed his arms tightly against his chest. *It requires only one usurper... one madman to set his mind on some lunacy.* "Drunk or drugged? People do mad things when they are under the influence of spirits. I have witnessed terrible acts performed by men in a stupor. Do not think for a second they will behave as expected when they are in this state of mind," he warned.

The young guard straightened, his gaze sweeping the full room intently. *Well at least he heeded my words.* Nirgali had become increasingly frustrated by the other guardians' inability to remain focused and alert at all times. He wondered if he was the only one who saw the endangerment a gathering of this size might cause. Yomadan apparently trusted his dedication, because Nirgali was always stationed in the throne room, and his shift always began right before supper—when the party regained its speed each night.

Nirgali spent the evenings alternating between checking each guest's face for a suspicious expression or a hand reaching for a hidden weapon. After he felt the room was secure, he watched the revelers—finding their behavior with food and drink fascinating. He had never partaken of such excess. There were celebrations after victories, of course, but he had never felt at ease enough after a victory to act as the other soldiers did—one well-hidden enemy could wreak havoc upon an encampment of drunken soldiers. Foods covered the tops of every table, servants bustled around the room, each carrying a different offering of drink. The king and queen were particularly fascinating to Nirgali. They spent half of each evening together, reclining side by side and enjoying those that were fortunate enough to receive the invitation to join them. The other half of the evening the queen took a turn about the enormous room with two of her ladies and two of her guards—greeting her guests and acting as the ideal hostess. Nirgali found himself quite enamored with the king and queen's relationship. They were certainly enraptured by one another, and whenever the queen left his side, the king spent more time watching her move throughout the room than he did speaking with those surrounding him. But Nirgali's study of his king and queen only lasted a few minutes at a time. Each set of new guests who entered the room brought his attention back to his duties.

On the ninth evening, well after midnight, Nirgali felt a prickling on the back of his neck. His eyes scanned each face in the room—hundreds of drunken people moved about, dancing, singing, or listening to the stories of others. Nirgali could feel something was amiss. "Watch this post," he commanded, grabbing a guard who was leaving the room at the end of his shift. "Something feels awry." The guard looked anxious—he was one of the swordsmen Nirgali had worried was too inexperienced when Yomadan selected him. "Ready your sword. You may need it." Nirgali watched the exhausted soldier snap to attention, his hand gripping the hilt of his weapon purposefully.

Nirgali pushed his way right through the center of the crowd, keeping watch for any swift movements or wary glances. The king lay on a large pillow at the head of the room, with platters of various foods and carafes of numerous varieties of wines spread around for him and his guests to enjoy. The queen was making her way across the room parallel to Nirgali—only a few steps away from his reach. He saw a man in the corner of the room thrust his hand into the air and perform a circling motion as movement sprung from each corner of the room.

"Guard the king!" Nirgali commanded as he reached the queen in two giant steps. "Drop, my queen," he growled as she squatted obediently, tucking her head in her hands. He had his sword raised in one hand and a dagger in his other, ready to protect the queen from whatever harm might be aimed toward the lady. Her ladies covered her with their bodies, and her two personal guardians took position so the queen was completely surrounded. Nirgali looked up and saw that six guardians encircled the king, while four very flustered attackers, equipped only with small daggers, looked around helplessly. Three more guardians rushed into the room as guests screamed and huddled by the edges of the room or ducked their heads in fear. The would-be attackers were disarmed and taken quickly from the room, followed closely by the king and his guards. Nirgali escorted the queen out right behind them, trailing the group in case more attackers emerged from elsewhere. When the attackers were locked in a room—for an interrogation which Nirgali was rather excited for— the king turned to Nirgali with an intense gaze.

"You knew. I heard you yell, but they were nowhere near me. How did you know?" the king asked with a glimmer of adoration.

"Something felt amiss. It was as if my body felt the threat before I saw your attackers. My hair stood on end," he confessed.

"And you protected my queen," the king shuddered, grabbing his wife and pulling her into his arms. He kissed the top of her head, nodding his appreciation to Nirgali.

Nirgali bowed his head, honored by the king's gratitude.

"Yomadan," the king called to the commander who had just arrived, still wiping the sleep from his eyes. "We will close this celebration in the morning and send everyone away. I believe the city has been properly christened."

"Yes, my king," Yomadan bowed as the guards accompanied the king and queen back to their private rooms for the night.

Yomadan turned to Nirgali, grasping his shoulder with a firm hand, and sighed. "Well done, Nirgali. Tomorrow we will deal with the attackers. For tonight, rest well. You will need stamina for tomorrow's interrogation."

Fifteen

Nirgali FLEXED his hands, rubbing each sore joint deeply. It had been a long morning. At dawn, he had taken the first prisoner into the center of the training courtyard and beat the man until his face was unrecognizable. He had not asked a single question. Nirgali simply wanted the man to bleed. The other guardians tried to stop him—asking why no questions had been asked of the man, but Nirgali knew exactly how to get the information he needed. He hid the first prisoner in a separate room with a guard.

"Give me a sword, a few daggers, and a spear," Nirgali told the confused guardians. Blood pooled on the ground in the center of the courtyard, and Nirgali wanted the other prisoners to feel intense fear when they saw the scene where their comrade had been. He ran the blade of the sword through the blood, taking care to make it appear as if the blade had pierced the skin of the prisoner. He did the same with the tip of the spear, and he placed a bloody hand print on the hilt of it, throwing it to the ground so the blood splattered in the impact. "Keep those daggers clean. I'll tell you when I'm ready for them. Bring out the other three prisoners now," Nirgali ordered as he wiped his blood-covered hand across his face and down his arms. He began pacing back and forth, breathing heavily, and doing his best attempt to appear insane.

As soon as the guards brought the three men into the courtyard, Nirgali watched as their gazes took in the scene he had created. Blood drained from their faces. He heard one man whimper in fear.

"Him," Nirgali pointed to the one who was whining. The guardians held back wicked smiles as the prisoner was forced to stand in the blood of his friend. Tears pooled in the corners of his terrified eyes. Shalmanisar bound the man's hands behind his back and stepped back to the other prisoners.

"I do not want to cut off another man's genitals today. Tell me who sent you, and yours will remain intact. Your friend was not so lucky. He suffered greatly before I allowed him to die," Nirgali remarked, punching the prisoner in the cheek.

"Please," the man begged. "We are from Tela. Your king flayed our fathers and burnt our mothers when we were only children. We sought to bring revenge upon his home. We sought to honor the memories of our parents and our city by bringing justice upon the one responsible for destroying our home."

Nirgali narrowed his eyes at the young man—he couldn't be more than sixteen or seventeen years of age. Nirgali had been in Tela for its destruction... he had commanded the leaders to be flayed and nailed to the city gates. Rebellion against the crown would not be tolerated, and the king had honored him for his decisions in dealing with the city and its leaders. *I would want justice if I was in this boy's place. But I would have executed my plans far more carefully. Stupid boy!* Nirgali paced back and forth, wishing he could force the boy to serve him. The boy needed training. Under Nirgali's tutelage, he could have made quite the mercenary.

"Pity," Nirgali shook his head sadly. "Because you were not prepared, you will die a failure. I gave the order to kill your parents. Now I must give the order to kill you as well." He raised a hand and signaled the other guardians. At once, the necks of the three boys were slit, their bodies shaking on the ground as blood poured from their veins. "Bring me the other," Nirgali commanded, clenching his sore fists. He had torn some of the skin on his knuckles beating the first prisoner's face earlier. He dreaded the bathing he would need to clean the blood from his skin—his knuckles would protest vehemently.

The first prisoner was brought back in, and Nirgali watched the boy's swollen features twist in fear and agony as soon as he saw his friends.

"You will return to Tela now. Tell them King Ashurnasirpal will not tolerate this kind of treachery. If any more of the Tela people are caught rebelling against the crown, we will hunt every one of you down. We will flay your children while you are forced to watch, and we then will put their bodies on spears and hoist them over the walls of your city as a reminder of your betrayal. And only after the bodies have grown rotten, we will lock your people within the walls of the city and burn it to the ground. Go now. Tell your people," Nirgali said as the guard took the crying prisoner away.

"Well done, Nirgali. I knew you would find the information we needed," Yomadan spoke with a tight smile. Nirgali gave a short nod and turned to leave the bloody courtyard behind.

He grabbed new garments from his basket, careful not to bloody them with his filthy hands, and he walked out of the palace and out of the bustling city without a word. He did not stop walking until he came to the canal that flowed along the west wall of the city. He stripped off his bloodied garments, removed his daggers and their new leather holsters, and walked into the swiftly-running water. As the liquid rushed over his body, he felt all the tension from the day release. He ducked his entire body underwater and screamed loud and long. Fury pounded in his chest, though he did not know why at first. He came out of the water for a breath, which was swiftly followed by him screaming curses into the heavens.

"Must I always be the bearer of death? Must I long for the feel of another's blood upon my hands? Why is this the only comfort I can find within this life? I want a moment of peace without bloodshed. Surely you cannot torture me with this life through all the ages to come!"

He grabbed a dagger from the ground and thrust it into his chest. *Please. Please let me die.* He did not feel faint as the blood poured from the hole he created. He sliced the vein on his left wrist, hoping perhaps the blood spilling from two places at once would kill him.

"No," he heard a booming voice from right behind him. He spun around, trying to see who had spoken the word, but all that surrounded him was the water that streamed over his skin. He looked down at his wrist and chest, and the wounds he had inflicted were gone. No marks remained as evidence of his attempt.

"No," Nirgali whispered as tears rushed from his eyes once more.

Sixteen

Kalhu, Assyria, 765 B.C.E.

NIRGALI ENTERED the throne room for his morning meeting with King Ashur-dan III and Khza Eil. Shortly after saving King Ashurnasirpal II and his queen's life, Nirgali was placed in charge of the Kalhu palace guardians. The Khza Eil whom he had first met upon entering the palace had been dead for almost a century. The man he now served beside—who also had the ability to see into a man's mind and soul—was a descendant of the Khza Eil he had met when first arriving in Kalhu.

In his time at the Kalhu palace, Nirgali had seen wise kings and foolish ones, brutal rulers and gentle, as well as those who simply warmed the throne for the next man who would fill it. He had grown rather fond of some kings, and quite despised others. Ashurnasirpal II would always be his favorite, though—the man who had put him in command of the palace security and had treated Nirgali with as much dignity as any man could dream. He often remembered his first weeks in the palace with fondness. His interrogation of the king's attempted assassins had given him the respect he deserved from the other guardians, and the stories of his brutality were passed from one generation of guards to the next—each story gaining a bit more fantasy and terror as it was retold. But he had no qualms with the other guards believing the embellished stories—the more he was feared, the more respect he attained from those in the palace.

Once Nirgali took charge of the palace security, the requirements for becoming a guardian shifted from difficult to nearly impossible. He invited soldiers who had a proven record of excellence in battle to come to Kalhu to audition for him. He only allowed those who could match him blow for blow with the sword and spear to continue to a psychological test. He gave each man an impossible scenario in which one would have to choose between saving the king, saving the queen, or saving the heir to the throne. After the first answer, Nirgali beat the man with his fists, asking if he was certain he was correct. If the candidates held firmly with their initial answers, they passed the test. If they wavered and changed their answers while under duress, they were rejected as guardians and sent back to the battlefield. The test was not about answering correctly. It was about having the mental fortitude in the face of fear and mettle to make a decision and stick with it at all costs. The ninety guardians that initially served in the palace when Nirgali arrived were quickly pared down to sixty. It was his belief that the quality of the guards was far more important than the quantity.

His guardians trusted his judgment, but they feared his wrath and were unable to relax in his presence. Many believed he *was* Nirgali, based solely on his immortality and imperviousness to injury. He sometimes heard guardians whispering prayers of protection and additional strength outside his door while he tried to sleep. He never allowed them to know how upsetting the men's words were, but his loneliness intensified with each passing year.

Please, he begged, *let me have a companion. Someone. Anyone to cure this loneliness. Please.*

"Are you ready to begin?" Khza Eil asked, pulling Nirgali from his dark thoughts.

"Of course," Nirgali bowed as the king entered the throne room, his gaze seemingly troubled. Nirgali had grown quite capable as an advisor to the king. His skills as a tactician and soldier on the battlefield had always been extraordinary, but after so many years serving in the palace and watching the diplomacy of kings, Nirgali felt he could easily lead in any fashion necessary.

"Tell me Khza Eil. My brothers have told me rumors. Are they true?" the king asked.

"Yes, my king. Plague has broken out across the land. There are several traders who arrived in the past few days and are now showing signs of infection. I believe we should shut the gates of the palace to keep the plague from entering," Khza Eil suggested far too calmly.

"I must go," Nirgali announced, feeling sick upon hearing the news. "I brought this upon the land. I do not know what I have done to cause this plague, but I beg you—command me to leave so you and your nation can survive."

The king exchanged a confused glance with Khza Eil. "Nirgali. You have been here for so long. You could not possibly have brought the plague onto my people. I will hear no more of this foolishness," the king commanded.

Nirgali gave the only response he could think of to force the king's hand. "I am Nirgali, child of the god of plague and war. If plague has entered these lands, it is by my fault and my fault alone."

Khza Eil stared at Nirgali silently for a short moment, his expression unreadable.

"My king," Khza Eil paused, searching for the right words, "Nirgali believes what he says. And though I do not understand why, I believe he speaks truly. He caused this plague."

Both men stared at Nirgali in bewildered silence. *I do not understand what I have done. Was I too happy here? Too comfortable? Is this punishment for living without the constant enmity of other men?* He wanted to rend his clothing and scream his frustrations.

"Then you must go," the king responded with the tone of a question. "Who is able to replace you as leader of the guard?"

"Rabila is most prepared. He will know how to lead," Nirgali answered without having to ponder the question.

"Then I ask you take your leave. A horse will be saddled for you at the palace door. And I beg you, take the plague with you when you go," the king asked, still perplexed at the entire situation.

"It has been an honor to serve Assyria and her kings," Nirgali bowed and left as Khza Eil and the king watched after him.

Nirgali did not inform his men that he was leaving. It would take too much effort to explain that he had caused the plague—though he was certain they would reject his culpability. He left the barracks without ceremony, taking only the clothes he was wearing and the daggers he always kept on his person. The leather holsters which had been made for him upon his arrival to Kalhu over one hundred years earlier would be his only keepsakes from his time with the Assyrians.

Nirgali did not know where he would go or what he would do, but the knowledge he took with him wherever he went still rang true—he would be despised by men. He had finally witnessed the proof of the promise that pain and destruction would follow him wherever he went, and the realization of that plagued him.

He sat outside the walls of the city, surveying the roads leading east and west. Perhaps he should next go somewhere he wished his plague would follow.

Seventeen

Castello San Romolo, Present Day

PRIEST LEANED forward in his chair, staring at his reflection in the small mirror on his desk as he reminisced about his time with the Assyrians. He had studied the fighting styles of the Mushku, the Arameans, the Mari, the nomads, and the Babylonians during his campaigns against them. When all was said and done, he had faithfully served nine Assyrian kings on the battlefield and served another seven as a guardian in the palace at Kahlu. The soldiers who had served under his command numbered in the tens of thousands, and those slaughtered by his hand and the hands of his soldiers numbered far more. For a time, Assyria had been his home.

Home was never a place, his mind chided him. *She was your only home.*

"Stop!" he yelled, punching the mirror that betrayed the depth of the emotions that showed in his eyes. It cracked under the impact, and with it, he felt his resolve to keep the past locked away shatter a little more. He snorted derisively at his blood-covered hand, knowing the cuts would reseal within a few hours, and the only remnants of his outburst would be the small shards of glass that littered his otherwise immaculate desk.

He was alone. The entirety of his Family was in the chapel next door, commemorating the lives of Elias and Samuel, while he sat in the empty castle he had built over the ruins of an ancient monastery hundreds of years earlier. But more than being the sole human in a castle meant for hundreds, he was alone in life. Even Saint, the one who knew him longest, did not truly understand the person Priest had become.

He looked again into the shattered mirror—at the disfigured face the reflection showed back to him with its misplaced pieces and numerous cracks —and wondered... *have I truly changed so much?*

EIGHTEEN

"TODAY IS A DAY of mourning and rejoicing. We mourn for the lives taken too soon from this Family who loved them. And we rejoice in the years we spent with them and the memories we will forever hold in our hearts." Saint paused, wiping a tear from his bloodshot eyes. "Today is not a day for anger, but a day for remembrance and honoring those lost."

Subtle reminder, Mattia thought bitterly, but he couldn't disagree with his great uncle's words. Samuel would not have wanted this day to be a rage-filled sermon on Priest's shortcomings as a father and as a human being. And Mattia took that into consideration when writing the eulogy he would soon deliver. But he wasn't going to lie or gloss over the truth of Samuel's life, and it didn't mean he wasn't filled to the brim with anger at the man responsible for Samuel's death… the man who had attempted to kill Mattia and his fiancée.

"I ask, first, for Gregorius to speak for Elias," Saint said, motioning for Gregorius to come to the front of the chapel. Mattia was relieved that he had time to bring down his level of anger before it was his turn to speak. He watched as Gregorius took his time walking to the front of the chapel, gathering his thoughts. He took several deep breaths before finally speaking.

"My brother. My blood. My soul." Gregorius was hardly able to whisper the last word before crumpling to his knees and wailing in agony. Everyone in the room had known the moment was coming, but finally, the floodgates had blown wide open. No one was immune to the effect of Gregorius's emotional eruption. After a few minutes, he stood and sighed forlornly before continuing.

"Elias and I shared our thoughts, our homes, and our lives more than any normal brothers. We were two halves of one whole, and without him, my life is incomplete. He was the best of us with a sword and a sniper rifle—and one of the most skilled tacticians. But more than that, he was a great man. He once planned a coup to overthrow Vlad III with the aide of the Turkish army, and he carried it out and killed the bastard without the permission or help of anyone in the Family." Gregorius chucked. "And when any of you asked for help or advice, he was always willing. He was an excellent husband and a loving father," Gregorius motioned to Elias's two sons. They looked almost as sickly as Gregorius, who had lost a considerable amount of weight in the past week. Both of Elias's sons had been mostly silent all week—barely even leaving their rooms except to eat. Mattia wondered if they blamed him for their father's death or if they blamed Priest, as they should.

"Elias took no pleasure in his final assignment. I had never seen him so distraught as before he left. And I knew whatever his contract entailed was horrific… for he did not share its contents even with me. I should not have let him go. And for allowing his departure, I will never forgive myself," Gregorius cried. Mattia wanted to comfort him and tell him it wasn't his fault, but in all honesty, Gregorius's words rang true. *If Gregorius had stopped his brother, neither Elias nor Samuel would be dead.* Mattia swallowed hard, wishing Gregorius could go back in time and change his actions. But it would do no good to wish for something that could never happen.

"And now I call Mattia to the front to speak for Samuel," he heard Saint announce. Lissie squeezed Mattia's hand, and he had to shake himself back to the present. He had apparently missed the rest of Gregorius's speech while his mind wandered, and his turn to speak had arrived too quickly.

Mattia walked laboriously to the front of the chapel, his legs trying to prevent the journey by threatening to lock up or give out. When he turned to face his family, he looked over the faces staring back at him. They were all grieving. Some for Elias. Some for Samuel. Most for both. The sadness in the eyes he met washed over Mattia like pouring rain. The constant stream running down his cheeks was unavoidable when influenced by the heaviness in his heart.

"Samuel was a character in his life. Like a living version of a sidekick in a story. He was clumsy and haphazard, and always in need of help," Mattia began. Heads nodded in agreement, and a few chuckles were heard throughout the room. Mattia sighed, knowing that would be the response to his opening words.

"But that wasn't the real Samuel." Heads jerked up, and all attention was focused on what Mattia had to say about the youngest of the Family's uncles.

"For centuries, Samuel was given assignments based on the reality that somewhere along the line, someone deemed him incompetent. He was forced to play a child at times. Forced to take on impossible contracts alone—contracts that would have been difficult for two or three people to complete together. Forced to live a life from his very birth without a single kind word from his own father." Mattia took a moment to bring his anger back down to a simmer. Every eye in the room registered shock, but Mattia knew the words had struck a chord.

"The funny thing is, I... I never once heard him complain. He bore the distrust, the jokes about his supposed incompetence, the lack of fatherly attention that he watched the rest of us receive. He looked on silently, content to be the brunt of every joke for hundreds of years in a Family of immortals who seemed only to remember the mistakes he sometimes made and not the triumphs he always worked for. The man was unlike any other person I've met. He smiled all the time, and even made jokes at his own expense to get a laugh from those around him. He didn't care what we believed about him. He was content to be himself. But I was fortunate to witness his genius. In a matter of weeks, he learned how to hack into any server without military-grade coding. I only gave him three lessons on how to do it, and a month later, he used that very skill to locate me and Lissie and save our lives. Samuel was not a fool or a screw up as you all believed. He was just too accommodating to try to change your minds. And now that he's gone, perhaps you'll do him the kindness of remembering all he did in service to this Family rather than his few shining debacles that seem to dictate the way his memory lives in our thoughts." Guilt was in every set of eyes Mattia looked into. Even his father and mother were guilty. Mattia sighed, not really sure if he could get through the end of his eulogy.

"Samuel. My favorite uncle," he looked up, his eyes closing as he imagined speaking with his lost friend. "Thank you for teaching me to laugh at my mistakes. Thank you for showing me kindness at every turn. You were always available if I needed advice or guidance. You were the one person I could always count on to hear my side of the story and honestly tell me if I was in the wrong or if I was justified in my anger. You were always there," he choked down a sob and breathed deeply. "And now you're gone, and I don't know what to do. I don't know how to get through a holiday without your jokes. I don't know if I can bear to drink our favorite scotch without you sitting next to me, telling me stories of past contracts. I don't know how I'll bear it. But somehow, I know I will, because it's what you would want. For us to remember you with joy. Not with anger or sadness. So I vow to you, I'll try. And every time I think of you, I'll force a smile, not a frown. I'll wipe away my tears, and raise my glass to the best man I've ever known. Thank you for the example you set. You've done so much to shape me into the man I am today, and I'll never be able to tell you how much I appreciate that. But somehow, I think you know." Mattia grinned and dried his cheeks. He sat down, unable to look into the faces of the men and women he had scolded. But it was the speech Samuel deserved. And Mattia couldn't let his uncle's memory remain tarnished the way it was before his death.

"I thank you both for honoring our dead. And I would now like for us to remain silent for a few minutes to reflect on who Elias and Samuel were to each of us," Saint added, lowering his eyes to the ground. Mattia knew there couldn't possibly be silence with the constant stream of sniffles throughout the room, but in a way, everyone's deep breaths and soft sobs and stuffy noses were honoring enough.

After a few moments, Saint motioned for the chapel bell to be rung, and the funeral came to an end. The silence continued, but Mattia was hugged or clasped on the shoulder by nearly every man and woman. None were cross with him for the truth he had spoken, and Mattia felt a glimmer of hope for the fate of the Family. *Perhaps we won't fall apart as I feared,* he hoped.

NINETEEN

THE DRINKS BEGAN to flow the moment the Family was seated around the giant dining table. Saint looked at the empty seat next to him and sighed. *Such a childish vendetta to cause so much grief,* he thought as he worried about Priest. His oldest friend was directly responsible for the deaths of Elias and Samuel, and Saint knew his friend was feeling the loss profoundly. Priest's exclusion from the funeral and feast would only fuel the frustration and anger he had been feeling over the past several centuries. *But this time, he will not have an opportunity to lash out at those he blames.*

Saint had watched silently on more than one occasion while Priest drew up a fake contract to remove someone who had upset him or threatened to expose Family secrets. He often drew up the fake contracts to kill power-hungry or militant leaders who wanted more from the Family than had been agreed upon. But any threats against the Family were bad for business—when every one of the most powerful leaders in the world used your "organization" to remove their competition, no one in their right mind would actually *want* to expose that organization. Nearly every government would collapse under the weight of the rampant corruption within. Of course, Saint was culpable for allowing Priest to operate that way for so long, and he may or may not have helped to write a few fake contracts himself. But both men knew the Family's very existence depended on it.

Saint's attention was drawn back to the feast as chairs slid loudly across the floor, and everyone stood to raise their glasses in a toast. He knew this part of the evening could take a while—many would have toasts for Samuel and Elias —and he felt appreciation for his family's love and closeness. If not for Priest, he would not be with the family. Though he supposed Priest could say the same of him.

"To our brothers," Claudius spoke first, "May you rest peacefully knowing the laughter you brought into our lives. Life would have been darker without you." Everyone grunted and took a drink from their cups.

"To Elias," Gregorius spoke with either a grimace or a smirk—Saint could not tell the difference on Gregorius's troubled visage. "For your ability to whip my ass into shape when I needed to improve a skill. For your willingness to listen when I needed to scream about a frustration. For your ability to know exactly what was wrong before I spoke the words. You were the best man I ever knew." Everyone drank again, and some already needed to refill their cups.

"To Samuel," Sergius spoke up. "You, my little brother, were my favorite mess. You brought joy into all our lives at a time when we needed it most. When mother passed away, we had you to take care of, to clean up after, and to raise. Every one of your brothers played a role in raising you, and we will miss you, our favorite little brother," he choked out, leaning over the table, gripping the edge for support.

"To Samuel!" Felix called out with a smile, hoping to lighten the mood a bit, and everyone joined him, most polishing off a full glass to recover for a spell.

The toasts continued for another twenty or thirty minutes, and everyone was thoroughly intoxicated by the time they were finally able to sit down and eat. The food was eaten over the course of several hours. After the first four courses were finished and the cheese and fruit platters were brought out, the stories of Elias and Samuel began pouring forth from those around the table.

Elias's sons told the story of how they had first learned to use a sword by attacking a tree on his command. Their mother had thrown a fit when she had walked into their garden, finding only stumps where her favorite trees had previously stood. "They needed to learn how to swing a sword without killing each other," Elias had muttered coyly with a shrug of his shoulders.

Antonio recalled the time he and the twins were sent to China to kill the son of an emperor who was too eager for his father's death. Elias was so sure he could pull off a disguise that made him appear Chinese. Antonio and Gregorius had watched out the window of their room as Elias walked down the lane, a full head taller than anyone he passed, thinking he blended in perfectly, while every local person stared up at him in utter confusion.

Felix talked about Samuel's love—and abject fear—of women. He had bedded hundreds, but had never had the guts to ask a woman for courtship or even for a stroll down a lane.

Saint stared at the table as he listened to story after story; his heart was pained for the men who had so needlessly died. *Oh, my old friend, how did you think this would end well?* he wondered as his mind returned to Priest, sitting alone in his room, missing the day's events.

"I think we must call it a night, gentlemen," Caterina announced with a slur as she poured the last of the grappa into her husband's glass. "We are out of food and drink, and we all know these lovely stories could go on for days."

Everyone became quiet once more as Sergius placed Samuel's dagger on the table and Gregorius placed Elias's next to it. The ritual which had only been performed a handful of times in the span of their lives began. Each man took his own dagger and nicked his skin with the point, smearing their blood onto the blades of both resting daggers. Once everyone had done so, they stood around the table solemnly. No one wanted to speak the words that would mark the end of the day.

Saint took a deep breath. He would lead once more, as he had been forced to do on more than one occasion. "We stand united," he began as everyone joined in, "Family of Immortals. Plagued by life. Cursed by the hand of God. We pledge our lives to this Family, and to the memory of those fallen, taken too soon from the world." It was the funerary pledge—only used a few times over their centuries of life. But all the men knew the words, and each spoke them with a promise of their truth. The silence that followed the pledge was overwhelming, and as Saint looked down at the crimson blades of the daggers, he felt tears fall from his eyes. *Priest will surely be next.*

TWENTY

SAINT WALKED BACK to his room after the dining hall emptied. He paused only for a moment in front of Priest's door before knocking and entering the chamber.

"What?" Priest groaned. He sat in a chair facing the open window.

Saint pulled a chair next to Priest's and plopped down beside him, not bothering to examine Priest's face when he already knew the dark expression buried there. They sat in silence for some time, looking out over the rolling hills bathed in moonlight.

"The weather was sunny today. The way Elias preferred it to be," Priest whispered, his voice strained.

"Yes it was. Of course, Gregorius honored his memory. It was a lovely remembrance," Saint added, unwilling to upset his friend by discussing Samuel's half of the day.

A long pause of silence hung in the room, filled with wariness and caution and fear.

"We begin preparations for the trial tomorrow," Saint said with the mask of calm which he had mastered centuries earlier. "I fear for you, old friend. I fear for what could be discovered when they begin digging into the past." Priest didn't respond. "And a part of me fears for *me*. You know I've done my fair share of putting my desires first."

"You needn't worry. I'll take responsibility for all of it. They trust you and your judgment. We've always kept it that way. You need to continue in your role—they must believe one of us has acted in the best interest of the world. And it is clear you are the more worthy leader between the two of us anyway," Priest inclined his head toward Saint and forced a corner of his mouth to lift a bit. It was nice to see the turn of countenance. Saint had missed their banter over the previous weeks. "Make sure you stay away after tonight, brother. I don't want anyone getting the impression you're on my side."

Saint shook his head. "This is too much for you to bear alone. I am more than willing…"

"No," Priest cut him off. "Blaming both of us for the Family's problems will only harm them. This Family must remain intact. If I am exiled or imprisoned or killed—that won't affect them. But if it's both of us… I cannot imagine what will happen. They have always trusted you completely—your counsel, your judgment, your friendship. No. You must remain innocent."

Saint nodded, though he knew guilt would rack his soul forever if he allowed the boys to believe he was not aware of Priest's actions. They sat in silence for a while longer, staring into the starry night sky, wondering what the coming days might bring.

Before he slept that night, Priest wondered about the decisions he had made that had brought him to this point. Surely certain men needed to be killed. *But others did not.* He felt heat in his cheeks. Over the centuries, he had become addicted to the power he held over life and death. It was like a drug—one that could only be found in the destruction of others who wielded enough authority or influence to challenge his place in the world. *You were not always this way,* he told himself. *There was a time when you still sought to see the good in yourself—when you hoped for redemption.* He knew that time was long gone now, though. Redemption was a pipe dream he no longer felt the need to chase. His life was full of death and destruction—and even his own "immortal" children could not escape it.

But in his quest for death and destruction, he had found Saint. And only after finding Saint, had he found *her.* A voice in the back of his mind whispered softly, *it was your quest for redemption—not death—that led you to her. Do not allow yourself to forget.*

TWENTY-ONE

Germen, Thrace, 520 C.E.

KASDEN SAT in his comfortable home in the center of the city, wondering if he should, at last, join the Roman army. He had not been a part of a proper army since he had fought with the Assyrians so many centuries before.

After leaving the palace at Kalhu, he had drifted across many lands and peoples, taking payment from kings, politicians, and other schemers in exchange for killing an enemy or two who were causing trouble in some way. It was astounding how much wealth one could amass by indulging the hateful whims of powerful men. After a few decades of bloodying his hands and earning a good bit of gold, he purchased a small plot of land by the Mediterranean Sea, and he set up a tent where he could live in peaceful solitude. Unfortunately, the solitude brought only boredom without the peace for which he had longed, and after only two years, he began his nomadic migration from city to city. He moved every twenty or thirty years, changing his name and heritage with each move. He decided after his time in Assyria that he would never again allow himself to be thought of as a child of a god—and that meant concealing his immortality to the best of his abilities. Wherever he was, he learned the culture, language, and history as thoroughly as possible—so when he moved into the next city, he could easily create a new identity for himself based on his previous place of dwelling.

His name changed so many times, and he often remembered, with wistfulness, his years spent as Nirgali and Ahuzzan. But it was better this way. He had been Lorik, Appius, Duilius, Vels, Thuxra, Arshaka, among many others. He felt his time as Kasden was coming to an end, and he longed for the battlefield—the hilt of a sword pressing into his calloused hands as they thrust the blade into his next victim. He needed death. And if he couldn't have it himself, then he wanted to inflict as much as he could on the poor bastards who would never know how lucky they were to have their wounds stay open while they passed into the next life. Death was the peace he longed for—the end he no longer knew if he would ever achieve.

Who shall I become? he wondered as he stood in the doorway to his home and watched Thracians scurry by on their way to and from the market. *I will be Belisarius,* he decided. He had known a few men by that name—it was common enough in the city of Germen to be believable. *I was born in Germen, where my mother and father were merchants. My parents died when I was in my youth, and I ran their booth until I was seventeen. Now I am a member of the Roman army, and my superiors decided to transfer me to another region where I can affect more damage upon our enemies. Yes,* he thought. *That will do nicely.*

TWENTY-TWO

Castello San Romolo, Present Day

SAINT WOKE AT TEN the next morning, his mind still swimming with the remnants of drink from the funeral feast and the guilt of his conversation with Priest. He stared at the ceiling as he often did, his eyes tracing the patterns in the wooden beams that spanned the room. He had loved Priest like a brother—called him a brother—for too long to lose him this way. Priest had aided him when none other could—rescued him from impossible situations. To now let him take the fall for their centuries of moral ambiguity seemed so… one-sided.

He rubbed a hand over his eyes, trying to force them into remaining emotionless as he waged war against the threatening tears behind them.

He still remembered the first time he met Priest. *I was so young. So arrogant. So naive.*

Pulling a sheet over his face to block out the sunlight, he squeezed his eyes shut and remembered the beginning of his life—the part of his existence before the concept of immortality was even a whisper in the back of his mind.

TWENTY-THREE

Constantinople, 522 C.E.

PETRUS STOOD beside his uncle, keeping a close eye on the proceedings as he always did. His poor uncle was as fit to be emperor as a sword was to be the commander of legions—he was useful only if wielded by a capable set of hands. Therefore, Petrus had become the silent puppeteer of his uncle since the moment he first rose to power. Justin trusted his nephew's council above all others. *And thank the Lord for that,* Petrus sighed, watching as his uncle continued a discussion with one of his army's commanders.

"My nephew tells me of the fame of one soldier in particular. It is said he is immune to the sword and the arrow, and that his brutality is unmatched in all the ranks," Justin said to the two commanders. The men's eyes narrowed at the mention of their greatest asset, and one nodded toward the other. Petrus found their reaction most intriguing. *Perhaps there is even more to this man that I have heard.*

"Yes, emperor. Belisarius is… as your nephew says," the first commander responded hesitantly.

"He came to us only a few years ago, but his skills far outweigh his claims of youth," the other continued. "Truly, I've seen no other fight as he does. And legends of his origins are already circulating amongst the men," the man added with a strange gleam in his eyes. Petrus couldn't tell if it was a gleam of jealousy or reverence—but the commander was incapable of masking his admiration for the soldier of whom he spoke.

"And is it true you consult with him when drawing battle plans?" Justin pressed.

"Yes, emperor. He has proven time and again his ability to strategize nearly flawless plans against any kind of enemy," the first commander spoke up again.

"Very well. You will bring him here. I want him as head guardian over my home. If he is as talented as you say, then I will be safest with him in command of my personal guard," Justin ordered—just as Petrus had suggested. The commanders exchanged a displeased glance, but they did not dare defy the orders of their emperor. Petrus felt a chill crawl slowly up his spine as he watched the two men bow before his uncle—before him—in compliance. *I control the greatest army in the world,* he marveled.

"Yes, emperor. We will send him to you at once," the first commander complied with a now-hardened look on his face. Certainly he would be losing his greatest commodity, but Petrus had plans for the young soldier. Belisarius would wage war again someday... but for now, there was work to be done in Constantinople which called for a man with his talents.

Within one month's time, Belisarius was brought to the capital city, ready to serve his emperor in whatever way was deemed necessary. Petrus was immediately inclined to like the fellow—he was not well-groomed for his introduction to the head of the entire Roman Empire. It was as if the man knew he had other things to do that were more important than wiping the grime and dust from his battle-hardened skin.

"Belisarius," Petrus greeted the man when he arrived. "I will take you to prepare yourself for the emperor. And I will give you some insight into how this place runs," he explained with a haughty glance. Belisarius's discomfort with the situation was palpable. *He has likely never been in such a grand place. I believe he is quite out of sorts,* Petrus pitied the man.

"I am the nephew of the emperor. My name is Petrus, and I will rule this empire after my uncle. It is I who requested you be brought here," Petrus gloated as he watched the undeniable expression of engrossed interest light Belisarius's eyes. "I believe you can create a much safer environment for the emperor and myself. When you meet with him later, my uncle will ask you for ideas on how to improve his protection. I thought you should have a bit of warning to prepare a thoughtful answer," he added as they walked through the large rooms of the palace to the guards' quarters. Belisarius appeared amused by the warning, but he remained silent.

"This is where you will stay for now, but don't get too comfortable. A change of guard is in order, and you are to be in command. I brought you here, and I need you to advise my uncle on a few key points that I believe you and I will agree on wholeheartedly," Petrus said with a raised brow, knowing the soldier understood his meaning.

"And would you like to discuss what my opinions should be now? Or will you stand behind me during my meeting with your uncle and whisper my responses into my ear?" the soldier rebutted with a false humility.

Petrus was taken aback. The first words from Belisarius's mouth were meant to shame him.

"I could have you killed for that remark," Petrus threatened.

The soldier had the audacity to snort a derisive laugh. "I wish you could," he bowed before turning to the guards' quarters to clean himself up.

Petrus stood still, waiting with a red face and racing pulse for the disrespectful guard to return. But he was taken off guard when the soldier emerged, cleaned and groomed. He did not look like a Thracian—which was the parentage of the odd-looking soldier before him. Petrus studied his face quickly. The man's grooming suggested he was from Persia, but his eyes, nose and skin tone were not indicative of that place. Possibly from the south? Certainly he was not of Egyptian blood. Petrus was perplexed, but as Belisarius approached, his mind moved from the man's ancestry to his age. He appeared more mature in features than Petrus expected.

"How old are you?" Petrus questioned.

The soldier looked at Petrus with a mischievous look in his eye before answering. "The rumor is that I am twenty-two. Others say seventeen. Although my favorite is thirty-five. So what age do you believe I am?"

"Are you incapable of giving a direct answer?" Petrus instantly remembered why he had been so furious with the soldier earlier.

"You do not wish to know about me. You do not want me to give you my own answers. So simply tell me what age you would like me to be. Tell me what opinions you would like me to have. And I will adopt them as my own. I will be your trusted guardian and your most faithful adviser—since all my opinions will only reflect yours," the soldier bowed again.

"My uncle is expecting us," Petrus turned to walk to the throne room, hoping his decision to bring the soldier into the palace would not prove to be his downfall.

TWENTY-FOUR

BELISARIUS OBSERVED from the corner of the small room as Petrus advised his uncle on matters concerning the importing of grain from the outlying regions of the empire. Petrus was always aware of the soldier's watchful gaze—it was as if the soldier was taking notes on every detail, every expression, every tone. It was unnerving to feel monitored every time he opened his mouth to speak, but he had brought Belisarius into the palace—so Belisarius was his own burden to bear.

"Uncle," he began when Justin had finally come to the conclusion Petrus had decided upon earlier that day, "would you mind if I steal away our new guardian? I need to discuss some plans for an upcoming change to our guard."

Justin waved his hand dismissively. His uncle had learned years before that if Petrus asked for something trivial, it was pointless to argue—Petrus was a master of debate and could usually come up with a viable reason for whatever it was he wanted. Justin rarely put his foot down in opposition to Petrus's requests.

Belisarius followed Petrus down a hallway into a small side room still in the emperor's wing of the palace. Petrus sat down and motioned for Belisarius to sit in the chair facing his. Petrus often frequented this small room to devise future plans and create infallible arguments to sway his uncle's mind.

"I need to know I can trust you," Petrus blurted out, realizing he had meant to be more regal with his statement. He cleared his throat and ran a hand through his hair. He had lived forty years. Why did he feel as if he was so much younger than the guard who stared at him so knowingly?

"I can be trusted with anything," Belisarius answered without pomp or emotion. Petrus had seen how power-hungry men would grovel and flatter to gain standing in life. He both loved and hated those kinds of men—they were easy to control yet spoke only to appease the one in power. Petrus sighed. Belisarius was not one of them. It was as if the man had no cares in the world— he was simply going along in life without a grand scheme to find fame and fortune. If he was a spy or had some ulterior motive, Belisarius would have an air about him or would give off the appearance of trying too hard. He did not seem to be driven by anything in particular, and thus his words were naturally to be believed.

"Have you bewitched me? Do you wear a talisman that imbues you with the ability to make others do as you want?" Petrus asked, confused by the comfort Belisarius's words brought.

"No. I do not believe in spells and magic. I believe that my sword and spear will always strike their target because I am guiding their aim. I believe that intelligence will always defeat the luck of incompetent leaders. And I believe that a brilliant tactician has much more power in the world than a mere foot soldier. Your uncle is the latter. You are the former. You brought me here to fulfill a purpose, and I am content to serve a man who thinks and acts the way you do, my lord." Belisarius gave a nod as he spoke the last word, and Petrus's heart leapt.

A slow smile crept over Petrus's face. He knew Belisarius was the tool he had been searching for to accomplish his goals. Petrus cleared his throat as his mind returned to the man facing him.

"I am glad to know my instincts were correct. We have a lot of work to do."

Within a year of Belisarius's arrival in Constantinople, more than half the schemes Petrus had spent years planning were accomplished. Justin's armies were strategically spread throughout the kingdom and beyond. Decrees now protected the rights of newly conquered citizens of the empire. Moneys had been secured for the expansion of the empire. And Petrus was on the verge of finally being able to take his beloved Theodora as his bride. Justin agreed to change the laws concerning marriage between social classes—Petrus now only had to wait for the death of his aunt to have the outdated law overturned. Theodora was the only woman Petrus would ever love, but she was well below the station of an empress. She was an actress and a dancer—one who excelled in the art of seduction. But she had ensnared Petrus's heart, and he would not relent unless he could have her by his side. Belisarius had quietly joined Petrus in mocking the old law, persuading Justin to believe that he would always be celebrated as the emperor who valiantly destroyed social stigmas by striking down outdated decrees.

Belisarius had also taken over the entire palace guard, forming a personal bodyguard regiment which he called the bucellarii. They performed their duties almost as if they were on a battlefield—complete with ranks, specializations in various weaponry, and daily training exercises to keep them in their best possible condition. They patrolled the palace and its walls armed with a spear, a bow, or a sword. Each man was personally chosen by Belisarius, forced to prove his worth in skill and battlefield knowledge before he was accepted into the bucellarii ranks. The guard presently numbered over eight hundred, but Belisarius was always increasing their ranks. The emperor and his family were safer than they had ever been—at least from an outside threat.

In their time together, Petrus had come to appreciate the occasions on which Belisarius voiced his own opinions—rather than simply echoing Petrus's thoughts. Belisarius was a wealth of wisdom and problem-solving—regardless of whether issues revolved around relations with warring nations, battlefield tactics, or personal discrepancies between uncle and nephew. It had taken months to pull Belisarius's opinions from his mind—after all, the man had sworn only to mimic Petrus. But once the floodgates were opened, Petrus could hardly make a decision without the guidance or approval of the palace's head guardian.

"Why does that cursed woman not die? She's suffered from headaches, backaches, stomach pain, and weak bones for years! Her body is trying to tell her to die. She simply… won't," Petrus complained, his head buried in his hands as he fought against the desire to scream his frustrations.

"She cannot die at this moment. Her death would seem far too convenient for you. Justin has only recently agreed to change the law for your marriage. Your aunt will die, but it is necessary for you to wait until she is taken naturally. If you are suspected of killing her, your death would swiftly follow," Belisarius warned.

Petrus groaned, pulling his head away from his hands to look into Belisarius's eyes. "I know!" Petrus yelled.

He watched as the guardian's jaw clenched, and his eyes grew hard.

"I am sorry for giving an unwanted opinion. I will leave you in solitude," Belisarius responded with forced propriety as he turned to leave.

Petrus was not sorry that he upset Belisarius. The man was only a pawn in his grand scheme, and he had spoken without Petrus's prompting. He felt his blood boiling as the words echoed in his mind. *It is necessary for you to wait.* "For her to be taken naturally? What if she lives for twenty years more?" he whispered to himself, knowing the guard's words rang true. "The world is against me. It is only a matter of time before another man asks for Theodora's hand in marriage."

He remained in the room for some time before determining to find Belisarius, but upon passing through the doorway, he found the head of the palace guard was already waiting for him.

"Good. I must see her tonight. Bring her to my chamber—through the front door this time. I cannot risk her passing my aunt's room again," Petrus commanded as Belisarius bowed and left for the theater to find the woman for whom Petrus pined without reason.

Two hours later, the knock at his bedroom door signaled the appearance of his future bride. Belisarius waited to be dismissed.

"Any problems?" Petrus asked without taking his eyes off the vision of beauty before him.

"None at all," Belisarius answered shortly. He knew better than to mince words when Theodora stood within Petrus's reach.

"That will be all," Petrus dismissed Belisarius and waited only for the latching of the door to jerk the cloak from Theodora's perfect figure. He loved when she came straight from the theater. Her wardrobe for the stage hardly left room for his imagination to guess at what was barely hidden underneath. As soon as her outer cloak hit the floor, Theodora's soft moan sent Petrus's mind into a furious need to have her naked in his arms. He crushed his lips to hers, and as her fingers grabbed at his hair and neck, he gently reminded her not to leave any marks this time. The glint in her eyes announced she would do as she pleased… and Petrus felt only excitement and more passion in her defiant stare. He easily picked up her light frame and tossed her onto his bed, stripping off his vestments. She watched in delight as he slowly pulled her clothes away from her skin, taking care to touch every piece of skin he uncovered—either with his hands or his lips. She played with his hair as he moved and sat up so he could pull the fabric over her head, freeing her body completely of the annoying coverings.

"When can we marry, my love? I have rejected three suitors only this week. And four earlier this month. Surely she can be poisoned. I will do it myself if you will not," Theodora pleaded with a tone of innocence that starkly contrasted her venomous words. Her relentlessness was only one of the reasons Petrus had fallen in love with her two years earlier. "I am only getting older. You know I wish to provide you an heir. How am I to do so if you do not show the empire I am yours?"

"In due time my little dancer. I promise. Do not accept another suitor. You know it does not bode well for other men to touch what is mine," he warned. A flash of excitement crossed her face as he spoke the words.

"Yes. And that is why I let them touch me. Right now, it is the only proof I have that I am truly yours," she narrowed her eyes and leaned so her mouth touched his ear. He felt the flick of a tongue over the lobe of his ear before she nibbled it softly. "And that is why I will continue to allow men to touch me until you show the entire empire who will be sitting at your side when your uncle is dead," she whispered dangerously.

Petrus could not control himself after her menacing and thrilling words. He ravaged her body for hours, until he could ravage no more. And when he finally felt the pull of sleep, Belisarius arrived to take Theodora back home.

Belisarius is a faithful servant, Petrus thought as he began to fade into slumber. *I pray Theodora will be as faithful a wife.*

TWENTY-FIVE

Constantinople, 524 C.E.

PETRUS WOKE to the sound of screams echoing through the stone halls of the palace. A man's wail sent his brain into a frenzy. He sprang from his bed, throwing a robe over his shoulders, and headed out into the hallway to investigate the confusion.

"My lord," a young guard addressed him as soon as the door opened.

"What has happened, Viator?" Petrus asked hurriedly, realizing his second guardian was missing from his post.

"Probus went with Belisarius only moments ago to aid the other guardians. I do not know what has happened—only that the emperor has been screaming for guards," the young man reported with tremors in his voice. Despite the fear in the guard's eyes, Petrus noted the watchful gaze that scanned for danger constantly. The man was well-trained.

"Accompany me," Petrus commanded as he set off to find the source of the wailing. After only a few steps, he broke into a full sprint without having consciously made a decision to run. He rounded a corner to find a mass of people huddled in front of his aunt's sleeping chamber.

"Uncle!" he called, pushing his way through the onlookers trying to steal a glimpse through the open doors. Petrus finally broke through the crowd to find his uncle's body protectively hovering over the lifeless body of Empress Euphemia. The noise that came from his uncle's body was unearthly—his mouth hung open as tears, slobber and nasal discharge dripped in equal measure from his face. Emperor Justin was the picture of grief from head to toe—his shaking fingers rapidly moving over the arms, neck and hair of his dead wife, searching for any hint of life remaining under his frantic touch.

"Please, Lupicina," he wailed, resting his forehead against her pale skin,

"Please no!"

Upon hearing the use of his aunt's birth name—a name only his uncle used in the privacy of their bedroom—Petrus realized he had been frozen in shock for far too long. He rushed to his uncle's side, wrapping the unusually fragile man in a strong grasp.

"Oh, uncle," Petrus cooed softly. "What has happened this night?"

The bucellarii quietly returned all of the weeping onlookers back to their respective rooms while Petrus remained with his uncle and the body of his deceased aunt. As his uncle wept in his arms, Petrus's eyes searched for the source of his aunt's death. The puddle of blood on the floor around her body was expansive. He found a bloodied knife resting in the open palm of her right hand. His eyes continued their appraisal of the corpse and found a deep gash on her left wrist peeking out from under the long, bloodied sleeve of her robe.

A gust of the chilly night air blew through the room, and Petrus looked up to see Belisarius had returned to the room. He searched the head guardian's face for a sign that he might have been responsible for the incident, but the face was cloaked in the same visage of determined protection that was normal in times of distress or urgency. Petrus looked more thoroughly at Belisarius's armor and skin in search of splatters of blood or signs of a struggle—but there was no evidence to indicate he was a part of Empress Euphemia's death.

"My lords," Belisarius spoke up, "I will begin an investigation this very night to find if there is any evidence of foul play at hand. I will act with the presumption that she has been murdered until I find no evidence to support that theory." He bowed and left the room.

A year had passed since he and Belisarius had last spoken of the desire for his aunt's death. Each time Petrus spoke the name "Euphemia" with even the slightest hint of disdain, Belisarius's warning glare reminded him of their earlier conversation. So he had waited patiently. Quietly. For more than one year. And without any warning or hint of the coming triumph, his aunt was dead in the course of one night.

She is finally dead. My God, Petrus mused, *if he is responsible for her death, he is more powerful a tool than I thought possible. With Belisarius in command of my armies, none will stand against me. Those who dare to challenge my authority will perish under the cover of the night sky; and kingdoms will crumble when, as day breaks, the threat of death swirls through whole encampments. Death himself has chosen to stand by my side.* He felt intoxicated with the power at his fingertips. The smile that threatened to curl at the corners of his mouth would have to wait. He held his uncle a little tighter as the man's moans continued.

"Oh uncle," he cooed. "How could this have happened?

TWENTY-SIX

Castello San Romolo, Present Day

SAINT LOOKED DOWN at his desk, memories of his first years with Priest occupying his thoughts. Had he known just how dangerous Priest was, he might never have invited the killer into his home. *That is a lie and you know it,* Saint chided himself. Saint's thirst for power was at its peak when he met Priest. The death of his aunt had only been the beginning of the mysterious deaths that surrounded Constantinople during the end of Justin's reign. People had to be displaced to make way for the new emperor—and no person was exempt from the threat of extermination. Save Saint.

He pushed his chair backwards, listening to the grotesque sound of its wooden legs scraping against the uneven stone floors. He usually picked the chair up to avoid the sound, but the discomfort of hearing the noise somehow made him feel a measure of punishment for the grand deception he would have to begin moments later.

His nephews had been gathering all of the contracts into the underground meeting chamber for hours—each scroll hand-written in ink, signed by the hiring party and Priest, and rolled and sealed with Priest's signet upon the contract's completion. There were tens of thousands in the Family vaults. Priest and Saint had taken great care to protect the vaults against temperature changes and moisture—they had studied the wine cellars of some of the greatest vintners in the Tuscan region to learn the best technique. Hundreds of years of secrets and concealed contracts would soon be revealed to the entire Family.

Priest was right—the Family would need Saint to play the innocent bystander if there was any hope of keeping the tiny fissures from fracturing into irreconcilable chasms. But the breaks had already begun to show. And so it was up to him to put on a performance that would leave no room for doubt. Priest was always the monster of the two, and though he tried, Saint had been unable to rein in his unruly brother. *What a ridiculous farce,* Saint snorted his frustration. *And if the rest of the Family believes such a lie, I am more capable an actor than I believed. Or else we raised the boys to be far too trusting.*

From the moment Saint had realized that Priest's sons were frozen in their late twenties, he had begun to construct the line of succession in the unlikely event that something removed Priest and himself from leadership—whether that be hiding from the law, mental breakdown, or the unlikely possibility of death. But though he discussed the plan with Priest, he never felt the need to disclose the line to the boys for fear of creating ill-will between brothers. The scroll of succession had been placed in the hidden crawl space under the main vault, along with other secrets he and Priest had hoped would remain hidden. They had gone to great lengths to conceal the loose stone that led to the most incriminating of records. Saint had, on numerous occasions, begged Priest to burn the scrolls, removing—fully—the threat of discovery. But Priest had insisted that their system of records be honored to the last. *You always knew the truth—he wanted to be caught,* the thought sent a chill up Saint's spine.

Saint made his way through the castle, listening to the low murmurs seeping out through the closed doors. The sounds of laughter that were typical only a few weeks before had since disappeared. The mood was somber—even a little angry. He entered the meeting room and eyed the stacks of contracts that now lined the rows of marble benches in the amphitheater. *Have they found the crawl space? Surely it was concealed well enough,* he hoped. Though there had not been a single moment for him to sneak into the vaults to destroy the chamber's contents, he knew it might seem more incriminating if the secret chamber was found to have been recently emptied. A sharp pang of fear ran up Saint's spine as he looked around. He felt sure the contents of the hidden space were somehow sitting in the hall, awaiting his nephews' discovery.

"I believe we are ready to begin," Thomas announced as soon as Saint crossed over the room's threshold.

"Sit down," Saint commanded as he made his way down the stairs to the large table his nephews had positioned in the center of the floor. They had moved his and Priest's chairs to make room for the table, and Saint gulped as he viewed the way their chairs had been pushed to the side. His nephews exchanged surprised glances as they shuffled to their seats. It was rare that Saint exercised authority over his nephews. He often acted as an adviser and confidant, but rarely more. His burning desire for power had disappeared with his wife's death so long ago—and since leaving Constantinople he had been content to stand in Priest's shadow. But with Priest locked away in his room, Saint was once again forced to act as the head of the Family.

"Sergius, Paulus, Felix, Alexander, and Demetrius—you will go through the contracts to decide which ones need further review. The contracts to be reviewed will be set at the front of the room. The contracts which you believe are justifiable will be placed back in the vault."

Thomas opened his mouth to object, but a raised hand and a stern look from Saint stopped the words from forming on his lips.

"We are all grieving, but you and Gregorius more than the others. You need to take care of yourselves first. We are capable of completing this task without you," Saint offered with kindness in his voice.

"And why am I not aiding?" Claudius questioned.

"Someone needs to be responsible for running the home and the Family affairs while we are stuck in here combing through thousands of contracts. You are capable," Saint lied. He would only have to worry about Claudius if the hidden contracts had been found.

Claudius accepted his role with hesitation, but apparently Saint's demeanor was such that his nephews knew not to press him further.

"Let's begin," Saint declared as he broke the first seal.

Saint watched as the men around the table broke countless seals and carefully unfurled the ancient parchments. The words were quickly skimmed— occasionally accompanied by raised eyebrows, sighs or grunts of frustration at the contents—before the documents were re-rolled and placed into one of the two piles. Saint noted that for every ten contracts read, at least two were placed in the "further review" pile. He inwardly groaned at the breadth of the task ahead. Priest's conviction of guilt seemed more and more certain as the day went on.

By the end of the first day, the stacks of scrolls lining the marble benches barely seemed to have been touched. But the looks of frustration and condemnation on his nephews' faces forced Saint's spirits even lower than they had been at the start of the day.

He returned to his room, trying not to drag his feet under the exhaustion he felt, and plopped down onto the edge of his bed, raking a hand through his hair. His heart was overwhelmed with guilt at the fall Priest would willingly take for their decisions. And, if he was honest with himself, the thought of going through life without Priest was terrifying.

Priest had, for centuries, served as the hand throwing the dice which decided the fates of kings, queens, dictators, and popes. But it seemed, perhaps, that Death might at last decide to reclaim his title from Priest's thieving grasp. Saint was unsure what the world might look like without the bloody tip of Priest's knife directing the tenor of the political atmosphere.

The idea that Saint might soon be abandoned to live out eternity without his closest confidant brought unwelcome tears to his eyes. He lay in bed and stared at the wood grains in the ceiling as he had that morning. *Was that only this morning?* He moaned, rubbing his tired, wet eyes. The upcoming weeks would only grow more difficult.

Priest had spent the whole day confined to his room. He alternated pacing and writing—as he often took comfort in jotting down short narratives or poems.

The fires of hell drawing closer in sight
Seem brighter than dark and more hopeful than light.
When sword's drawn at last over head bowed in shame
I will feel only peace at the end of this game.

His latest poem felt juvenile and contrived—a pouting child's fit after being caught picking on a younger sibling. A corner of his mouth lifted as he held the parchment over his candle to destroy the words at which he scoffed. He hated writing in English, French, and Italian. But writing in Arabic and Latin had grown tedious after a few centuries. He sometimes enjoyed writing poems in Japanese or Thai—but his understanding of the script was abysmal, and he rarely completed a poem before the parchment was destroyed because of a fault in his calligraphic attempts.

As the remnants of the page drifted away and disappeared, he felt a sliver of joy in the act. He wrote only to ease his own mind, not for the enjoyment or ridicule of others. There were only a few pieces which he loved enough to keep —and none would see those if he had his way. This day had seen at least fifteen short stories about the untimely deaths of certain sons and grandsons—and each of the stories was hastily incinerated. He wished he could find an excuse for his odd writing habits, but the only real explanation was that he enjoyed the simple act of watching his thoughts and dreams float away in ashes.

The day had dragged on far too long. The castle was too quiet. And his stomach had begun growling its hungry protestations hours before. He knew it was imprudent to walk about the castle with tensions so high, though, so he waited until silence was the only sound echoing off the cold stone walls.

As his door creaked open, he listened for the hint of anyone still awake. Nothing, he thought as he proceeded down the hallway. His steps were silent on the stone floors covered in long, narrow rugs. The only sound he heard was his own heartbeat. He breathed a sigh of relief and walked swiftly to the kitchen.

It wasn't that he feared his family—far from it. He simply did not wish to add discomfort to those of the Family whom he still loved. Gregorius, in particular, did not need any grief added to his already-overwhelming sadness. And Priest knew how torn his beloved boy must be at this juncture.

Priest opened the refrigerator in the pitch-black room to remove some of the prepared food that had been left by someone earlier in the day. He suspected that Caterina had been setting aside the portions of food specifically for him, though he could not for the life of him figure out why she would go to such lengths for a man she hated so vehemently. Even so, the food was waiting for him in the same spot each night. He thrust the bowl into the microwave and turned it on. He had grown accustomed to having all the modern conveniences present in the castle—electric lighting, heating, and kitchen appliances in particular. But he still found himself in awe of the microwave and refrigerator on occasion. The bell sounded and he removed the food, ready to return to his room with his dinner. But as he turned to go, a shadow blocked his way.

"Father," Priest heard his eldest son whisper in a pained voice.

"Sergius," Priest replied through tight lips. This was not an encounter he wanted to have in the dark of night. His love for his firstborn son was something he could not describe. Sergius was loyal yet righteous, brutal yet gentle. He was the best of his father and his… *mother.*

"I wish things were different. I wish I understood why you've done the things you've done. I wish…" Sergius's voice cracked.

"It's better this way. My decisions affect only me. No one else need shoulder the blame for the wrongs I've done—the sins I've committed," Priest rested his free hand on Sergius's shoulder. "You've only carried out my orders."

"It doesn't feel that way. I think we should all share this burden," Sergius's voice began to rise.

"Hush. You will not voice that opinion aloud. Promise me. Whatever blame is found, whatever judgment is cast. It is mine alone to bear," Priest urged his firstborn. He did not wait for Sergius's response. He pushed his way past Sergius and returned to his room, locking the door behind him.

He stood with his back against the door for some time, thinking of nothing and everything at once. When he finally came to his senses, the food in his bowl had gone cold, and his appetite had vanished. He tossed the food into the trash and climbed into bed, hoping to find some respite from life in the nothingness of sleep.

TWENTY-SEVEN

Constantinope, 527 C.E.

BELISARIUS MARCHED to Petrus's chambers to deliver the news. He did not know how Petrus would respond to the death of his uncle, but Belisarius was hopeful he would see the monumental opportunity that had been laid at his feet. Petrus would be named emperor within a few days—this was the defining goal that had pushed Belisarius forward for years. He breathed deeply before knocking twice at the door.

A few moments passed before Petrus opened it, a candle in hand. Belisarius could see he had woken Petrus from slumber.

"Out with it," Petrus's whisper commanded as he rubbed the sleep from an eye with his free hand.

"The emperor is dead. He passed in his sleep—the physician said it was peaceful," Belisarius reported.

Petrus exited his room and shut the door softly behind him, so as not to disturb Theodora's slumber.

"He is dead?" Petrus queried, his face looking stricken with pain and a bit paler than normal.

"He died within this hour. He was surrounded by servants, guards, and physicians. My guards informed me only moments ago," he reported.

Belisarius saw Petrus's eyes searching his face for any sign that his head guard had been involved in his uncle's death. Belisarius felt tension leave his body as Petrus's face relaxed slightly. *Apparently I'm doing a good enough job of appearing innocent.* Belisarius had been careful to keep himself away from searching eyes while he had poisoned the emperor over the previous months. He needed the emperor's death to appear natural, and he wanted to rejoice at his success. Nonetheless, he kept a grave expression carefully plastered to his visage.

"I should pay my respects," Petrus whispered almost inaudibly.

Belisarius could see the tumult in Petrus's eyes. He was sad for the loss of his uncle, yet the sickness had been coming on for months. He was finally emperor, yet he must mourn for his uncle's death before he could celebrate the momentous accomplishment. He did not automatically have the throne, yet he did not think any other would dare to challenge him. Petrus eyed Belisarius quizzically for a short moment before nodding his thanks for the gentle delivery of the somber news and heading toward his uncle's bedchamber. Belisarius followed him, keeping a close eye on any movements in the dark corridors.

Petrus stood in the doorway of his uncle's chambers, bracing himself against the thick stone wall as he breathed deeply. Belisarius felt a slight pang of guilt as he watched Petrus grieve, but this was the goal for which Belisarius had been brought into the palace. His next steps were simply to protect Petrus and Theodora.

The next morning, Petrus emerged from his chambers with his wife holding his arm in support. His red-rimmed eyes and the dark circles beneath them were evidence of a teary, sleepless night. Belisarius was shocked by the man's reaction.

"Were you so surprised? He's been growing sickly for months," Belisarius muttered as they walked toward the throne room. Petrus stopped, and Theodora glared at Belisarius with the most confusing combination of accusation and admiration as her husband spoke quietly yet furiously.

"You should not be so obvious, Belisarius. My intention was never for you to kill my uncle. He would have died eventually—the man was advanced in years as it was. And do not deny your involvement, Theordora assures me you had been poisoning him for weeks, if not longer."

Belisarius raised his eyebrows at the revelation Theodora was aware of his interference in the emperor's life. *If she knew, why did she not speak up?* he wondered, but promptly remembered the hint of admiration in her eyes. *She wanted this too.* And if he asked, she would likely help him in a future endeavor. He filed the thought away.

"I do not deny it. Your goals have always been my goals. Your reign begins today, and I have secured the palace grounds and guards so that you and your wife may live without fear as you rule. I trust every one of the bucellarii with my life and yours. You are the undisputed ruler of the Roman empire, and I will always serve in whatever way you deem necessary to further your purposes," Belisarius finished with a small bow.

Emotions danced across Petrus's face—anger, confidence, fear, excitement. But there was also a measure of distrust which Belisarius could not understand. Petrus masked his emotions with a blank calm before resuming his walk to the throne room.

"I will be declared Justinian I tomorrow. After I am emperor, I will decide the punishment for your actions… and if you are worthy to remain head of my guardians," he spoke evenly. Belisarius shook his head in disappointment but said nothing. *After all I have done to secure the throne for him, he no longer believes I am worthy of his trust.*

TWENTY-EIGHT

Castello San Romolo, Present Day

SERGIUS GLANCED around the cavernous room filled with dozens of men combing furiously through contracts. After the first three days of reviewing the details of the never-ending stacks of scrolls, he and his brothers had convinced Saint to bring in more of the family to aid in their task. Saint had agreed that the five brothers assigned to the task could bring in their sons and grandsons to help—which brought their total number to forty-seven. Now, after a week with the extra man power, they were through about half of the contracts.

"I'm taking these back to the vault," Sergius muttered as only a few heads nodded in acknowledgment that he had spoken. He piled the scrolls his family had deemed "acceptable" that day onto a platter he had found in the kitchen—transporting them that way was easier and far quicker than carrying the scrolls by hand, ten at a time. Saint had decisively shut down the idea of burning the acceptable scrolls after it had been suggested by numerous people.

"This is a fine-tuned system. Stop pestering me, or I'll send the extra help away, and you five will have to do *all* the work like I originally planned," Saint threatened. No one had spoken another word on the matter, and Sergius had volunteered to run the scrolls back to the vault whenever the stack in the center of the table grew too large.

Sergius entered the vault, careful to close the door tightly behind him as soon as he was inside. He was astounded that the scrolls remained in such excellent shape after all these years, but Saint and Priest had ensured the conditions were ideal for the moisture and temperature when they had built the castle centuries earlier. Sergius felt a chill run down his spine as he thought about the size of the room and the number of shelves necessary to house all the contracts the Family had fulfilled. "So much death," he whispered. He sighed and went to the farthest corner of the room, placing the scrolls on the last shelf on the left side of the long vault. *Halfway sorted,* he thought with some relief. He dropped a scroll, grunting with worry as he bent to grab it and checked to make sure it was undamaged. But when he picked it up, he felt the stone beneath his right foot shift a little. *That is odd,* he thought as he reached down to examine the loose stone. As he pushed on it to see if it was secure, the dust between it and the surrounding stones began to fall through cracks, leaving a crevice exposed. *What on earth?* His mind began to speculate over the possibility of another space existing beneath this one. This vault was the lowest point on the entire castle grounds. It was down a set of stairs off the underground amphitheater. With the effort it took just to dig this room, he had not entertained the idea that the vault concealed a chamber set even deeper into the hill where their castle rested.

He pulled the stone up and four others moved a bit, exposing a space just big enough for someone to crawl through. He dropped a bit of dirt into the dark crevice, unable to see how large the space was in the dim light coming from the front of the room. He listened breathlessly as the dirt hit the bottom of the dark space far more quickly than he had expected. He wished he had brought his cell phone with him so he could have use of a flashlight, but if he returned to the amphitheater only to grab his cell phone and return to the vault, someone might suspect he was up to something. Sergius stared for a moment more into the shallow space before lowering his body into the dark hold, feet first. When his feet hit the ground, his shoulders and head were still outside the now-open chamber. He squatted down, feeling around blindly with his hands. The lighting in the vault had always been dim—which Priest had attributed to the conservation of the ancient scrolls. But now, Sergius suspected it was also to conceal the hidden space. After a few moments in the darkness, his eyes adjusted so he could make out what was stored in the small hole. He saw a few scrolls, books, and boxes in the space, but he would have to come back again with a flashlight so he could look more thoroughly at the hidden contents.

He crawled out, now covered in dust, and sat next to the opening. If whatever was hidden was important enough to keep secret from the rest of the family, perhaps it was exactly the concrete evidence they needed to confirm Thomas's suspicions about Priest's mental instability. He sat for a few moments, staring into the dark hole filled with ancient secrets. *Do what you know you must,* his mind commanded. The fear he felt in the pit of his stomach was overwhelming.

"If you reveal what you have found, you are condemning your father to death," Sergius jumped at the sound of his uncle's voice.

"Uncle," Sergius blinked, not sure whether he could shoulder the weight of the decision before him. "Do you know what that chamber contains?"

"I do. And if I have been able to conceal it for all this time, you, too, are capable."

Sergius stared at Saint—rage, fear, and despair taking turns pulling at his mind.

"You have known of the corruption all this time and done nothing?" Sergius asked.

"Oh Sergius. You are more intelligent than that. We have all known and done nothing. Do not now have the audacity to blame me for this entire family's willful ignorance," Saint warned.

Sergius stayed unmoving as he pondered the truth of those words.

"I simply ask that you think on it. Replace the stones. I will remove the dust from your clothing. If you decide it is necessary to search the contents later, I will not stand in your way. Only know that you will find all the evidence you need within its walls," Saint added, helping Sergius to stand and dusting him off as he deliberated over the situation. He narrowed his eyes at his uncle, wondering if Saint might try to destroy the scrolls if he left them. *But they've been here all this time. Surely if he meant to destroy them he would have done so already.* He left the room, though he felt as if he had left his mind within the hidden chamber.

Sergius barely slept for the next two nights. He heard his uncle's words echoing in his mind like the clanging of pots and pans before breakfast—the words called to those who could hear, begging them to arise from their slumber and tend to the call. *If you reveal what you have found, you are condemning your father to death. Do not now have the audacity to blame me for this entire family's willful ignorance.* How had he and his brothers and nephews and Saint allowed his father to go on with such corruption and arrogance?

Since the time he was old enough to play the role of "big brother," Sergius had prided himself on standing up for what was right, correcting wrong behavior, and helping his brothers and nephews find their way back to reason and righteousness if they were lost. Because of this, the failure to identify and stop his father's actions weighed on him more heavily than the rest of the family. *It is time to make this right,* he decided as he quickly emerged from his bed, grabbed a flashlight, and marched to the vault.

Priest had made a decision to leave the door without a lock and key—it would have been pointless to try to keep the rest of the Family from entering the room. And Sergius now believed Priest's intentions were to keep any feelings of suspicion away by outwardly showing an air of transparency. The entire house was asleep as he entered the dark room and flipped on the dim light. He closed his eyes, listening for the sounds of anyone stirring above, and only when his senses told him he was completely alone, he began.

The stones shifted easily as he pushed them aside to clear the opening. He shone the flashlight into the space, checking to make sure everything was still where he had found it, and breathed a sigh of relief. Everything was there, exactly as it had been two days earlier.

He found a stack of thirteen scrolls which he decided to examine first. He opened the first, reading about the assassination of Pope John XXI as planned and carried out by Gregorius and Elias. Sergius wondered why Priest felt it necessary to hide the assassination of a prominent religious figure (as it was quite normal for the Family to accept contracts for such people), though he assumed it had been concealed due to some of his brothers' feelings of love and appreciation for that particular pope. John XXI was actually one of the good popes from an era of corruption and villainy in the Catholic Church. Sergius put it aside, relieved that the first contract was not as incriminating as he expected.

The second and third he looked through were politically-related. Not so out of the ordinary to be deemed condemnatory. He pulled a fourth from the stack, and as he opened it, his heart sank. It was the contract Sergius himself had completed to kill Anamaria's family. He had never seen the contract, but his father had assured him that killing whomever was in the home at that exact time would fulfill the contract and put the Family dispute to rest. Sergius had not known he was killing Mattia's betrothed, and the guilt of his actions had forced Sergius to flee the company of his family for nearly a century. He had gone to Portugal where he met his third wife. They had lived together in peace for a few years before she died in childbirth—along with the child. He had accepted her death as punishment for his sins against Mattia, but as he looked at the contract, he felt all the sorrow of that loss once again. The contract was meant only to kill Anamaria—not her entire family, as Mattia had been told he must do. And the reasons given for the assassination were petty, at best. Sergius wiped his tears with the sleeve of his shirt, careful to not let them fall upon the old parchment. He rolled it slowly, knowing that particular contract would be important in his father's conviction.

The next contract unfurled was for Pope John Paul I, the thirty-three day pope that was apparently murdered by Elias's eldest son in 1978. Sergius had presumed the Family's involvement at the time of the pope's death, but the Family was so spread throughout the world, there was no way to know for sure if anyone had been in Rome during that particular moment. Pope John Paul I had been a threat to the entire infrastructure of the Catholic Church, and a group within the Vatican had requested the pope's murder. Sergius rolled his eyes—the corruption of that particular institution had driven him away from Catholicism a few centuries earlier. Nothing about the Vatican—good or bad—

was capable of surprising him anymore.

Next, he unrolled the scroll contracting the Family for Sir Thomas Urquhart's death—which had been secured by Oliver Cromwell for the sole purpose of "disposing of a thorn in the Kingdom's side." There were no political gains. No attempts to make the death seem important. Simply that the Crown wished the man dead, and Priest was too happy to oblige. *That's evidence enough,* Sergius sighed at the idiocy of such a contract.

The seventh was clearly the newest of the scrolls. Sergius knew what would be written upon the parchment and had little desire to read it, but he opened it nonetheless. A breath caught in his throat as he read the words condemning Mattia and Lissie to death for "the dissemination of ill will against Priest within the ranks of the Family." Sergius quickly re-rolled the scroll and set it in the pile with the others.

The next four scrolls were almost too much for Sergius to cope with. He had been under the impression that Mattia and Lissie were Priest's first attempts to kill members of the Family. But that was simply not the case. Three of the contracts were signed and fulfilled by Priest himself. The fourth was carried out by Samuel—who most certainly did not understand the crime he was committing by setting fire to the inn where Elias's youngest grandson had spent the month wasting away in debauchery and drink. Sergius doubted Priest had explained anything to Samuel except that the inn needed to be razed to the ground while those inside were asleep. *The Family will be devastated by the contents of these scrolls,* he realized as his head began to ache. "Why would father not destroy these?" he heard himself asking aloud.

The final two scrolls would be examined the next day. Sergius could not continue on his own. He set the thirteen scrolls outside the crawl space and continued to search the contents of the small room. He thumbed through a few of the books, realizing that Priest had, at various intervals, kept diaries of the events in his life. However, Sergius did not recognize the language and therefore could not read them. The third and most ancient-looking book contained pages covered in rows of lines and dots. The scribbles lent themselves to proving Priest's apparent madness as Sergius could find no rhyme or reason to the incoherent scratchings. He would look through the journals' contents more thoroughly in the light of day to see if there was any possibility of comprehending what was hidden within them.

The only items left in the room were two wooden boxes sitting side-by-side on a stone ledge. He opened the larger box to find loose papers, letters, and a few small paintings. He picked up an old piece of parchment folded and sealed with Priest's signet. Without hesitation, he broke the seal and carefully unfolded it. "Line of Succession" was written clearly across the top of the page. Sergius felt his breath catch in his throat as he read the first name: Paulus. *Father hasn't even given me the benefit of leading the family in the case that he and Saint are incapable of leading?* Sergius's heart pounded against his chest, breaking as it did its best to burst from its cage of bone. He couldn't bear to look any more. He refolded the parchment and placed it back in the box.

He shut the box and stacked it with the journals, forcing his eyes to look away from the most crushing item he had found in the secret room. He examined the smaller box—which required a key. Sergius rolled his eyes. *Anyone in this house could have this open in seconds.* He grabbed the room's contents and dragged himself out of the tiny space, stretching and moaning at the aches his body now felt after remaining hunched over for so long. He checked the hour and found he had sat nearly unmoving for three hours, bent over uncomfortably the entire time. He took the scrolls to the center of the table in the amphitheater so he could review the contents with his brothers the next day.

He carried the boxes and journals up to his room and turned on the small reading light on his desk. He felt the pain of betrayal from his father—the man who had given him life, the man who had given him so much love—for choosing another to lead in his stead. And for behaving in a way so contrary to the heroic image Sergius had created in his mind of Priest. "We only accept contracts that will shift the world toward more stability. Both good and bad men become corrupt when they find great power within their grasp. Without our Family, such power would go unchecked. We are the scales of justice that keep the world from tipping off its axis," he heard the speech that Priest gave to each young member of the Family as they began their training to enter the ranks of the Family assassins. Sergius hung his head at the lies he had believed for too long. *It was right there in front of me. Always. Right there.* He leaned forward to rest for a moment as he thought of all the noble speeches his father had delivered over his life, and somewhere in the haze of his past, his body gave in to exhaustion.

TWENTY-NINE

"WHERE DID THESE scrolls come from?" Saint heard Paulus ask as he entered the amphitheater. He felt his heart begin to race at the words. *It seems Sergius has chosen to condemn Priest to death.*

"I found them last night," Sergius began. "There was a small crawl space in the back of the vault under a loose stone. As soon as I found it, I knew it could only contain information pertinent to father's guilt."

"Under the vault?" Saint heard several voices mumble as everyone stared worryingly at the new scrolls.

"I do not think it is necessary for us to continue combing through the rest of the scrolls. Everything we've feared is contained within these," Sergius pointed to the stack with weariness in his eyes.

Saint walked down the stairs reluctantly. He lamented over how the day would unfold.

"Gentlemen," Saint began, clearing his throat, "why don't we review these with just the five of you that I originally selected. I would like to keep the rumors to a minimum until we decide on a clear course of action."

With his nephews' nods of approval, their offspring left the room begrudgingly. Every man in the Family would soon know of Priest's most scandalous actions—it was best if he could keep the Family's anger to a minimum until the inevitable trial. He thought it certain the date of the trial would be set by the end of the day.

Saint sat at the head of the table as Sergius, Paulus, Felix, Alexander, and Demetrius sat in the chairs closest to him. Sergius picked up the first scroll and unwound it, reading the details of Pope John XXI's death. Paulus and Demetrius were outraged, having been faithful followers of the Catholic faith for over a thousand years. They were even more furious when Sergius revealed that the second scroll outlined the execution of Pope John Paul I.

"How could these great leaders' deaths possibly be to maintain balance in the world? Was the world too 'good' because of them?" Demetrius growled as his brothers nodded in agreement.

Saint did not acknowledge the question, he was too busy trying to act surprised as the contracts were read aloud. "Shall we continue?" he asked as Sergius grabbed the next scroll.

The third and fourth contracts were glanced over as they were political assassinations, though none of the brothers could imagine why Priest had felt the need to hide them with the other concealed scrolls. The fifth was the murder of Sir Thomas Urquhart, which confused and frustrated the men around the table.

"This has no merit. Was father bored? Did he think he needed to find favor with the British Crown? Surely there must be some explanation for this level of stupidity," Felix scoffed.

Saint watched as Sergius carefully picked through the scrolls, clearly having decided upon the order in which to read them to his brothers the night before.

"This is the contract on Mattia and Lissie's lives. Priest had the audacity to draw up his own contract and write, in third person, that the reasoning for the murders was linked to their 'dissemination of ill will against Priest within the ranks of the Family.'"

Paulus rubbed his eyes roughly, his frustration growing with each revelation. *What have you done, Sergius?* Saint thought over and over again, as if his brain was stuck replaying a loop of only those five words.

Sergius picked up two scrolls in his hands and his eyes flitted between them. He set one down and broke the seal on the other. *So he still has not read them all. What joys will this one contain?* Saint thought darkly, feeling a fleeting moment of relief that the words in his mind had shifted to form new thoughts. Sergius looked a little surprised, rather than angry as he read over the words in front of him.

"This outlines the murder of the American president, William McKinley, by his vice president, Theodore Roosevelt. Hmm. It seems that this one was quite rushed. Roosevelt seized the opportunity to kill the president after another man had shot him. This clearly goes against our policy to keep power in check. In fact, this serves the opposite goal," Sergius sighed. He picked up the other unopened scroll and shook his head as he read the words within.

"What is it, Sergius?" Paulus leaned across the table and snatched it out of his brother's hands when he remained silent.

"For stirring discontentment and anger amongst his brothers, and for vocalizing an outcry against Priest, this contract details the imminent death of Thomas, fifth of Priest's sons. Upon completion of his services to Hernán Cortés de Monroy y Pizarro, the fulfillment of the contract would be completed only by the death of Thomas," Paulus choked out the last word. "Saint, please tell me you did not know of this."

"I would have stopped him if I had known. This comes as a great shock to me," Saint lied, shaking his head in a show of concern for his brother's decisions as Sergius picked up the next contract from the pile.

"This outlines the death of Anamaria Serrano. *Only* Anamaria Serrano. Not her entire family as Mattia was led to believe. And its purpose was to exact petty revenge on a political opponent who was causing a minor inconvenience to another in the Spanish court." There was a collective sigh around the table, but Saint could see everyone was waiting to hear the contents of the four remaining contracts.

"I cannot read the last four," Sergius mumbled, looking physically exhausted. As Paulus reached for them, Sergius grabbed his wrist with a speed that made everyone jump in their seats. "Not you, brother," he warned as he slid the contracts to Felix. Paulus's eyes narrowed at the implications.

"For continued debauchery and uselessness to the Family and the world, Borvin, fifth grandson of Elias, is to be killed in his sleep by way of accidental fire," Felix stopped reading as he and his brothers exchanged worried looks. Saint could see that they were now remembering those that had been lost to the Family, wondering whether their deaths had been planned or accidental. Paulus snatched the contracts and opened them quickly, searching for one name in particular.

"No!" he yelled as he threw the contract at Felix. "Read it," he commanded, pointing his shaky finger to the parchment rocking back and forth on the table as it rerolled into its learned shape. Felix slowly picked it up, closing his eyes briefly in dismay before opening his mouth to read the words everyone already knew were written there.

"In order to purge the Family of those who believe they are above the task of killing for the good of the world, I, Priest, have taken upon myself the responsibility to remove Lucius, firstborn of Paulus, for choosing a life dedicated to the church," Felix could barely finish.

Saint buried his head in his hands in disbelief, having never known that Priest had taken these steps. Had he known, he would have kept Paulus from this meeting, as he had with the others who were directly connected to the contracts.

"Paulus. I had no idea," Saint whispered, seeing the grief in every part of the man's being.

"Finish them. Please. Let this be over," Paulus begged, pointing at the final two contracts.

Sergius picked up one of the two when no one moved to comply with Paulus's request.

"Maximus, second son of Claudius, must be eliminated from the Family for refusing to carry out a contract given him."

No one reacted. They simply wanted to hear the contents of the one remaining scroll and be finished with this emotional undertaking. Felix read the final parchment.

"Kadir, fourth great-grandson of Gregorius, must be put to death by the hand of Priest for showing blatant disrespect to his elders, including both Gregorius and Priest, and for remaining out of contact with the Family to put the needs of his wife above the needs of the Family," Felix finished, placing the scroll back down on the table.

"I need a strong drink," Alexander announced after remaining silent for the entirety of the day. His brothers nodded in agreement, leaving Saint to sit alone in the amphitheater and worry over what would come next.

THIRTY

PRIEST HEARD a soft knock after midday. He put his pen down and sauntered to the door, only opening it enough to see who stood on the other side.

"I thought you might want these," Sergius said without looking Priest in the eyes. Priest's gaze drifted to the stack of items in his son's hands, and his heart gave a heavy thump.

"You found them," Priest stated matter-of-factly. Sergius nodded once, finally looking into his father's eyes.

"The trial is set to begin as soon as the rest of the Family arrives. No one knows these exist," Sergius thrust the pile of books and boxes toward Priest. He took them out of his son's hands, wishing there was some explanation that might make sense to his eldest son. But there simply wasn't a way to explain.

"Thank you, Sergius," Priest whispered as his son walked away. Sergius's body looked as if a yoke was set upon his shoulders, each step burdened by his perceived betrayal.

"Did you read them?" Priest asked as Sergius paused without turning back around.

"Only the line of succession. I cannot read the language you used in the journals," Sergius whispered.

"You know why I chose Paulus, right?" Priest asked as he looked upon Sergius's trembling shoulders.

"I do not think I could understand even if you explained. I trained them in your absence. But it is now clear that I was never good enough," Sergius walked briskly away.

Priest shut the door and returned to his desk, setting the stack of items down gently. He knew Sergius would not understand if he discovered Paulus was to lead in his place. But Paulus's moral code was the same as Priest's—he would do what needed to be done no matter the cost. Sergius simply could not fill the same roll, however excellent of a leader he may be.

Priest felt gratitude, relief, and disappointment in equal measure over Sergius not having been able to read the journals. He wished someone could somehow know the sordid history of his life without his actually having to speak the words. He touched the cracked leather covers of the ancient journals, feeling a fondness for the companionship they had provided to him during some of his most trying moments in life. The journals were sacred to Priest. He did not allow himself the luxury of dwelling in the past, but with only three days until his trial, he felt an urgency to relish every memory.

He flipped open the oldest journal, searching for a specific page, and when he found it, the images flashed through his mind as if he was there once more.

THIRTY-ONE

Dara, 530 C.E.

BELISARIUS INSPECTED the battle plans he had drawn, smiling at the nearly perfect execution of those plans by his soldiers. The victory had come as a surprise to many—Belisarius's soldiers were heavily outnumbered. But his officers had followed his instructions without question, resulting in a victory Belisarius knew was inevitable. He was even able to join his men in battle for a few moments—which was still one of his favorite pastimes. He found supreme enjoyment in killing the Zhayedan (or "immortals," as the Persians liked to call them). He still found humor whenever he killed one of the mislabeled lads. They were excellent fighters without question, but they were most assuredly mortal. He relaxed more with each "x" he added to the map, identifying the enemy's defeated regiments. Now was the time for his soldiers to chase after those who had escaped during battle—and to kill them before they could regroup with the Persian army.

"General Belisarius," he heard a messenger call from outside his tent.

"Enter," Belisarius shouted. Only a yell could cut through the din of the soldiers' revelry.

"Your presence has been requested by the Emperor. You are to return to Constantinople immediately," the messenger gave a nod and exited.

Belisarius sat down on the chair beside the table covered in maps and battle plans. Defeating the Persians would have to wait. He rested his head directly on the table, his arms hanging limply by his sides. "Ahhhhh!" he growled in frustration, his right hand finding one of his daggers and driving it into the table without any thought. The unwelcome interruption into his military campaign had broken through the calm he tried to maintain as a commander of the Roman army.

"Ready my horse," Belisarius yelled to the servant stationed outside the tent.

As he mounted the horse an hour later, he put a stop to his commanders' protests about his determination to ride alone. "Unless you have orders to return to the capital, you are to remain here. Continue with the daily sparring exercises. And don't let my men get fat and lazy," he warned, only half-joking, as he rode away from the encampment.

"Welcome back, Belisarius," Empress Theodora greeted him the moment he walked through the doors of the palace.

"Empress," Belisarius bowed with as much sincerity as he could muster. He was aware that Theodora had been the one to appoint him to the battlefield. And though he was extremely grateful for the position—and for the return to battle —he was rather upset that the woman had made Justinian distrustful of his intentions and allegiance.

"Follow me," Theodora commanded as she turned without waiting for a response. She was flanked by four women, who each stole glances at Belisarius while offering coy smiles.

She led him into the throne room where Justinian was dealing out a punishment to two servants having a dispute over a matter that obviously annoyed Justinian. He dismissed the men as soon as he saw Belisarius, and the room was rapidly cleared.

"My victorious general, come home again after three long years! Oh how I have missed you, old friend!" Justinian clasped Belisarius on his shoulders and pulled him into a firm hug.

This is new, Belisarius marveled.

"Thank you, Emperor. All credit for victory goes to you," he bowed. Justinian glanced smugly toward his wife who seemed utterly unimpressed by Belisarius's words.

"I am sure you are confused as to why I would call you away from the battlefield at such a time. But my wife has not been at ease with your present state. It is her decision that you should be wed. And she has chosen four women whom, she assures me, have all the qualities that a man desires in a wife. So. I will let you choose from amongst them." Belisarius's gaze followed Justinian's outstretched hand to the women who had accompanied Theodora when he first arrived. All four were pleasant in their appearance. They ranged in age from late teens to mid-forties (as far as he could tell). But Belisarius had no use for a wife when he was engaged in the war.

"I do not have time for a wife when I am on the battlefield. Will I be wed only to leave my wife here and never see the woman?" Belisarius could not understand the reasoning behind Theodora's decision.

"Why no! Of course not! Your wife will remain by your side no matter what. That is why these four have been chosen—none shy away from difficulties," Justinian winked. But Belisarius finally understood. He was too capable on the battlefield—was held in too high a regard by the soldiers and commanders alike—to remain unwatched by the emperor.

"May I speak with you privately, emperor?" Belisarius asked.

"Of course, of course," Justinian waved his hand, dismissing his wife and her ladies before any protests could be formed.

"Justinian," Belisarius shook his head, not really knowing what he wanted to say.

"Believe me, Belisarius. I think this is as ridiculous as I'm sure you do," Justinian sighed, returning to his throne and slouching in it comfortably. "But she simply does not trust you. After killing my aunt and uncle, she worries you will be at liberty to kill me and take my place as Emperor."

"But that is ridiculous. Every strategy we drew—every plan I carried to fruition—was for the sake of making you the head of the empire!" Belisarius protested.

"I know. Trust me. It only took a few weeks for my grief to subside after

Justin's death for me to see everything clearly. And by that time you were already in battle. But Theodora has never gotten past her distrust, and if placing one of her spies as your wife will allay her nerves, what is the harm? I want you to know that I had nothing to do with this decision other than bringing you here to choose one. But at least you will have someone by your side as you continue your campaign. The warmth of a woman in bed is usually a welcome alternative to an empty bed, is it not?" Justinian prodded.

Belisarius raked his fingers through his hair. The emperor was not wrong, and he had nothing to hide from the emperor and empress. What could the harm be?

"Which one is the most skilled? If I must do this to keep peace in the Empire, I want to make sure I receive enjoyment from it."

"That's the spirit!" Justinian laughed. "There is Caelia, who is quite lovely, but extremely shy. She is young, which might be useful in traveling between Constantinople and the battlefield. Take into consideration, your travels to the capital will occur regularly now that you have a wife," Justinian warned.

"And the others?" Belisarius wanted a full explanation of all the options before he chose one.

"Titiana is… spirited. Always enjoying life within the palace in whatever way she can find. Though she will make a good wife, I believe she would have a terrible temperament away from parties and her friends. She will not do for your purposes. Then there's Antonina. She's older than the others. She already has a few children from various men, though no one has any idea whom. She is conniving and will likely sleep with as many of your soldiers and fellow commanders as possible in an effort to annoy you or make you jealous—depending on whether or not she likes you that day. She would be difficult. Maybe too difficult for a man such as yourself."

"And the last?" Belisarius asked, becoming engrossed in the prospect of having to choose from such vastly different women.

"Horatia. Lovely woman. Well-mannered, excellent company, and one of the most diabolical schemers you'll ever meet. I'm convinced she's the reason for half of Theodora's fears," Justinian warned.

"I will take Antonina. I have no preconceived notions of loving any of these women. And since it appears that she is the oldest and brings the most history into the relationship, maybe we will be on a more even playing field," Belisarius gave a mirthless chuckle as Justinian's eyebrows furrowed in confusion.

"Very well," Justinian nodded, calling for the ladies to return.

"But remember, Belisarius," Justinian whispered warningly, "if she dies while you are wed, you will lose more than your rank and my goodwill."

Belisarius nodded in understanding, but killing his new wife was not something he had even considered.

As the women rounded the corner, Belisarius eyed Antonina—who was by far the most progressed in age. There was a regal beauty in her age though, and Belisarius felt intrigued at the idea of being tied to a woman with no less than forty years of life experience and her own family from previous relationships.

"Belisarius has chosen Antonina," Justinian announced much to the surprise and chagrin of the other women. Antonina beamed at the triumph over her younger competitors, and Belisarius hid a smirk at Antonina's gloating. "We'll leave you two to become acquainted with one another," Justinian muttered, leading his wife and her ladies away.

"General," Antonina bowed.

"How lovely to make your acquaintance, Antonina," though Belisarius was uncertain if he was actually happy about the development. "I am certain the Emperor will arrange for our union to take place at the earliest possible moment. We must return to the battlefield as soon as possible. Justinian told me you have children."

"Yes. I have three children—Photius, Vita, and Drusa. Vita is my eldest. I was married when I was quite young, and she was our only child." Belisarius liked the way Antonina spoke about her history as if it belonged to someone else. She was emotionless—which was a positive trait in Belisarius's mind. "Vita has a daughter, Laurentina, who is nearly six years old now. Drusa, my second, was born a year after my first husband's death, following my return to the theater." She searched Belisarius's face for a reaction to her confession of debauchery, but he was unaffected, and she continued. "And finally there is Photius. He is my sweet youngest child—only fourteen years of age and a gentle boy."

"Good. Photius will join us on the battlefield. I will train him to fight, to lead, and to win," Belisarius was excited to pass his knowledge on to a "son," even if the child was not technically his own.

Antonina looked as if she might object, but held her protests behind the tight line of her mouth. "As you wish. I desire he will learn all you have to teach."

Two weeks later, everything had been settled, and Belisarius was finally on his way back to the battlefield with his new wife and her son. Photius was a scrawny little thing, rather in need of some hearty food and physical training. But Belisarius and his men would whip the little stickling into proper condition soon enough. The return journey took nearly three times as long as his solo ride on horseback. Antonina and Photius rode in a heavy carriage together with far too many belongings. Belisarius sighed. *This is to be my life from now on, but at least I can rest knowing my end surely must be near. There will be no more silence in my tent to think of battle plans. No more sleeping alone in my bed—I wonder what she will think of my night terrors?* His mind barely rested as he rode. He rather enjoyed the silence and nothingness of long journeys, but he could not find a way to stop the thoughts that continued to question what his life would look like with a wife and children.

The twenty-two-day journey was nearly finished, but the last night of the journey would be forever burned into Belisarius's memory. They had stopped for the night to rest for a few short hours, everyone in agreement that they should finish the trip as soon as possible the next morning. Everyone but Belisarius had fallen asleep, and as he sat over the fire, watching the ashes from the scorched branches float listlessly into the air and then return to the earth to join the dirt from whence the tree had once sprouted, Belisarius lamented what the future would bring. He was bound to this woman now. He was responsible for her well-being and that of her children. But he would not age. He would not be able to explain to Antonina why he remained youthful as she grew old. He looked above at the stars that peered down at him, mocking his eternal frustration. He stood and kicked dirt into the fire, swearing in his native tongue at the situation in which he was now stuck.

"In what language do you curse?" Antonina asked, emerging from the carriage.

"A dead tongue. One my mother taught me." He did his best to dodge a real answer.

"I understand you have your doubts about this marriage. You were forced into it, as was I. But I would like to be your partner in life. You are the great general, known for your excellence as a commander, superior skills as a tactician, and your inability to die in battle. I think you will find I am equally resilient in life," Antonina flashed a smile that almost touched her eyes.

"You are quite good, I will admit. But your racing heartbeat and disingenuous expression have me doubting the sincerity of your words," he replied calmly.

Antonina shot him a venomous glare before composing herself.

"I suppose I will have to work on that."

Belisarius looked up at the stars once more, trying to decide how to proceed. He hoped Antonina would be amenable to his conditions.

"I do not expect that you will change your... habits—especially in an encampment full of soldiers. But I require two things from you. First, you will sleep in my tent each night, preferably in our shared bed, though I will not force that matter. Second, you will not make my name into a mockery. The great and un-killable General Belisarius will not be made a fool by rumors of his unfaithful wife. If you suspect one of your lovers will not remain silent, either you will kill him or tell me so I can deal with it. I will provide a list of commanders and soldiers who are too valuable to the Roman campaign to risk their deaths, and you will not so much as send a flirtatious glance in their direction. Do we have an accord?" he asked, turning to observe his wife's response to the terms. She seemed a bit shocked, but there was also a hint of relief behind the surprise.

"We have an accord," she agreed as she walked over and snaked her hands up around his neck, pulling his mouth down to meet hers. The kiss was not gentle, not loving, but fueled by something violent and desperate. They had not yet consummated their marriage bed, and under the hot wind of the starry summer sky, they allowed need to overtake judgment. Any moment, one of the servants accompanying them (or Antonina's son for that matter) could awaken and find them entangled, but the thrill of the risk seemed only to excite them further. Belisarius laid Antonina on the hard ground, yanking her skirting up as her hands struggled to remove his clothes. The joining was rough and far too fast—it had been more than a year since Belisarius had slept with a woman— but Antonina seemed pleased nonetheless. Belisarius laid on the ground breathing heavily as Antonina stood and fixed her cloak.

"I look forward to the moment your stamina returns. You've not felt a woman's embrace for too long my dear," she whispered as she disappeared back into the carriage.

Belisarius didn't sleep at all that night. His brain could barely comprehend the complexity of the new situation in which he found himself. He did not love Antonina, and he was fairly certain he never could. But he was very much intrigued by her. An hour or so later, he woke the servants so they could finish the final leg of their journey.

They arrived just after dawn, the noise of the carriage announcing the onset of a new day. Soldiers emerged clumsily from their tents, still carrying the remnants of sleep in their half-opened eyes. Everyone rushed to the carriage as it came to a stop, eager to see who accompanied their general to the encampment.

"General," Belisarius heard the voice of Hermogenes behind him as he dismounted his horse.

"Hermogenes. Please tell me the soldiers haven't gotten fat," he teased as they grasped each others' forearms in greeting.

"We kept our word," Pharas and Sunicas emerged from the crowd of soldiers and greeted Belisarius in the same way.

"I am happy to hear it. Now, there is a tiny bit of business to which we must attend." Belisarius walked to the carriage and opened the heavy door, putting a hand out for Antonina. "This is my new wife."

THIRTY-TWO

Constantinople 532 C.E.

"PLEASE!" Antonina screamed, tears rushing from her angry eyes.

"By the gods. You have dozens of lovers already, Antonina. Do you know how many men have died in the wake of your seductions? I have killed ten at least in the past year alone. Why this?" Belisarius groaned.

"Because I *want him*," she sighed wiping the tears from her cheeks. "And he needs us," she snuggled up to his side.

"I love Theodosius like I love Photius, but this is pushing the boundaries of right and wrong even *for me*. You know it is something truly wicked for *me* to feel such a way. Does Theodosius favor you in the same way?" Belisarius asked, feeling nauseated.

"I've only made a few initial passes to gauge his responsiveness, but he has welcomed the attention." She perked up at the small headway she had made.

"Adopting a son solely so you carry on an affair within the comforts of your own home is a new level of reckless licentiousness, even for you," he rebutted with the shake of his head.

"It's not my fault you're a *priest*! You barely look at me. And God forbid you glance at another woman. You act as though you are being punished by our agreement. But it's only you whom you're hurting. Stay celibate. I don't care. In fact, I think I'll start calling you Priest Belisarius. How is that?" she pointed a finger right in his face.

Belisarius felt his hands move before his brain registered the action. He grasped Antonina by the shoulders and pushed her against the wall with a thud, his face burning under the heat of his rushing blood.

"Do not speak to me that way, and do not dare call me a priest," he commanded in a terrifying, quiet voice.

"Finally, the commanding general has reappeared," she beamed, pushing his bottoms down from his waist and pulling up her cloak as he kept her top half pinned to the wall. She lifted her legs around his mid-section and tried to get him to respond.

Belisarius calmly released her shoulders and removed her legs from his waist. He pulled his bottoms back up, tying the string in a knot to make sure she couldn't release them again.

"You simply do not arouse my affections any more, dear, cunning wife. Besides, I fear I may catch a nasty disease you have contracted from one of your other lovers." He walked away, listening to his wife feign sobs that would not even fool a young child.

Castello San Romolo, Present Day

Priest shook his head at the torture he had been forced to endure under the tyranny of Antonina and Theodora's incessant plotting. He had corresponded throughout the marriage with the emperor—about battle plans and the reckless actions of their wives. Justinian had always remained calm and reassuring that everything would be all right. *Easy for him to say. He had an historian commissioned to paint a flattering version of his life with the tip of a pen into the pages of history.* He huffed out a breath, wishing desperately that he had slit that sniveling Procopius's throat when he'd had the chance. *Procopius, you swine. I would have made your death unimaginably painful if I had known the words you would pen after we left Constantinople.* But despite Procopius's version of what happened during his time in Constantinople, Priest was appreciative that in real life, Justinian had always supported his military endeavors—even the more risky or foolish strategies. He had been the kind of emperor one only dreamed of serving—fair, power-hungry, yet careful with the lives of his soldiers and those over whom he ruled. It was the last time Priest had served in a real military under the rule of another. And, for the most part, he remembered his time in Constantinople fondly.

He flipped a few pages forward in the book and all pleasantness drained from his face. *But then I remember the conniving witches,* he thought humorlessly.

<u>THIRTY-THREE</u>

Rome, 537 C.E.

"**WELL, THAT IS MADNESS,**" Belisarius paced the floors of the tent.

"I agree with you, husband, but it is signed and sealed by the empress herself. Have I any choice but to obey?" Antonina actually sounded distressed, which bothered Belisarius… along with the command itself.

He had never, in all his years of fighting and killing, kidnapped or taken the life of a holy man. He felt that some lines were not to be crossed, and this seemed like one of them. But an order from the empress was not to be ignored, and so he would help Antonina in the daunting task.

He and Antonina had discovered they succeeded greatly in life by heeding the advice of one another. They were each skilled, in their own way, in planning deceptions and murders. They found a sort of camaraderie in one another that blossomed in the sharing of information and consulting during times of scheming. He was pleased by her understanding of the battlefield, and was glad to advise her on the many uses of poisons and daggers when the need arose.

After securing the affections of Theodosius, Antonina had stayed true to the boy, which only irritated Belisarius a little. He had proposed the agreement in the beginning of their marriage, and he would stick to it. Unfortunately, it seemed Antonina was growing more cavalier with the public nature of her relationship. He hoped she would not break her promise and make him the laughing-stock of the empire.

"You must obey. You are more than capable of seducing a Pope. Surely you do not doubt your ability to lure the man into a trap. We just need to make sure a secure plan is in order before we proceed," he assured her.

"You mean…" she looked up at him with a rare gleam of gratefulness in her eyes, "you will help me?"

"Unless you wish it otherwise," Belisarius offered.

"No! Of course not. If you are willing to give counsel and aid, I will be comforted. Theodora has never truly forgiven me for taking Theodosius as a lover. Maybe this will help me win back some of her approval."

"I hope it does, my dear. How do you intend to lure him in?"

Antonina lay on a couch in the center of the domus in which she and Belisarius were living while in Rome. She had sent a special invitation to Pope Silverius and Bishop Vigilius to join her for a "special evening". Belisarius knew enough of the pope to believe he would attend—and the man certainly did not disappoint. Belisarius's guards blocked the doors quietly once the men entered the dwelling.

"Come, Pope Silverius! Sit here with me," she patted the couch as she moved her legs to make room for him. Belisarius watched the fool slide right into the trap. The pope sat down, and without missing a beat, took a drink of the wine Antonina offered.

"Now tell us, Silverius, what the emperor and empress have done to you and the Romans that you would choose to betray us into the hands of the Goths?" she asked innocently.

The pope turned grey as the blood rushed from his face. "I have done no such thing!" he protested, jumping up from the couch. He wavered a bit on his feet as the effects of the tainted wine began to take hold. He sat back down just as quickly as he had stood to avoid falling. The wine had been laced with a sedative that worked quickly but left an aggressive and lasting headache in its wake.

"Oh? But we have a letter written in your hand proving correspondence with the Goths! And we have many witnesses that say you have done such a thing. In fact, we've even secured bishops and deacons to assure your guilt. Don't worry," she reached up, stripping his papal vestments away as he sat paralyzed, "you're not going to die yet—you'll simply be living in exile. Empress Theodora sends her best wishes for your new life."

Belisarius stepped out from the door where he had been observing and helped Vigilius—who would soon be the pope in place of Silverius—put the robe of a monk onto the drugged man. He was transported to Patara in Lycia for keeping, and Antonina earned a well-deserved period of good graces from the empress.

Only one year later, Belisarius and Antonina were called on once again to permanently dispose of Silverius by placing him somewhere no one would know nor find. Belisarius chose the Isle of Palmarola for the task, and despite his misgivings about killing a holy man, he felt far more fear of Theodora's wrath if he did not obey. He charged two of his personal guardians to accompany Silverius for a maximum of two years. If the man had not died at that point, they were commanded to end his life and return to Belisarius's household.

Belisaius felt only the slightest pang of distress when his guards returned after only six months to report Silverius's death, and though they claimed he died of self-imposed starvation, Belisarius thought it far more likely that Silverius's death was directly related to the boredom of his guards.

For weeks Belisarius had night terrors of Silverius writhing in pain, angrily accusing Belisarius for all his suffering. But as weeks turned into months, the dreams lessened in frequency. *Men will always die—by natural causes or by the hand of another—so why does it matter if they die sooner rather than later?* Belisarius asked himself. The realization began lifting the weight of centuries of deaths dealt by his hands. *A mortal can only be mortal, and a single life is meaningless when compared with the whole of the world.* He felt the corners of his mouth quirk up as the thought truly set in, and for the first time in what felt like centuries, he found peaceful sleep.

THIRTY-FOUR

Lazica, 541 C.E.

BELISARIUS WATCHED as Photius approached with a worried look on his face. He knew what his son's concerns were, and he could no longer play the role of "bewitched husband." Antonina had completely given up her side of their agreement over the course of the previous three years.

She now paraded her lover around wherever they went, even kissing him in public. Everyone believed Belisarius to be so madly in love with his wife that he was blind to her indiscretions. But the truth was, he loved Theodosius like a son and could not bear the idea of killing him.

"Father, this has gone too far unchecked. Mother has begun telling everyone that Ioannina is Theodosius's child!" Photius whispered, afraid that the rest of the encampment might hear of Antonina's behavior and mock their general.

Belisarius growled in anger. "She is what?" Ioannina was the five-year-old daughter of Antonina and Theodosius. Belisarius knew immediately that the child was not his... the evidence lay in the fact that he had not lain with Antonina for more than four years prior to her pregnancy. But he had claimed the child as his own nonetheless, allowing Ioannina the position of sole heir to his estate upon his "death"... though he still did not know how that would come about.

"It is the truth. Please. We must kill him before the truth of the child's parentage becomes known. Theodosius is no longer trying to deny what Antonina claims. He will ruin our family. Are you deeply injured by her betrayal?" Photius's tone turned to concern.

"I'm wounded by her spitefulness. We agreed her affairs would stay hidden from the public. But it's clear she no longer cares about our agreement. Now, she will hate me for killing her lover, and I must cast her aside publicly for her indiscretions! Surely she knows her treachery will have consequences."

"You mean, you knew all this time?" Photius's forehead wrinkled. Belisarius had played the role of loving, ignorant husband quite well. Maybe too well. She had made him appear foolish—Belisarius: the blind fool in love with the heartless, wandering harlot-wife. He would be written in the histories as a cuckold. He punched the thin, wooden table where his maps of the battlefields lay, the noise of the wood cracking under the impact, echoing the sound of the bone in his knuckle breaking. He paid it no mind; it would be good as new in a few weeks, and he would enjoy a little feeling in his life until the pain subsided.

"Yes. I've known. I have never loved your mother. She was placed in my life as a spy for Theodora. We have not had relations for nearly ten years," Belisarius said as Photius tried to comprehend the new information.

"But you are madly in love with her. You've been denying her affairs for years! How is this possible?" his voice squeaked.

"We do things we do not always like for those we serve. And sometimes your mother and I even partner with one another." Belisarius gave a half-smile as he remembered their numerous collaborations throughout the years, but his memories faded as he thought about the way she now mocked him openly. "She arrives in a few days. I will arrest her, and you must find Theodosius and lock him up until I can join you and take my revenge. Now that all is known, I have no choice but to play the scorned, vengeful husband."

"You cannot do this to me!" Antonina screamed from the post where Belisarius had shackled her outside his tent. His soldiers did not dare laugh at her plight while she hurled obscenities at her husband. Belisarius ignored her, tired of the game they had played for too long.

"You made your choice. I have been nothing if not understanding for these past ten years. But you chose to ignore my rules and run my name through the mud. Therefore, you and Theodosius must pay the price for your actions," Belisarius answered her protests calmly.

"What will you do to us?" she feigned sadness. Belisarius knew all of his wife's false looks and empty smiles. She fooled many, but not him. Her insincerity in almost all of her relationships had astounded him at the beginning, but now he saw clearly her lust for power and prestige. The more people who favored her, the better her life became. And the more she pleased the empress, the more liberties she could take without repercussions. *But not even the empress can save you from your fate now,* his lips curved, overjoyed at the prospect of being free from the lie he had been forced to live for so long.

"Photius already has your lover imprisoned," he whispered as her false grief turned to true fear.

"Don't. Please don't do anything to him. I will do whatever you wish. Let us leave! We can pretend to escape together and you will never see us or have to speak our names again," she began to sob, her voice desperate and shaky.

Belisarius took a step back from her, studying her expression and body language. "Real emotion," he breathed. "It's refreshing to see you're able to have a sincere feeling. I apologize for my doubt. I thought you incapable." He walked away while she continued to sob, and he felt nothing but pleasure in having finally seen his wife truly upset.

Unfortunately, only a few days later, a summons came from the empress. Belisarius and Antonina were required in Constantinople immediately.

"You cannot expect me to continue in this way," Belisarius growled as Theodora and Antonina exchanged wicked smiles.

"Oh, but that is exactly what I expect you to do. You will announce that you have made a grave error, and that all is forgiven. Antonina will continue being your wife, and you will continue to do what is expected of you in service to your emperor," Theodora narrowed her eyes, waiting for his response.

"Very well," he rubbed his eyes hard, wishing he could simply take a knife to his chest and be done with it. These women were killing him anyway—removing the pride which he had always held in high regard.

"And you will tell me where Photius has taken Theodosius. I have tortured Photius for days, and still he does not tell me," Theodora slammed a fist down on the arm of her throne.

"You… you are torturing *Photius*?" Belisarius felt his blood begin to boil. Photius was truly his son. He loved the man as much as he was capable of loving someone, and Photius cared for him in return. Photius was an excellent tactician and commander. He was not, however, a fighter. He was a bit soft, and always took great pains to care for his grooming. He took only male lovers, and though Belisarius did not understand the appeal of such a thing, he had no qualms with the choices his son made. The mental image of Photius being tortured by Theodora's minions made his stomach churn. "I do not know where Theodosius is being kept. I would not hesitate to tell you if I knew." He hung his head, fearing for the damage the torture would do to Photius's psyche.

"Very well. The torture will continue," the empress said through gritted teeth.

Belisarius glanced at Antonina to see an admiring grin of approval for her friend's words. *Absolutely disgusting. She is so desperate to find Theodosius that she does not care if her son—her own flesh and blood—is tortured. She is deplorable. I pray I remember this moment, and I swear I will never use torture of any kind to further my own selfish goals.*

Photius did not give up the location. And when, at last, the empress's guards found Theodosius, Photius's broken body was delivered to Belisarius's home. Physicians and servants tended to him for months as he recovered under careful supervision, but Photius would never again be the same man.

"I had no idea such a thing was occurring... and right under my nose!" Justinian yelled, allaying Belisarius's fears that the emperor had allowed his son to be tortured without interference.

"I know you do not want to hear it, and forgive me now for the words I must speak, but Theodora does too much in secret. She dreams and plans with her ladies for her own purposes, and I must admit that I fear they do not align with the good of the empire," Belisarius muttered with his eyes fixed on the ground. He could be sentenced to death for such an accusation... not that he could actually die. But he worried about the favor of the emperor nonetheless.

Justinian paced back and forth angrily, his face turning purple and then returning to its natural coloring several times. After a few silent moments, he plopped down to the ground.

"I cannot deny her anything, Belisarius. I am simply incapable. Is it possible to love someone too much? I fought so long and hard to have her as my wife, it is as if those years of fighting depleted my will to deny her a single wish. She has ensnared my very soul," he sank his head into his hands and rubbed his temples.

"And..." Belisarius did not know how to proceed.

"I will do nothing. I will ask her not to interfere in your marriage again, and I will demand that she apologize to you and Photius. But that is all my heart can stand by way of punishment. I suppose it will humiliate her in some small way —though I am unsure if she is able to feel that emotion," he admitted.

Belisarius had foolishly hoped the emperor would command him to kill the empress. Nothing would have pleased him more in that moment. But he accepted the apology as best he could and hoped the empress would leave him out of her future schemes.

THIRTY-FIVE

Castello San Romolo, Present Day

PRIEST TURNED the page angrily, still upset over the torture Photius had endured for such a ridiculous reason. He thumbed through several pages of his musings, reading a line or two here and there, and allowing his mind to be swept back to his days with Antonina. She had never been worth the grief she had caused—the history of Belisarius was still written as that of a scorned, idiotic husband whose downfall was caused by undying love for his unfaithful wife. But every interaction with the witch had been exciting. At least there was that.

He turned the page and read the first sentence. *Ahh. Here it is,* his jaw clenched as he read each word carefully so he could remember the gory details.

Constantinople, 542 C.E.

Belisarius read the letter once more, urging his horse to run faster without really thinking about his feet kicking the sides of the beast.

General Belisarius,

Our Emperor has fallen under the fateful whims of the great plague. I fear he is lost to us. He begs you return as quickly as possible. He is desirous to see his great general once more and deliver unto you the instructions for his successor. I urge you, come quickly.

Empress Theodora

He cannot die from the plague. The thought gave him a terrible headache. He had received the letter when, thankfully, he was only one day's ride from Constantinople. He mounted his horse and set off immediately, riding through the night to get back to the emperor.

"I must see the emperor!" he yelled as he rushed to the doors leading to Justinian's private chambers.

"There is great risk of becoming infected. We fear the emperor has only one or two days left in this world," the physician warned outside the room.

"I will not become infected. Let me in," Belisarius commanded. The physician offered an ointment of protection, but upon Belisarius's refusal, the man bowed his head and backed out of the way.

The smell of the room assaulted Belisarius's nose, and memories of a past life rushed over him. He came back to the present as quickly as possible, closing the door tightly and hoping to never remember that time again. But it did not detract from the fact that the smell of death and plague swirled violently through the room, mixing with the strong scent of the ointment the physicians and servants wore as protection.

He ran to Justinian's bedside and looked down at the man. His sleeping friend was afflicted by open sores on his neck and arms. His fingertips were blackened as if he had pushed them into the remnants of a dead fire. Belisarius felt his knees buckle beneath him. *Not again. Please. Not again.* He pleaded, knowing there was no one listening to his cries. There had not been anyone listening the first time he watched a village die of the plague. His pleas had fallen again on deaf ears as plague overcame an encampment of soldiers a few hundred years earlier. Watching death overtake others only reminded him that he could never join them in the easement from his unending life. His veins pulsed with jealousy as he watched Justinian's hands shake with fever. The jealousy warred for a fleeting moment with sympathy for his friend's suffering. *Friends. Is that what we are?*

"Belisarius," Justinian moaned, trying fruitlessly to move his hand to touch Belisarius's.

"Shhh. Do not trouble yourself, emperor. I am here. What do you wish me to do?" Belisarius asked in a hushed voice.

"Accept the decision I have made. I have dictated all to Procopius and signed the scrolls relating my wishes for succession. You will not be named emperor. You were never the type to rule from a palace," Justinian rasped painfully.

"I had not even thought it a possibility. I thank you for naming another," Belisarius heaved a sigh of relief.

"I worried you might be hurt," Justinian's mouth curled in a grimace that was supposed to be a grin.

"By the gods, no. You have given me great joy by passing the title to another. But you will not die, emperor. I will remain here until all hope is lost," he swore.

"The time for lost hope has already come and gone, my friend."

Belisarius blinked at his use of the word. That fabled idea of friendship which Belisarius had forgotten the exact meaning of. *Friend.* He felt the oddest tightness in his chest, and his eyes began to leak awkwardly. *Tears? I am crying?* He wiped the moisture away quickly, but more of the wetness appeared where he had removed the previous tears.

"Justinian, please. I beg you not to go. You can live. You can survive. I have survived too many plagues to count," the words flowed from his mouth as rapidly as the tears from his eyes. "You can overcome this. You are my only friend. For centuries. And I only just realized that's what you have become to me. You are more than my emperor. You are my friend," he choked out, his head hanging on the last word.

"I am glad to have a friend with me," Justinian groaned as his breathing evened out and he succumbed to sleep once more.

Guards pounded on the chamber door. Their fear of the plague was the only deterrent from barging through the doors and physically removing Belisarius from the room. He had barred the doors shut the moment Justinian had breathed his last breath two weeks earlier. He would not give in. His friend could not be dead.

"You promised me this!" Belisarius growled in rage as he paced around the room, destroying whatever happened to be in his path. A vase shattered on the opposite wall as a familiar rumble announced the emptiness of his stomach. He had eaten only the broth that the physicians brought for the emperor ever since Justinian's heart had stopped beating. "You said you would give me this," he whispered, pleading for his friend's life once more. "He didn't despise me. He never despised me. He trusted me. You promised."

The physicians knocked on the door once more, asking for an update on the emperor's condition as they did each morning and evening.

"He is unchanged. Still holding on by a thread. I need more broth. I believe he will begin improving soon."

"Please let us come in and examine him. Surely there is more we can do than you are capable of doing," they pleaded.

"He needs broth! Only broth!" Belisarius yelled as footsteps scurried away in fear of the general.

Belisarius walked over to Justinian's body. The body remained exactly the same as it had when Justinian died. Belisarius did not know if the unchanging condition was because the body was already so decayed from the sickness that there was nothing left to deteriorate, or if his demands for Justinian's life were being heard by another.

"Wake up," he commanded his friend as he had several times each day.

He walked away and sank into a chair wearily. His body was beginning to waste away from the meager nutrition it was receiving. His hands shook all the time, and his muscles protested each time he rose from his chair. He had tried starvation as a means to death on two occasions—and both had been met with failure and pain. His body would not die. *He* could not die. But it had taken months for his body to fully recover. He shivered as he remembered the physical pain connected to those particular attempts. He dared not starve himself again. *So many unfulfilled promises,* he thought as he drifted to sleep.

THIRTY-SIX

A SWELTERING DESERT breeze swirled around Belisarius's body, the sand sticking to his sweat-covered legs and arms. The sun was hotter than it should have been, and he couldn't remember why he was there. *How did I get here?* he asked as he looked around the barren wasteland. There was nothing. No trees, no water, no people, no horses. He was completely alone. *Why am I here?* he wondered as he began to walk east. He didn't know where he was heading, but he supposed east was as good a direction as any.

"Help me," he heard a faint whisper from just behind his head. He whipped around, the feeling of comfort and terror combining in his mind to create a confusion he could not name.

"Who are you?" he asked to the invisible caller.

"Help me. Please," the whisperer groaned behind Belisarius's back again. He spun around, searching the sky and the ground fruitlessly for the origin of the voice.

"Where are you?" he tried a different approach.

"Wake up," he heard a very different voice command. His hands flew up to cover his ears—this new voice was so loud and terrifying, he felt the urge to fall to the dust and cover his head with his hands. But he stood firmly, still searching the barren landscape for the source of both voices.

"Wake up now!" the voice demanded as he felt his feet get swept out from beneath him. Just as his body was about to land painfully on the ground, he opened his eyes. He was once again in the dark, silent chamber where Justinian had died two weeks earlier. But now there was a rasping sound coming from somewhere in the room.

"Help me," it called. "Where am I?"

Belisarius stood, rubbing his eyes in disbelief. He walked slowly to the bed, searching the covers for movement. *Is this a trick? Am I dreaming still?*

"Belisarius?" Justinian's voice asked as their eyes made contact.

"My god," Belisarius choked, his eyes fixed on his friend's face. He couldn't bear to look away for fear he was dreaming.

"Where am I?" Justinian asked once more.

"You're in the palace. You died. You were dead for two weeks. They wanted to take your body away, but I told them you were still alive. I wouldn't let anyone in. You were dead, Justinian. You were gone. Show me your hands," Belisarius breathed, knowing he was stuck in a dream that felt far too real.

Justinian held up his hands for Belisarius to examine. The fingertips were a purplish-blue color, reminiscent of bruising. The open sores on his neck were scabbed over—healing. Belisarius realized this couldn't be a dream. Everything was too real, and each minute scrape and wound was right where it should have been. He sat with his mouth open for a moment, not knowing what else to do after witnessing such a miracle.

"You must be starving," he stated without need for a reply and went to the door to summon food for the emperor. He opened the door to find the guards were nowhere in sight.

"You there!" he yelled to a servant passing by. "I need fresh water, fruit, and hot broth. The emperor is regaining his strength!"

The servant stared in disbelief for several seconds before breaking into a full sprint toward the kitchen to do as he had been commanded.

He shut the door again, not bothering to lock it now that the emperor was finally alive, awake, and showing improved health. He walked back to his friend, feeling overwhelmed at what this might mean for him. Was Justinian to be immortal as well? Would he, at last, have a friend with whom he could live his life?

"Belisarius," Justinian's voice barely a whisper, "what has happened to me?"

Castello San Romolo, Present Day

Priest smiled down at the words written in his journal. It had been one of the happiest days of his life—realizing that Justinian would be immortal with him. That day marked the beginning of hope in his life. Hope that the foretold prophecies might actually come to fruition. All the centuries of solitude had made him unstable, and having someone to ground him had kept his mind from slipping into a state of constant madness. He was still a bit mad, of course—but with Justinian as a permanent fixture in his life, he was able to put the rest of his life in perspective.

He had known within a matter of days that Justinian had joined him in immortality. Every wound had healed fully—without even scars as reminders of the plague he had endured—within a week of Justinian coming back to life.

Priest snickered when he remembered explaining immortality to Saint for the first time.

Constantinople, 542 C.E.

"Immortal?" Justinian's eyes narrowed. "I am either sleeping or you are lying to your emperor."

"It is neither of those things, I swear to you. How do you think I was able to live through so many battles? They call me invincible for a reason, my friend," the corner of Belisarius's eyes crinkled with humor.

"But… how long have you lived?" Justinian's acceptance of Belisarius's words was evident once the questions began to flow from his lips.

"I have lived for centuries. I will say only this, I served King Ashurnasirpal II of the Assyrian Empire. I was the head of his palace guard in Kahlu. Everything I have done with the palace guard here, I had already done centuries earlier," he offered as the emperor's incredulous stare remained fixed on his face.

"I have been alone, without true companionship, for hundreds of years. Your life is a miracle," he felt his throat cough with emotion on the last word. He did not cry. Ever. And this was the second time he had felt the unfamiliar and unwelcome feeling in a short period of time. However, he felt compelled to continue as he rubbed his eyes hard. "Nothing and no one can kill me. I have tried every way imaginable to take my own life: drowning, bleeding from multiple wounds, starvation, a self-inflicted stab to the chest. I have been cursed with the solitude of immortality. Until now."

"You do not paint a very pleasant image of what my life will be like if I am, indeed, immortal," Justinian narrowed his eyes. Belisarius was impressed by the emperor's acceptance of this revelation—he himself had not welcomed the news with such a calm demeanor. However, his friend should be prepared for the brutality of an immortal life.

"It is not pleasant. Your friends and family will pass into the next life without you. You will be forced to leave the life you've always known to keep from being discovered," Belisarius began to describe the unfortunate details of their future when Justinian held a hand up to silence him.

"Why would I leave? I can be worshiped as a god here! 'The Eternal Emperor' has a beautiful sound, does it not?" Justinian's eyes gleamed with hope.

"Oh Justinian. I beg you, no. Immortality comes with far too many complications without adding 'rule an empire for all time' to the list of hardships. Empires rise and empires fall. If there is anything I have learned in my life, it is the truth of that statement," Belisarius warned.

Belisarius was unable to persuade Justinian to give up his idea of becoming "The Eternal Emperor" until six years after that first conversation. It was the empress's death that finally convinced Justinian to abandon the scheme. There was nothing left for him in Constantinople but empty power. Belisarius wanted to leave the empire right after Theodora's death, but Justinian was too grief-stricken to make any decisions that large. Justinian had loved Theodora to her final breath—despite her constant conniving, manipulation, and inability to bear an heir to the throne. Belisarius understood that level of adoration in theory, but he had only experienced something similar to it once—a very long time before meeting Justinian. It wasn't until several years later that he would finally understand why Justinian's heart broke so completely for so long. When Justinian and Belisarius finally "died" in 565 C.E., Justinian left the empire with the worry of a parent leaving his child for the first time.

"Let the empire fall when its time comes. Another will rise in its place, and Constantinople will have reigned supreme for long enough," Belisarius pleaded with his friend.

"What will the scrolls of history say about the fall of my empire?" Justinian asked with a pained voice as the city grew smaller in the horizon.

"Do not grieve yourself with such thoughts, Justinian. This moment is only the very beginning of your history. I can tell you quite frankly that you will always remember this time in your life fondly. But there is so much more life to live—so many more things to accomplish and places to see. You are free from the burden of leadership—from the confines of ruling. We can go wherever we want, do what we wish. Do not dwell on what has passed. Dream of what can be. We will live forever—through every era to come. Imagine that, my friend. Look now to the possibilities of the future."

THIRTY-SEVEN

Castello San Romolo, Present Day

LISSIE ENTERED the dining hall with the last of the platters for dinner and quickly read the tone of the "discussion" (as Mattia liked to call Family arguments). Two weeks had passed since the funeral, and it seemed the Family had begun shifting back toward their normal rambunctious way of life. The sense of anger over what had happened had not lessened in the least. But the somber cloud from the deaths of Samuel and Elias had somehow dissipated a little. Lissie had even seen Mattia and his father share a laugh the day before—which, for those first few days, had seemed unimaginable.

This conversation, however, appeared to be resting safely between perturbed and exasperated. She set the platter down and took her seat next to Mattia, who absentmindedly grabbed and kissed her hand while remaining engrossed in the conversation.

"But the question is, will we continue taking contracts? I feel like the answer to this is a given. Why would this incident change anything? We've been doing this for centuries! And we've lost people before," István, the third son of Paulus, offered.

Lissie had met all of Mattia's cousins on multiple occasions, but learning each of their names was proving increasingly difficult. She had tried to decipher which of the men were brothers based on their looks alone, but so many of the brothers had been born from different mothers in different cultures throughout the past fifteen centuries that she had given up that idea quickly. Antonio's offspring were the perfect example of her dilemma: six sons from six women hailing from Italy, Poland, France, England, Spain, and Japan. Four of them shared Antonio's striking height—but that was about all they shared. Light skin, olive skin, blond hair, black hair, green eyes, gray eyes. There was hardly anything to link them as brothers besides the air with which all the members of the Family seemed to carry themselves. She shook her head a little, coming back to the present conversation.

"You truly mean that?" Marcus barked out.

Oh no. What did I miss? She worried about the venom in Marcus's words. He was usually so level-headed.

"I think a system of checks and balances should be introduced. One man making decisions for everyone is indisputably dangerous," Tielo—the eldest (or was it second eldest?) grandson of Elias offered, as if it was the obvious choice.

"Your grandfather is dead. Your great uncle is dead. This Family is in turmoil. Because of what we do," Marcus punctuated each statement.

"And I disagree. I think it's because there wasn't a proper system set up to check each contract for merit. One terrible incident doesn't void all the work we've accomplished over the years," Tielo sat back and crossed his arms with a huff.

"Or you could, I don't know, stop murdering people?" Lissie heard the snarky words break out of her mind and escape through her lips before she could stop them. She squeezed her eyes shut and felt Mattia's hand tighten over hers.

"You think it's that simple? That what we do is a matter of right and wrong?" Alexander narrowed his eyes at her and spoke in his quiet, terrifying voice. "You are obviously too naive to comprehend the full situation. Do you have any idea how many lives have been saved by this Family? We have assassinated tyrants, murderers, and dictators. Child-molesters, thieves, and rapists. How can you possibly call any of their deaths 'murder'?"

"Because that's exactly what it is. You have served as the judge, jury and executioner since the 7th century. You have killed innocent women, children, and men in the name of... what? My boss was guilty of being successful. And he's dead. Anamaria was guilty of being the object of affection of the wrong man, and she, along with her mother and brother, were killed. Elias is dead.

Samuel is dead. Mattia and I are supposed to be dead. How is it even possible that this topic is up for debate? Are you so blind to your own shortcomings that you cannot see murder for what it is?" her voice squeaked on the last word, her hands shook violently with the emotion that now pulsed through her body.

"So if I'm understanding you correctly, I am a murderer. And I should have simply allowed myself to be raped multiple times. Because, by your standards, murder is murder, and we don't have a right to play judge, jury and executioner."

The blood drained from Lissie's face when she heard Caterina's icy rebuttal. She hadn't even thought about Mattia's mother. The woman was as deadly a fighter as any of the men in the room, and everyone knew it. She had killed numerous men without aide. *But self-defense was something entirely different.* Lissie looked to Mattia for help explaining her point, but her fiance's discomfort with the situation was tangible. His back was straight as a board, and his eyes were fixed on the table in front of him. *Okay. I'll do this alone.*

"If I was in your situation, I would probably have done the same. Though I'm quite sure I'm not nearly as capable of using a knife as you," Lissie muttered, more sheepishly than she wanted.

"But she brings up a valid point," Marcus agreed, ignoring the tension between his mother and soon-to-be sister-in-law. "We are not a court of law. We are not officially authorized by any world government. We have done the dirty work for governments, religious leaders, and the richest of the world for too long. What right do we have to choose which contracts are worthy or not? And what right do those contracting us have to even ask us to carry out their wills?"

Lissie still shook, but she couldn't hold back what was tugging at her heart.

"Do any of you believe that mortal lives are precious?" she asked, looking at every set of eyes she could find. Most of them looked away to avoid her gaze, but several of the glares defiantly declared "No!"

"I just... I just see life as something that's already short enough without cutting it off even earlier. I know there are terrible people in the world. And they should absolutely be locked away. But I will never be able to agree with murdering another human being. And I will not apologize for feeling like anyone who disagrees is horribly wrong," she finished, pushing her chair back and exiting the room.

She ran to her bedroom and climbed into bed, tears streaming down her face as she sobbed into her pillow. *This is the Family I'm a part of now. I knew what Mattia was before I decided to become a part of it. I could have walked away in New York. I could have never looked back. Am I just as bad as they are? I chose Mattia before I knew he hadn't killed. Am I just as guilty as everyone in the dining hall? And now even Caterina is against me. And Mattia didn't say a damn word to defend me against them.*

The door opened and shut as she fumed, and she felt Mattia slip into bed and put his arms around her.

"Don't you dare try to comfort me now," she pushed him away roughly with her elbow.

"What? I didn't do anything down there!" Mattia sounded hurt and upset, but she wasn't moved.

"That's exactly right. Your uncle and your mother openly attacked me for my opinions—the same opinions that *I know* you share with me—and you couldn't say a single word in my defense. Your *brother* had to step in to deflect the attention away from me!"

"Yes, but then you spoke up again!" Mattia sounded like he was scolding her now. She sat up and looked him in the eyes.

"Because *someone* needed to ask that question. If no one in that room believes that mortal lives are precious, then none of them should be allowed to take another life. Ever. I would sooner call in a military group to arrest and lock each and every one of them away. That is dangerous, sociopathic behavior, and I will not be a part of it. If you won't stand up against that kind of reckless, murderous behavior, then I will walk away right now," she held her hand out to Mattia with the engagement ring sitting in her palm. "It's your choice."

"Oh my God, you cannot be serious. Lissie, I will always stand beside you," he fumed, grabbing the ring and pushing it back onto her finger.

"When it's convenient? When it's not your whole family against me?" she snapped back, fighting the urge to take the ring off and throw it in his face. She looked up at him and saw the emotion in his eyes, and her heart softened a little.

"Lissie," he breathed the word reverently, "please don't forget that I stood in front of every one of them to walk away from that life. I didn't do that for me." He shut his eyes and his head hung, his expression one of devastation. Lissie's outrage shattered in the length of a heartbeat. She moved to him and wrapped her arms around his waist as he grabbed her as if she was the life-raft keeping him afloat. They cried together, exorcising their anger and sorrow over the events of the past few weeks.

"Please never threaten to leave me," he rested his forehead against hers and caressed her cheeks with his thumbs. "I cannot take any more heartache."

"I'm sorry, Mattia. I'm so sorry. I was hurt, and I didn't mean it. I won't do it again. I promise," she swore, closing her eyes and wishing she could rewind the clock to a few minutes earlier.

"And I'm sorry you felt betrayed. I froze down there, and I know I let you down. I swear I will do my best to prevent you from feeling that way again," he promised.

She kissed him lightly at first, and then their kisses grew more urgent. Her eyes flickered with lust as he began unbuttoning her top and kissing each new inch of exposed skin, and she didn't want him to stop. She needed a momentary reprieve from the world that existed outside their bedroom door.

THIRTY-EIGHT

LISSIE WAS AWAKENED by a quiet knock at the bedroom door. Mattia shot up from the bed and raced to answer it—his reflexes to protect her were still in high gear after their near-miss with death.

"It's for you," he mumbled groggily as he lay back down and immediately fell back to sleep.

She dragged herself from the bed and wrapped a heavy robe around her body—it never ceased to amaze her how cold the castle got each night, no matter the season. The stone walls and floors clung relentlessly to the chilly air. Only the stones that were directly hit by the sun's rays were able to hold their heat, but just until the light released them back to their natural state of cool.

Lissie cracked open the door and fought against the urge to gasp at the sight of Mattia's mother. Lissie hadn't expected to speak with Caterina until she had given some serious thought about how to explain her point of view. But it seemed the conversation was going to happen immediately. She looked at the worried expression on Caterina's face, and felt some tension release from her body. Each time she looked at the youthful face of Mattia's mother, Lissie felt an odd sensation she couldn't explain. Lissie was nearing thirty with the beginning signs of wrinkles forming on her forehead and sides of her mouth, while Caterina's skin was eternally, perfectly twenty-year-old smooth. It didn't bother Lissie so much as it kept her in a perpetual state of near-confusion. Would she ever be able to think of Caterina as "mom"? She didn't know if it would be possible.

Caterina silently motioned for Lissie to accompany her, and Lissie followed her all the way to the kitchen before a word was spoken by either. Caterina pulled a bowl of grapes from the fridge and offered some to Lissie before setting it on the table and sitting down. Lissie felt the discomfort rolling off

Caterina, but there didn't seem to be any hostility.

"Caterina, I swear to you I was not trying to imply that you were a murderer. You caught me completely off-guard..." Caterina cut Lissie's pleading off with an upheld hand.

"Please do not apologize, Lissie. I am sorry that I attacked you in such a way—and in front of everyone like that. I've felt absolutely dreadful all night. I couldn't sleep until I'd apologized. Please forgive me," Caterina's worried eyes searched Lissie's face for a sign of forgiveness.

"Of course, Caterina," Lissie reached across the table and gently squeezed the relieved woman's hands. "I need you to understand that I believe you were in the right. Self-defense is completely different than a planned assassination. And while I'm sure many have died that probably deserved it, I still stand by my belief that it's wrong. Believe me—I know that makes me a hypocrite for knowingly choosing to be with Mattia even though I thought he was an assassin at the time. But sometimes love chooses us and we can't choose to walk away. It would have been worse than death to live without him," she finished.

"I understand," Caterina nodded. "And I agree that this Family needs a new purpose. I think the time for accepting contracts is over. But there will be much debate on that matter, and if Priest remains alive, I'm not sure what will happen to the Family."

"If Priest remains alive? You mean they're actually proposing to *kill him*?" Lissie sat back in her chair as her eyes flitted around the room. She needed something to calm her down. "I'm getting a bottle of wine, do you want a glass?"

"Sure. That sounds nice," Caterina agreed.

Halfway through the bottle, Lissie finally found the words she was looking for.

"So murdering the man who's responsible for all the murders is the logical choice here?"

"I don't necessarily think it's logical so much as it's merciful. Would you rather Priest remain locked up here under constant supervision for the rest of eternity? He would go mad," Caterina shook her head a little at the thought.

"How is being killed more merciful? And he stays in the castle nearly all year of his own accord. How would his life be any different than it is now?" Lissie wondered.

"Because right now he has purpose. He's always working on the conditions of a new contract or making the assignments for the boys. Everything goes through him. If that changes, he'll have to leave to stay sane," Caterina offered.

"I suppose he could potentially slit the throat of whomever might be on guard duty to escape if he was confined to the castle," Lissie mused.

"You've never gotten to know him, have you?" Caterina looked saddened.

"I know enough. He wants me and my husband dead because we're annoying to him. He had no remorse whatsoever over the death of his youngest son while, at the same time, grieving the loss of the son who willingly killed his brother and was happy to kill me and Mattia. And adding that to the first time I met him, I'd say I have a pretty solid understanding of his character."

Caterina looked almost distressed by the tirade. Her eyes stared off in the distance, as if she was seeing something in another time and place. She came back to the present and took another drink of her wine.

"Elias was an absolute wreck before he left. But his loyalty to his father was worth more to him than his own happiness. That's why Priest assigned the contract to him." Caterina took another sip before continuing. "He was such a good grandfather," she grinned almost imperceptibly. Lissie noted for the first time that the painting in the Louvre bore a striking resemblance to Caterina when her mouth curled that way. "He was not the 'come sit on my lap while I read you a book' kind of grandfather, but he was so proud of their skills and accomplishments. He told the boys all the time how much enjoyment they gave him. Hugs and smiles and tears and laughter have never been his way. But I did not doubt for a minute that he loved all three—until Anamaria's contract. And even then, he was more disappointed that his incredibly skilled grandson had defied him openly than he was about Mattia falling in love with the girl. It was an unfortunate turn of events that set many things in motion. I believe that incident was the first spark that has led us to where we are now," Caterina sighed.

"You care for him? Like a father?" Lissie's eyebrows creased in confusion.

"He allowed me to enter his Family. I know it might not seem like a reason to care for him, but I was completely alone until Thomas found me. And to be welcomed—even if it was reluctantly welcomed for a time—gave me the incredible life that I've lived. He could have turned me out. He had that power. But he embraced me as daughter. He even had one of his wife's rings engraved with Thomas's crest, and he gave it to me on our wedding day," she held the ring out for Lissie to see. The ring looked like it belonged in a museum. *But I suppose anything from the history of this Family would fit into that category,* Lissie mused.

"You're right. I don't know him at all," Lissie took another gulp of wine.

Caterina's gaze snapped to the doorway, and Lissie followed suit without understanding what they were looking for. She hadn't heard a sound, and nearly a minute passed before a figure stepped into the room. *Priest.*

"You should consider yourself lucky, Lisette. To know me is only to know pain," Priest's hard stare held a look of remorse.

"That is not true, Priest, and you know it. Your plate is here," Caterina went to the oven and pulled a plate from the warming tray. "And I chose this bottle for you if you'd like wine tonight."

Caterina is preparing him meals? And choosing wine pairings to go along with his dinner? Confusion clouded her thoughts as she watched Priest place a kiss on Caterina's forehead and silently leave the room with his plate and wine bottle.

"He is wounded, Lissie," Caterina whispered as she rubbed her eyes and fought against the exhaustion behind them. "He is a murderer, and a sociopath, and he is misguided—do not think I am dismissing his faults. But he is also terribly wounded. Once he is gone I will tell you what I know about Thomas's mother," she assured Lissie. "But for now, I think we both need some more sleep."

He is wounded. Terribly wounded. The words repeated in Lissie's head as she fell back to sleep, but the idea of Priest being anything but the horrible man she had known the past year was simply too difficult to comprehend.

THIRTY-NINE

PRIEST ATE more slowly than usual as he heard the women's conversation replay in his head. He did not want nor deserve any kindness from Caterina. He had tried to kill her son and his fiancée. He had tried to kill her husband—though he wasn't sure she was yet aware of that fact. But each night, she proved she cared for him by preparing a meal just for him, keeping it in the warmer until he could take it without interacting with others in the castle, and leaving him bottles of wine paired perfectly with each meal. She had even brought it to his chamber a few times when the boys were up later than usual.

He dropped his fork onto his plate and sat back in his chair abruptly. *And she is advocating for my death. It is too much to hope for.* The uneasy feeling in his chest was unwelcome. He could not dare to hope that an end might finally arrive after so much time. But alas, there it was.

He snatched a journal from the bottom of the stack on his desk and flipped to the first page. He had avoided the memories for long enough. She would not let him keep her locked away any longer. Especially if he was near his end. She needed to be remembered.

FORTY

Rome, 617 C.E.

THE MORNING MARKET was crowded—the way that Belisarius liked. He and Justinian had left the lands of Justinian's empire immediately after their "deaths" and spent the next forty years roaming the territories belonging to the Southslavs and Bulgars. They hadn't been able to agree on a location to live permanently, so they had continued to move around until a few years earlier. Justinian had always wanted to spend time in Rome during his reign, so after his suggestion that it might be a nice place to call "home," Belisarius had agreed. He knew of the debauchery for which Rome was famous, and wherever there was debauchery, he always seemed to find steady work. The anonymity he now maintained meant he could hire himself out as a guard, sell-sword or assassin. He could move through the streets of Rome without drawing unwanted attention—as always seemed to be true of life in the largest cities he visited.

People swarmed all around him in their own worlds, purchasing food, sacrifices for the temples, clothing, and other textiles. The brightly-colored fabrics tied to the posts of the stall selling linen and wool waved lazily in the hot summer wind. Women called for people to come look at their wares while men haggled over the prices of livestock to be uselessly slaughtered at the temples.

It had been many years since Belisarius had worshipped anything or anyone. He knew his life was not in his own hands—so why try to please this god or that in an attempt to bless something already cursed. He wanted to spit on the sacrificial animals as he passed by, but he refrained to keep from drawing attention to himself.

He found the stall where he always purchased their household's grain. The old woman who ran it sat silently, watching his every move. It was as if she could see into his darkened soul. Her eyes too knowing—too wise. But she sold her grain for the best price, so every few weeks he came back.

"One bag this time," he said as he threw the heavy sack over his shoulder.

The woman nodded and held out her hand. She didn't waste the words he already knew—he had come to her long enough to know exactly how much he owed for the purchase. He handed her the coins, careful not to make contact with her skin. There was something about the woman that reminded him of the Assyrian palace. As if she had the same aura encompassing her body as the Lamassu carvings on the door frames at the palace at Kalhu. He felt a chill crawl up his spine as he turned to leave. *Maybe spending a little more for the grain would be all right.*

"You can redeem yourself," she muttered in a low voice from behind that made him stop in his tracks. "If only a little."

He turned quickly to look her in the eyes, trying to surmise what she meant and how she knew he was in need of redemption. But she didn't meet his gaze. Her eyes were trained on the dirt around her feet. A rushing wind blew through the market and swirled around his body. The sensation of being watched prickled on the back of his neck and made him want to flee the market at a sprint. He turned, his eyes searching for any watching eyes, and walked away— leaving a little more briskly than usual. He had not seen anyone suspicious in the crowds, and he felt a bit foolish for allowing himself to become panicked by a harmless old hag.

He started to turn down the alley where he always walked, but some unnatural force pushed him onward. He felt his feet carry him to the next, much more narrow alleyway, and he turned without hesitation. He paused, feeling alarmed by the break in routine. *What drives me to this place?* he puzzled.

He knew the way back to Justinian like he knew how to draw breath. But his legs seemed determined to forge a new path—as if they acted independently from his mind. He turned down another small alley, trying to make his way back to the path on which he normally walked, when he suddenly stopped in his tracks. The scene before him made his stomach churn, and he quietly placed the sack of grain on the ground, drawing a knife from its holster.

"You worthless whore!" a man growled over a tiny body curled into a ball on the ground. "You think you can get away with this? You think I haven't noticed the way you have been avoiding your work?" The man kicked the body, and Belisarius watched as blood splattered from the brutalized frame. The girl must have already taken a severe beating before the last kick. She looked as if she might already be dead, her body unresponsive to the subsequent abuse.

Belisarius's blood boiled, and his eyesight was bathed in a cloak of red. He had sworn he would never become entangled with another whore—the years spent cleaning up after Antonina's sexual escapades had made him all but swear off women for the rest of his life. But as red pooled around the helpless creature, he could not stand idly by.

He rushed toward the man from the side, keeping his footsteps quiet as he approached. When he fell upon the man, the coward yelped in terror. Belisarius pinned him on the ground in a matter of seconds. The man tried to fight him off with swinging arms and kicking legs, but Belisarius's practiced technique kept him unmoving in the dirt.

"You think it's enjoyable to beat a woman to death?" Belisarius growled in a low voice.

"She is mine to discipline in whatever way I see fit. I own her. She is my whore to sell to whomever I please," the man hissed as he spat in Belisarius's face.

"You are a monster. And for *me* to say that is quite something, considering how many men have been slain by my hands," Belisarius whispered as he wiped the spit off his left cheek and rubbed it onto the man's face. "Now, I will torture you for your transgressions. You will suffer, and you will not live to regret your actions."

The man's defiance faltered. Belisarius knew the man was calculating how much truth was in the promise, and the true cowardice of the man's character washed over his pitiful face. He let out a loud cry for help before Belisarius hit him so hard in the side of the head that he was knocked unconscious. The struggling body sagged, and Belisarius easily hoisted him over his shoulder where the sack of grain had previously rested. He searched for a secluded corridor—one that was far enough removed from the main paths that no one would happen across them or hear the man's screams of pain as he peeled flesh from the limbs of the dumb beast. For that was what this man was—an ignorant creature begging to be put out of its misery from his worthless existence.

Belisarius found the dark dead-end of a narrow alley that was nicely suited to his particular needs. He ripped off part of the unconscious man's tunic to use as a rope to bind the man's arms behind his back and to tie his ankles together. *The girl...* he remembered her limp body was lying just a few lanes away. He quickly retrieved the injured female—though it seemed likely she would be dead before he finished with her master's torture—and brought her into the alley where his victim awaited a slow and painful death.

Why are you doing this? Belisarius's mind screamed in protest. But as Belisarius looked back and forth between the broken body and the fiend who beat her, his rage grew once more. *As long as the man is conscious, he will know why he is suffering,* the corners of his mouth turned up in a wicked smirk.

"Wake up!" he yelled, slapping the man's face to revive him. The man groaned and opened his eyes slowly. "I once swore I would never torture another for my own selfish gain. Fortunately, I have nothing to gain from this," Belisarius smiled as understanding flashed in the man's gaze. "I want you to feel everything I am about to do. I want you to keep your eyes fixed on her— the reason you deserve to suffer—whenever you are conscious. And I will continue to wake you until you can no longer wake," he promised. Fear filled the man's eyes and he tried to scream once more. Belisarius ripped another piece of the tunic and shoved it into his mouth. He then wrapped a second piece all the way around the man's head and mouth to ensure he could not spit out the first. Belisarius tied it more tightly than necessary—furthering the man's discomfort while effectively shutting him up.

Belisarius took his knife and ran it down the length of the man's arm, teasing at the horrors to come.

"You will regret every moment of your worthless life by the time I have finished with you. I have lived for hundreds of years and never wanted to torment someone the way I long to torture you. I will enjoy this. You most assuredly will not," he whispered in the man's ear as tears dripped from the terror-filled eyes.

By the time Belisarius was finished, not one piece of the man's tattered tunic was left unbloodied. He was missing several fingers and toes and a few of the nails from his remaining digits. One ear was entirely cut off—the man had passed out during that one. But Belisarius was quick to revive him and start again. The final moment of glory that Belisarius had kept for the finale was the removal of the fiend's manhood. He waited until his knife was dull from cutting through bones. And as he sawed through the final bit of flesh, the man's screaming ceased and his eyes rolled back into his head. Belisarius stabbed him several times in the heart for good measure, but he was overjoyed to know the man died losing what was surely his most prized possession.

He turned to leave, wiping the blood from his knife and hands as best he could, and he saw the tiny body curled up on the ground behind him.

He swore. He had forgotten about her. *I cannot leave her here. If she is dead, her body will lie here rotting. If she is alive, she will die without a healer. Maybe Justinian will have an idea of what to do with her.* He picked her up as carefully as he could, worried that he might worsen her injuries simply by carrying her back to the home. He covered her body with a part of his tunic, shielding her from the eyes of passers-by. When he arrived at their dwelling—without the grain he had forgotten in the alleyway—Justinian opened the door and his eyes flashed with shock.

"What have you done?" Justinian asked, moving out of the way to let

Belisarius in.

"She was nearly beaten to death when I happened upon her. I foolishly took too long ripping apart the man who did this, though."

"I'm sure it was deserved," Justinian spoke with a gleam of his old mischievousness in his eyes. It had been a long time since Belisarius had glimpsed the more brutal side of his friend, and he couldn't help but appreciate Justinian's response. It was nice to know Justinian maintained some of his violent tendencies from his time as emperor. "But why is she here? Could you not have left her? Or taken her to a physician? Having her in our home is unwise. Surely someone saw you bring her this way."

"Have I ever made a decision that was not in our best interest?" Belisarius hissed, narrowing his eyes at Justinian.

"No, of course not," Justinian moved slightly away, shaking his head.

"I am not sure how to proceed," Belisarius admitted. Justinian looked at Belisarius from the corner of his narrowed eyes as he shook his head slowly.

"Well I certainly have no idea," Justinian snapped. "I always had physicians to care for me and my wife. You must act as healer. Did you ever treat wounds on the battlefields? I'm willing to go out and find a physician if you wish," he offered.

"No. I will do what I can for her, and if she survives, we will let her go free. I believe she is a whore, and the man I killed claimed to be her master. A physician is too risky. If one were to recognize her and discover that her master is missing, I might be thrown in prison or she might be accused of the murder. No... we cannot allow anyone to know she is here," Belisarius explained as he placed the pitiful body on his own sleeping pallet. "I'll need some supplies, though."

Justinian took down the list of items Belisarius might need to help the woman survive and left without another word.

The girl remained unconscious while Belisarius bent her joints and poked and prodded at her bones and skin. He was grateful she did not wake—she would have screamed in agony if she was conscious for the examination. He cringed at the sight of her shredded garment and brutalized frame. He needed to clean and cover her wounds if there was any chance for her to live.

He could immediately tell she had two broken bones in her right arm—and many more in her right hand. One break caused a fragment of bone to push straight through her flesh. There were at least three ribs on the right side of her body that seemed to be broken. The massive bruise on her abdomen would need to be bled to reduce swelling. And it would be a miracle if the left side of the woman's face was not permanently mutilated. Belisarius guessed that her face had been the point of impact from the man's brutal kick. Her mouth was filled with dried blood, and it seemed that no matter where he looked, he found more blood and bruising on another part of her body.

"I do not think that I can save you," he whispered in her ear. "But I swear I will do my best to keep you alive."

FORTY-ONE

BELISARIUS STOOD over the pallet where the woman lay. His pulse raced, and he felt panicked and jittery—feelings which were both unwelcome and uncommon in his life. *How do I keep her from bleeding to death if I cannot tell where her wounds begin and end? I should simply slit her veins and let her die in peace while she remains unconscious. That would surely be more merciful.*

He had spent years aiding soldiers with wounds on the battlefield when no physicians were available. But this felt entirely different. This was a citizen—not a soldier. A female instead of a male. He had never looked at a woman's body in such a capacity. What if sewing up the gashes was somehow different? He breathed a heavy sigh and rubbed a hand across his face, letting it linger there for a moment. He knelt down and spoke, hoping she would understand his pleading.

"If you are awake for any part of this, you will be in such excruciating pain that I will not be able to keep you from doing more harm to yourself. I am begging you. Stay asleep."

He pulled a knife from its holster and cut away the remaining pieces of her tattered frock. The blood-soaked garment had dried to some of the cuts, and as he pulled it away, blood began to leak from the reopened wounds. Her body was smeared red, with spots of purple and blue darkening her skin where the blood was not as prominent. She should have been dead, but her quiet moans and jagged breaths kept him assured that life still flowed through her veins. Justinian arrived back from the market just as he was ready to begin working.

"I need the alcohol, the thread and a fish hook," Belisarius commanded somberly as he looked down at his shaking hands. He never had shaky hands. Shaky hands were signs of nervousness and indecisiveness. Nervousness and indecisiveness were signs of weakness. And weakness was not a part of who Belisarius was. *Stop shaking this instant,* he commanded his disobedient hands.

"Here." Justinian handed him what he had asked for and stared down at the woman. "Who would do such a thing?"

"A monster," Belisarius answered with venom in his voice as he felt his hands go immediately steady. He would save this woman. He had to. The old woman's earlier words reverberated in his mind. *You can redeem yourself... if only a little.* Had that really been earlier in the same day? The words were connected to the broken woman on his pallet. He knew saving this girl was the redemption she spoke of. *I have to save her.*

He wet a cloth and began to gently wash the dried blood away. Her condition was even worse than he originally thought. Her deeper cuts were still bleeding, and the swelling around her abdomen spoke to the possibility of deeper injuries which he would not be able to fix. He took the alcohol Justinian had purchased and poured it over each bloody wound. He took the small fishing hook and tied a piece of string onto the end. He started with the largest cuts and sewed those shut first. Then he worked his way down until he was satisfied she would not lose any more blood. He covered each wound with small strips of honey-soaked linens to keep dirt out of the cuts and hasten the healing process. Then he checked each bone for a break and marked the injured places with a dot of Justinian's ink. Justinian had gathered tree branches to use as braces for the broken limbs. Six branches for her right leg—two for the top part, two for the bottom part, and two to keep the leg perfectly straight—were wrapped with linens and secured to the leg. He used the same technique for her right arm, except he bent the joint at her elbow as he had seen many physicians do when his soldiers had suffered arm injuries. He wished, now, that he had paid closer attention to the battlefield physicians.

When, at last, he was finished, the woman looked like one of the Egyptian mummies, all wrapped in linen cloth. Belisarius sat back against the wall, exhaustion finally taking its toll on his body. A full day had passed in the time he had worked on her, and the first rays of sun were beginning to peek through the home's courtyard. He looked at his shaky hands once more. They had been steady for the duration of his stitching, but now that he looked at her lying so still, his fear for her life returned in full force.

"I have to keep her alive," he mumbled to himself.

"I think you did, my friend. I've never seen anything like that. What possessed you to save her? You know she will die in a few years anyway, and you will continue on as you always have. It's either now or in a few short years," Justinian shook his head.

The words rang true, but Belisarius felt his temperament bristle at the way Justinian spoke in relation to the girl. The events of the day were evidence (at least in his mind) that the girl was anything but some mere mortal woman who would pass away without being remembered. Any chance for a moment of redemption for the life he had lived felt important. But he did not want Justinian to worry he was going soft.

"I don't know. I felt that it was something I needed to do," he explained with a nonchalant shrug. His response was apparently convincing, because Justinian nodded and walked away, seemingly happy that the drama had died down.

Belisarius found he could not bring himself to leave the girl alone. He feared for the coming days and weeks. Her recovery would be long and drawn out. And there was a very real possibility she would not wake. He cringed at the thought but remained ever watchful.

Days passed, and she did not stir. Justinian offered to help with the girl's care, and they took turns looking after her throughout the day and night. They poured a few drops of water under her tongue every hour or so and put tiny crumbs of food on her tongue to attempt to nourish her body without any effort on her part. But after so much time without a response, Belisarius feared she was lost.

Each time he looked at her, he felt guilt that he had possibly done something wrong. For a moment while he had sewn shut her broken skin, he had felt a glimmer of hope at the opportunity to redeem himself a little—but with each passing hour the glimmer grew more and more faint.

"I'm going to sleep, Belisarius. If she does not wake within the week, I do not know what else we can possibly do. She is wasting away without food and water," Justinian said as he went to his room to sleep.

Belisarius had barely slept since she arrived. And Justinian's flippant willingness to dismiss her life as lost did not sit well in Belisarius's gut. He sat over her all night, hoping for some kind of response that would let him know she would be all right. "Wake, young one. You need to eat," Belisarius whispered as he watched her face for a response of any kind. Nothing.

He traced his finger over the bruises on her neck where the monster had nearly strangled her. He ran a finger over her bruised jaw and cheek. He thought she might be fourteen or fifteen. She was of marrying age for certain, but whores rarely found men to take them as wives. Had he not killed the man, and had the woman somehow survived the day under another's care, she would have likely lived out the rest of her days taking beatings from her master.

She stirred under his touch of her cheek, and he stood, watching her breathing quicken a little.

"I hurt," she groaned brokenly—he thought her speech might be impaired from the injury to her neck. Her right eye was still swollen, and she did not attempt to open either eye.

"You were badly beaten. Don't worry. You are safe here, but you must eat and drink."

He placed the tiny pieces of bread and fruit on her tongue one at a time and watched as she struggled to swallow even the smallest crumb of nourishment. He poured water into her mouth a little at a time, not wanting her to choke or cough—which would only cause her more pain.

When she fell back asleep an hour later, she had eaten two figs and a few bites of bread. Belisarius wanted to shout for joy. She was alive. He had saved her.

FORTY-TWO

THE WOMAN'S EYES opened carefully, squinting against the dim flickering of the candle next to where she lay. She looked around tentatively, seeming only slightly alarmed that she did not recognize her surroundings. As her searching gaze met Belisarius's, he watched confusion flash in her eyes before she closed them once more. She mumbled something unintelligibly.

"What?" Belisarius asked.

"Are you a physician?" she whispered, barely loud enough for him to hear.

"No," he answered.

"A priest?"

"No," he shuttered.

"Then who are you? And where am I?" she pressed quietly.

He thought for a moment about what answers he should give. He had not given any thought to what name he should be called in Rome. There had been no need for him to create a new identity up to that point. But the broken woman before him had been on the brink of death when he saved her, so in her eyes he must seem like a priest. He cleared his throat and said the first thing he could think of.

"You can call me Priest," he agreed. The young woman nodded—barely—and fell back to sleep.

He had waited for some time to ask her about the man he had killed and was a bit irritated that he would have to wait even longer. He wanted to know where she was from. He wanted to know what to call her. Was there someone looking for her? Would she want to return to her family? The questions rushed to his mind one after another. But there she was, still asleep, unable to answer his queries.

"What did she say?" Justinian asked, having noticed the exchange.

"She asked if I was a priest," Belisarius admitted without turning to look at his friend.

Justinian made no effort to hide his amusement.

"And what did you tell her?" he looked incredulous.

"I told her she could call me Priest. I know, I know. But I had not thought of a name to give her before she asked, and I do not want to continue using the name 'Belisarius'. Even though we live in Rome, and even if it has been seventy years, if Justinian and Belisarius are rumored walking around Rome together, who knows what kind of attention it might bring," he pointed out. "And it is not as if I will always be called Priest. I can choose something less pious once we figure out a more permanent situation for the girl," he kept his eyes fixed on a spot on the ground.

"My god. If you're a priest, then I'm a saint," Justinian shook his head slowly.

"That's perfect," Belisarius nodded, finally looking up. "'Saint' is ambiguous enough of a name. You were considered a saint during your reign."

"Yes… called a saint by only the most loyal of subjects. Others would have had you believe I was a demon cloaked in human form, only capable of death and deception," Justinian scoffed.

"We do not speak of that spineless worm. Procopius was jealous of your power… and the way you trusted me implicitly," Belisarius pointed out. Justinian rolled his eyes.

"Regardless. If I will be called Priest, then Saint would be the perfect companion. We are two holy men, doing our good deed for the century," Belisarius knew he had meant words as humorous, but they rang true nonetheless. *No. I am not Belisarius. I am Priest, son of no one. Hailing from nowhere,* he told himself firmly.

"I suppose it will do. You shall have to remind me to call you by your new name," Saint warned. "I have spent so long calling you Belisarius."

"I will. And I will only call you Saint from now on," Priest promised.

Priest remained by the woman's side, and each time she opened her eyes, he felt more relief flood his veins. She said nothing, but the gratitude in her gaze was almost too much for him to bear.

When finally she awoke for more than a few fleeting moments, Priest took the opportunity to ask her some of the questions that had pulled at his mind since he found her. She still had not moved from lying on her back, but her coloring looked promising. Her bruises were changing from bright red and purple to a dark blue. She was healing little by little, and he was glad for it. He tried to make his voice sound as caring as possible.

"What is your name?" he asked.

"I am called Alexandria here," she answered with a wounded glint in her eyes. "But that is not my name."

"Then tell me your name, and I shall use it," he spoke reassuringly.

The woman paused briefly, as if studying his face for some ulterior motive.

"Basina."

"Where are you from, Basina?" he asked.

"I was stolen as a child from Hispania. I am fifteen, but I have lived in Rome for the past six years," she answered.

Priest swallowed hard at her words. A nine-year-old forced into prostitution was not uncommon for the time, but that did not make it any less horrifying. He had been raised in a home with a loving mother. His father had died in battle when Priest was only seven years old, but Priest's memories of his parents' relationship were of unfailing love and devotion. When his father was killed, Priest's mother became a hollow shell of a woman, barely able to care for Priest and his younger sister and brother. For three years, Priest worked and provided for his family. And when, at last, his mother returned to her former self, Priest —at only ten years of age—had already become a man.

His relationship with his mother was never easy after that time, but he had firmly established himself as the head of their household. Against his mother's wishes, he became a soldier—as an homage to his father's memory. And at ten years old, he vowed to become the greatest warrior his people had ever seen.

Priest's mind returned to the present, and as he looked down at the young woman, he felt his fists clench. *What if my sister had been stolen away and forced into this life.* His pulse raced, and he took deep breaths to calm his pounding heart.

Basina watched silently, but he felt as if her eyes pierced through his mind and understood the war raging within him.

"Who was the man beating you?" Priest asked through gritted teeth.

"My master. I have not been myself lately. They cut a baby out of me last month, and I have not felt well since," she muttered brokenly, squirming in the discomfort of her candor.

"He is no one's master any more. I… I rid the world of his filth," he revealed, waiting for her response. Her expression didn't seem to change, so he continued. "You can remain here and recover for as long as it takes for you to regain your health," he stated more harshly than he intended.

Basina lowered her head in deference to his proclamation, but Priest thought he saw the hint of a smile playing at the corners of her mouth.

"Do you have family or friends in Rome?" he asked, not quite finished with his questioning.

"No," she responded without emotion, her eyes fixed on the ceiling above.

The slow blinks of her eyelids told him Basina had revealed enough for one day. He sat back and remained silent, hoping she would fall back to sleep soon so he could speak to Justi… *no*… Saint about the young woman without her overhearing the conversation.

When he was sure she was asleep, he left her alone and joined Saint in the main room of their small abode. He sat on the crude wooden bench situated in the center of the sitting room. They had rented the smallest domus they could find on the outskirts of the busiest part of the city. They allowed a family to run the shop in the front room of the home and took only a small portion of the profits (since their wealth was sufficient to live comfortably for hundreds of years). The home was a far cry from the palace in which they had lived before, but since leaving Constantinople, they had suffered far worse. He had initially worried about Saint's ability to cope with the change—Priest had lived in squalor on more than one occasion over the course of his unending life—but the emperor had adjusted to the simple life much faster than Priest could have hoped. He looked around the dwelling and sighed. *We cannot stay in this tiny place with the woman.*

"Did she tell you anything about herself?" Saint asked, apparently for the second time.

"I am sorry, my friend. I was lost in my thoughts," he apologized. "Her name is Basina. She has no family and no ties. Her master is… was… the man I killed. And she has been a prostitute since the age of nine." He sat back and rubbed his forehead roughly with his fingertips, frustrated with their current situation. "What do we do with her? She has nowhere to go. And I have already told her she will recover here for as long as it takes to make her healthy. I spoke without thought. What are we going to do with a young woman?" Priest worried as his mind whirled over the girl's lot in life.

"How long do you think her recovery will take?" Saint asked with the familiar gleam of scheming hidden in his eyes.

"I do not know. A month or two?" Priest offered without a real estimate. "She had a baby cut out of her last month and still has not recovered from the trauma. She is in worse condition than her exterior wounds might suggest."

Saint shook his head sadly. "Poor girl," he muttered with an absent stare.

"What if she were to stay once she has recovered? We can pay her to cook and clean. It would be nice to have a housekeeper for a short time," Priest suggested.

Saint's eyes snapped to Priest's. "And I'm sure she has other skills."

Priest felt fury bubble up from his chest at the implication in Saint's words.

"We would never lay a finger on her, my friend. If she *wants* to stay, we will treat her kindly, and she will have an income. We can move into a villa or a larger domus where she can have her own space. And she will be able to afford whatever she wants because she will have no master. We will allow her to stay for one, maybe two years at most. She will have plenty of time to recover, find another job, and move on with her life as a free woman."

Saint seemed irritated by the authority with which Priest spoke. *He was an emperor and my superior for many years. I suppose it will take him some time to get used to a reversal of roles.* Saint had followed Priest's lead upon leaving Constantinople, knowing full-well that Priest had all the experience they needed to create a new life for themselves. He wondered if Saint would continue to trust his judgment.

"Is that safe? To have another person living with us? What if one of us uses the wrong name? Or refers to something in our pasts in front of her? Will she not wish to know our histories if she is to live with us?" Saint pressed.

"We will tell her what we wish her to know, and if she feels she needs more, she can leave. She will not be bound to our home. And we are not bound to Rome, you know. If any suspicion is cast upon our lives here, we will relocate. And next time we move, we will create our identities *before* we go. I am dumbfounded by my oversight on that matter," Priest chided himself.

Saint sat quietly, thinking for some time before speaking. "I don't know. It seems an unnecessary risk. But if you think she will not pry into our pasts, I cannot deny her a short time here to recover and earn some income. She has no one else, and, as you know, I am a saint," he snickered.

Priest eyed Saint. If he even looked at Basina the wrong way, Priest would make his friend pay. But it was, he supposed, possible that Saint had other reasons for agreeing to the idea. *Perhaps my friend has grown tired of our meager lifestyle after all. Maybe he has been searching for a reason to move to a larger home.*

"I want to ask her if this is something she even wants. She was brought to Rome against her will, forced to sell her body against her will, and forced to have a baby cut from her stomach—most likely against her will. I refuse to make any decisions regarding *her* life without first consulting her," Priest said with finality.

Saint's eyebrows rose. He quickly replaced his surprise with an approving nod, but Priest saw his friend eyeing him with interested glances throughout the day.

Priest found his thoughts wander to his past while he waited for Basina to awaken. He did not often allow himself to reminisce, but the unique situation in which he now found himself recalled memories he had long since buried in the darkest corners of his mind.

He had married a fourteen-year-old girl when he was sixteen years of age. Priest's father and mother had arranged the marriage when Priest was a small child, and though he had not liked the decision, he respected it. His wife was found murdered two years into their union—and Priest had not been sorry for the loss. She had neither respected him nor given him any offspring. Most of their two years of marriage had been spent ignoring one another completely. She was uninterested in him, and her plain looks and lack of skill in bed did nothing to entice him into pursuing her more fervently. They did not argue or fight because neither acknowledged the other's presence except when they were attempting to produce a child. At the time, he had suspected that his mother had arranged the murder—she had not liked the girl and often hinted that his wife's infertility was a product of her many sins. But he had discovered a few years later that it was his mother, herself, who had killed the girl. She had not meant to tell him, but it had slipped out during an argument over his recklessness on the battlefield.

Priest took a deep breath as he thought of his mother's silent determination. She had not been at peace with Priest's decision to follow in the footsteps of his father. She wanted him to become a fisherman or an artisan—the most respected and much safer vocations within their tribe. But Priest's vow to honor his father by becoming the greatest warrior his people had ever known was one his mother had to respect. And though she had not spoken the words, he could see she was proud of his accomplishments.

After Priest's first wife died, he spent a few years focused solely on the battlefield. And when he was once again ready to take a wife, he married a woman of his own choosing. The girl he selected was the widow of one of his soldiers. Her name was Safira. She was barely seventeen—too young to be a widow—and had been joined to her husband for only a few short months before he was killed in battle. She was pretty enough—not so beautiful that he would worry about other men trying to seduce her while he was away fighting—but he found her figure quite pleasing. He remembered her late husband speaking about her as a good wife, so she seemed a logical choice after his untimely death.

A few days into the union, she proved that his second marriage would be just as difficult as his first. The only prior experience he had as a husband was with a wife who ignored him, so Priest had no idea how to act with his new bride. They had consecrated the marriage on their wedding night, but after that, he was unsure how to proceed. The first morning of their married life together had been unbearably silent and awkward. He knew the woman was uncomfortable, but could not imagine what the reason could be for her mood. He had made a single demand before walking out of the home that morning— that meals be on the table at a certain hour each night. After he left, he assumed things would be normal by the time he returned for dinner. But that evening, Safira proclaimed her disobedience by placing uncooked ingredients before him when dinner should have been served. He did not know how to respond, so he simply ate the unprepared ingredients, hoping his suffer-in-silence approach would dissuade her from continuing her scheme.

When he finished eating, he took Safira by force since she would not willingly lie with him. He was not proud of his actions, but at the time, he thought she was merely a possession to do with as he chose.

However, the next night, Safira made it quite clear she would not behave as a wife should. He remembered thinking that all women must be intolerable witches with the power only to infuriate men and wreak havoc upon the world.

The second night of uncooked ingredients landed on the table in front of him, followed by a vicious argument. After what seemed like hours of hurling insults at one another, he felt his self-control collapse. He did his best to beat the disrespect out of her, and though she fought back for a time, his strength easily overwhelmed hers. Furious with both Safira for her disrespect and himself for losing control, he left the woman's body crumpled on the floor. He stayed away for several days, trying to focus his energy on the anger he felt at his wife's disrespect. He fought against the fear in his chest that made him wonder if Safira was all right... and failed miserably.

When he finally returned home, Safira was waiting for him. The side of her face was black and blue, and one of her arms did not look as it should have—he thought it likely her shoulder was popped out of its joint. He felt sick that he had done so much damage, but he wondered if perhaps he had succeeded in ridding the woman of disrespect. She had cooked dinner, and as he sat down and looked at the meal before him—thrilled that his wife could, in fact, cook a meal—she smashed him over the head with the very pot she had used to cook. He fell to the ground in a daze, his chest burned from the stew and his nose bloody from the impact. Safira took the opportunity to sit on top of him, beating his face until every inch of it was bloodied, screaming as her shoulder protested the movement. He grabbed her arms as she screamed, doing his best to hold her injured arm still to minimize her suffering. When he pushed her shoulder back into place, she stopped fighting. He was furious with her, but the overwhelming emotion he felt was awe that she had been able to not only surprise him but also break his skin with the swing of her fists.

It had taken them months to get past their initial marital problems, but she had eventually provided him with a son to carry on his family line and a daughter with whom they could arrange an advantageous marriage with another powerful family. She had shown him that he was capable of loving another person in a way he had not thought himself capable.

Safira showed Priest how valuable a good wife could be. She was capable not only of bearing children and making delicious food, but also of giving great pleasure and friendship in matters one could not discuss with men. She gave him support and encouragement in times when it was most needed. And they shared an emotional intimacy he had not felt since.

Priest returned to the present, cringing as he imagined his wife and daughter being stolen and sold as whores in a foreign country. He suddenly felt shame for all the times he had purchased a whore for a night of pleasure. What if they had been stolen just as Basina? He stood, his breathing heavy with the anger he felt toward himself and anyone involved in Basina's life of slavery. He paced for a moment until he could no longer wait for her to wake up.

"I have an offer for you," Priest began loudly, waking Basina from her slumber. The woman's eyes popped open in surprise, but she remained silent.

"We would like you to work for us. We are preparing to move into a larger home, and it will need cleaning and care. We want you to live in our home—in your own room—and cook and clean for us. Do you know how to cook?" he asked.

"Yes," she replied cautiously.

"Then do you accept the job?" he pushed.

Her brows furrowed as she studied his features for any hint of dishonesty in his offer. He continued to look at her with the same hopeful expression.

"Only to cook and clean?" she asked, still confused.

"Yes. That is all. You will not be used for anything more," he promised.

"I accept," she answered as more of a question than a statement. But it was good enough for him.

"We need to find a bigger home, Saint," he announced as he left their domus to search for a new place to live.

FORTY-THREE

FOUR WEEKS LATER, the three moved across the city to a large domus situated in the heart of Rome. The home was much too large for just three people, but Saint insisted it would make Basina feel at ease if she had more work to do. There were four bedrooms, a study for Saint, a dining room, a large atrium, and a vestibule in the front of the home that housed a shop. The shop was run by a family with four children over the age of ten, and Priest and Saint paid the children to cook and clean while Basina continued her recovery. A large courtyard with a pool comprised the center of the domus, with all the rooms encircling it. Priest knew swimming would help Basina regain some of her leg strength without the pain of resting her full weight upon it. When he was a child, his sister had fallen from a tree while playing, and he remembered the way the healer had used a local body of water to assist in the healing process. He had watched as his sister walked back and forth with only her head showing above the surface of the water. She had gradually been able to increase her speed as she regained the full use of the leg. Priest hoped Basina could heal as quickly as his sister had.

Basina was walking around the house a little each day with the help of a stick Priest carved into the correct shape to allow her to rest her body on it comfortably while keeping the weight off her broken leg. He had cut the thread out of most of her stitched up wounds a week earlier, but the bright pink skin was still a reminder of the deep gashes she had suffered. The bruises on her face and ribs were nearly gone now—only a pale yellow color remained that announced the last of the injuries. The only wounds that lingered were on her legs, covered by her robes. She almost looked like a healthy young woman again. Almost. Priest knew the scars on her skin would forever remind her of her violent past. And he hoped her broken limbs would heal properly so she would not have to live out her days with a limp or a useless arm. He pictured Basina having to always walk with a cane and swore under his breath. Saint and Basina's eyes snapped up to his.

"Apologies. I was lost in my thoughts," he said, walking away without explanation.

The three of them fell into an easy routine over the weeks together. Basina grew more at ease with the two men every day, though Priest still caught the occasional glance from the corner of her eye that announced she was wary of them both. But after the beating she had taken from another man, he was not upset by the distrust. She barely spoke a word that was not in response to a question. But in her silence, Priest knew she saw much. Her eyes took in *everything*. She carefully measured the tenor of Priest and Saint's voices as they spoke about the latest happenings in the city, and she studied their expressions as they discussed political uprisings. They were careful not to speak about their pasts, but Priest suspected the ever-watchful girl knew they were hiding information from her.

Basina rested on a chaise in the vestibule or in her bed for most of each day, and Priest took care of her as best he could. Saint went to the market a few times a week while Priest stayed behind.

"No one is searching for me," she assured him once she understood the reason for his protectiveness. "Even the brothel's patrons hated my master, and some of the other women tried to get me to run away before he had the physicians cut out my baby. No one will blame me for his death... nor for my disappearance," she said thoughtfully.

Priest pondered her words for a moment, wondering if she understood that she was not bound to him and Saint in any permanent way.

"Once you have recovered, you may leave any time you wish," he said as her forehead wrinkled in confusion at the change in subject.

But even as he spoke the words, a pang of fear rushed up his spine at the thought of her being unprotected. She watched him, the expression on her face unreadable as she pondered his words for a few silent moments.

"I would prefer to stay here and serve in the home," she answered, looking down at her still-bandaged leg.

Priest nodded. He understood her gratitude, but he hoped she would acknowledge her debt was repaid after a short time working so she could live a real life. Neither he nor Saint could offer her a life beyond protection and employment.

A few days later, Basina grew unexpectedly distant. Her eyes darted to every movement he and Saint made, and when she was not with them for a meal, she remained hidden in her room.

"What do you suppose caused the change?" Saint asked Priest one evening as Basina walked slowly back to her room following dinner.

"I will not begin to act as though I understand what she must be feeling. She has not lived a decent life. Surely she is in shock that there is a place where she can be at peace. The mind takes time to adjust."

Saint merely nodded, but the calm expression on his face seemed forced.

After a few days of her strange behavior, Priest determined it was time to take action.

"I believe it is time to remove the thread from your legs. I want you to begin using the pool to help you recover," Priest announced. Basina nodded silently, lying down on her bed with a small wince before lifting her robe to reveal the bandages that wrapped both her legs.

"Are you in pain?" he asked, worrying that something had suddenly gone wrong with her recovery.

"Only a little," she responded without lifting her eyes to meet his. He knew she was hiding something, but he could not begin to guess what it might be.

Priest carefully unwrapped the bandages from each of her legs, happy to see that he was correct about the wounds being healed enough to remove the thread. Basina remained stoic as he cut the thread and pulled it carefully from her skin. Priest was proud of her for staying calm and silent—he had seen grown men whimper in pain from the same.

He pushed lightly on the scars that were no longer sewed shut, hoping to discover the source of her new pain. He knew how dangerous an infection could be if left without treatment. Many a good soldier had died from such wounds. But as he pushed on each spot, Basina gave no sign that there was pain under the surface.

"Basina. I need to know the source of your pain. This change in your attitude is…" he did not know what it was. It concerned him more than he understood. "Unexpected."

"I am not in pain any longer," she lied without looking into his eyes. She pushed her cloak down with a wince and turned onto her side.

Priest stood angrily and looked down at her. *Why does she not tell me what the problem is?* He wanted to grab her by the shoulders and demand that she reveal her secret, but as he looked at the back of her neck—a place he could not normally see because of her long hair—he noticed a bright, new bruise along her spine.

"What is that?" his voice transformed into something that was terrifying even to himself.

She sat up with a wince, looked at his gaze, and pushed her hair back into place.

"What is what?" she replied with a hint of fear in her voice.

"Basina, please show me the bruise on your neck and explain to me how it came to be there," he pleaded as sweetly as possible.

"I fell," she offered innocently, her eyes subtly darting to the doorway.

"Can I please see your neck?" he asked once more.

She turned silently and pulled her hair out of the way. Priest sucked in a sharp breath as he realized the bruise went at least a little way down her back under her robes. *You fell? Unlikely. Was this Saint? Could he be so cruel?* But it was obvious she was afraid for a reason. *Is it possible she is protecting the shopkeepers and their children? Perhaps this was truly an accident?*

"Did one of the shopkeepers do this to you on accident? Did you trip over one of the children?" he pressed. "They will not be fired from their post if it was accidental."

"Umm. Yes. I stepped backwards without realizing one of the children was behind me. And I lost my balance and fell," her eyes flitted to the doorway once more and her face paled a little.

Priest had heard Saint approach silently, but he was now certain his friend had caused the injury. Whether on purpose or by accident remained to be determined, but he would find out the truth. He was outraged that Saint had acted as if he was unsure why Basina's mood had suddenly changed. He had always been excellent at playing the role of innocent victim. *Nothing has changed. But you forget I know all your secrets.* He glanced sideways at his friend, who seemed concerned over Basina's health.

"Do not worry, Saint. I will look after her," Priest said pointedly. Saint shrugged and left the doorway. Only after Priest knew his friend had moved too far away to hear him did he turned his full attention to Basina.

"Tell me this instant what he did to you," Priest hissed.

Priest paced back and forth in the courtyard, trying futilely to calm down before confronting Saint. The fool had made Basina feel that she should repay him for his kindness in more than just housekeeping. And when she had responded negatively to his suggestion, he had grabbed her and tried to force a kiss. Basina was fortunately a fiery little woman and landed a slap on Saint's face before he threw her down onto her back. She had allowed Priest to see the entirety of the damage Saint had caused, and Priest had not been able to remain in the room with her once he saw the extensive bruising. "He will pay," Priest had spat as he rushed out of the room. It had been the only recurring thought in

Priest's mind for the past half-hour. But once he realized he would not soon calm down, he decided to confront Saint and lay the matter to rest once and for all.

He barged into Saint's study where the man was looking over the monthly expenditures the shopkeepers had recently provided. He grabbed him by his throat and slammed him against the wall, knocking the air out of him. Saint tried to inhale, but Priest's hands were cutting off his supply of air.

"I told you we will not lay a finger on the girl. Her entire back is a solid bruise because of your idiotic behavior," Priest yelled as Saint clawed fruitlessly to free his neck from the tight grip.

"If you look at her in a way that I find displeasing, I will tie you to a chair and torture you slowly for years. Just because I cannot kill you does not mean I cannot make your life the most miserable existence possible. You are not in command in this home. You are an equal to everyone living here. Remember this for the rest of our lives. If you understand me, tap my hand," he commanded. A desperate tap on his hand announced he should release Saint, but Priest found he had to mentally tell his hands to release their hold before he could let his friend go. Saint gasped in as much air as he could while glaring at Priest with a combination of fear and mistrust.

"Do not attempt to touch her again," Priest commanded as he walked away, unable to care if his friend was in pain or not.

As he made his way back to his room, Basina watched, wide-eyed, from her chaise in the vestibule. Priest paused for a moment, nodding once to her as a sign the issue had been dealt with. The corners of her mouth turned up slightly as she bowed her head and closed her eyes.

She had nothing to be thankful for. He had brought her into his home under the guise of healing and protection, and instead he had brought her more pain. He wished he could send her somewhere safer—but he knew, or hoped, Saint would not attempt to touch her again.

Why is there nowhere safe for her? He paced in his room that night, unable to sleep. He had lain down several times without finding sleep. *Surely there is somewhere she can go.* After hours of unrest, he moved a chair from the vestibule to the doorway of Basina's room and sat down. Once he knew the room was inaccessible to Saint, he fell straight to sleep.

FORTY-FOUR

"PRIEST?" A SMALL voice whispered right behind him. He burst up from the chair, embarrassed that Basina had found him blocking her doorway. He had expected to rise earlier than she so he could put everything back in its place.

"I am sorry. About this. And about what happened with Saint," he cleared his throat and picked up the chair to return it to its normal resting spot.

"Thank you," she balked for a short moment before resting her small hand on his left arm. He nodded and moved slightly out of her reach. Her touch had felt like hot coals on his skin—hot coals without the searing pain that usually accompanied them. He rubbed his right hand over the spot where she had touched, just to be sure there were no physical signs of the heat her hand had produced. But there was nothing. He wanted to say *something* to rid the encounter of the awkwardness he felt.

"You should do some exercises in the pool. We need to get you walking without that stick." He looked at the pool as he spoke, avoiding her gaze. He did not know how she was feeling—some mixture of gratitude and fear and other emotions constantly swirled in her eyes.

She emerged from her room a few minutes later wearing the outfit he had purchased for her. It was a heavy, dark cloak that would allow her to remain fully covered while moving in the water—and the weight would add some resistance which would aide in her exercise. Each time she stepped into the water, he could see the determination in her eyes. She needed little encouragement from him to succeed in her recovery.

The three carried on in an awkward truce for weeks: Saint sullen and standoffish, Basina full of silent determination, gratitude, and occasional worry (over what, Priest had no idea), and Priest fearful of what his house mates might do next.

Basina's limp was nearly unnoticeable. After two full months of equal parts rest, exercise, and healing, Priest was happy she no longer winced with each step. She cleaned and cooked and even joined him on trips to the market every once in a while. Priest had purchased several tunics for her in various styles and sizes—all of which did not fit. Finally, she had protested against his failed attempts and convinced him she must join the trips to the market so she could choose for herself. He did not understand the way robes fit women, but at least he finally knew Basina's size. Saint gave him some grief over how much Priest spoiled Basina, but Priest knew his friend was not actually upset over the money spent. It seemed as if the men's relationship was finally finding its way back to the ease they had had before Basina came into their lives.

Basina became relaxed once more with Saint—the single episode graciously forgotten. Most days, joy filled the rooms of their home, and at night Saint sang songs from his childhood and Priest told battlefield stories. Basina begged for new stories each night, believing that his imagination was filled to the brim with delightful tales. Priest and Saint eyed each other mischievously each time her eyes lit with wonder at the fanciful tales.

"I am going to get fat if she keeps cooking so much food," Saint admitted as he sat next to Priest late one evening.

"I do not mind at all," Priest confessed. "Do you see how much joy it brings to her? She becomes happier and more relaxed each day."

"What do we do when she asks us where our income is from?" Saint asked.

"We will tell her we trade goods and services. It has been my source of income all my life. She need not know *what* we trade," Priest answered.

"You told me you are not a priest," Basina said one morning.

Priest looked at her determined expression and felt his hands involuntarily clench into fists.

"That is correct," he answered, forcing a smile.

"And Saint is certainly not a saint," she added with the roll of her eyes. "Then who are you? And what are your names? I have lived with you for months—surely you can tell me your names," she pushed.

"I am called Priest. And he is called Saint. We have no other names."

"Your parents must have hated you," she muttered in an accusatory tone. But she didn't press the issue further.

"And where are you from?" she asked.

Not even Saint knew Priest's age and origin. He certainly wasn't going to divulge the information to a mortal woman who would soon leave them. But a few ambiguous answers might satiate her need for information.

"I was born in a sea village to the east. I am in trade," he replied vaguely.

"And what brought you here?"

"Most in my village were killed," he answered, effectively ending her questioning.

Though she looked at him with pity for the rest of the day, he knew she was too courteous to push him for more details of his tragic past.

He watched her as she moved about their domus tidying messes and arranging furniture. He did not want Basina to feel pity for him—in all honesty, he did not want her to feel anything for him. He was a poison to those who grew too close to him—Saint's immortality was evidence of that. Before becoming immortal, Saint would not have made a complete ass of himself in such a distasteful way. He had loved Theodora passionately, even after her death. But now he was growing colder, more inhuman. Basina was too innocent to be swept up into their sordid, miserable life, and Priest found himself hoping she would leave before he drained the goodness from her as he too often did to those around him.

FORTY-FIVE

PRIEST WAS AWAKENED by someone breathing over his bed. He could hear the intruder's heart beating wildly, and he waited for the inhale that would announce the moment right before the attacker's knife descended upon him. The attacker waited—Priest did not know why, but he did not dare stir. If the intruder followed through with his attack, he would be killed before his weapon could draw a single drop of blood. Priest grasped the hilt of the knife holstered on his left leg, preparing for the intruder's next move.

A finger touched Priest's right shoulder, and his reflexes responded before his mind could tell his body how to react. His right hand shot up to grab the arm of the person who had touched him. Priest slid from his bed as his armed hand found the intruder's throat. He used his momentum to swing the body around and throw it down hard onto the pallet in one swift move, keeping the knife pressed firmly to the intruder's neck without cutting too deep. He wanted to know the motive for this attack before death was dealt to the attacker. Priest's knee pushed down on the invader's legs as he used his full weight to keep the man from moving. He felt the familiar crunch of a breaking bone and inwardly beamed that the unwanted guest would need time to recover if he made it out alive. Priest's mind raced with possibilities of how the intruder could have entered his tent undetected—he was sure that his soldiers would not fall asleep while on duty. The punishment for that kind of lapse was greater than they would be willing to bear.

Priest's eyes focused in the dim candlelight—candlelight which had not been present when he fell asleep earlier. He blinked in confusion, the rage draining from his mind as his eyes finally caught up with his body's actions. Basina looked up in terror as she kept her neck pressed as close to the bed as possible, doing everything in her power to keep her bleeding skin away from his blade. She breathed quick, shallow breaths, never taking her eyes off of Priest's. Not once had she screamed or even made a sound of panic. The only indication of Basina's fear and pain was in the tears that pooled in the corners of her eyes, though even they were too afraid to drip down her cheeks.

Priest's mind grasped what had happened, and he jumped away from the woman who now had blood dripping down her neck, throwing his knife against the far wall. He raised his hands in the air to show her they were empty. He backed up to the wall opposite his bed, their eyes never breaking the strained connection.

"What possible reason can you have to come in my room in the middle of the night?" he yelled. He had been dreaming of the battlefield, as he often did. She knew he screamed in his sleep from nightmares. Surely she was not stupid enough to try to awaken him from his dreams. Her tears finally slid down her cheeks, and his anger faded as he realized he had wounded more than just her body. "I…" he stammered.

She did not move from the spot on which he had thrown her. She still had not made a sound. She only stared at him with her terrified eyes and heaving chest.

"Are you all right? Did I open your scars? I broke your leg," the words flowed out in a rush as he took a hesitant step in her direction. Her eyes narrowed and her head turned slightly away from him—he had seen the action many times before, always as he approached a man who knew his life was about to end violently. Priest sucked in a breath and slammed his body back into the wall, his emotions raging. His head ached as he pounded the back of it angrily against the hard stones that made up his bedroom's wall.

"Gods!" he spat. "I am so… I am sorry, Basina. I thought you were… I thought you came to kill me. I was dreaming I was on the battlefield. I thought you were an enemy. I would never knowingly hurt you. I would never…" his voice faded when he realized she wasn't going to speak.

"Why did you come in here? I've wounded you. I promised I would never lay a finger on you, and now I've injured your body," his voice cracked as his knees buckled beneath him, and he slid to the ground. He had not shed tears since the hopelessness he had felt as Saint lay dead decades earlier, but he felt the unfamiliar wetness run down his cheek. He buried his face in his hands in shame.

He heard uneven footsteps shuffling toward him, and he looked up. Basina was limping—dragging her broken leg behind her… putting her weight painfully on the wound he had inflicted… to walk to him. He had damaged her healing body. *You are the monster,* he chastised himself mentally. He could not look into her eyes. He wished to rush to her, snatch her up, and put her back on the pallet so he could tend to her injuries. But if he moved, she would flinch away. He could not bear to see that expression again. So he remained seated, helpless, unable to help her without first terrifying her.

"I am a monster," he spat, his face twisted in a grimace.

"No," her unsteady voice replied from above his head. He refused to look up. The soft touch of her hand felt like searing coals once more on his wrist, and he flinched away. "No," she growled more fiercely as she grabbed his wrist and forced him to look at her. "Get up," she demanded, and he did what she said without question. "Get back into your bed and go to sleep," she commanded, releasing her hold, and limping toward the door. Priest listened to her labored breathing and hisses of pain with each step she took and felt as if he might vomit.

"No," he groaned, watching Basina stop in her tracks. He walked around her, careful not to touch her broken body. "Stay in my bed. I will sleep in another room. I can tend to your leg right now if you wish," he offered. But the look on her face told him he should not approach her. He turned to leave her alone, looking back to see her grimacing face. "If you want me to look over your wounds in the morning I will," he offered quietly. "But if you wish to leave our home, Saint will take you to a surgeon in the morning and provide you with enough coin so you will be able to live comfortably until you can work again. Call out if you need anything in the night," he whispered as he left Basina alone in his room.

"Basina is in your bed," Saint began, sitting across from Priest in the tablinum. "And she has requested you come look at her wounds. Did something happen between you two last night?"

"Not what you're implying," Priest snapped, unable to look Saint in the eyes.

Priest had not slept after the previous night's events. He sat awake in the atrium all night long, keeping his eyes on the entrance to his room where Basina was hopefully sleeping. He cursed, wondering how many times he would feel this renewed hatred for himself. *How could I have ever believed redemption was attainable? Is this what immortality does? Are we ruined and hateful and unredeemable for all time? This price is too high to pay.*

"Are you going to check on her?" Saint asked, pulling Priest away from his self-loathing for a moment.

"I do not know if I am able," Priest answered. He had seen the fear in her eyes after Saint hurt her. He could not bear if her eyes regarded him the same way.

"I wish I knew what was going on. But she isn't moving, and she would not tell me why. I was too afraid to ask if I could look her over—more of you than of her," he muttered as an aside. Priest's gaze snapped up to his when he mentioned Basina was not moving. "I suggest you do as she asks," Saint warned with an accusing glare in his eye.

Priest had hurt Basina as badly as he feared. He had saved her life only to snatch it away.

He walked slowly to his bedroom, hoping Basina would be walking around when he entered. But when he peeked into the room, her fragile body looked helpless to move on its own yet again. He groaned, rushing to kneel beside the bed, moisture threatening to leak from his eyes as it had the night before.

"Forgive me," he whispered with his head bowed, careful not to touch her with his folded hands. He felt Basina's hand cover his clenched fist. She turned his hand over and pried his fingers open. He did not fight her, allowing her full command. He would gladly do whatever she asked—even if she commanded he stab himself in the heart. But she gently placed her hand in his open palm and squeezed. He looked into her eyes for the first time, now unsure of what he would find there.

"The fault was mine," she spoke softly as he shook his head back and forth. "I came into your room unannounced and woke you from a nightmare. Your reaction was not inappropriate, and I am in no way upset by your response. But I do need you to look over my leg, ribs, and back. I do not know if I should move," she admitted with a pained grin that was meant to be reassuring. Her eyes were bloodshot from a sleepless night, and with every breath she winced a little at the pain in her ribs.

"You cannot be serious," he choked out after a few moments of disbelief. "You will not shoulder the blame of these injuries. I am to blame. Fully. Do not dare speak of your fault again," he commanded in a terrifying whisper. He would have shaken her if she was not injured.

Basina did not respond verbally, but the look in her eyes told Priest she would not comply with his demand. He had seen determination exuding from her during her recovery, but this was the first time she had stood up to him in any way—not that she had needed to at any point in the past. But it was unsettling to his mind to be at odds with her this way. He crossed his arms and set his jaw, unwilling to move until she agreed.

"I will do no such thing. And if you refuse to admit that I am to blame? Then I suppose I will continue to lie here and starve. Do not examine me. Get out," she ordered, clenching her jaw and looking away from Priest's glare.

He stood and stared down at her, simultaneously bewildered and conflicted. She was his to safeguard, and he had failed to protect her against even himself.

He could not allow her to lie there in agony, refusing care. He bent down and grabbed her face gently but firmly, turning it toward him so she would have to look him in the eyes.

"I am going to look at your wounds with or without your permission," he growled. Her arm flew up from the bed, her open hand slamming against Priest's cheek loudly. She hissed in pain, her entire body recoiling from the effort, and Priest stumbled back, releasing Basina's face. Basina's eyes filled with the threat of tears, but Priest could only stare.

Basina slapped me. For trying to help her. She refused to admit that I am to blame for her injuries, then slapped me when I told her I was going to look over her wounds. He turned, let out a frustrated growl, and marched from the room, hoping he might understand the situation more clearly if he was not in her presence.

"Did you check her wounds then?" Saint asked when Priest sat down in the kitchen once more.

"She would not let me," Priest yelled.

"But she just asked..." Saint began as Priest cut him off with a raised hand and a shake of his head.

Saint read his mood and left the room, and Priest was grateful he could wallow in his frustration and self-loathing in peace once more.

FORTY-SIX

FOR TWO COMPLETE DAYS, Basina refused food or care. She only took water when Saint offered it, and Priest's anger finally gave way to fear. The wounds needed to be checked—if her bones healed incorrectly, she could be crippled for the rest of her life.

"This is your fault," he growled as he stomped into his bedroom, ignoring Saint's confused stare. "And I am not to blame."

"Now, wait a moment. What…" Saint began to ask as Basina cut him off.

"It is about time," she yelled back at Priest. Both men were dumbfounded by Basina's outburst. They had never heard her speak at a volume greater than a soft voice—even when she was upset, she usually whispered her anger. "Now check my wounds, you stubborn ass," she commanded, her voice returning to its normal volume.

Priest was too angry to laugh at her words, but he was humored nonetheless as he pushed up the bottom of Basina's tunic to look at her leg. Saint left the room silently, confusion plastered on his face. And Basina let out a cough to hide a giggle. Priest smirked at Basina, but all amusement disappeared when he saw the color of her leg.

"I re-broke your leg." He swore under his breath. "In the same place it was broken before, I believe. I must bind it again—no walking for another month at least."

"All right," she agreed without any hint of irritation. "And my ribs and back?" she asked, rolling onto her side and hissing in pain. He had been surprised when he first brought her to their home that she did not mind his examinations of her bare skin, but he reminded himself that she had been in a whorehouse for so long, the nakedness must have been commonplace to her. Since that terrible first day, she not been fully naked in his presence, and he was careful to keep everything covered during examinations apart from the exact area he needed to see. Her indifference to the situation had irked him at first, but it made his examinations so much less awkward, he had come to appreciate her lack of a need for propriety.

Priest pulled her tunic out of the way, his eyes narrowing in anger. The soft, lovely skin on her back was black and blue from the impact of her body on the hard surface of the bed.

"I think it is only bruising. It will dissipate in time. I am so…"

"If you even think of apologizing, I will get up and walk out of this room right now," she promised, and he knew she was determined enough to follow through. He glared at her, unable to form a response that wasn't rife with swearing. It took him some time before he was calm again.

"I am so grateful you allowed me to look at your wounds," he growled through gritted teeth.

"And I am grateful you came to your senses and realized this predicament is *my* fault," she grinned.

Priest wrapped her leg without another word or glance at the brat's face. He couldn't bear to see her triumphant smile.

Saint returned with a fresh plate of food soon after.

"Thank you. I'm starving," Basina responded with a pointed look in Priest's direction. He cleared his throat to keep from yelling at her and stormed from the room.

It was another full month of recovery before Basina could once again stand on her leg for a few moments each day. Her limp was worse than Priest had hoped, but it wasn't so bad it would draw attention. He cursed himself thinking that she would always have a slight deformity in her right leg because of him. The rest of her body was in perfect condition—bruises gone and insides healed. He wanted nothing more than for Basina to fully heal and leave their home forever.

The relationship among the three housemates was admittedly strained, though some days were a little better than others. Priest realized that at some point over the previous few months, Basina had become... important. He was afraid to look her in the eyes, worried that she might see the regret and fear that mixed relentlessly and caused him constant worry for her future life. At some point she would go. He wanted her to go—to live a real life without his presence threatening the possibility of more injuries. But each time he imagined her walking away from the domus with her limping gait, he felt his stomach churn and bile creep up his throat. He kept his eyes fixed on the ground whenever she walked about the home or tried to make conversation with him. She surely despised him secretly but was too kind to tell him so—probably out of some misguided gratitude from when he saved her from dying the first time. The conflict within him was intolerable. He despaired when he thought of how she must hate him, and he hated himself for the attachment he felt toward her. He could not allow her to stay, yet could not bear the idea of her leaving. *What have I done, bringing this woman into my home?*

FORTY-SEVEN

"ARE EITHER OF YOU hungry? I was thinking of preparing our dinner," Basina asked, making her way toward the kitchen.

Saint had been watching Basina and Priest tiptoe around each other for weeks. Priest knew his friend was aware of the way he and the woman avoided direct eye contact with one another, jumped when the other got too close, and rarely had a conversation lasting longer than a few short moments (almost entirely limited to the weather, meals, and their health). The moment things had changed was the night Basina had mysteriously been re-injured, but neither he nor Basina would speak about it. Saint at last grew tired of the awkwardness, his calm shattering in an instant.

"I refuse to live one more day in this home, until this..." he pointed back and forth between Priest and Basina, "is discussed. I must know what happened. I cannot take any more of these horrid conversations about food and weather. And can we speak about something other than Basina's leg? Maybe we can talk about how awful it is to wake up to Priest screaming from night terrors every night. Or how nice it would be to get out of Rome for a picnic. Or why the two of you cannot seem to look at one another without blushing or fleeing the room. Please. I will happily settle for lies at this point over one more conversation about how the poultry was seasoned for last night's dinner."

Priest exchanged a quick glance with Basina—who seemed slightly amused by Saint's exasperated outburst—and they both looked back at Saint.

"Whatever are you speaking of?" Basina asked innocently, continuing into the kitchen, leaving Saint and Priest alone.

"I think you have lost your head," Priest agreed as he stood and walked to his room, leaving Saint alone.

"This is not over!" Saint yelled in a rare moment of unchecked anger. He exited the domus quickly, slamming the door loudly to let his house mates know the extent of his displeasure.

FORTY-EIGHT

A FEW WEEKS passed, and Basina had begun using the pool multiple times a day on her own accord. Priest often caught glimpses of her dark robe floating through the water, and he was glad they had moved into the large domus so she had use of the pool.

The awkwardness between Basina and him had lessened a little. Without directly addressing the issue, he was sure they had both come to the conclusion that, for Saint's sake, they needed to attempt to behave more naturally around one another. Their conversations came more easily now, and they only spoke about Basina's leg when he saw her grimace or if Basina mentioned the injury.

Priest lay in bed one night on the verge of sleep when he heard the sounds of water lapping against the side of the pool. *Someone is swimming?* Whether it was Saint, Basina, or an intruder, he did not know. He grabbed his knife and quickly made his way to the courtyard. The summer air was hot and thick, and the moon was bright overhead. The atrium and courtyard were well-lit under the cloudless sky, and Priest's vision strained to adjust to the refraction of light bouncing off each of the crests that formed on the surface of the water.

He did not think the swimmer was Basina—the dark robe she usually wore was not moving along the surface of the water. But a head covered in dark, short hair bobbed about from one side of the pool to the other. As the intruder swam in the opposite direction of where he stood, Priest made his way to the side of the pool, squatting down with his knife in view. He hoped to quietly escort the intruder away from the home, leaving enough of an impression that they would not risk returning.

When the bobbing head turned back to where Priest was, it stopped moving.

"Damn it, Basina," Priest whispered angrily, recognizing the female with her hair tied up into a bun on the back of her head.

She narrowed her eyes and swam over to him, not saying a word.

He could see that she was naked, and turned his back to her hastily.

"I felt smothered by the heat and could not sleep, so I decided to go for a swim. Am I not allowed to use this pool when I feel the need?" she asked, scolding him with her tone.

"Of course you are. But in the middle of the night, when the house is asleep, is a rather odd time to go for a dip in the pool. You should not be up and about like this. Especially without your cloak," he rebutted, still facing away from her.

"Perhaps I was hoping you would awaken and join me." He could not tell if her tone was a challenge or an invitation. *Her meaning does not matter. It is out of the question.*

Priest snatched Basina's discarded cloak from the ground and held it up between them to block his view.

"I told you I will never use you in that way." Priest swore under his breath. Basina made no reply and the stillness of the water was an announcement that she had no plans to exit the pool. He dropped the cloak back to the ground and left her alone once more. But with her enticing words replaying again and again in his mind, he could not find peace to fall asleep the rest of the night.

FORTY-NINE

"PRIEST," HE HEARD Basina whisper from the entrance to his room. He sat up, panicking that something was the matter. Her body was fully functional after a five-month recovery—in spite of the extra leg-break. Things had not been easy between them in the weeks following the incident in the pool, and Priest thought it likely she would leave their home soon.

"What is the matter?" he asked, rushing to Basina.

"Nothing is the matter. Please, sit down. May we speak?" she asked, motioning to his bed. He sat down warily on the edge. She sat next to him, her eyes searching his face for a sign she should begin. He nodded.

"I am happy here," she began. Priest felt his chest tighten, waiting for the words to come that would announce her plans to move on with her life. He nodded, gritting his teeth for the inevitable sentence to follow. She was a quiet presence that—despite their hardships with one another—brought a kind of peace to the house that he and Saint had not realized they needed until she moved in. But their lives were unending and aimless. Basina deserved a full life —a real life.

He wished there was a way he could keep her in his life *and* protect her, but he had centuries of evidence to prove she would only continue to be hurt by even the tiniest connection to him.

"And I was thinking maybe I could remain with you after this year," she finished, her voice so hushed he had difficulty hearing the words.

Priest was at a loss as to how he should answer. He and Saint had only discussed Basina *leaving*. There was never any doubt that she would want to move on. Especially after the strained relationship she had suffered with him over the past months.

"Why?" he asked more harshly than he intended.

Basina's expression fell.

"Never mind," she whispered, standing to leave his room.

"I meant… why would you want to stay with two lifeless, old men?" he asked, stopping her with his question. She barked out a quiet chuckle and turned back to see he was sincere.

"Old men? You are hardly old men," she spoke matter-of-factly while he inwardly groaned at her naivety. "I mean, Saint is a bit progressed in age, but you are…" she hesitated, "full of life."

"What reason can you possibly have to stay?" he pushed.

"Because you rescued me," she admitted.

That was a good enough reason, he supposed. But it was not a reason to throw away her potential life. She had so much more to see and do now that she was without the shackles of a master.

"I did what any decent man would do. He was going to kill you," Priest tried to keep his breathing normal, but just the memory of the man wounding Basina was enough to bring him to a rage once more. Basina sat back down next to him, placing her hands on top of his clenched fists to calm him. It had almost the exact opposite effect. His blood rushed more fiercely at her soft touch. He stared at the tiny hands, wanting to hold them within his much larger ones. He fought the urge to bring her hands to his mouth so he could cover them with his lips.

"I meant you rescued me from my *life*. Before you, I had not known freedom or companionship or kindness. I was neither respected nor free to do as I wished. My life was one of servitude alone. I've experienced more happiness in the past five months than in the past five years. And I barely remember life before I was taken. You rescued me, and I would be grateful and honored if you would allow me to stay. I will continue to cook and clean. And I will take care of you in whatever way you wish," she whispered the last sentence, running her finger in light circles on Priest's wrist.

He jumped away from her, realizing what it was she was offering. Her expression grew discouraged once again as she looked down at her lap.

"You must never do that again. Neither Saint nor I will ever use you in that way. You are not a whore any longer, Basina. I will speak with Saint in the morning to discuss your staying," he said, holding his hand toward the door.

She sniffed quietly, leaving him alone in the candlelight. If she was going to stay, they would have to find more duties for her so she didn't feel that she owed the men anything. He swallowed hard, trying to calm his anger over the years of life that were stolen from Basina, but when he lay down, he could not stop imagining what horrors she had lived through. The lingering sensation of her touch on his wrist made him restless. But no matter how long he tossed and turned, he could not stop wishing she was curled up beside him.

"She wants to stay?" Saint asked a third time. Priest didn't know how else to answer... 'yes' didn't seem to be sinking in.

"Why?" Saint asked, finally moving to a new question. Priest repeated what Basina had told him the night before, and Saint nodded understandingly. Priest left out the part where Basina offered to service them in every possible way. Saint had left his less gentlemanly actions in the past where they belonged.

"Then I suppose we should allow her to stay," Saint agreed quietly.

"What? You just... agree?" Priest asked in disbelief.

"I admit I thought it was a bit strange in the beginning. I thought she would come and go quickly—that she would want to go back to her old life in some capacity. And that is why I behaved the way I did, though you never thought to ask," he glanced at Priest out of the corner of his eye. "But after all this time, I rather think life would be dull without her presence. And I do not think you could stand the separation. You are already intolerable if she's out of your sight," Saint shook his head.

Priest was taken aback.

"You cannot be serious. I am no such thing. Of course, I want to protect her

—I saved her life and am therefore responsible for her now. But aside from that, I don't understand your meaning," he huffed.

"You are either having a nice joke or you are completely blind. You are well on your way to being in love with the girl, my friend. Unless you are already—which is entirely possible. Only two emotions produce your behavior: love or obsession. I do not believe you capable of obsession over a human being that isn't the object of your love. Obsession with a plan or an idea? Certainly. But a woman? You simply are not capable." Saint looked smug at his little discourse, and Priest wasn't sure if he had any grounds to be upset.

"Maybe we should make her go. Do you think it is wise for me to become attached? We would not be able to conceal our condition from her if she stayed. And life could become rather complicated if we are living with just one mortal. Surely people would notice that she would age while we would remain. I am not even sure she would be willing to leave Rome if we needed to avoid discovery," Priest warned.

"Really? That is the best excuse you can conjure? She is mortal, Priest. She will only live for a few decades, and I truly believe we can trust her with all our secrets. With her, I think the risk is quite small. If she thinks she will be happy with us, then why not let her stay? She will keep us fed at the very least," Saint shrugged.

Priest walked away feeling uneasy. Was he in love with Basina? *Only one will love you,* he heard once more. He could not think about the second part of the prophecy—the idea alone threatened to tear a hole in his chest that might remain always unhealed. He felt his breathing quicken and his heart pound.

"Are you all right?" Priest jumped at the sound of Basina's voice combined with the soft touch of her hand on his arm. He had vaguely heard her approach but was too lost in his thoughts to realize she was paying attention to him.

"Yes, yes. I was merely thinking over some things. But I do need to speak with you," he motioned for Basina to sit on the chaise where she usually preferred to sit, and he took the small bench that faced it. Basina's expression was clouded by worry as she sat on the edge of the chaise and leaned forward, waiting for him to begin.

"I have spoken with Saint," he said as her expression became shrouded in disappointment. "And we have agreed that we would like you to stay."

He could not help but grin at the turn of her countenance. The day held hope and possibility for Basina—he could see it in her eyes. She leaned over and squeezed his hand, thanking him again and again while he remained still and awkward. *This might be more difficult that I thought.*

Basina spent the next week eying Priest either warily or gratefully. Apparently she had not forgotten his scolding from the night she had expressed her wish to stay. He could see she was avoiding conversation with him when it did not pertain to meals or trips to the market, and he assumed the behavior was born out of embarrassment over her scandalous offer.

"Priest," she whispered at his door late one night.

"Are you speaking to me again?" he asked, turning to look at her. He hoped she could see the relief in his eyes. He hated when things were awkward between them.

"Maybe," she replied with a look on her face he did not recognize. She walked to the edge of his bed and sat down. She pushed her hand through his curly dark hair, and he grabbed her wrist firmly.

"I told you. You are not a whore," he hissed through gritted teeth.

"I am aware of that fact. But you must realize that I *am* a woman, and you said I was free to do as I please," she growled back at him, pulling her arm away from his grip.

He stared at her, unmoving, while angry tears dripped down her cheeks.

"I never meant that I intended to offer myself to you *and* Saint," she spat. "I *want* to be with *you*," she admitted with a furrowed brow. Her eyes searched his face for his reaction. "Is my past so repulsive that you cannot think of me in that way?" she asked, her voice cracking in pain.

I do yearn for her touch. I cannot sleep until I know she is restful, and I cannot accomplish anything in the morning until I have checked if she is all right. Basina was more than some fleeting obsession, and he could no longer ignore his feelings now that he was aware they existed. Old prophesies echoed in his mind, but he began speaking to drown out the words.

"No. Of course not," he whispered, pushing a stray piece of hair away from her forehead as tears spilled from her eyes. "I simply had not imagined you could feel this way. I assumed you thought I was too dangerous or unruly or old," he admitted. His words were not untrue. It was easy for him to forget he wore the face of a thirty-one year old. Centuries of time lay between him and the man he was when he had stopped aging.

"I do not think you are too old. And I certainly don't think you're dangerous… at least not to me," she whispered, her tiny hands grasping his arms. "You are handsome. And kind. And although you are a bit unruly, I don't think you…"

"You do not know what kind of man I am," he cut her off and pulled away before she could continue listing his qualities.

"I know exactly what kind of man you are," she spoke passionately, her hands reaching up to hold his face. Her gaze flitted between his eyes and lips.

"No," he breathed, looking away from the naive eyes that gazed up at his. She could not understand the depths of his wickedness—the inevitable thirst for blood and destruction which, even now, he felt clawing at his chest to get out. He grasped Basina's shoulders to push her gently away, and he stood to walk away.

She was stubborn, though, and quickly repositioned herself in front of him, grasping his jaw firmly, forcing him to look into her eyes. Her expression faltered from determination to fear and back to determination again. She took a deep breath and lowered her voice to hushed whisper.

"I saw *everything*," she set her jaw. "I was not unconscious when my master was beating me. I felt every kick, every tear in my skin, every drip of blood running down my face."

Priest's breathing quickened. His hands had somehow found their way to Basina's shoulders as if he was holding her like she was a bit of driftwood floating atop rough waters, keeping him from slipping under the surface. And with each word she uttered, his fingers dug a little deeper into her skin without his permission. He did not want to hear her next words.

"I watched as you dragged him away, and I silently pleaded for you to come back and get me so I could watch. I rejoiced when I saw you return, and I felt how careful you were when you picked me up. I knew your kindness in every step. You did not jostle me once, and when you placed me on the ground, you positioned me so I could bear witness to my master's demise. I saw your power in every movement. I reveled in your brutality as you peeled the skin off his body and cut the fingers from his filthy hands. I was elated each time blood formed a new puddle on the ground. It took every ounce of strength in my body to keep my eyes open, but I did. And I fell in love with you before I even knew your name," she finished, keeping her eyes locked with Priest's.

He could not speak. Words were absent from his mind. She understood. His heart beat too rapidly, and his cheeks were full of heat. She knew. She had witnessed one of his darkest moments, and she loved him *for* it… not in spite of it. He ran his hands through her long hair and down her back, pressing his forehead gently to hers. He breathed in her lovely scent as his fingertips ran along her spine.

"You cannot be real. It is impossible for a woman like you to exist. Have I created you in my mind?" he breathed as he searched her face for any signs of the regret or fear or hatred that he had come to expect from the faces of the women in his life. His mother, though proud of his accomplishments, always hid the gleam of regret in her eyes for the life he had chosen. The last time he saw his sister, she had looked at him only with fear and anger. And Antonina had looked upon him only with hatred. Even when she "made love" to him (if one could call it that), she kept a mask of adoration and joy plastered over her hateful, deceptive visage.

But with Basina, there was only love. In her mouth, in her eyes, in the hollows of her cheeks, in the touch of her fingers. She was as deeply wounded as he, and she recognized him as a kindred soul. He knew she would share his desire for bloodshed, and he would gladly slay thousands to see her look at him the way she did in that moment—with admiration and love.

"I am real. And no matter your words or actions, you will not be able to rid yourself of my devotion. I can keep my feelings a secret no longer. I love you," she stated matter-of-factly, without the girlish grin of a woman who thinks herself in love when she's only infatuated.

For only a fleeting moment in time… he heard that dreadful voice again. If he was only allowed this moment of joy for a short time, he could not waste a single breath.

"I love you," he gasped as desperation pushed his mind in a new direction. He held her tightly and began placing kisses on her forehead, her wet cheeks, and her neck. When his lips found hers, he felt his desperation reflected in equal measure. She grabbed at his arms, his back, his hair, trying to pull him as close as humanly possible.

He pulled slightly away, realizing the speed at which they were moving. And though she fought to pull herself closer once more for a moment, she soon nodded with a heavy sigh, agreeing they need not move too quickly.

He could not take his eyes off of her—he loved the way her long, dark hair fell over her shoulder. He loved that her height allowed her head to rest perfectly against his chest. He loved that she was not a foolish or frivolous woman who giggled at every little thing as flirting women often seemed to do. She was somber yet happy. Wounded yet content. She was his match, and she had actually found a way to love him.

Basina stepped away from him, and he fought the urge to grab her and hold her tightly against his body once more. But she did not leave his room. She lay down in his bed, leaving plenty of room for him to join her. He crawled into the bed facing her, yet keeping his distance—his body could easily betray him in his sleep even if his intentions were to repress his desires. Basina did not touch him—she simply looked into his eyes with a knowing gaze.

Her eyes were deep brown, and even in the dim light of his candle, he could see their vibrancy. Her skin was pale olive in color and perfectly soft to the touch. He ran a finger down the length of her arm, enjoying the gleam of contentment in her eyes from the simple act. Her long, straight hair was a rich brown color. And her tiny hands were lovely—she motioned with them to emphasize her points when she spoke, and he often caught himself noticing how graceful they looked. *She loves me.*

They stayed that way through the entire night—staring at one another until sleep overcame them. In the morning, Basina left a soft kiss on his lips before returning to her room to prepare for the day. They went about their lives as if nothing had changed. But Priest's thoughts strayed very little from Basina as their eyes met with flashes of longing throughout the day.

When night fell, Basina found her way back to Priest's room. He moved so she would have plenty of room to lie down, but he didn't say a word. He needed her to know everything before he could allow himself to lie with her. She needed to fully understand the life she was agreeing to before he ensnared her. But he was enjoying the peace of her company too much to ruin the moment. He did not know how long he could resist the perfect curve of her smooth neck while they lay so close to one another, but his mind warred with his body that she might leave if he revealed the truth. They continued the sleeping arrangement for a week, never speaking a word or touching—only studying each other's faces until sleep overcame them.

"Tell me about your past," Basina whispered as she walked into Priest's room. She finally broke the silence that had become their nightly routine. She had caught him unaware, and she appraised his shirtless body for the first time. His breath caught as she walked closer, studying the numerous scars that marked his body, gently tracing each. He tried to control his emotions, but her touch was like the first ray of sun in the morning sky after a moonless night.

She slid her hand up his side, finally resting it on the mark that branded his chest.

He remained silent, fearing any noise that might escape his mouth would sound more like a moan than actual words.

"Who were you before?" she asked quietly, running her fingers over his sensitive skin. She knew exactly what she was doing.

He took a deep breath, trying to flush away the panic that he felt tighten his chest. This could be the end of her time with him. But Basina's touch made him feel alive for the first time since becoming immortal. He could almost imagine Basina reaching into his chest and removing his heart to keep it as her own.

"I fear you will not like the answer," he whispered, searching her face for any sign of fear.

"I already know who you are. I want to know who you were before you rescued me," she pressed, laying her hand on his cheek. He placed his hand over hers and heaved a sigh. *If you want her, if you want to fully love her and know for certain that she can truly love you, she must know everything.*

"I will tell you only if you swear to never repeat the words to another soul," he offered. She swore without a moment of hesitation, and he began to reveal his life story to her—from the very beginning.

It took four nights to get through the major points of his life. But the fact that Basina returned each night for more reassured him that she had no intention of changing her mind and fleeing. She hung on his every word, always ready for more and forlorn when he announced he was too tired to continue. When at last he caught her up to the present, he looked deeply into her eyes, wondering if she would still want to stay with him.

"Now. You decide. Am I a monster? Or do you think I am a liar? Or am I delusional? But more importantly, am I worthy of your affection? Because that answer is resoundingly evident in my own mind," he admitted sadly, sitting up on the edge of the bed. He could not bear to look into her eyes if she rejected him the way he deserved. She slid to his side, clasping her hands into a ball on her lap.

"It is as I said before. I already know who you are. I simply wanted to know how you came to be the man I know. I know you would not create such a lie for me. And if you are delusional, I simply don't care. But I must make one point absolutely clear. You are, without question, worthy of my *love*. Affection does not do my feelings justice," she said pointedly.

She did not despise him. She *adored* him for who he was—even the parts of himself that he loathed. And though he knew he was not worthy of that level of devotion from anyone, Basina's troublesome past had prepared her for the sort of love he could offer. What he offered was imperfect and broken. But it would be unconditional.

He looked down at her, knowing absolutely that Basina was the woman who had been promised to him so long ago. She was his one great fleeting love. *How long will we have?*

He reached over and touched her perfectly smooth cheek. He had wanted to caress her skin for days, but he had staid his yearning until she heard his full history and made her decision. Her face lit up with joy the moment they touched. He ran a hand through her silky hair and down her neck. She had a slight frame, but her attitude and personality made her seem much larger in stature. He held her small frame and pulled her close, his left hand pressing her to his body, and she wrapped her arms around his neck in response, pulling his head down to hers.

"I will only truly love one woman in this lifetime," he whispered. She angled her head back to search his face for the words she needed to hear. "I cannot imagine you being any more perfect," he confessed as his lips tentatively brushed hers. She exhaled, her body relaxing into his arms, and she kissed him back with unbridled passion.

Fifty

PRIEST PULLED his lips away from Basina's and looked into her beautiful, brown eyes. He had no desire to touch her in the way she had been touched while she was still a slave. He would do everything in his power to make her forget her past. He wanted to worship her, to clothe her in only the nicest garments, to lavish her with gifts befitting of the power she unwittingly wielded over him. He would make sure she understood her value in his life as something more than a physical object.

His lips crushed against hers once more as she pulled his head back down so she could reach him. The longing that rushed through his body was so intense, he wondered if it could ever be quenched. His hands grabbed at her shoulders, her back, her hair—whatever allowed him to keep her body and his from separating.

"Basina," he whispered as he began trailing kisses from her forehead down to her neck. The noise she made when he nibbled on the curve of her soft neck set every sense in his body on fire.

"I need you. Please," she moaned, placing her perfect lips upon his shoulder, clavicle, and chest.

He pulled her night dress over her head and gently laid her body down on the bed. He allowed himself to actually look at her for the first time—when he had treated her wounds, he had managed to look upon her only as an object requiring medical attention. But now… this was something entirely different. He didn't *appraise* her body—that would suggest there might be something wrong. No. Everything about her was magnificent. From the way her skin had healed from her beating to the way her hair lay next to her on his bed—every part was uniquely *her*. And she was more than he could have dreamed. He kissed the shiny, pink scars on her stomach, chest and arm. He continuously repositioned himself over her so none of his weight would cause her pain, but she didn't allow that for long. She pulled him down on top of her, wrapping her legs around his waist so he couldn't get away. And that was the end of his self-control.

His body lay limply on the bed a few moments later while she traced the lines of the mark on his chest with her finger. She looked as if she would burst with joy. His eyes tried desperately to force their way shut, but he could not sleep until Basina had known real pleasure.

It took a full hour to coax her body to appeasement, but he had found more pleasure in each of her sighs or moans than he had in his own moment of satisfaction. She slept deeply next to him, each of her soft snores delighting him. He had heard her sleep for many months now, and never before had her sleep sounded so deeply content. He kissed her temple and wrapped her in his arms. And with Basina in his bed, sleep found him more easily than usual, and his nightmares of the past remained tightly locked away.

FIFTY-ONE

Castello San Romolo, Present Day

PRIEST SUCKED in uneaven breaths and looked down at his tear-drenched shirt. His eyes would be swollen for days if he kept this up. But he knew he needed to remember every part of their relationship. He had written something about her every single day after that night—what she wore, what she cooked, if she hummed a tune, if she felt sick. Every detail of her short life was precious, even those another might deem mundane. Priest scoffed at the word even as he thought it. *As if any part of Basina could have ever been considered mundane.* No. Every breath she took was a gift. A gift that he had always known would be ripped away from him.

He remembered the way he had reacted when Basina first told him she was with child.

Rome, 618 C.E.

He felt as if someone had thrown a massive rock into his chest, pushing all air out and keeping new breath from entering his lungs. *This is how I will lose her. Please! Not yet!* He begged internally as he fought against the pangs in his heart.

"You cannot treat our life as if it is always slipping away," Basina's forehead creased in worry as she wrapped her arms around Priest's waist. "You will miss all the best parts if you are constantly fearing what may come next."

"You are right—I know you are. But I do not want to put your life at any higher risk than it already is. It has been so many years since I have been a father, and it did not end well for me the last time. I hope our child will not share my same fate. I hope he will age. Will grow old and die. But another side of me fears he will wither away with old age as I remain young, forced to watch his suffering. But if he is like me—cursed with eternal life—it may be more than I can bear. Life cannot be so cruel. Can it?" Priest nearly choked as he asked the question.

"I hope our children will be exactly like you. Then, when I am old, I will know that you are surrounded by loved ones. I will easily lie in peace if our children are with you when my time comes," she smiled. But Basina's words felt like another blow to his chest. *She is at peace with her end already, and she speaks of children as if we will have many. Each child is an unnecessary risk.* He held Basina tightly, hoping he could somehow keep her safe with the strength of his own grasp. Years of transgressions, thousands of murders by his own hands—now he would feel the weight of his actions in full force. He realized his own unending life was not his punishment. The true punishment would be watching Basina's life end while he remained, never able to join her in the afterlife.

"Ahuzzan," Basina whispered. "My love, you are crushing me," she squeaked as he released her and smirked guiltily. He felt his cheeks flush each time she used his true name. She was always careful that no one else heard it spoken, but in their private moments together—especially in the heat of passion —her beautiful mouth whispering his name gave him unspeakable pleasure. He kissed her gently and laid a hand on her stomach. She was so tiny in every way, that even this early into the pregnancy, her stomach was showing signs of the child within.

"I think it's a boy," she said, placing her hand over the top of his. "In fact, I have the oddest feeling that all our children shall be sons."

Priest felt a flicker of recognition at her prediction.

"We should focus on one child at a time, Basina," he shuddered.

She kissed his lips softly once more and spoke gently, "As long as I am able, I will provide you with children. I want this for both of us, and I know, without question, you cannot resist me in bed. So it seems we will likely have many children."

Priest opened his mouth to refute her words, but his mind could not form a coherent rebuttal. She was right, and he knew he should grow better acquainted with the fear—it was not likely his fears would be quenched if she survived this pregnancy.

FIFTY-TWO

Rome, 619 C.E.

"YOU HAVE A SON," Basina beamed at Priest as he pulled himself up from the floor. He did not even feel the shame he should for his actions over the course of the day. His emotions had fluctuated from panic to excitement to fear to resentment and back to panic so many times in the hours leading up to the birth of his first son, that he had finally lain on the mat in the corner of their chamber and faced the wall. Basina had ordered him away after her first real pain began. He had stood over her with so much anger in his eyes that she had yelled at him. Of course, he wasn't angry with Basina—he was furious with himself. He was the source of her pain. He was the reason she was in peril.

But the labor had ended, the screams and moans had passed, and Priest was the father of a baby boy.

He walked slowly to Basina as she held the child out for him to take. He carefully took the boy from her, and there was something in that moment that changed his entire world. Suddenly his heart had been cloned. All the love and devotion he felt for Basina remained, but his heart had somehow swelled to make room for the love and devotion he had added for the child in his arms.

"What do you think about the name 'Sergius'?" Basina asked, smiling up at Priest's awed expression.

"Sergius. Yes, I think it's a strong name. A Roman name. Do you know the meaning?" he asked.

"It means 'one who attends.' He will be his brothers' keeper. He will tend to the needs of the family. And he will have the strength that the eldest requires to keep his siblings in order," she smiled knowingly.

Priest's gaze snapped to Basina's. "Have you been given a vision of what is to come?"

"No visions. Just a feeling," she said as she took Sergius from Priest's arms and placed a kiss on her son's forehead.

"I have a son named Sergius!" Priest ran from the room to tell Saint the good news.

"All is well? Basina is healthy?" Saint asked with a knowing grin on his face.

"Yes, yes. Everything is as it should be. And you are an uncle," Priest clasped Saint's shoulders and pulled him into a firm hug.

"Uncle," Saint smiled widely. "I quite like the sound of that."

FIFTY-THREE

Rome, 640 C.E.

"NO, BASINA. Do not dare close your eyes. Do not give up now!" Priest yelled as he watched Basina's eyelids flutter weakly.

"I love you, Ahuzzan. You gave me the best life I could have imagined—a home of my own filled with love and peace. Promise me you will love him the same as our other sons," Basina whispered feebly.

"No. This isn't enough. I haven't had enough time with you. Stay. Stay with me, Basina. Thirty-eight years upon the earth is not enough. You are not finished in this world," he begged.

"His name is Samuel. Remember how I begged for one more child? I am like the woman in the stories Saint reads to the boys. I begged the gods for this child, and now he is here. Let me hold him," she said as the midwife stepped forward and handed Basina the newborn.

Priest refused to look at the child. With every son before this one, he had held the baby just as he had done with Sergius—feeling the instant, unbreakable bond. There had always been an expanding of his heart for the new, beloved child and a joy that his beautiful Basina was strong enough to bring a child into the world. But he could not look at this Samuel. He had no intention of holding the tiny beast.

"Promise me you will take care of him," Basina's eyes began to close, the droopy lids blocking her beautiful brown eyes.

"I promise," he muttered, giving the midwife the silent command to remove the child from Basina's arms. As soon as the babe was gone, he slid Basina's body into his arms and cradled her against him gently.

"Do not go yet, Basina. Please, I am begging you not to leave me. I cannot survive without you," the tears dripped down his face and onto Basina's chest as she struggled to inhale and exhale. Her hand raised to his cheek as she gazed up at him.

"We had longer together than either of us deserved. And you have ten handsome boys to take care of you now. Do not cry, Ahuzzan. The life we have lived has been extraordinary."

"I will never love another," he whispered the promise as he placed his lips on hers. She kissed him back as best she could manage in her weakened state.

"I do not think I would be able to leave you if I thought you might replace me someday," she tried to smile. She was trying to make him happy in her final moments, and his heart broke even more at her attempt.

"Even if I wished—and I do not—no one would compare to you. I love you more furiously than I long for my own death," he grimaced, knowing that was a paltry comparison.

"I love you," she let her eyes shut, and her head nestled into Priest's chest. She was making herself comfortable for the end. He gently covered her face with kisses as her breathing grew slower and more labored. He whispered "I love you" between each kiss, wanting her final moments to be wrapped in as much comfort as he could provide.

He did not know how long he sat with her after her chest stopped moving. His eldest sons—Sergius and Paulus—came in and coaxed him away from their mother's lifeless body. He did not hear anything. Did not see anyone. He allowed himself to be led wherever they took him. He ate whatever they fed him. But unless someone explicitly told him what to do, he was devoid of understanding. There were no words to describe the nothingness that followed Basina's death. But he remained in the emptiness until Saint shook his shoulders violently while declaring Priest must leave the domus.

"It has been three months of nothing but your lifeless body taking up space. For God's sakes, brother. Your sons are spoon-feeding you meals! Get a hold of yourself. I forbid you to sit here any longer!" Saint growled loudly.

Priest was unsure of whether Saint had tried the tactic before, but he heard every word his friend spat during this particular tirade. *Three months? Surely she has not been gone for so long.* But he knew Saint was right. He could not sit in the home any longer. He looked around and felt the emptiness in the home without Basina's presence. He needed to get away. To do something with his life once more. He needed to fight. He needed to feel the satisfaction of his sword thrusting into the chest of a mortal man, and if Basina was ripped from his life, then he had every right to rip others from the arms of their loved ones.

He stood, nodded his thanks to Saint, retrieved his daggers and sword, and left the villa as his sons and Saint looked on silently. They did not follow him. They did not ask where he was going. But he could not have answered even if they had. He did not know exactly where his feet would take him, but he knew he was searching for a war.

Fifty-four

Castello San Romolo, Present Day

PRIEST SHUT the journal carefully and wiped his face clear of the tears that drenched his skin and clothes. He had not been able to properly record the events in his life after Basina's passing. He had not wanted to write about her end. She was his whole world—his only reason for existing. And without her guidance, he had floated from place to place aimlessly for decades.

Upon leaving his family's villa outside Rome, he had walked until he was too exhausted to stand—and then he had walked some more. He continued until he found someone in need of a soldier. And after he was finished with whatever battle he had fought, he continued to the next.

He had not allowed himself to think of Saint and his sons—to think of them would be to think of Basina. So he fought and trained and killed and strategized and fought some more. He had set a goal for himself to make sure his focus was always on the battlefield—five thousand lives must be extinguished by his own hand before he would consider returning home. Basina's life was worth at least five thousand lives. He had counted every kill—made tallies of each death so he knew exactly how many lives he had taken. And when he finally reached his goal and allowed himself to remember his sons, he hoped he would return to find their graves. He had wanted a clean slate—to start anew without the remnants of his short happiness to haunt his days.

Priest stood from his desk and took a turn about the room. The shock of returning to a house full of grown sons had not been easy for him to overcome. Saint had concocted a story to cover for his long absence, but Priest had fought an inner battle over whether he had wreaked enough havoc upon the earth to honor Basina's memory. It was the realization that Basina had given him immortal children to aid in his vengeance that had ultimately convinced him to stay. Priest was built for causing death—and Saint had taken it upon himself to begin the boys' training to follow in their father's footsteps. He had begun with the basics—swordsmanship, hand-to-hand combat, the art of blending into one's surroundings, strategy, and archery. Sergius had taken the lead in training his brothers once Saint had imparted his own limited knowledge, and he had done a fine job preparing his brothers for Priest's return. Priest came home to a small squadron of sons who were ready for their final steps of training. They needed only to understand the art of concocting and delivering poisons without detection, the proper way to stake out a victim, and the best way to hide a body and escape a scene after the assassination was complete. Of course, the boys' skills still needed some adjustments, but aside from that, the Family was nearly ready to jump into action. He set a higher goal for the number of lives he would extinguish, taking into account his new army of sons, and set them to work to help him achieve it.

Priest's mind returned to the present as he walked quietly to the kitchen. The sounds throughout the castle had quieted, and his stomach was empty. He had stayed hidden in his room for a few days after his last trip to the kitchen— hoping to remain in Basina's world for as long as he could. He entered the large room and found Lissie warming two plates of food in the microwave.

"I thought you might be ready for dinner," she said without looking. Priest balked a moment, impressed that she knew he had come into the room.

"You thought correctly. Will you be joining me?" he asked.

"If you'd like the company," she smiled weakly. He could see she was trying to maintain a courteous attitude despite his earlier attempt on her life— and he found a sense of true gratitude for her effort.

"I thank you, yes." He took both plates of food to the table as she grabbed a bottle of wine and two glasses.

They ate in silence until their plates were mostly empty, neither seemingly able to conjure an appropriate topic for dinner conversation.

"I was beginning to think you wouldn't come out again until the trial,"

Lissie murmured before taking another bite.

"There were some items that needed attention before the trial. I still have a few phone calls to make, but the most important things have been done," his eyes shut as Basina's beautiful face flashed in his mind.

"Are you feeling okay?" Lissie sounded worried as he heard her hand slide over to touch his. He kept his eyes shut as he listened to her hesitation and then the quiet rustling of her clothes as her arm pulled back without having made contact.

"My body is healthy," he answered without further explanation. He knew Lissie would understand the underlying meaning. She reached over once more and gripped his hand tightly. His glanced down, surprised by the gesture, and stared at her blankly, unsure of what response she might be hoping for.

"I thought about what Caterina told me the other night, and I think I finally understand some of the pain you must be experiencing. I've tried to imagine losing Mattia, and I feel like I could throw up at the idea of living without him. To love someone the way you must have loved your wife, and then to have to live without her for so long—you've never recovered. I'm sorry, those words probably seem thoughtless," she stopped speaking and tried to pull her hand back, but Priest squeezed her fingers, not quite willing to lose the physical contact of a human being who seemed to care for him. Her gaze jerked up to meet his, but she didn't try to pull away.

"I thank you for your kindness. You've nothing to apologize for—it has not been easy since her death. But Basina was not my wife in the technical sense. We did not need such titles to be faithful to one another, and we did not dare risk having our names in the Catholic church's registry," he chuckled once. "But I do thank you for your kindness… and understanding," he kissed Lissie's hand sweetly and released it as she looked on silently, her face cloaked in disbelief at the exchange.

"Mattia will be wondering where I've disappeared to," she mumbled, taking her plate and glass to the sink as she tried to make a quick escape from the room. She paused at the door and glanced back at him. "Enis arrived today. The trial will begin either tomorrow or the next day. I thought you should know," she whispered, leaving him to sit in silence at the table he had built with his own hands—perhaps for the last time.

He breathed deeply, thankful for the quiet moment of reflection.

I could be dead by the end of tomorrow, he thought as a slow grin stretched across his face.

FIFTY-FIVE

SERGIUS SAT on the edge of his bed in silent reflection. The light bulb of the lamp beside his bed had begun flickering a few days earlier, its signs of life growing weaker as it fought to stay lit. It reminded him grimly of his father—an immortal soul who wanted death but couldn't help but fight for life.

Sergius couldn't understand why he felt so betrayed by Priest's parchment outlining the chain of succession. He hated trying to fill the role as head of the Family. He had filled it once before—however feeble the attempt had been. He rubbed his tired eyes and stood up, feeling too restless for sleep. He often reminisced about his first twenty-one years of life—the years before his mother died and his father fled their home. The years following his mother's death—the ones without Priest's guidance—had been some of the most difficult of his existence. Saint, however fatherly he tried to be, could simply not fill the role of father for Sergius and his brothers. The responsibility had fallen squarely on Sergius's shoulders. And even though he was mature enough to have children of his own, he most certainly wasn't ready to have a home full of adolescents who needed to be trained as soldiers. The responsibility had nearly crippled him in the beginning, but the first time Samuel had called him "papa", he had felt his strength rise to the task before him.

Rome, 642 C.E.

"Lunge! The thrust and lunge are simultaneous. If you do one without the other, the tip of the spear will never break through the ribs of your opponent. Watch me once more," he commanded as he demonstrated the proper technique on the straw-stuffed enemy in the center of their villa's courtyard.

They had moved into the massive villa on the outskirts of Rome after

Thomas's birth. Mother had decided the boys needed space to run and play, and father had agreed on the condition he could find a home with a courtyard large enough to keep the boys enclosed within the home's walls—as if the walls had ever kept the boys contained. Finding a large enough villa had not been difficult near Rome. Father had found an abandoned property that was formerly used to train slaves as gladiators. The villa had needed more than a little work to feel like a home, but father and uncle had taken great care to transform it exactly to mother's specifications. Mother had, shortly after moving into the space, announced her plans to fill every one of the fifteen bedrooms with a son for father, and another brother for him. Of course, father argued whenever mother spoke about having more children. But the teasing glances and loving embraces between his parents were the glue that made the villa feel like home. Without his parents in the home, he was desperate to provide a similar environment for his youngest brothers to grow within. But with each passing day, he felt more and more like a failure.

Sergius glanced around at his bickering brothers as they gave each other advice on how to better use the spears with which they were equipped. His mother's quiet voice and knowing eyes had disappeared from the world in the blink of an eye, and his father's discipline and leadership had walked out of the home a few months later without a backward glance.

He sighed, doing his best to swallow down the fear and sadness he could feel churning in his gut. Father had left him in charge—or at least that is what Saint claimed. More than a year had passed since father left, but he still waited each night, hoping to hear the voice of the man who had taught him so much. *You've done well, Sergius. I thank you for picking up the mantle of responsibility in my absence. I could not have done this without you.* His father's imagined voice echoed in his mind. Taking care of Samuel had been the most difficult task. The lack of sleep alone had been the most overwhelming part of the process, but a few days earlier, Samuel's first word, "papa," had come while Sergius gave him a bath. The word had instilled a new level of resolve in his mind to succeed at the task he had been assigned by his father.

"Take a break and eat some lunch. You have done well this morning," Sergius acknowledged as he released his brothers from their morning training session.

"Sergius," Thomas motioned that he needed a private word. "Have I been making progress with my spear?" Thomas asked with a furrowed brow.

"Yes, and I have noticed," Sergius smiled encouragingly.

"Would it be possible for you to teach some more advanced strikes to me and the twins? I don't want to keep doing the same exercises as the younger boys when I know we can do the more advanced thrusts and throws like you and Paulus know."

Sergius nodded. Thomas was not thrilled to be stuck in training with a nine-year-old.

"Certainly. Tomorrow I will have Paulus take you three aside for more strenuous training. Will that be agreeable?" he asked.

"Yes. Thank you." Thomas walked away with a satisfied gleam in his eyes.

Sergius felt a bit deflated that he had not come up with the idea before. *I should have done this months ago. I cannot be a brother and a father and a trainer all at the same time. Please, father, come home. I cannot do this without you.*

Rome, 667 C.E.

"Happy birthday, Samuel. You have officially joined the ranks of immortality. Twenty-seven," Sergius toasted his youngest brother as Thomas jabbed their baby brother in the arm.

"I hope I do not disappoint you, brothers. You are such glowing examples of immortality," Samuel tried to keep his face serious, but a chuckle escaped as the men all burst into laughter.

"Immortality never looked so young," Demitrius raised his glass and took a long pull of his ale.

"Twenty-seven will never again seem so young," Felix toasted again.

"Nor so immature," Claudius added.

Thank God Samuel knew how to take the jokes from his brothers. They were relentless, but Samuel simply chuckled along with them.

The festivities continued well into the evening, despite the fact that Samuel had passed out from drunkenness before the sun had set.

Sergius felt his feet take him into Saint's office without his having made the conscious decision to have the discussion that weighed daily on his mind.

"Hello Sergius. Is the party over?" Saint asked, looking up from whatever book he had been reading.

"We need to move on. And we need to begin searching for work. We are all restless, purposeless. Your stories do not fool us any longer. Father has abandoned us to our own devices, and it is time we move on with our lives. Your hope for his return will not bring him back. Traveling throughout the Empire has been good. But we need jobs. Please, I will inquire about training soldiers. Surely there is a need for men with our skills *somewhere*." Sergius knew he sounded desperate, but at this point, he did not care. His voice was but a shadow of the true desperation he felt within.

"I have not lied to you. Your father is supposed to return soon. He has been fighting and training and making contacts for your work. I assure you of that," Saint said. But Sergius knew his uncle was as weary of lying as he and his brothers were of listening to the lies. "If he has not returned within five years, we will send him word that we are moving to a new city. But surely you agree we can spare five short years when we have an eternity ahead of us," Saint tried to sound reassuring. His tone was unconvincing.

"Fine. Five years. But my brothers and I are all grown, and we have the right to make the decision to move on if we feel so inclined. I will tell my brothers we have five years left here, but honestly, I am finished waiting for a man who has abandoned his children. We don't need him anymore. And when we did need him, he wasn't here. I won't allow my brothers to carry this false hope much longer."

Sergius heard Saint sigh as he turned and stormed from his uncle's office. But he knew Saint could not feel surprise at his outrage. The conversation had been inevitable.

Rome, 670 C.E.

"Saint?" a familiar voice called from the vestibule of the villa. Sergius felt his breath catch in his throat as every sound in the courtyard ceased. He could hear his brothers' hearts beating wildly—though whether from the exercises they had been practicing or the sound of the familiar voice, he did not know.

"Brother? Are you here?" the voice called out once more.

Paulus made a move toward the passage into the vestibule, but Sergius put a hand up to stop him. He silently motioned for his brothers to form a line for inspection. No one disobeyed. They stood at attention from eldest to youngest, awaiting appraisal.

"Priest?" they heard Saint's footsteps descend the stairs to the vestibule and the sounds of the brothers embracing. Sergius had expected to feel only anger and disgust at his reunion with his father, but he instead was consumed by nervous excitement. He wanted Priest to praise the work he had done to prepare his brothers for battle. He wanted his father to grab him by the shoulder and tell him how he had been missed. He tried to calm his racing heart to no avail. The voices of the two men inside the vestibule were muffled for a moment more before their footsteps neared. Sergius commanded his body to remain in place, fighting the urge to run to the door to see what was taking so long.

Priest and Saint stepped into the courtyard to a collective inhale from all ten brothers. Priest's fists clenched slightly, and Saint watched with an expression of amusement. Priest stepped first to Sergius, his hands clasped behind his back as he strolled from one son to the next, assessing each of the grown men his sons had become. Sergius could not understand how his father remained silent for so long. But the expressions of pride and excitement were intermixed with sorrow and disappointment—only in quick flashes, but enough to let Sergius know there was more behind his father's eyes than the man wanted to reveal.

"You have trained fine soldiers, Saint," Priest finally spoke as he turned back to his brother.

"I have done very little," Saint shook his head. "Sergius has led in your absence, with the help of Paulus of course."

Priest turned to face his two eldest boys, and as the corners of his mouth twitched to form an almost-smile, Sergius could have sworn he felt his heart burst right from his chest.

"You have taken it upon yourself to train the others? Very well. Let me see what you and your brothers can do."

FIFTY-SIX

SERGIUS WATCHED his brothers perform every drill perfectly with spears, swords, bows, daggers and fists. They parried attacks with perfect form, landed surprise blows on one another, and fought brilliantly. He could not have been more pleased if they were actually his own sons. But Priest barely reacted.

"You are ready for your final steps of training. There must be a few adjustments to your stances and form, but all-in-all, you only need a bit more work to reach your potentials." Priest turned and walked away with Saint.

Sergius seethed internally. He was not the type to need someone to hold his hand and tell him "good job"—he knew when he had done well, and the wasted breath telling him as much seemed redundant. But Priest did not even seem to notice that it was Sergius's training, leadership, and skill that brought his brothers to this point.

"Go prepare for dinner. We're done here," Sergius whispered as his brothers eyed him with sympathy. None of them moved except Samuel, who walked over and placed his hand firmly on Sergius's shoulder.

"You made us what we are, brother. We all know that," Samuel assured him. "At least he acknowledged your existence."

Sergius blinked, realizing that their father had neither spoken to nor even glanced at Samuel all day. He shook his head in frustration.

"We should have left years ago. I will speak with them to see if there is any real work for us or if it has all been a complete waste of time," Sergius turned to the villa as his brothers whispered behind him about the day's strange events. He was so disappointed with… everything.

He heard his father and uncle's voices coming from Saint's room. He crept quietly, hoping they were too lost in their conversation to hear him approach.

"I hoped they would be mortal. I thought I might be returning to an empty villa—my sons out in the world, living mortal lives. I cannot be their father," Priest sighed.

"That is not your choice. You *are* their father, and you will fill the role that you should have been filling all these years. If you try to leave again, I will send them after you to bring you back and lock you up. Do not test me, brother," Saint threatened in a tone Sergius had never heard from his uncle.

"I do not plan to run. But I have forgotten how to be a parent. I cannot even bear to look upon…" he didn't finish.

"Yes. Samuel looks like his mother. Same eyes, same hair, even his height is the closest to hers. But you promised Basina you would look after him, and up to this point you have done nothing for him. Sergius has done every single thing you should have done. He raised Samuel from infancy. He has taught all his brothers the way to fight. Sergius *needs* you. They all do. But I see it in his eyes most of all. Be a father. You have done it before—and well."

"But I had her to show me the way. I feel entirely lost. I'm drifting farther and farther away from who I was with her, withering all the while. She kept me grounded. She is why I could be a father. Without her…" Priest cleared his throat.

"Without her it will be more difficult. You'll try harder. But your sons are grown now, and they don't need you to parent them. They do not need anyone to hold their hands. What they need is a push in the right direction, and you will give it to them. Please tell me you have contacts for work. The boys need to work, and I have a plan as long as we have connections with the right people."

"Yes. I have been… everywhere since I left. I will have no trouble finding work for all of them."

Sergius backed away from the door, not wishing to hear more. He had known his father grieved for his mother's death, but this was something different. Sergius did not recognize this kind of pain—could not understand how Priest continued to mourn her loss as if it was yesterday. Almost thirty years had passed. Of course Priest would still miss her, but his words—the anguish in his tone—it was as if his mother had died days or weeks earlier.

He sank into his seat at the head of the dining table and put his head in his hands. *He needs me more than I need him. I must find a way to lessen this burden for him.*

FIFTY-SEVEN

Rome, 671 C.E.

"YOU ARE AS ready as you will ever be," Priest said to Sergius and his brothers as they sat around the table for dinner. The past six months had been grueling. Shortly after returning home, father had announced that the brothers would act as assassins.

"We will only accept contracts that will balance the powers-that-be in the world. Both good and bad men become corrupt when they find great power within their grasp. Without our aid, such power could go unchecked. You might say we will serve as the scales of justice that keep the world from tipping off its axis."

Sergius and his brothers had loved the idea. Assassins with a purpose. They would finally have a purpose.

After the announcement, Priest had thrown the brothers into impossible situations that they had to find a way out of. He locked them in rooms without exits and made them escape. He grouped them into teams of two or three and made them find a way to defeat the other team using a mixture of skill and wit. He made them stay awake for forty-eight hours straight to test their ability to function without sleep. He made them watch various people going about their daily life in order to discover the time the person slept, woke, left their villa, returned home, and ate meals. They were also required to gain an understanding of each subject's personal tastes—whether they drank a certain type of wine, ate a unique food, or slept in a certain spot on their bed. Every detail might be important. Any tiny peculiarity in the person's life might be the exact factor in planning the perfect assassination.

The mental exertion took its toll in the beginning, but the more they practiced, the easier everything became. It was a gut reaction now for Sergius to count how many people were in a room when he entered and find two different escape routes in case he needed to leave quickly. What started out feeling a bit like paranoia now felt like logic—if he was sent to kill someone, then he needed to be ready for every contingency.

They were also trained in the art of poisons—what to use for the desired effect, how much to use, how to apply it to skin or drop it into a drink without being caught.

But now the training was complete.

"We have our first set of contracts," Saint smirked as he casually made the announcement as if it was of no importance. Sergius's and his brothers' eyes lit up as they looked from one face to another around the table. *Finally.*

"Will we all work together? Or separately? Or in smaller groups?" the questions from each man around the table jumbled into one incoherent sound, and Saint chuckled as he held a hand up to quiet them.

"Your father is deciding right now which of you should be put into pairs. He will make the decision based on skill sets and the specific requirements for each job. You will know by this evening who is going where and with whom," Saint finished as he went back to eating his bread.

Sergius and his brothers worked together all day in the courtyard, doing their best to calm their nerves and excitement over what the evening might bring.

"Do you think we will travel very far?" Demetrius asked as he and Elias sparred with their fists.

"Father surely knows many important people in parts of the world we cannot imagine," Elias stated without giving an opinion of his own. Most of the time, he was happy to wait for instruction rather than force a conjecture that might be incorrect. Of all Sergius's brothers, Elias was the most eager to please those he respected—and of course Gregorius followed in his twin's footsteps.

"I wonder what kind of men we will eliminate. Surely they must be vile if someone is willing to pay a fee to remove them from the world," Samuel interjected thoughtfully.

"Of course they are vile—father would not accept a contract on a good man's life," Paulus assured him as all the brothers nodded in agreement.

By the time the sun set, the brothers had worked themselves to exhaustion. They sat around the table, eying each other, Priest, and Saint throughout dinner, each one unwilling to break the silence and ask the question about where they would be traveling in the coming days. Priest and Saint both smirked as they ate, failing to hide their amusement at the brothers' anticipation. Finally, when Priest finished the last bit of food on his plate, he pushed back from the table and stood as if he might leave.

"But you said…" Thomas stopped himself as a full smile crept over Priest's face.

"I must retrieve the contracts from my room before I can inform you of where you will be going," he spoke matter-of-factly as he left the room.

The silence was deafening as they waited for Priest's return. They had waited so long for this moment, they could barely stand the final moments before their new lives began. Everyone sat a little straighter as the sound of Priest's footsteps grew louder.

"First things first," Priest began as he stepped back into the room. "You already know we have no family name. Those who hire us will know us only by "the Family," so for each job you take, you must choose a new family name and create an identity for yourself. For now, you should keep your history to local areas with which you are entirely familiar. The more you travel, the better your linguistics and knowledge of different cities and regions will become—this will allow you more identities. Always expect that someone will be familiar with the city you claim as your own. If you plan your personal story wisely, you will be able to convince anyone that you are from the region you profess. Second, do not reveal the identities of your targets to anyone. That includes your brothers.

We are hired under the condition of discretion and silence, and I expect each and every one of you to respect our clients' privacy."

He unrolled the first scroll. "Now we can begin. Sergius."

Sergius's mouth went dry and his stomach did a flip as he waited for the next words.

"You and Samuel will travel to Ephesus in the morning. The details of the assassination are in this," he held up a second parchment on which he had written the specifics of the job. I suspect the trip will take some weeks. Once you arrive, you should have at least one week to prepare—and remember to make a plan for every contingency. I know you will do well."

Sergius and Samuel's eyes met, and both were excited to share this first contract together. Samuel was like a son to Sergius, and this would knit their bond even closer.

"Paulus, Felix, and Thomas," Priest continued as he unrolled the next scroll and pulled out his own instructions. "You are leaving for Athens by boat in four days. You will have a month to prepare once you arrive in Athens," he handed Paulus the parchment and moved on to the next scroll. Gregorius and Elias would be leaving for Pavia in a few days' time. Finally, Claudius, Alexander and Demetrius would leave the following week for Alsace. Every contract required at least two of the brothers, and they were thrilled to experience their first taste of death with a trusted partner.

"The more contracts you do, the better understanding you will have of your propensities for weapons and various skills. I expect each of you to be forthcoming after each contract concerning the successes and failures, strengths and weaknesses—of yourself and whomever you work with. We must all work to improve whatever is required to become better in every aspect of our work. And I will do my best to guide you every step of the way." Priest sat down and organized the scrolls into a line as Saint stood up and glanced around at his eager nephews.

"Make sure you pack enough food and water, don't forget to take enough coin and gold to barter for as long as you are away, and remember your weaponry. Do not forget you may need to secure passage on a vessel for easier travel. Pack your clothing appropriately for the personal history you create. Take care that your horses are ready before your journey. And remember—we are watching your progress. We want to see you succeed," Priest nodded.

"Say your goodbyes before you leave," Saint warned. "It may be many months before we are all here together again. And get some rest—two of you leave in a few short hours."

They all stayed awake far too long discussing what trials they might need to be prepared for. And even after Sergius was in bed, he could barely keep his eyes closed.

When he woke the next day, he felt every bit as exhausted as he had dreaded the night before. He and Samuel said their goodbyes and filled their horses' saddlebags with gold, clothing and supplies. Though Priest had given them specifics for what they would need, he had also told them to prepare for every contingency— so they took more than Priest recommended. Sergius knew this first contract would serve as a sort of plumb line for Priest—a way to measure their abilities and potential. And Sergius had every intention of setting the bar for all future contracts to be judged by.

FIFTY-EIGHT

Rome, 673 C.E.

SERGIUS'S HEART raced as Thomas's and Demetrius's horses came down the road. They had been waiting for this moment for nearly two years. All the Family was together again at last.

There had been much to learn over their first several contracts. Mistakes were made, injuries were had by some mortals who were in the wrong place at the wrong time, and injuries were endured by several of the brothers as they were caught unawares by a target who was more able than they expected. But every mistake was an opportunity for growth, and Priest was willing to sit down with each of his sons to work through any difficulties they might experience.

Sergius had never felt closer to his father. It was not that Priest praised him or his brothers for their triumphs—no, he expected them to excel. It was simply a joy to Sergius that their father took the time to speak with each son about any problems or failures without the anger or disappointment one might expect from an experienced assassin. And when a contract was finished without any hardships, there was a look of calm on Priest's face that could almost be deciphered as pride. Sergius lived for that expression.

Sergius embraced his brothers as they dismounted their horses. "It went well, then?" he asked.

"It was not without its difficulties, but it is finished," Thomas said, looking at Demetrius with a tight smile.

Priest emerged from the front of the villa with two glasses of wine for his returning sons. "Come into the vestibule for a meeting. Tonight, we will celebrate our accomplishments for the first time as a complete family."

Castello San Romolo, Present Day

That had been the night Priest introduced the Family pledge to his sons. Sergius remembered the way his heart overflowed with pride at all the criminals and tyrants he and his brothers had eliminated from the world. They celebrated for three days, cheering for stories of their triumphs and poking fun at their missteps.

Sergius wished that period had lasted longer. Priest had chosen their contracts wisely in the beginning. They had removed a tyrannical dictator who threatened the stability of all European powers, had eliminated several corrupt bishops who were known child molesters, and had prevented three military coups planned by power-hungry generals in Francia, Saxony, and Liburnia. Each contract further convinced them of Priest's scrupulous judgment, and Sergius and his brothers had not felt the need to question the value of later contracts—they simply *knew* Priest was serving the best interest of the Family and the world as a whole. *When did the madness begin to set in? Or was it always there, and I simply chose not to see the truth of it?*

He sighed and turned the light off next to his bed. The next morning, the trial would begin. And the dread of all that would take place over the following days made his stomach churn with nervousness. He would not enjoy a single moment of what came next.

FIFTY-NINE

SERGIUS KNOCKED on Priest's door. He had volunteered to bring Priest to the trial. The night before, he had realized that he was one of only a handful in the Family who would maintain enough self-control to keep his thoughts to himself. Priest was deadly no matter his age. His eternal youth, penchant for staying fit, and regular sparring with his sons and grandsons meant he was still in perfect fighting form. Sergius knew that it was not in his father's nature to remain silent when others attacked—he would fight back if someone provoked or threatened him… no matter how much he wished for his own death.

Priest did not respond to the knock, but Sergius could hear him speaking to someone behind the closed door. He opened the heavy wooden door slowly as the thick iron hinges groaned in protest. His father did not turn around to acknowledge the intrusion, so Sergius took the liberty of entering the room without invitation.

"I am sorry as well. I had not planned for our agreement to come to an end, but it seems my role in this fragile game of ours has expired. I imagine you would like the details buried with me? Certainly. If anything changes, I will be in touch," Priest spoke in perfect English on the cell phone pressed against his ear. Sergius watched as Priest nodded, silently agreeing with whomever was on the other end of the line.

"It was an honor doing business with you. Please know I have always held the utmost respect for you and your country. I hope you find someone just as capable for your future endeavors." Sergius remained silent while Priest hung up the phone, disassembled it, and crushed the insides with the heavy wooden bowl he always kept on his desk. Priest turned to face him.

"Now that my affairs are in order, I suppose we should make our way to the trial," Priest announced, walking to his door with regret tugging at the corners of his mouth. Sergius did not know what to say—whether comfort or kindness or harsh words were what his father craved in the moment. "Sergius," Priest whispered, turning his back to his son, "You may be amazed by the state of the world we live in if this Family ceases to serve in the way we always have. We have done far more good than any of you know. Without my guidance, without someone willing to make the difficult decisions, you will witness the tipping of delicately-balanced scales, the overthrowing of righteous leaders, and the commencing of great world wars that will make the previous wars seem like child's play. Each moment in history where an evil leader took power was the direct result of another being too fearful to address the problem before it grew too large. Imagine the world collapsing under the burden of war. That is what happens without our contracts—without me to take on the weight of responsibility someone must shoulder. Are you willing to bear that responsibility?"

Sergius felt the words tug at his heart. Priest wanted to fight for his life, just as Sergius had known. But there was nothing to be done—most of the Family had already made up their minds… and those who felt differently before would surely want Priest's head after the trial revealed his shameful actions against the world and the Family themselves. Priest himself wanted the Family to kill him. He had tied up all the loose ends before the trial—which meant Priest, at the very least, *hoped* to be dead within a day or two. It was an inevitability everyone in the Family knew was coming.

There was no denying it was time for the family to forge a new path with a dramatic change in leadership.

SIXTY

SAINT STOOD at the front of the chamber as the Family filed in. He looked concerned, but not overcome with grief or sadness—which, Thomas surmised, came from years of Saint expecting this outcome.

"Gentlemen and ladies, sit where you wish—fathers and sons, uncles and nephews, husbands and wives. I only ask that those bringing evidence or testimony against Priest come to the front when you are called upon to present your complaints," Saint announced.

Everyone sat quickly and wordlessly. There were no whispers or conjectures about what might come to pass. They had spent weeks guessing at the outcome of the coming events. Now their father's judgment day was upon the Family, and the mood of the chamber was eerily dark.

Thomas waited restlessly for Priest to walk through the door. He listened to the unnerving symphony of racing hearts and jagged breaths of those filling the seats around him.

Caterina squeezed his hand, reminding him that he was not only surrounded by those who felt the same anger and grief he was feeling, but also that she was by his side—supporting him in whatever came next.

He felt the corners of his mouth lift slightly. This was the first time in his life that Caterina would sit next to him at one of the Family gatherings. The physical contact with his wife was more reassuring than he had expected. He felt her finger rub across the back of his hand as her gaze locked with Lissie's. The women had a silent conversation that revealed their sadness. Thomas loved his wife's tenderness, though he could not understand how she could possibly feel compassion for Priest after what had happened to Samuel.

Caterina's eyes flashed to Thomas's, and her small nod assured him she was prepared for what would come next.

Sergius entered the chamber with Priest trailing behind, and the deafening silence felt unnatural as the two made their way to the front of the room. Thomas watched his father closely with a mix of emotions raging through his body. How had his father become a crazed madman? And how long had his decisions put the lives of the Family and innocents at risk? Priest sauntered to the center of the room and stood facing Saint.

Saint rose from his chair at the head of the room—Priest's chair remaining empty for the first time in the Family's history. The rest of the Family followed suit and spoke together.

"We stand united, Family of Immortals. Plagued by life. Cursed by the hand of God. We pledge our lives to the Family."

Most voices faded out during the word "family", and none finished the original pledge. The men had been unable to come to a unified decision over how to proceed with their Family's pledge for the meeting. Some wanted everyone to remain silent. Others had thought it more effective to change the ending from "to the Family" to something more concrete like, "to the good of the world" or a more aggressive version like, "to exterminating those who deserve death." In the end, the only point that the majority had been able to agree upon was that they should not complete the ending of the pledge as they had for so many centuries. Their father had lost the trust of nearly everyone in the Family.

The Family sat back down while Priest and Saint remained standing, their eyes locked in an emotionless stare.

Thomas listened to the intake of Saint's breath as he opened his mouth to begin, hoping the meeting would go as he and his brothers hoped and planned.

"Many years have passed since our beginning," Saint began. "Our story is not one of ease or joy. Its path was paved with loss, regret, and hardship. With war, murder, and betrayal. Our Family has overcome all of these things," he stopped to clear his throat, looking down at Priest's feet. "But evidence has come to light that condemns you, my brother, of betraying the Family you created. This Family you pledged to protect," Saint whispered. He looked back into Priest's eyes with determination. Thomas wished like hell he could see the expression on his father's face. "And your children have decided you are no longer worthy of *their* loyalty and devotion."

Thomas glanced around at the scowling faces around him. *Interesting choice of words, Uncle.*

"What have you to say about these accusations of disloyalty to the Family?" Saint asked after a short pause.

"I have always done what I thought best for the Family," Priest answered, his voice rife with the arrogance he somehow always maintained.

Even at the door of defeat, he claims he acted in the Family's best interest. Pigheaded fool! Thomas's mind yelled.

"Unlike past matters, the outcome of this trial will be decided by the Family as a whole," Saint said, looking at each person seated in the chamber. This was the first time anyone outside of Priest or Saint would have any *real* power in deciding an outcome pertaining to the Family, and every man straightened in his seat as Saint made the announcement. He pointedly looked at each woman in the chamber as he spoke the next words. "That includes you, ladies. You are as much a part of this Family as your husbands."

Priest made no verbal protest to Saint's announcement, but instead turned and nodded at Caterina, who returned a reassuring smile. Thomas's heart dropped to his stomach. *They have some unspoken pact? Or bond? Have I missed something while I have been grieving for the loss of my brothers?* He glanced at Caterina and Lissie, who were now holding hands in either a show of solidarity or comfort. Thomas narrowed his eyes at the women, hoping they still intended to side with their husbands, but neither noticed him, their gazes fixed on Priest.

Mattia looked across the two women at Thomas, seeming just as confused by the women's behavior as he. *At least I am not alone in missing whatever has happened there.* Mattia gave an unconcerned shrug and turned his attention back to the front. Thomas hoped his son's lack of concern was valid, but his stomach still flipped with worry.

"I call Sergius to the front to read the charges measured against you," Saint announced. Sergius stood, looking every bit as determined to bring Priest to justice as Thomas felt.

"Here is the list of charges compiled against Priest, the immortal father of this Family: attempting to divide Family loyalties, murder of innocents, accepting contracts only for personal gain of power or money, and conspiracy to kill members of this Family. I call Gregorius to the front to address the first charge," Sergius finished, returning to his seat.

Gregorius looked intensely uncomfortable and conflicted as he stood before his father. His hands shook visibly, and he shoved them into his pockets before opening his mouth to speak. Thomas felt compelled to stand beside him and hold him up, but he knew his brother did not require real help.

"Priest. Father," Gregorius fought against the emotion in his throat. "You sent Elias on a false mission that you yourself concocted and drew up in an attempt to rid the Family of two valued members. Knowing full-well that Elias would not question your command, you manipulated him into doing your bidding. The contract you drew on the lives of Mattia and Lissie was not only self-serving and childish, but the loss of Mattia's expertise in the field of security and technology is considered by all to be detrimental to the efficacy of the Family."

Thomas looked around, content to see his brothers and nephews confirming their approval of Gregorius's words with grunts and nods.

"Furthermore, you were aware that Samuel might be present at the appointed time Elias was to carry out the assassination on Mattia and Lissie, and not only did you fail to present Elias with this important information, you hoped that Samuel would be embroiled and killed in the process.

"For as long as I can remember, you have done your best to separate myself and Elias from our brothers. As twins, you knew our loyalty to each other would always come before our loyalty to anyone else, and you not only encouraged our bond with each other, you made us feel that we were superior to all the others because of that bond. You paired us together for nearly all our contracts—often keeping us alienated from the companionship of our brothers, and inflating our egos in a way that made us feel that you valued us as your sons above any others. And while you may have actually valued us above any of your other sons or grandsons, it was not for our abilities—it was because we blindly allowed you to brainwash us into trusting you unfailingly. Your actions, and yours alone, caused Elias's death. And I will never be able to forgive you these wrongs.

"For the count of treachery against two of your sons, a grandson, and a granddaughter, how do you plead?" Gregorius asked, his voice hard.

"As you have already decided and are well-aware, you know I plead guilty," Priest answered in a heavily-accented Arabic dialect.

There was a collective murmuring through the chamber at his answer. They had expected non-compliance—at the very least—from their father. Thomas found himself scooting to the edge of his seat.

"And on the count of purposely dividing the Family ranks, causing dissension and unrest among the Family, how do you plead?" Gregorius continued.

"As your testimony shows, I am guilty," Priest answered in the old Latin that he and Saint still used when they spoke together.

This time, everyone looked around at one another, confusion splattered across every face—save two. Caterina and Lissie gave off the impression that they were utterly unsurprised by Priest's admission of guilt. Thomas raised his eyebrows in question at his wife, but Caterina only shrugged, her expression one of sadness. What is going on here? Thomas wondered.

Gregorius returned to his seat, his face expressionless, as Sergius returned to the front.

"I call upon Paulus to address the murder of innocent victims," Sergius sat once more and Paulus stood directly in front of his father.

Thomas gave his full attention now to Paulus, and saw that his brother's eyes were bloodshot.

"This is not easy for me to say, and I wish there could be some explanation other than the obvious. But our father has been accepting contracts on innocent lives simply for political trust or favors, financial gain, or out of mere boredom for hundreds of years.

"As you all know, for the past weeks, Demetrius, Felix, Sergius, Alexander and I have been examining contracts from the past thirteen hundred years. During that time, we found some truly troubling things which I will now bring to your attention." Paulus pulled a piece of folded paper from his pocket and opened it.

"At least thirty-five women were killed because their husbands held grievances against them. More than fifty young men were assassinated by either an uncle, brother or some other connected party to keep the boys from having a claim to the thrones for which they were in line. One contract removed an entire family of benevolent royals so an opposing family could take power. Three contracts were to rid wives of their husbands so the women could marry someone more politically powerful. And there are no less than fifteen contracts to remove bishops or cardinals from within the Catholic church for no reason other than those certain men would not push aside their moral convictions for the sake of the church's political gain."

Paulus folded the paper and pushed it onto his father's chest, finally looking into the face of the man he had trusted for so long.

"For the charge of accepting contracts on innocent victims, how do you plead?" Paulus's jaw clenched tightly, and Thomas could see he wished to say more to their father.

"As you already know, I am guilty of what you say," Priest sighed, seeming weary of the whole process.

Thomas saw his own pain mirrored in his brother's eyes as Paulus looked quickly away and returned to his seat.

Sergius stood once more and faced his seated brothers and nephews. He looked terrified, and took far too long to speak. Thomas's stomach churned in anxiousness at what might come next. Sergius had not given him any ideas of what information might come to light during the trial.

"During our time combing through the contents of the vault, I happened upon a hidden chamber under the stones in the farthest corner of the vault," Sergius began. There was a collective intake of breath across the chamber, and pulses began to race. The sound of Thomas's own pounding pulse in his ears was loud enough to give him a headache.

"Thirteen scrolls were concealed from us, and after reviewing their contents, we knew we no longer needed to look through the other scrolls," Sergius's voice faded as the seated family began looking at one another worriedly.

"I call forth Alexander to discuss the first six scrolls," Sergius sat as Alexander walked to the front with the scrolls under his arm. He set them on Priest's empty chair and picked up the first.

"The death of Pope John XXI is contracted for his secret acts of necromancy and for forming an alliance with the Eastern Church that threatens the stability of the Holy Roman Empire. His death should appear accidental." Alexander rolled up the scroll while a few of the Family whispered their frustrations. He unceremoniously moved onto the second scroll, obviously hoping to get through the reading of the scrolls quickly so he could sit down once more. Alexander was not one to enjoy being the focus of others' attention.

"Pope John Paul I should be put to death by means of untraceable poison." The room erupted when Alexander re-rolled the scroll, some asking for further explanation of the reasoning for the contract and others yelling angrily over the death of a beloved pope. But Alexander unrolled the third scroll and tried to continue, beginning to read, though unsuccessfully, several times before his shoulders sagged and he lowered the scroll to wait. As the shouting continued, Thomas watched his younger brother pull a flask from a pocket and take a long pull of whatever spirit resided within it. That brought about some chuckles, though most still shouted.

"Enough!" Saint yelled, the chamber echoing the single word as the yelling softened to mere murmurs. "We can further discuss these contracts once Alexander has had the opportunity to read through all of them. Let him finish in peace."

The room quieted, and Alexander took another drink from his flask before reading.

"The death of Sir Thomas Urquhart is requested by Oliver Cromwell in order to dispose of a thorn in the Kingdom's side." Alexander quickly moved to the next contract, shifting his weight back and forth as he read.

"By request of vice president Theodore Roosevelt, it is requested that American president, William McKinley, should be put to death while recovering in the hospital from gunshot wounds. The death should give the appearance of an infection from the prior injury."

More murmurs and confused glances were exchanged amongst those listening. Thomas couldn't understand why these contracts would ever have been accepted. They were petty, at best. Alexander continued.

"Jan Masaryk should be assassinated by means of 'assisted suicide' in order to aid the peaceful transition to a communist Czechoslovakian state." The confusion persisted, though the discussions amongst the Family were limited to shrugs and questioning glances.

"For acts of indiscretion, for disgracing the dynasty, and for ruling in place of the former emperor's chosen successor, the death of Zhu Changluo, Taiching Emperor of the Ming Dynasty, shall die from a painful poison of the assassin's choosing." Alexander rolled the scroll as a cry of anger came from someone across the room. Everyone's heads turned to the left as Alexander's fourth grandson, Arcadia, pulled a knife out from a holster and was barely stopped by his brothers before he could heave it toward Priest.

Thomas looked back at Alexander, who was taking a long pull from his flask. *What on earth is happening?*

Arcadia continued his barrage of insults and profanity as his brothers restrained him.

Priest turned toward Arcadia and began speaking in his great-grandson's native dialect of old Castilian.

"Did you honestly think your relationship with that man would go unnoticed? The moment the emperor's family discovered there was a romantic connection between you, they began seeking an assassin who would kill you both. I convinced them only the emperor needed to be killed," Priest offered casually.

"Arcadia, sit down. That's enough information, father," Alexander grumbled through gritted teeth as his hands grasped his father's shoulders and pulled him around so he no longer faced Arcadia.

It took several minutes for the Family to quiet enough for Alexander to present the official charges against Priest. The Family was so shaken by the murder of Arcadia's lover that there was no further questioning over the first five scrolls Alexander had read.

"On the count of accepting contracts that clearly do not fall under the categories of 'maintaining the balance of power in the world' or 'protecting those who need aid', how do you plead?" Alexander asked.

"Guilty," Priest spoke in Mandarin—the official language of the Ming Dynasty. Alexander groaned in frustration before continuing.

"On the count of intentionally doing harm to one of your offspring, how do you plead?"

"Doing harm? Truly? The emperor would have died eventually. And I convinced the rest of the emperor's family that Arcadia did not need to be killed. But I suppose you wish me to admit some kind of wrong-doing here, so I guess I must plead guilty," Priest answered with a dismissive wave of his hand.

The profanities continued from Arcadia as Alexander returned to his seat, taking yet another pull from his flask. Thomas wished he could tell his little brother he'd done well, but Alexander was doing his best to maintain self-control as he stared hard at the ground by his feet.

"Finally," Sergius's voice quieted the room, "I ask Felix to come up and read the remaining seven contracts."

Felix walked to the front of the room, set the scrolls down in Priest's chair, and balled and unballed his fists before turning to stare at the man responsible for their contents. Thomas felt his stomach lurch in anticipation. *They've saved the worst for last.*

SIXTY-ONE

FELIX PICKED up the first scroll and began reading.

"To exact revenge on a political inconvenience and create a greater sense of unity amongst servants of the crown, the death of Anamaria Serrano is requested."

Caterina glanced at Mattia, who was holding Lissie tightly as he fought against the anger he was clearly feeling. She knew he was in pain, but she would have time to comfort him later—once all of this mess was dealt with.

"No part of the contract pertained to the rest of the Serrano family," Felix finished as he looked up at Mattia.

Antonio and Marcus tensed as Mattia's breathing quickened and his face reddened, but he remained planted in his seat as Felix unrolled the next scroll and read.

"To quell the dissemination of ill will against Priest within the ranks of the Family, Priest calls his most reliable son to remove Mattia, third son of Thomas, and his fiancée, Lissette, from the Family. Their bodies should be hidden and never found."

Caterina felt Thomas pull her closer while she involuntarily shook with anger. She knew each of the remaining contracts could only get worse—and there were still five to go. Felix's eyes locked with Thomas's, and there was a quick flash of fear in Felix's eyes before he breathed in and began reading.

"For stirring discontentment and anger amongst his brothers, and for vocalizing an outcry against Priest, this contract details the imminent death of Thomas, fifth of Priest's sons. Upon completion of his services to Hernán Cortés de Monroy y Pizarro, the fulfillment of the contract will be completed only with the death of Thomas."

Oh no, Caterina's eyes began leaking tears—of anger or grief she did not know.

"Bastard," Thomas breathed quietly. "You have been treating us as if we are your play things? Are we so worthless to you? Is your life so pointless that you cannot even see what is before you?" His voice had swelled from a whisper to a yell as he spoke, but Caterina held him tightly to keep him from charging to the front of the room to engage with his father physically.

She rubbed her hand up and down his back, trying to calm him, but he sat on the edge of his seat, hands braced against his knees, breathing heavily as his face remained flushed. Priest did not turn around to face Thomas. He stood still, seemingly unconcerned with Thomas's outcry. Felix grabbed the next scroll and read.

"For continued debauchery and uselessness to the Family and the world, Borvin, fifth grandson of Elias, is to be killed in his sleep by way of 'accidental fire'."

A knife planted itself in the ground between Priest's feet as soon as Felix finished reading. Caterina had heard the knife fly, but she was so focused on Thomas, she didn't know who had thrown it. Priest picked it up and turned to Gregorius, his face showing no response to the threat.

"You missed," Priest drew in a long breath before tossing the knife back to Gregorius—whose expression was even more murderous than Thomas's. *Please let us get through this trial,* she sent up a desperate prayer. She was as furious as the rest of her Family, but Caterina knew her husband and his brothers needed the trial to follow the proper course or there would be discord amongst them. The past weeks, months, and years of bickering had taken its toll on the entire family.

"In order to purge the Family of those who believe they are above the task of killing for the good of the world, I, Priest, have taken upon myself the responsibility to remove Lucius, firstborn of Paulus, for choosing a life dedicated to the church."

"Oh my God," Caterina breathed as more of the Family hurled insults at

Priest for his crimes against his own sons and grandsons. Felix now hurried, sensing the trial was nearly to its breaking point.

"Maximus, second son of Claudius, must be eliminated from the Family for refusing to carry out a contract given him."

"What? No! MY SON!" Claudius wailed as his body flew down the stairs toward Priest. Caterina watched as Claudius's fist flew at the back of Priest's head. But in a fluid movement, Priest not only avoided the contact, but also grabbed his son's fist and twisted his arm painfully. Claudius collapsed to the ground, and Priest's face twisted into a remorseful grimace as he quickly returned to the position in which he had stood since the beginning of the trial. Claudius kept wailing as his sons dragged him unwillingly back to his seat.

She began to worry that the day might end in a bloodbath rather than a verdict.

"And the final contract," Felix regained control of the trial. "Kadir, fourth great-grandson of Gregorius, must be put to death by the hand of Priest for showing blatant disrespect to his elders, including both Gregorius and Priest, and for remaining out of contact with the Family to put the needs of his wife above the needs of the Family."

Caterina watched as Gregorius turned his knife over and over in his hand, trying to control his impulse to kill the man who had destroyed his family.

Felix set the scroll down with the others and faced his father directly.

"For the charge of deliberately destroying the lives of your own sons and their families, how do you plead?" Felix's gaze was eerily self-controlled.

"The evidence has been set before all to see. I am guilty of all you say," Priest responded in Latin.

"I would now ask you to turn and face your accusers, your victims, your pawns, your family," Felix sneered at the last word as Priest turned around and looked from face to face of his offspring. "Are you satisfied with the life you have lived?" Felix asked pointedly.

"I am as satisfied as I am capable," Priest said nonchalantly.

Felix shook his head slowly in disbelief at the tone of his father's answer.

Sergius was as frustrated with his father's dismissive words as Felix seemed to be. He had hoped to see some remorse—even a little—from his father.

"She would be so disappointed in you," Felix breathed only slightly louder than a whisper, but everyone had heard him.

Priest's eyes filled with regret and sadness—it was the first true show of emotion from Priest all day.

"That may be true, but your mother knew exactly who I was the moment we met. I do not think my behavior would have ever surprised her," Priest smiled a little, his mind seeming to drift to another time and place.

Saint finally stood and walked to stand beside Priest.

"My brother, you stand accused and have willingly proclaimed your own guilt," he clasped Priest on the shoulder, his expression wistful.

"Sit down, uncle," Sergius barked out as he moved to Saint's side. "I am in charge of this trial, and we will deal with you next."

"I have been nothing but supportive and helpful since your father left after your mother's death. You know me, and I am not the one on trial here," Saint rebutted with a hint of anger in his tone.

"Not now, uncle. Let us finish one trial before beginning another," Sergius warned.

Saint and Priest exchanged a glance—Saint appeared shocked while Priest looked a little proud—and Saint returned to his seat, blindsided by the meeting's change in direction.

"Father. Do you have any excuse, any reasoning, anything at all to say in your defense?" Sergius questioned.

"I will only say this—that I have always acted upon what I deemed best." He kept his head held high, maintaining eye contact with his children.

"Then it is time for us to take a vote," Sergius announced. "All those in favor of conviction and punishment?"

Everyone in the room put a hand up except for Priest and Saint.

"And those in favor of pardoning our father?" Sergius did his best to control the emotions that were racing through his body. He was relieved and saddened that no one defended his father. But the man had given them no reason whatsoever to stand in his defense. *Is that by design?* he wondered, not knowing if this was part of an elaborate scheme his father had concocted.

"What punishment fits the crimes of which our father is convicted?" Sergius questioned.

"Kill him and be done with it," Claudius hissed out while most of the room nodded or grunted their approval.

"Imprisonment would be less merciful," Gregorius chimed in as eyebrows around the room were raised at the suggestion.

"By the gods, kill me," Priest interjected. The room fell completely silent.

"What?" Saint asked in a fearful whisper.

"Please," Priest sounded weary, and Sergius's heart ached in response. His father's pleading didn't stop there. "Please kill me. I have lived *far* too long, and I was promised an end." His voice cracked with emotion.

No one knew how to respond. Everyone was looking around, waiting for someone to speak up.

"I have turned my own children against me. What life do I have left? I led you as faithfully as I am capable for more than one thousand years. And I have wished for death for a long time to no avail. I have only one request before you kill me."

"Priest. Brother," Sergius could hear the pleading in Saint's voice.

"I ask that you let me tell my story—my whole story. When I am gone, you must carry our Family history with you through life and pass it on to your sons."

When Priest had first told him about their immortality, Sergius had not believed a word. But as time passed, he had seen himself and his brothers remain young and healthy. He had asked only twice how the Family became immortal, and both times the question was met with outright hostility. There was no "maybe when you are older," no allusion to a future telling of the history. The only response had been, "That is none of your business." Sergius knew his father well enough to realize there would have been no point in asking again. He wondered if Priest imagined his sons would feel differently about him if they knew his history. *Perhaps this is a final attempt to regain our devotion.*

"Then we will vote," Sergius announced. "All in favor of listening to our father's story before deciding his fate?"

Sergius was surprised to see a few people were uninterested in knowing their history. But the majority ruled, and so they would hear the story nonetheless.

"We will hear your story tomorrow, Priest. Now we will have a break for lunch and reconvene after to put our uncle on trial," Sergius began to walk toward the door, but no one moved.

"We know it isn't possible for Saint to have been ignorant of Priest's actions," Felix spoke up. "We all heard his heart race when he lied about being ignorant of the hidden contracts. Am I wrong?"

Sergius desperately needed a short respite from the trial, but he could see in his brothers' faces, he would have to wait.

"You are not wrong, Felix. We all heard it, uncle," Sergius turned to Saint. "Do you have any defense against the accusation that you were aware and complicit in the drawing up and concealing of the contracts brought forth today?"

"Surely you cannot believe I would be a part of such a scheme. You all know me. You come to me with your grievances. I have served as an adviser and as a loving uncle to you for centuries. Please," Saint begged.

"Uncle," Sergius shook his head a little. "We all know when you are lying. We can all hear your heartbeat rise. Perhaps father should have taught you how to control yours as he does his." Sergius's frustration was seeping out.

"Fine. Then you know I am guilty," Saint stared hard at the ground. "But before you sentence me to anything, I want to hear Priest's story as well."

Sergius looked between Saint and Priest as the two men exchanged a look. He had never really known what the two men were to each other genetically, but he had always assumed their story was one and the same. As he glanced at his brothers and nephews, his own surprise was mirrored in the others' faces.

"All those in favor of conviction and punishment of Saint for his involvement in the contracts brought forth today?" Again, Sergius felt a small jolt of surprise that everyone didn't agree with his belief that their uncle should be convicted; however, the majority raised their hands. "Very well. We will listen to Priest's story beginning tomorrow morning, and afterward we will decide both of their fates."

SIXTY-TWO

PRIEST SAT in his room, listening to his family stir in the dining hall downstairs. He felt an unfamiliar flutter in his stomach as he considered how his sons would respond to his history. The day had been… strange.

He had assumed his sons would have figured out Saint's involvement in the accepting and drawing up of contracts. And Saint's shock was a bit naive in Priest's opinion. His friend should have known the boys would think critically enough to realize Saint was embroiled in all the Family affairs.

He lay down on his bed, staring at nothing in particular as he began to think about where he should begin his story. There were so many key points in his history—points that were unrecorded by historical documents. And he felt it his responsibility as the last true descendant from his people to relay as many details of his culture as he could remember.

A thought flickered in his mind, and he darted to his desk and pulled a pen and paper from a drawer. He opened his old journal that contained the secrets of his past and began with the first page. He translated the first three pages into Italian—that way his sons would be able to make a cipher to translate his native tongue into a modern language. *Perhaps Marcus will undergo the task,* he wondered as he finished writing a note to explain the translation, folded the pages, and pushed them into the front of the journal.

He poured himself a glass of wine and walked onto his small balcony. The sky was so clear and the moon so bright that every vineyard in the surrounding hills was visible. He remembered that, when they had first purchased the old monastery that sat on the spot where their home was now situated, there had been only one other vineyard visible from their hill. He rubbed his shoulder as he thought of the loads of stones they had carted up the dirt roads to build the castle. Saint had drawn the plans over and over again, making calculation after calculation to ensure the walls were thick enough to support the structure. They had studied the famous Tuscan vineyards to see how their cellars were made, then he and Saint had made adjustments to the designs to prevent moisture from seeping into the lower room where their scrolls would be preserved. They had visited stone buildings that had stood the test of time to analyze which construction would endure. After years of planning and preparation, the whole Family had come together to construct the castle that Priest had lived in for the better part of the past millennium.

He ran his hand along the smooth stone surface that framed the door to his small balcony. He would not miss the room or the view or his sons. He would be dead, and hopefully—finally—at peace somehow. He hoped there was nothing after life. He didn't want feasts and streets of gold and angelic songs. He didn't want fire and screaming and darkness. He simply wanted... the end. The vast nothingness of *after*, never to wake from an endless slumber.

He returned to his bed and lay down. He squeezed his eyes shut and felt relief knowing that the end of his life on earth was close at hand. The combination of exhaustion and wine pulled his body toward slumber. But before he succumbed to sleep, he broke his only rule, and sent a prayer upward. *Surely, after this endless life from which I have been cursed, you can give me this one kindness. Let me die tomorrow. And let it truly be over for me.*

SIXTY-THREE

THE MORNING SUN poured through the doors Priest had not shut the night before, and Saint was pacing back and forth through the bedroom.

"Finally," Saint breathed as Priest pushed himself up groggily. "I swear you have not slept like that since we met. I thought maybe someone had knocked you unconscious."

Priest smiled at the idea that someone could actually achieve such a thing.

"How long have you been in here?" Priest asked, finally recognizing the panic in Saint's features.

"Since before dawn. I scaled the wall between our rooms so the boys would not stop me from coming to see you. I almost fell a few times, but I made it in," Saint gave a small smirk before resuming his panicking.

"That must have been noisy. I did sleep rather soundly, didn't I?" Priest rubbed the sleep from his eyes as Saint rolled his eyes. Saint pulled a chair next to the bed and sat facing Priest directly.

"I think we should leave together. Let the boys have all of this, and we can start over somewhere else." Saint waited for Priest's response.

"No." Priest would not attempt to calm Saint down or allay his fears. This was their final day on earth, and Priest had experienced the best night of sleep he could have ever imagined.

"You must accept that this is our end. And the world will go on without us. And the boys will live differently, but I'm certain they will survive. Make peace with it. Make peace with your actions. If you feel so inclined, make peace with God. Then let it be over," Priest felt he had said enough and hoped the words would comfort his friend.

Saint sighed and shook his head. "I do not understand how you are so calm in this moment. I cannot find peace." Saint whined, and Priest looked up, wondering if Saint's sanity was intact. "The boys slept all night. I did not need to climb about like an idiot. They were all in their beds soundly asleep."

Priest broke into a small chuckle at the visualization of Saint trying to traverse the weathered castle's stones. Saint joined in, and they laughed harder than Priest had laughed since Basina lived. They carried on for a few minutes until the door to the room opened and Sergius looked in with a furrowed brow.

"Uncle. I did not hear you enter father's room this morning," Sergius said with a questioning glance—which set off Priest's and Saint's guffaws once more. Sergius left with a confused shake of his head as the two continued their uproarious laughter.

Saint's expression shifted and he quieted rapidly. Priest gripped his friend's shoulders firmly and looked into Saint's eyes.

"We have earned this death. And I intend to die well."

SIXTY-FOUR

PRIEST LOOKED AROUND the chamber at his offspring, and the curiosity and wonder on his children's faces reminded him of another time. Priest sat, for the last time, in the chair from which he had conducted Family meetings for over nine hundred years. Saint was, of course, next to him, and Priest realized he felt only fondness for the men and women that surrounded him. He was determined to make this a memorable day for everyone present. He wanted them to know *everything*. He had spent his life documenting pieces of his history in journals so he would be able to tell his children their heritage when the time came. He heaved a sigh as he allowed his memories to overwhelm him. He closed his eyes as the hazy scenes began unfolding in his mind.

"I was born in a seaside village on the Mediterranean coast. The city was called Ashkelon, and based on historical accounts of battles and events, I believe the year was 1081 B.C.E." he began, watching even Saint's eyes light with excitement. "I am a descendant from the isle of Crete, and you would know my people—*your* people—as the Philistines. My people's history was not properly recorded, and what was recorded was destroyed over time by warring nations. There was actually a great deal written about us in the Library at Alexandria—our people dealt at great length with the Egyptians—but unfortunately, we all know what happened to the scrolls in that place. The short history of my people is that my ancestors were forced to flee our homeland in Crete to make a new life on the mainland. But wherever they went, our people were so great in strength and in number that they were forced into battles in which they did not wish to participate. Our people were mainly tradesmen. We were fishermen, shepherds, and exceptionally skilled craftsmen—weavers, potters, sculptors, and painters. Only the most strategically gifted and strongest became warriors. Our army was rather small in spite of the shadow of terror other nations saw when they looked upon our people. But we were a generally peaceful nation, until... until we came up against the Israelites." He sighed, allowing himself a moment to remember the details of the spoken history he was taught as a boy.

"The Israelites inhabited a land quite close to where my people settled. And *they* chose to war with *us* for centuries. My father was a warrior, and his father before him. When I was only five years of age, my father and grandfather were killed in the same battle—leaving my mother a widow with three small children. In honor of our father's sacrifice, and because my mother was the daughter of the lord of Ashdod, the Philistine leaders moved our family to Ashdod so we could be well-cared-for in the capital city.

It was there that, against my mother's wishes, my purpose in life became singular: to honor my father's memory by becoming the greatest warrior in Philistine history. I began my training at ten and became a soldier at twelve—the age Philistine boys were considered men. I served under a highly regarded commander for two years before asking to lead a small group of soldiers on my own. We were constantly at war with the Israelites, and I wished to do more than participate in open battle."

"I know which soldiers will serve me best," Ahuzzan assured Ekosh, the chief commander of the Philistine army.

"And what do you plan to do with your soldiers?" Commander Ekosh asked.

"Anything our commander wishes. If you choose to place us at the front, we will fight at the front. If you allow me to choose the soldiers I have chosen most suitable to the task, we could deal more damage than regular soldiers. We could deliver accurate reports on enemy movements without detection. We could easily infiltrate enemy encampments and neutralize targets, escaping unnoticed. And if we fail, you will lose only ten men," Ahuzzan assured the commander.

Ekosh stared down at his battle plans for a short pause. "And if you don't approve of my orders?"

"We would carry out whatever our commander wishes without objection," Ahuzzan promised once more. He felt irritated that he needed to repeat himself, but did not let his emotions show.

"You show great ambition and even greater courage, young one. Tell me which men you want under your command, and I shall take your request into consideration."

"I led those ten men for only three months, and our success was widespread. The commander placed four additional teams of ten under my group's command, and I became a commander—all at the age of sixteen," Priest said, remembering each man who had served beneath him during that first year. He had commanded men from the ages of fourteen up to twenty-eight —his proven intelligence and leadership on the battlefield and in scouting were so admired by the entire Philistine army, others regularly requested a transfer to his command.

"My mother was proud, even though she didn't want to admit it. I was an ideal soldier—and that was a great honor in our tribe even though the profession was not as highly lauded as others. I exercised absolute control of my men while maintaining their respect. Only twice did I have to kill one of my soldiers for disobedience on the battlefield. The other commanders envied my skill, and though I was respected, I was also feared. The chief commander used my group's abilities to disrupt enemy plans. Often, our enemies were defeated before they knew we had infiltrated their encampments.

"On my order, each group of three will enter from a different location. These oafs have two entrances into their encampment on each side—they have sent us an invitation to slit their throats and drink their wine," Ahuzzan growled as his men grunted in agreement. The thrill of an attack had no match. Even on nights like these, where the enemy would fall within minutes, there was a feeling of overwhelming gratification that accompanied victory.

Ahuzzan watched from a hill as his men spread out to their respective hiding areas. Once the soldiers were in place and the enemy still showed no sign of suspicion, Ahuzzan let out a loud screech that mimicked a hawk to announce the onslaught should begin. With swords drawn, he watched his soldiers slit every throat in the camp, never once hearing a yelp of pain or a cry for help. He puffed out his chest and grinned at the easy victory, and his second-in-command, having waited for the grin which immediately followed the enemy's defeat, yelled their victory cry, his men joining in with raised swords.

"When the chief commander felt I was accomplished enough to command more troops, he placed a greater mantle of responsibility upon my shoulders and moved two hundred more soldiers under my command," Priest lifted his chin, remembering the pride that rolled off of his entire body as he accepted the sword that marked him as a high commander in the army. "I was twenty years of age that year, and that was the year I married my second wife—Safira. My first marriage was arranged when I was sixteen, and I had no kind feelings for the woman. She was sheepish and scared. And though we tried for a while, she could not bear children. However, she died, and I married Safira, the widow of Makati, one of my fallen soldiers. I thought she would be different from my first wife, but our first several months together were not at all what I had expected."

Ahuzzan paced the floor, staring at his new wife. She had refused to cook him a meal *and* denied him his husbandly right. The woman had placed uncooked ingredients on the table in front of him and pulled away when he tried to take her to bed. The fury that stirred in his chest was overwhelming.

"You will lie with me, or you will suffer the same fate as my first wife," he growled in a haze of anger. Safira glanced up at him defiantly, unwilling to budge on her decision.

"You do not own me. Makati treated me with love and respect, and you would do well to do the same. My husband has been dead for only three months. When I am ready to be touched, I will come to *you*," she spoke with a quiet resolution.

Ahuzzan's blood boiled. No woman would ever tell him how to act.

"You are *mine* now. *I* am your husband, and despite your first husband's manner of behaving, I am not he. You will do as I say. Now remove your cloak immediately or I will tear it from your body," he commanded.

"No!" she growled, sitting up straighter.

He rushed at her, grabbing her wrists and tossing her to his sleeping mat. She was unable to fight back under his weight, and he thought she might have momentarily lost consciousness from the impact with the thin sleeping mat on the floor. He didn't care. She would recover, and he would have what was owed to him. He ripped her cloak all the way down her front as she whimpered quietly, aware that any screams would go unanswered. None of the other Philistines would dare to stand against Ahuzzan. Safira was not used to this kind of treatment. Her father had been loving and gentle toward her mother, and her first husband had been adoring and kind. A tear dripped from her eye. Ahuzzan was none of those things. He was a cruel beast, accustomed to the life of a commander who led attacks on enemy encampments and the villages of those who stood against his people. He and his men plundered, killed, and raped wherever they wanted. That was the man Safira had married. A man who would not let anything stand in the way of what he wanted.

She lay still, quietly praying to the gods it would be over soon. But in his passions, he was not rough with her. He knew she expected brutality, but he did not feel the need to punish her any further. He finished and turned to walk away.

"Next time, do not fight me," he muttered without a backward glance.

The next evening, there were, again, uncooked ingredients on the dinner mat when Ahuzzan sat down to eat—a raw fish, a bowl of flour, a few uncut herbs. He could not believe the woman was capable of such stubbornness and disrespect. She astounded him—and impressed him a little. He ate the food without a word, displaying his superior form of stubbornness with pride.

But the next night, when Ahuzzan walked into their home to eat dinner, there were once again uncooked ingredients waiting for him. His could not hold back his anger, and he began screaming at her.

"How dare you disrespect me in such a way. If you wish to please the gods, you should give unto your husband that which is due him," he yelled.

"That which is due? I should drive a knife into your loin—that is what is due after your behavior two nights ago!" she screamed.

They continued to accuse each other of wrong-doings, threatening the curses of the gods for all the terrible sins the other had committed. Finally, Ahuzzan had heard enough.

"You think so highly of your dead husband, but perhaps he could not tolerate you and that is why he allowed himself to die in battle." Safira quieted at the callous mention of her husband's death, and even Ahuzzan felt a little guilty for reducing Makati's death to petty insult. Makati had been an accomplished soldier and a good friend.

"How should I know if he even died in battle? If your first wife's demise is any indication of your character, my husband likely died by your knife while he was asleep," she whispered in a furious tone.

Ahuzzan could take no more. He was a trusted leader—and he never laid a finger on a soldier who did not deserve punishment.

His shaking hands grabbed Safira by the shoulders and threw her roughly against the wall. In a stunned silence, she didn't move, and he walked to her, slapping her hard across the face.

"Is this what you want from me?" he asked, slapping her other cheek. She didn't respond or even make a sound as her cheek began to swell. He threw her down onto the ground, her shoulder violently hitting the dusty floor. He stood over her shaking body, his blood pumping wildly through his body.

"If you wish for this marriage to continue, I suggest you practice a little obedience and respect," he said, his pulse beginning to slow down. She looked up at him with eyes as full of fear as a man about to die by his sword on the battlefield. Tears streaked her cheeks, but she still did not let out even so much as a whimper. As the bloodlust subsided, Ahuzzan began to understand what had just happened. He turned his back to Safira's crumpled body and made his way to their door.

"I will be away with my soldiers for the next three days at least. When I return, I expect to be properly fed." He left the home, feeling like the coward Safira had accused him of being. He had just beaten a woman—a smaller, weaker creature who was incapable of defending herself against him. And before that, he had taken her against her will. Even worse than that, he was *supposed* to be her husband. Though his father had died when he was a child, his memories of his father and mother were of care and protection and love—not abuse and insults. As he began to see his actions of the previous days more clearly, Ahuzzan's shame covered him like a thick fleece of wool on a sweltering summer's day. *What have I done?*

His duties kept him gone for four days. His shame kept him away for seven.

When at last he was ready to face his punishment, he went home to Safira, hoping she would be willing to forgive his lapse in self-control. When he walked through the door, Safira forced a smile—her face still covered in bruises. He tried not to wince when he saw the damage he had caused. She told Ahuzzan to sit on the cushion where he usually ate, and she moved awkwardly to retrieve a pot. He watched as she picked up the pot with one arm—he thought her other shoulder looked a bit out of place. She set a large bowl before him and filled it with stew. She did not sit down with him or attempt to eat, and though he feared the food might be poisoned, he hoped she was too intelligent to think she would get away with murdering one of the highest-ranking commanders in the Philistine army. He sniffed the soup, trying to discern if anything was amiss, and slurped up a spoonful. It was delicious, and he sighed in relief that Safira could, in fact, cook a decent meal.

"It is very good," he admitted, eating another spoonful. Safira stayed silent, waiting until he finished the first bowl, then pouring the remainder of the stew into his empty bowl.

"I am happy it pleases you," she said quietly. She moaned softly whenever she had to move her right arm. *Dislocated, if I had to guess,* Ahuzzan thought, wondering if she would allow him to push it back into place.

As he raised his spoon to his mouth once more, the pot Safira used to cook the stew smashed into Ahuzzan's forehead and nose. His body flung backwards, the bowl of hot stew spilling onto his chest. He didn't know if the liquid had burned him because all he could think of was the blood that poured from his nose... or was it from a gash on his head? Ahuzzan lay, stunned, flat on his back. Safira sat down on his chest and began beating his face, shoulders and chest with her fists. She screamed with every movement, the pain in her shoulder begging for a reprise. For a few seconds, Ahuzzan forgot how to move, but after his senses returned, he grabbed Safira's wrists, doing his best to be gentle as she thrashed about. He sat up, pulling her close, and pushed her shoulder back into place. She shrieked in pain, but did not fight him any more as her pain began to subside. He massaged her shoulder gently with one hand and held her shaking body tightly with the other. As the intensity of the moment began to wear off, the pain in his head, nose, and chest grew unbearable. He released Safira from his arms and lay flat on the ground, wondering if she might finish what she started while he was incapacitated. He felt blood dripping down his throat from his broken nose, and he turned his head to spit. But the movement only worsened his headache, and his entire body began to shake. Safira watched his struggle for only a short moment before rising to her feet and leaving him alone. He closed his eyes, feeling the weight of remorse for ruining his marriage and realizing his lack of self-control might be his undoing. He could no longer keep himself awake. Safira would soon be free of him.

He awoke to an unbearably painful swipe across his burned chest, and the moan that emerged from his mouth was akin to a war cry. Safira jerked her hand away, and Ahuzzan heard something hit the ground. His vision was blurred by the tears that had involuntarily sprung in his eyes; he wiped them away quickly—though even that motion was painful enough to create more tears in his eyes.

Safira picked up the bowl she had dropped and resumed smearing a salve over his burns. The damned tears returned, though this round was from a combination of regret and gratitude rather than pain.

"You would treat my wounds after…" he couldn't finish the question.

"You are my husband, and you are a respected commander of our armies. What kind of wife would I be if I left you to fend for yourself after I caused you harm?" she glowered down at him, and tears of shame ran down his cheeks. He had fled after injuring her, and now she would stay to give him aid.

"I wish there was a way to express my shame. I am sorry for the pain I have caused you. I have treated you abominably, and you have every right to accuse me of wrong-doing and to ask the priests for an annulment. I know my grandfather would be able to persuade them with coin if it is what you wish," he offered, unable to meet her gaze. He saw her jaw tighten determinedly before speaking.

"I am not a weak woman. I do not run when I am faced with something terrible. I do not trust you. I do not love you, and I am certain I never will. I doubt I will ever allow you to touch me again—and if you try, I will have my knife at the ready. But I have committed myself to you, and I will honor my vow. It is up to you to prove whether or not I am foolish for remaining attached to such a monstrous ass."

Safira finished rubbing the salve on his chest and set clean strips of cloth over the burns. She then cleaned the blood from his broken nose and pushed the crooked part back into place as he winced. He watched her movements in awe. This was a woman he could respect. And he felt a longing deep inside for *her* respect, though he doubted he could ever make up for the mistakes he had made.

Priest recalled the moment with perfect clarity. Safira had nursed him back to health, and he had fashioned her a sling to keep her arm immobile while it healed. He had done whatever he could to help her with cooking or with chores around the house—something he had not done since he was a child. But he always made sure not to touch her as he moved about their home. The problem was that the more time he spent with her, the more her appeal grew. She was a formidable woman who filled whatever space she was in with her quiet, yet powerful, presence. He wished he could go back and start over. But he could not undo the past—only attempt to correct his behavior going forward.

It had been five months of unbearable longing for the wife he could not touch. Ahuzzan had been away for two full weeks on a scouting trip. When he walked into his home, Safira was cooking dinner and humming one of the fishermen's songs her father had taught her. Her voice was terrible, but it was the sweetest sound Ahuzzan could imagine. He wanted nothing more than to hold her and tell her she had been a distraction that had almost gotten him killed while he was away, but he knew the rules—and he had done this to himself.

Safira looked up and as she realized Ahuzzan was watching her from the door, her eyes lit with joy.

"You are back!" she smiled, and his heart nearly exploded. He cursed the rules as he walked purposefully to his wife.

"I could not focus on my mission because of you," he grumbled, and Safira's brow crinkled in confusion as she took a small step away from his intense gaze. "All I could think about was that you were here, alone, without my protection. What if someone attacked while I was away? What if you had an accident and I did not know you were injured? I cannot keep my mind where it should be when you are here and I am away," he breathed the words, hoping to convey his meaning as clearly as possible.

Tentatively, she raised a hand to push a stray curl away from his forehead. It moved to rest against his cheek, and he wanted to cover it with his own hand. But she had vowed she would stab him if he touched her again, and her word was not to be tested. He closed his eyes and memorized the feeling of her hand against his cheek, knowing it would soon be gone, but his eyes flew open when he felt the soft touch of her other hand against his right cheek.

Safira's thumbs caressed his cheeks softly as her gaze combed over each detail on his face. He reveled in their closeness, and fought with every speck of self-control to keep his hands at his sides. Her hands slid to the back of his head, combing through his hair in the most sensual way Ahuzzan could imagine. He moved willingly as he felt her hands pull him closer until her forehead rested against his. His eyes squeezed shut as he breathed in her lovely scent—freshly baked bread and olives. When he felt the soft brush of her lips against his, he nearly collapsed.

"Safira," he whispered her name, unable to say more.

"Touch me. Kiss me," she commanded. Her lips were an assault on his mind, his heart, his ability to breathe. His mouth crushed hers as she grabbed at his hair and his back. He pressed her against the wall, his hands cupping the back of her head, protecting her from knocking her head against the hard surface. He could not bear the thought of injuring his wife. He would rather kill himself than wound her physically or emotionally ever again.

He made love to a woman for the first time that night, and completely lost his heart in the process. Before Safira, he had no concept of what sex could be. With her, it was a spiritual awakening—a different form of worship. And it changed him forever.

Priest leaned back in his chair. Of course he left out the more graphic moments in his retelling—those memories were only for him. He had stayed devoted to Safira for the rest of her short life. Her strength and determination had changed his perception of women. He began to see the way his mother and wife hid their fear each time he went away on a mission or to fight a battle. The way his wife managed their home without a single complaint. And how she silently bore the weight of the household water basins on the long walk to and from the city's well. He himself had made the trip once and hated every step. Safira had been a force of nature.

Priest looked up at the men and women listening to his tale and was met with varied expressions. Fascination, disgust, humor, anger, anticipation. All were deserved. He had behaved monstrously, been bested by a woman, and fallen madly in love. Any censure was to be expected, and deserved.

"My relationship with Safira changed my life. I understood happiness. We brought children into the world. It was a brief, yet wonderful moment in my mortal life. And then one foolish decision ruined everything."

SIXTY-FIVE

"IT WAS MY THIRTIETH year. And I was on my way back to Safira after winning a brutal battle over the Israelites. We happened by a small contingent of Israelites doing a poor job of hiding, and I realized the group was half made up of soldiers and half of holy men. You have to understand that we lived in a superstitious time, and the Israelites always carried with them the golden box we all know as The Ark of the Covenant," Priest looked around as he uttered the words. A few rolled their eyes or scoffed at his inclusion of the mythical box in his story, but the rest were either shocked or awed.

"For years I had witnessed the luck that the box bestowed upon the Israelites when they took it into battle. Our people feared and respected its power as much as or more than the Israelites. But I knew without the box, our enemies would fall more easily, and I hoped that ownership of the box would give us the same luck it had bestowed upon our enemies. So I did what any logical commander would do in the same situation. My men and I slaughtered the group and took the box to fully break the spirit of our enemies. We took it all the way back to Ashdod, singing over our decisive victories. I'm sure you all know the story. Saint pounded the Bible into your minds from the time you could read," he glanced at Saint who was too shocked to be amused by the jab.

"We have set the Israelites' box at the feet of our most high god, Dagon!" Ahuzzan roared to the crowd that had gathered in front of the temple. The people cheered wildly, some dancing or singing or jumping. The city's leaders were even joining in the revelries. Ahuzzan's men were hugged and kissed, greeted as the city's champions. The people knew of the secret power the box held for the Israelites in battle. Perhaps there was a way to destroy the box, a way to bring peace to the warring nations once and for all.

Safira raced toward him, and his thoughts drifted away with the wind that rushed past him as she jumped into his arms.

"My husband is celebrated by our whole nation. What an honor you have brought upon our home," she marveled before kissing him, holding his head firmly to her lips. "Your children have missed you as well." His son and daughter raced to him in a thinly-veiled competition which his son—who was three full years older than his sister—won without difficulty. He hugged them both while whispering a gentle warning to respect his sister in his son's ear. Ahuzzan still lived for the battlefield. But he lived, in equal measure, to hold his wife and children in his arms at night. It was a constantly vacillating pendulum. If he was at home, he wished for the battlefield. If he was away on the battlefield, he wished to be at home with his family. The divide plagued him, but he had learned to embrace the duality of his life by means of killing on the battlefield or enjoying his wife's body at home.

That night, the ground shook violently as pots shattered in their home. Ahuzzan and Safira clung to one another in their bed, the commotion waking them from their slumber. Ahuzzan's heart beat thunderously as he covered his wife's head to protect her from the dust falling from their roof. The disturbance lasted only a short time, but the moments following were filled with screams and cries for help from beyond the walls of his home.

"What do you think has happened? We should see if anyone needs aid," Safira stood, dressing quickly.

"Wait here. I will check to see if something can be done. Make sure the children are all right." Ahuzzan kissed her and walked out into the night. He could see that none of the homes were damaged nearby, so he continued toward the center of the city. There were people awake everywhere, some crying, some arguing about what the earthquake meant, and others seemingly asleep while standing in the open air.

Gusts of wind rushed through the city, chilling his bones and setting his nerves on edge. The wind blew so fiercely at times that it sounded as if a woman was howling in pain. As Ahuzzan glanced around, he saw that everyone sensed what he felt as well.

"He is angry! Dagon is angry with us!" a priest ran by him, yelling to no one in particular. Ahuzzan felt his feet sprinting in the direction of the temple.

He charged in, and shock ripped through his entire body. Dagon's statue lay face down in front of the golden box. As a child, he and his ten closest friends had sneaked into the temple on numerous occasions to climb the stone statue of the city's most high god. They had hung from its arms, pushed against it, dared each other to try to push it over. But they would have had equal success had they attempted to push a mountain onto its side. He regarded the felled statue incredulously.

"We must set it upright before the people see what has happened. It is one thing for them to *know*, it is entirely another for them to see Dagon prostrate with their own eyes," the high priest announced.

It took more than fifty men to put the statue back upright—a fact that set everyone on edge. *How could an earthquake knock him over?*

The priests and city leaders assured the crowds that had gathered outside the temple that the earthquake had been powerful enough to knock over the statue and that the people had no reason to be afraid.

"We must move the box out of the temple. Dagon is displeased. He does not like this Israelite god, and we would do well to heed the warning before Dagon removes his blessings from our land," one of the temple priest's argued the next morning. The city leaders and priests had joined together to decide whether anything should be done about the previous night's incident.

"We need to show our people that we are not afraid of this little box. Our gods are more powerful than the gods of our enemies. I do not see why a single earthquake should strike fear into our city. It is nothing!" another priest grew agitated over the conversation.

"For now, it will stay where it is," the lord of Ashdod announced with finality. He was responsible for the city, and his word was final. Ahuzzan turned to leave the temple and the high priest of Dagon grabbed his arm forcefully—almost painfully. Ahuzzan whipped his head to make eye contact with the man, unsure of how to properly react to the aggression.

"You were a fool to bring such a thing to this place," the man spoke without looking into Ahuzzan's eyes. It was as if the high priest was not himself—almost as if someone else spoke the words through his mouth. "Take the ark, return it to the Israelites, and save yourself from the repercussions of what will come next."

Ahuzzan watched the man's gaze come into focus as he loosened his hand and turned a questioning eye to Ahuzzan. "Did you ask me something?" the high priest wanted to know.

Ahuzzan shook his head and left immediately, returning to Safira and his children, wondering what the warning meant. He barely spoke a word the rest of the day.

That night, Ahuzzan was awakened by a soldier calling to him from the front room of his home. He jumped up, dressing as he moved toward the door.

"What has happened?" he commanded from the young soldier. But the boy simply stared up at him, fear whirling behind his eyes. "Where am I going?" Ahuzzan asked, snapping the boy from his inactivity.

"To the temple, commander," the boy said, turning to exit.

Ahuzzan sprinted toward the temple without waiting for the boy, and when he entered, the atmosphere was nothing shy of chaotic. His mouth hung open as he gawked at Dagon's statue. There had been no earthquake. There had been no intruders into the city. But there Dagon lay, prostrate, his head and hands severed from the rest of his body as if they had been cut by vinegar ropes. The break was not jagged as if the statue had fallen and the head and hands removed by the force of the impact. They were *cut off,* deliberately.

"How is this possible?" Ahuzzan breathed, his heart racing violently in his chest.

"We sat awake, praying all night. Ten of us were here when it happened. It was as if the statue was pushed over, and the head and hands were *removed* with a popping sound. We saw no one there, but we all know this was the work of some unseen force. It is *you* who brought the ark into our sacred temple, Ahuzzan," the high priest narrowed his eyes.

Ahuzzan would not take responsibility for the incident. He had been asleep in his bed, and the priests must have been drugged with a potent incense.

"I do not know why you all look so terrified. This is only a box that creates false confidence and fear. Soldiers fight more bravely when it goes into battle with them because they believe it will help them win. Enemies fear those victories, and so they fear what is contained within. But can you not see, it is only an artifice? A contrivance of the mind. I do not fear such things, and I will show you—neither should you." He walked purposefully to the box. Even he had allowed himself to fear it, but he could not show any sign of weakness now. He grabbed the top of the box and pushed the heavy lid aside so he could look at the contents within. But the flash of light that emerged from the inside blinded him, and the screams of those surrounding him faded to silence.

SIXTY-SIX

PRIEST BLINKED BACK to the present. The memory of that moment was so intense, he could still feel the searing heat on his skin, the absolute silence painful in his ears, and the white blinding light against his eyes.

"I had not known utter uselessness in my life until that moment," he whispered. The suspense of what came next was palpable in the air. His sons and grandsons looked on with intense curiosity in their gazes, breath held for what was to follow.

"I was paralyzed, blinded, and in pain so intense I wished I could wretch. I do not know how long I stayed suspended in that moment, but it felt like an eternity. Then my fear of never being free from that place morphed into a fear I dare not put into words. One moment I was alone for an eternity, then in the next moment there was a voice so powerful I thought my ears might deafen to all sound."

"Ahuzzan," a voice boomed around him. It was so loud, it hurt even the skin on his feet. It was as if the sound wasn't spoken from a single place, but instead from everywhere all at once—perhaps by the air itself. *What do you want?* his mind screamed in response, though he could not respond with his own voice.

"I cautioned you to return my ark to the Israelites. But your choice not to heed my command has been your downfall and the downfall of your people. Even your god knew to bow to my glory, but you could not see. I knew you would not, and yet I still hoped. You stole my ark, placed it in an unholy temple, and acted with such brazenness that you not only touched it with your bare hands, but also gazed within at contents not meant for any but those cleansed from all sin. You, Ahuzzan, must now feel the fullness of my anger."

If Ahuzzan could have moved, his body would have been convulsing with tremors. The spoken words held the power to physically convey their meaning, and he felt the fear and desperation of a man who wished to go back in time and change every action. No god had ever held a power over him. He had not given credence to the fanciful words of the temple priests and the religious sects who yelled their doctrines in the streets for all to hear. The only god he had ever known was the power of the sword, the strength of the physically able over the weak. He had worshiped the battlefield—the rush of looking mortality in the face and snuffing it out, the pounding of his heart after a victory, the feeling of looking down over the bodies of one's defeated enemies. That was his god.

But *this*. This entity was something else entirely. He was, in every sense, overwhelmed. And he knew his mistakes would be so great in number by the account of this entity, his punishment would be unbearable.

"I curse you, Ahuzzan," the voice began, and the pain consuming Ahuzzan's body somehow intensified. He thought he would die before the entity continued, but he was not so lucky.

"You stole from the Almighty One. You took a precious gift meant only for my chosen people. You disobeyed my command to set right your offenses. And in arrogance, you deigned to look upon my holiness. This is as you deserve.

"Because of your actions, I curse you with unending life. You will survive everyone around you. You will find no peace among mortals. You will be despised by all men. And though you may seek to end your life, no attempt shall succeed. Because I am holy and you opened my ark in an unholy place, you have unleashed a plague upon the earth that will last for all time. By your hands, millions upon millions will know death while you stand by, unable to help, unable to change the course, condemned to life. Wherever you set your eyes, death will soon follow. You will run from my glory, try to hide from my wrath, but I will always know where you are and where you are going. You will know friendship only once. And you will know love for one fleeting moment. You will remember the feelings of mortality for a second in endless time. I will give you sons who will share your same fate, and they will know the loneliness and desperation you feel. You will carry a brand upon your chest that will mark you as cursed for all time. And only when I am satisfied with your time on earth will your life come to an end. You will be the last remnant of my true wrath— the only human on earth incapable of redemption. This is the word of The Lord."

Priest's chest heaved in pain as he recited the words that plagued his nightmares so often. His body was covered in the familiar sweat that broke out upon his skin whenever he remembered that voice. He looked up at those in the room, at every set of eyes that scrutinized his words and thought over their meaning. Never before had his children known of his offenses against the earth, yet in speaking the words aloud, he felt lighter, freer. The only person he had shared the story with before this day was his beloved Basina. And she had not judged him for his actions, but instead supported him, loved him, cared for him. *Her love was worth all the pain.* He smiled, remembering the details of her beautiful face. Someone cleared their throat, breaking the silence that had rested peacefully in the chamber for the past several minutes while everyone digested the information he had shared.

"I think we should take a break for lunch, then return to hear the rest," Sergius announced in a shaky voice.

Priest remained seated as everyone exited the chamber quietly. He knew it might be some time before they could truly grasp the history he had finally revealed.

"You should join us for lunch," Caterina approached him with a sadness in her eyes. "Your sons may have questions. And if this is your last meal with your family, I think they may regret your absence in the future. Please," she held out a hand, and he could not refuse her. He took it gently between his own and stood.

"I am so grateful I was able to have an immortal daughter, even if you are not my blood. I am sorry for any grief I caused you. I believed I did everything in the name of keeping our Family's secrets and in keeping the balance in the world. But I am cursed. Unredeemable. Unforgivable. And if I'm being honest, I felt that if I had to live without Basina, others should be forced to know the pain of losing their loved ones as well. Forty-two thousand three hundred twenty-eight lives in total. Though I think Basina might have even deserved more from me," he looked her squarely in the eyes to gage her reaction to the figure.

Caterina only nodded and took his arm, silently contemplating his words as they joined the family in the great hall for one final meal. He had always liked her. She had a bit of Basina's fire concealed behind her sweet face—though he thought Caterina hid her darker side a little better than Basina.

The room fell silent as Priest made his way to the head of the table and sat in his place for the final time. He could not help but reminisce about the conversations that had taken place over the very table. Tales of contracts, jokes at the expense of brothers and cousins, tears over lost loved ones, and plans for a future he no longer shared. A smile crept over his face, and he could not help the words that came from his mouth next.

"I am proud that you are my children," he said as he glanced at the family surrounding him. No one else spoke for the remainder of the meal, but he noticed two or three of his family wipe tears discreetly from their cheeks.

SIXTY-SEVEN

WITH ONLY THE remainder of his father's story to be told and no trial left to adjudicate, Sergius took a seat between Gregorius and Thomas when they returned to the chamber. His mind was overwhelmed with the onslaught of information they had received, and he wished he had recorded his father's words so none of their history was forgotten. *I will write it all down later,* he decided as his father picked up the story where he had left off.

"When I awoke, I was buried some fifteen feet under the ground, in a mass grave of those who had died from the plague while I was... wherever I went. The guards told me I had been dead, everyone who saw me cursed me or thought me a ghost, and I was sent away from Ashdod immediately. Most of the city died in the plague that was unleashed when I opened the ark. My wife and children were among the first. Only my sister survived, and she hated the sight of me. Everyone knew it was I that had brought the plague upon our people, and I left in shame.

"My life was nomadic in the beginning. I attempted to hire myself as a mercenary, but people suspected I was a spy. Assyria was the first nation in which I remained for any length of time. I served sixteen kings, either on the battlefield or in the palace at Kalhu. My time there prepared me for many future endeavors, including when I served Emperor Justinian in Constantinople." Sergius watched his father and uncle exchange a look, and understanding shook him in his core.

"I had been roaming the lands for a time, and I could not stand the peace of a normal life, so I went to the Roman army and climbed the ranks until the nephew of Emperor Justin took notice of the rumors of an un-killable soldier and brought me to the palace to serve as the head of the palace guardians and as his personal assassin. When his uncle died..."

Saint cleared his throat loudly. "You mean when you murdered him?" he interjected, unamused.

"Very well. When I murdered Emperor Justin so his nephew could take his rightful place as the Emperor, *Saint* Justinian—as some of his more loyal subjects called him—kept me by his side or in command of his legions. When plague struck Constantinople, I selfishly begged God for Justinian's life. He had died, just as Caterina died. But he came back, immortal like me, and he's been stuck with me ever since." Priest and Saint exchanged a nod as Felix spoke up.

"*You* are Emperor Justinian? The last true emperor of the Roman Empire? That is you," Felix asked what everyone wanted to know, but his questions came out more like statements than actual questions requiring a response. Saint spread his hands and turned in a circle.

"In the flesh. I am Emperor Justinian. And your father is the great Belisarius," he looked at Priest out of the corner of his eye while conversation erupted throughout the chamber. Sergius nearly choked on that bit of information. Justinian was shocking, but Belisarius's fall at the hands of an unfaithful wife did not match with the idea he had of his father.

"My wife was forced on me by the empress, no thanks to this bastard. And I knew from the beginning that she was a conniving wench. They forced me to stay with her and play the role of idiot cuckold. I have still not forgiven you for that, brother," Priest raised an eyebrow at Saint, but the emperor only shrugged.

"I was the emperor. You served me however I chose. Oh, to have life back in its proper order," Saint looked away from Priest and leaned on the opposite armrest of his chair, obviously ready to move on.

"We 'died' after Saint had lived long enough to get his affairs in order, and we chose to settle in Rome. It was there I met your mother," he was barely able to whisper the last sentence. But Sergius had wanted to know their story for centuries, and it took all his willpower not to press his father to continue without delay.

"When I found her, I thought she was already dead. She had been stolen when she was nine years old from her family in Hispania, raised to be a whore, and then nearly beaten to death by her master because she was too sick to work after a forced abortion. I saw him kicking her tiny body, and my vision went red," he paused.

"I peeled the skin from his body, cut off fingers and toes. I waited for him to be conscious each time I moved to a new body part. But I saved the best for last. I cut off his genitals and watched him bleed to death. Your mother fought against death and endured more than most men I had fought beside. She was the most powerful tiny creature I had ever met. She was only fifteen, but her life experiences had been such that I found I could relate to her on every level. I was scared to death to get close to her," he smiled, and Sergius couldn't help but imagine the two of them together.

"It was uncomfortable on a level you could not imagine," Saint interjected with a short burst of laughter. "Watching them tiptoe around each other and pretend there was nothing between them was infuriating."

"Hush, brother," Priest waved a hand at Saint and continued his story. "She had told me she wanted to be with me, and I thought it would not be possible were she to know who I truly was. But she had been conscious when I ripped her master apart. She had seen me in one of my darkest moments. And it was that moment she fell in love with me. She was my match in every way," he wiped a stray tear from his cheek, and Sergius gawked. He could not think of another moment when he had witnessed his father crying. It seemed everyone in the chamber was as dumbstruck as he, some getting emotional from the sight. Caterina sniffled on the other side of Thomas, and Thomas held her close. *What an incredible day this has been,* Sergius marveled.

"After your mother died, I lived as a mercenary. I set a goal for how many deaths I had to deal before I could return to you boys, though I had hoped and prayed you would not be immortal. I do not know why I hoped such a thing— every other part of the curse had come to fruition. But still, I hoped. I never wanted this life for you. It is too demanding, too intolerable, and too heartbreaking. But alas, you were all waiting, my army of assassins," Priest sighed, closing the book on his story once and for all.

Sergius stood and walked to the front of the room. He didn't know how to proceed. He did not want his uncle or father's deaths on anyone else's hands. As the eldest, he would perform the kills.

"Do you have a preference?" Sergius asked both men, barely able to speak the words.

His father stood and grasped his shoulders, giving him a single nod. "Any clean and quick death by a sword will do. Just make sure I'm really dead," he smiled tightly.

"Tonic and poison, please. I do not wish to be conscious," Saint grumbled, his eyes never leaving the ground in front of his chair.

"Claudius, did you bring it?" Sergius asked. They had suspected Saint would prefer that method of death.

"But I brought my own," Saint held up two small vials of clear liquid, and Claudius shook his head as he brought over the poison he had prepared.

"Uncle, if you think we're going to let you skirt your own death by using a non-lethal concoction, you are sorely mistaken," Claudius took Saint's vials and pushed his own into Saint's empty hand. Their uncle did not look amused. But he drank both quickly and without protestation. As the tonic took effect, he glanced around the room with a furrowed brow.

"I hope you all know I am not happy about this. I raised you, and became your confidant and adviser. This is an act of betrayal," Saint groaned as he grew groggy with sleep.

Thank you's were spoken from a chorus of voices around the room. Saint had been as close a confidant and friend as anyone could have asked for. He would be mourned over the coming weeks and months, despite his involvement in the contracts.

"We know, uncle. Thank you for your guidance," Sergius nodded, doing his best to comfort Saint as he passed painlessly into an endless sleep. The moment felt surreal and wrong. Sergius began to question their decision, but his father stepped forward and smiled at him.

Mattia watched Sergius as he struggled to hold himself together. Priest was at peace with his end—Mattia had watched the calm that had settled over his grandfather's face the moment they had agreed to end his life the day before. The same peace was nowhere to be found in Sergius's expression. He looked as if he might pass out any moment.

"Please tell me it is finally my turn to leave this life," Priest sighed, his face one of absolute serenity.

"That it is," Sergius struggled to form even that sentence.

Priest knelt facing all of his sons while Caterina and Lissie openly wept, holding each other, inconsolably. Priest took his time looking at each person in the room, returning nods with anyone who first gave him the acknowledgment. He looked up at Sergius when he was finished and gave a quick nod that he was ready. He turned his face to the floor in front of his knees and waited for the end.

This could not happen as it was happening. If Sergius was the one to take Priest's life, he would relive the guilt every night. Mattia had to stop it.

"Father," Mattia leaned over and nudged his father's shoulder. Thomas turned to look at him, understanding the anxiety in Mattia's expression without explanation.

"Sergius," Thomas called out, standing and making his way to the front of the room. "You cannot do this," he insisted as he clasped Sergius on the shoulder. "Everyone knows I'm much better with a sword. I think Priest has suffered enough without you making a mess of things," Thomas grinned sadly as he watched Sergius's tears spill onto his cheeks. Thomas grabbed the sword out of his brother's unmoving hands and moved into position.

"Thank you, Thomas," Priest whispered, his eyes still fixed on the ground.

Mattia reached over to wrap his arms around both his fiancée and mother as they wept. Lissie buried her head into his shoulder, unwilling to watch.

Thomas lifted the sword over Priest's neck and then breathed deeply.

"We stand united," Thomas began. Mattia listened as his brothers, cousins, nephews, and uncles joined in the chorus around him. The beautiful words echoing off the walls of the stone chamber one last time. "Family of immortals. Plagued by life. Cursed by the hand of God. We pledge our lives to the Family, the Priest," Thomas's sword slid into his father's spine and down into his heart as he said the word, "and to the Saint." He pulled the sword out, and everyone watched as Priest's breathing slowed to a stop and his eyes closed as his heart gave one final thump.

Thomas staggered backwards, and Sergius's body dropped to his knees, burying his head in his hands as he wept. The room was quiet as Thomas took a handkerchief from his pocket and cleaned the blood off the sword, sheathing it and setting it on the ground next to Priest's body. Only the sounds of jagged breathing and crying cut through the silence in the room. Mattia kept his eyes fixed on the pool of blood under his grandfather's body, unable to process everything that had taken place—not sure if he truly wanted to.

The Family had seen thousands upon thousands of deaths over the centuries. They had dealt them without emotion or hesitation. But this death— the death of their leader, father, grandfather, and the first immortal—was something entirely different.

After he began thinking coherent thoughts—he wasn't sure if it had been minutes or hours—Mattia looked around and found nearly every set of eyes fixed on his father. Thomas stood, dumbfounded, clearly unsure of what to say or do. Mattia didn't know if he should try to comfort his family or let them grieve in silence. But he could not bear the quiet any longer, and spoke the phrase that had been repeating in his head since Priest's lifeless body had collapsed to the ground.

"What do we do now?"

SIXTY-EIGHT

Castello San Romolo, One month later

THOMAS AND HIS brothers sat at the head of the table in the great hall as the rest of the family watched expectantly. They had given everyone one month to grieve, celebrate, or ponder—whichever each individual needed. But it was time to make a decision.

"As you all know, we have come together once more to determine the future of this family. We must each choose our own path—whether that be the path Priest and Saint set before us or something entirely new. We want to hear from anyone with an opinion, and we want you to be honest. We would prefer that everyone would come to an agreement, but we will not dictate your futures in the way father dictated our past. It is as simple as that. Thomas will speak first," Sergius finished.

Thomas nodded to his eldest brother before speaking. He had been practicing the speech for days, and he hoped he could inspire some of the undecided family members to consider all their options in life.

"First, I have to say this. You know that I will support you all in any decision you make, even if I do not fully agree with or understand it. That being said, our lives were controlled from the moment we entered this world. We had no choice in what we became—and those who tried to forge a new path were either murdered or the victims of attempted murder. Do not remain on the same path merely out of habit or because of the deep-seated fear of what happened to others who chose a different path. No one here will judge you for choosing a new life. Caterina and I have decided to stay in Tuscany, but we are choosing to reject the idea of continuing in Priest's footsteps. We are planning to purchase some vineyards throughout Italy to create jobs for some of the villages that are on the verge of disappearing. And we will need partners in this enterprise, so we open our arms to any of you who wish to join us," he breathed deeply as he finished, hoping the idea would spark some interest among the others. There were so many opportunities to do good in the world, one needed only to reach out and seize them. Antonio stood to speak next.

"I have created a plan with Alexander and two of our sons. We are setting up a foundation to fund the improvement of living conditions and the creation of job training and employment opportunities in the refugee camps in Syria, Turkey, and Jordan. We will not only use our own money, but will host fundraisers all around the world to show the investment opportunities and benefits of job training and creation within the regions. Right now, there are only four of us who have made the initial plan, but for our success to be attainable, we need at least ten to pool our resources. Talk to me after the meeting if you're interested," Antonio sat back down, and Thomas could not have been more proud. He had only known that Antonio intended to work with refugees. This plan reached far beyond what he could have imagined. Claudius spoke up next.

"I intend to create a private security group. We will offer protection for groups entering high risk areas for both work and leisure. I know you are all qualified," he guffawed once. "So if any of you want part-time work, let me know, and whenever a job becomes available, you'll get a call."

A glimmer of hope crept up Thomas's spine. He knew many of Claudius's sons and grandsons would follow his lead. Thomas started doing a mental tally of how many were already headed down a new path. Demetrius stood up with a scowl on his face.

"I am retiring for now. I have no idea what I will do or where I will go, but I have plans to discover a remote beach I haven't yet visited, do some scuba diving, and drink a lot of colorful drinks with tiny umbrellas. None of you are invited along. I'm sick of you lot," Demetrius kept a straight face, but the whole room roared in laughter in response.

"Okay, okay. Calm down," Paulus waited as the final guffaws died out.

"It seems my brothers have already walked away. I thought we had intended to discuss the future of the Family, not present a multitude of other job opportunities to try to pull everyone away peacefully," Paulus shook his head sadly. "Just because father and uncle made horrible mistakes and unwise decisions for this family, that does not dictate that if we continue, we would walk the same path. Assassins is what we truly are. We were raised to follow those steps, because that is the path we were meant to take. And I, for one, am not going to throw that away," he sat back in his chair, frustration coloring his cheeks.

"Here, here," Felix chimed in. "I'm with Paulus. I have no desire to change my path. And while I respect your decisions to live your lives freely, I feel no guilt whatsoever in continuing on my own journey. My life is what it is because of our father's influence and direction. I am not ashamed of who I am, and none of you should be either."

Thomas gulped as a rumble of low voices whispered throughout the room. Paulus and Felix were respected by everyone present, and it was possible their pleas would sway some of the men on the fence over what to do.

"What about Sergius and Gregorius? What are you going to do?" someone called from across the room.

Gregorius cleared his throat and mumbled, "I'm moving to the United States," without further explanation. Thomas wasn't sure what his brother's plans were, but he would talk to Mattia about making regular, unscheduled check-ins to be sure Gregorius was taking care of himself.

"I have decided to stay in the castle and take care of it. Of course, this home belongs to all of us, so if you choose to stay here, no one will argue," Sergius began. "But I would ask that the past of this place dies with our father and uncle. I am begging for this castle to represent the closing of one door and the opening of another. If you would like, we can take a vote on whether to leave the castle as the training grounds for those who wish to continue or to allow this place to live out its days in peace."

"Stop being so dramatic, Sergius. My home outside of Rome is big enough to act as the new headquarters. I vote that Castello San Romolo become a regular castle where we can gather for holidays and whenever else we want," Paulus rolled his eyes at the dramatic plea Sergius had put forth. "All those in favor?" Nearly everyone voted in favor. "There you go, brother. The castle is yours to tend," Paulus grinned, and Sergius nodded at the breaking of the tension between them. As first and second born, they had been at odds too many times to count, and Sergius was always grieved when there was a lack of peace between himself and any of his brothers. Sergius's expression was of pure relief.

"Remember," Sergius began, "that from here on, none of you are locked into any single decision. If you choose a path and do not enjoy it or find fulfillment in it, you have the freedom to move to another. I only want to encourage you to challenge yourselves. Seek out a path that gives you purpose and joy. Find a goal, and stop at nothing to attain it. We are immortal—use that immortality to better the world. We have a gift, and I challenge you to make a difference."

Thomas smiled at Sergius's words. They were exactly what he expected from his wise eldest brother.

"Enough of all this. I propose a toast," Sergius lifted his glass and the rest of the family followed suit. "To the incredible life we've lived and the unknown future ahead. And to us, the Family!"

"To the Family!" everyone chimed in as glasses clinked around the room.

One month later

Caterina stood in the open window and looked out over the clear Tuscan sky. The moon was so bright, and the cool wind felt nice as it blew into the bedroom. She had not been able to sleep a wink all night. After the Family went their separate ways a month earlier, she and Thomas had chosen to stay in the castle with Sergius to do some reorganization. Two of the largest rooms in the home were now vacant, and when Gregorius had decided to permanently leave Italy to reside in the United States, his and Elias's room emptied as well. A few days into the process, she had become a bit lightheaded, which was not only uncommon—it was unheard of. She chalked it up to not drinking enough water, but strange physical occurrences continued over the next few weeks. She hadn't wanted to worry Thomas, and therefore hadn't complained about the physical weakness, lightheadedness, or stomach cramps. She had been at a local shop buying some headache medicine when she spotted the pregnancy test. She put the medicine back and instead purchased a few tests.

How could I be pregnant after all this time? she pondered as she stared into the night sky. She and Thomas had tried to have more children after Mattia, but they were unable and had stopped trying after a few years. Her heart had broken in the beginning—she had adored raising her boys and had hoped to have many opportunities over her immortal life, but God had had different plans for her and Thomas's life, and she had come to accept that part of her life as complete.

She brushed a hand over her stomach—which showed no signs at all of a possible pregnancy—and marched back to the bathroom where she had left the little stick on the counter.

A plus sign. Her eyes widened as she stared at the indicator and then re-read the instructions to make sure she was reading the results correctly. "It's a plus sign," she could not keep the words inside. She ran and jumped onto the bed as Thomas shot up from his sleep.

"What? What's wrong?" Thomas yelled reflexively.

"It's a plus sign!" Caterina squealed as she jumped up and down on the bed and Thomas looked at her as if she had lost her mind.

"Caterina. I have no idea what that means," he said with his brows scrunched together.

Sergius pounded on the door, coming to make sure everything was all right.

"Everything is wonderful! It's positive!" Caterina ran to the door and threw it open, giving Sergius a big hug then returning to Thomas to give him a kiss.

Thomas put his hands on her shoulders and pushed her away from the kiss gently.

"What is positive? What is a plus sign?" he asked.

Caterina beamed as she handed him the pregnancy test. His breath caught in his chest when he realized what was in his hands.

"Truly?" he whispered, a look of joy washing over his face.

"Yes. We're going to have another baby!" she squealed as Thomas pulled her into his arms and held her tightly, showering her with kisses while she giggled.

"Congratulations," Sergius muttered as he backed quickly of the room and shut the door, knowing he would not want to witness what happened next.

SIXTY-NINE

New York City, Three months later

LISSIE HAD JUST snuggled up under a blanket with a freshly-poured glass of red wine when her phone rang.

"Hi handsome. This is a nice surprise," she answered the phone and took a sip.

"Hello back. Can you do me a favor?" he asked.

"That depends on the favor. I just got under the blanket with a glass of wine," she teased and heard Mattia's breath catch on the other end of the line. Lissie stayed quiet, knowing her fiancé's imagination was running wild. A few seconds later, he cleared his throat, shaking himself from his daydreaming.

"I just got a call from Gregorius. He's asked us to meet him at San Romolo on Friday. I need you to book us a flight and call Sergius to see if he'll pick us up when we get in."

"But you've been gone for two weeks," Lissie whined. She hated when Mattia was away for work.

"I'm taking the red-eye tomorrow night. We'll have thirty-six hours to enjoy each other's company before we jet off again. Will that suffice, my love?" his voice adorably pleading.

"I suppose," she teased as she took another sip.

"It's going to be weird," Mattia whispered after a short pause.

"What is?" Lissie worried over the trembling in his voice.

"It will be strange going back to the castle and having so few people there. I hadn't thought about it until just now," he cleared his throat. "And my mother is going to be pregnant," he huffed a sound of disbelief.

"You know these are all good changes," Lissie tried to assure him as she took another sip of her wine. The end of the era of required participation in the

Family business was, by Lissie's estimation, the best possible outcome for the world as a whole. When Priest was alive, she had made peace with the idea that the Family was assassinating to maintain the balance of good and evil in the world—even though she had always known that was a giant pile of crap. But with the Family's paths each branching in new, mostly peaceful or helpful directions, she was truly at peace with the idea of marrying Mattia and becoming an official member of the testosterone-heavy clan. "And you'll have a little brother to spoil," she tacked on.

"Yes, I know. And I have every intention of whipping him into shape. But all of that doesn't make the idea of the castle being empty any less... weird."

"I know. I'm sorry." She needed to get Mattia's mind out of the funk he was in. "I've been lonely at night," she whispered seductively. Lissie was ready for her bed to not be so cold when she climbed in each night. Mattia had been gone for two weeks installing a new security system for one of the biggest tech companies on the West Coast. He had done the consultation, shown them his plans for an increase in security for the company, and been hired on the spot. His consultations each included a demonstration of the time it took for him to personally hack into the company's security system and servers—generally the clients hired him immediately to fix the glaring weaknesses.

"I've been lonely too. I'll wake you when I get home tomorrow night," Mattia promised.

"Perfect. I'm counting the hours." She hung up and grabbed her laptop to buy their tickets to Florence. She picked up the tv remote while her computer started up. *One more viewing of* You've Got Mail *before he gets home couldn't hurt,* she smirked as she navigated to her still-favorite movie and hit play.

Mattia was glad Lissie had slept the whole ride from the airport to the castle, sprawled in the back seat of Sergius's new Range Rover. Sergius had decided to settle permanently at Castello San Romolo, selling his flats and vehicles in Moscow, Sarajevo, and Kiev. He had always preferred the Russian and Eastern European cultures and languages, so he had stayed mainly in those regions for his work. Lissie still hadn't forgiven him for selling his flat in Sarajevo—it was one of her favorite places to visit.

As they pulled onto the drive, Lissie woke up, pushing the tangled mess from her slobber-streaked cheek.

"Sorry guys. I hope I didn't snore too loudly."

"No problem, Lissie," Sergius glanced back at her. "You only kept us from being able to have a conversation. No big deal," he teased. After Lissie came into the family, Sergius had decided to become fluent in English. It had taken a while with all the other matters to attend to, but Mattia was impressed by how far he had come.

Mattia noted how many cars were parked in front of the castle and shot a questioning glance toward his uncle. Sergius shrugged and said, "Gregorius," but gave no further explanation.

Lissie opened the door before the car was in park and rushed to hug Caterina, who was sitting in a chair on the front lawn, waiting for them to arrive. Mattia heard the women chatting exuberantly together as he and Sergius grabbed the suitcases from the back of the car.

"Congratulations, mom," he smiled as he set down the bags to embrace her. "I can't believe I'm going to get to be a big brother after more than four hundred years. That's such a weird thing to say," he shook his head, still in disbelief.

The doors opened, and dozens of Mattia's cousins and nephews came out to greet them. He was genuinely happy the house was full. It only felt normal when it was full of his loud family.

"We waited for you two," Gregorius said from the door. "If everyone could come into the great hall, I want to show you what I have been working on these past months," his eyes lit with excitement—a look that gave Mattia more relief than he had realized. Everyone had been terrified for Gregorius's health after Elias's death. But Gregorius looked genuinely happy. Everyone hurried inside to figure out why Gregorius had brought them together.

"Sit down and be quiet," Gregorius barked only half-jokingly. Mattia looked around and counted more than fifty people in the room. Without the consistent training exercises and regular check-ins, Mattia had worried he wouldn't see his family as much as he liked. But here they were, only a few months after they had last been all together.

"I have always loved the sciences. This is something I kept very quiet— only Elias knew how I would research and study. But he always encouraged me to pursue that passion. So when he was gone, I thought I should honor him by doing exactly that. I have been studying our DNA for the past twenty years, trying to unlock what makes us immortal and incapable of suffering from sickness or disease. I made a few discoveries on my own over the years, but after the trial I sent proposals to some of the world's greatest disease researchers—and all of them responded positively. So I purchased a medical facility in Virginia and shared my findings. Of course, I had to be a bit vague about the antibodies in my blood, but they've signed confidentiality agreements. And I think they've grasped the idea that I'm a dangerous man to cross." The room rumbled with quiet laughter.

"My business is called the Experimental Laboratories for the Investigation of Advanced Sciences—or E. L. I. A. S. for short," Gregorius smiled and Mattia couldn't help but mirror the expression. "I plan on expanding once the first project really gets going. I'm going to do cancer research as well to see if our antibodies have any effect if introduced into a sick host. And that is why you are here. If any of you would like to invest, I'm opening the floor to you all for partial ownership. Of course, I'll remain in charge of all operations and research, but the results should be rather lucrative—or so I'm told by my market researchers. And I'm also accepting blood donations. I'm interested to see if there are any differences in the healing properties between each generation, if there are other genetic influences depending on your mother's origin or race, or if all the blood is the same. I am also interested in studying Caterina's blood specifically since she is not from our lineage. So there you have it. Let me know if you're interested or have any questions," Gregorius finished with his chest puffed proudly.

Everyone congratulated him on his new venture, and the questions began to flow. Mattia was excited to hear that there had already been interesting results with cells from people suffering auto-immune diseases like lupus and multiple sclerosis. The opportunities seemed endless. Lissie gave Mattia the "we would be crazy not to say yes" nod, and he began discussing the company's needs with Gregorius and the other interested family members.

SEVENTY

New York City, Four months later

"HEY! A REALLY intense courier delivered a box for you today," Lissie called from the shower as soon as Mattia stepped into the apartment. "He really didn't want to leave it with me. I had to show him a bank statement with both our names on it before he would let me sign for it. It was super weird."

"We don't have time for that," Mattia ran into the bathroom and Lissie stuck her head out of the shower door. "I need you to get out and help me pack the bags. We're on the next flight out," he exclaimed. "Mom started having contractions, and the midwife is on the way to the castle."

Lissie squealed, turned off the shower, and sprinted out of the bathroom, dripping wet with a towel haphazardly wrapped around her body. Mattia couldn't help but stare open-mouthed at her speedy exit. She had gone from rinsing in the shower to packing the suitcase in under a minute.

"If we forget anything, we'll just borrow from the others or buy it there," she yelled, not realizing Mattia had followed her into the room.

"Sounds good," he agreed as she nearly fell over from the scare of his unexpected nearness.

"Oh my god! Don't scare me like that!" she growled, continuing to pack as she recovered from the panic. "What time do we need to be at the airport?"

"We're probably okay to get there in an hour and a half," he handed her a stack of shirts to put into the suitcase she was leaning over.

"Okay. So we need to leave now in case of traffic. Jesus, Mattia. That's way too close for comfort. Should we take the train instead?"

"I already checked the traffic reports—everything seems clear. I'm calling a driver to pick us up in five. Go get dressed. I'll finish this," he had to physically pull her away from the suitcase and push her back toward the bathroom to get to the suitcase. "I am capable of packing our suitcases, you know," he teased.

"That's not true! Every time you pack for me, I end up with only the most uncomfortable underwear I own. That stuff is only for special occasions, okay?" She walked back in with her hair fixed and makeup on, and Mattia found himself frozen in place and incapable of thought.

"How did you do that? You were gone for a minute and walk back in here looking like a supermodel!" he marveled.

"Shut it. And don't forget this." She tossed him her makeup bag, and they zipped up the suitcases and ran out the door.

Thomas looked down at the tiny baby girl in his arms. He and Caterina hadn't even considered that they might have a little girl. No one in his family had *ever* had a daughter. *She's the first of her kind. I wonder if it's because your mommy is so special?* he marveled. Thomas's cheeks hurt from smiling for so long. Marcus and Antonio were already there, and Mattia and Lissie would arrive at any moment. Caterina had made the brothers promise not to spoil the surprise for their brother.

"Sorry we're late," Mattia and Lissie rushed into the room exchanging hugs with everyone and gushing over the baby. "What did you decide to name him?" Mattia asked as Lissie held the baby tightly.

"We decided to name her Vittoria, after my closest friend from my youth who married my brother, Giovanni. I think the name suits our little girl, don't you?" Caterina smiled as the words sank in. Mattia and Lissie gawked in silence, their eyes searching for any sign of a joke being played.

"A sister? Truly?" Mattia took the tiny bundle from Lissie and brushed Vittoria's cheek with the tip of his finger. "She's perfect."

Lissie embraced Caterina in a careful hug, worrying over her and asking about her health.

"This was not the same as the deliveries I had with the boys. I hurt after their births, but this is more intense. I think I may need to take some medicine for the pain," Caterina looked up at Thomas with worry that paled in comparison to his own. Caterina's pregnancy had not been as easy this time, and he knew that for her to ask for medicine, her pain had to be excruciating. She never let anyone fuss over her.

"Let me check what's best for your body after you've given birth, and I'll have someone drive to the pharmacy to pick it up this afternoon," Lissie pulled out her phone and began searching articles on the topic. Lissie and Caterina quietly discussed the options as Thomas joined his sons while they cooed to their baby sister and took turns holding her.

"Have you noticed anything strange with your health?" Thomas asked, hoping there wasn't a terrible, unknown side effect from this pregnancy. He was overjoyed to have a beautiful baby girl, but all he could think about was Caterina's health.

"Yes!" Antonio shouted and Vittoria's arms flailed in fright. They returned her to Caterina, and Antonio continued, "There's a new line on my forehead. At first I thought it was from sleeping the wrong way, but I've tried everything. It's there permanently." Antonio shook his head in disbelief as Mattia and Marcus made fun of his vanity. But Thomas wondered if there was truly something to the new wrinkle and if something was affecting the whole family without their knowing. Thomas left the room to make a call to Gregorius.

"Gregorius. I think there's something wrong with Caterina's health. Can I send you a blood sample to analyze? Will that tell us anything?" Thomas whispered, emotion catching in his throat.

"I have people who can analyze it to check for any abnormality. Does she have specific symptoms? Or is it a more general health concern?" Gregorius's voice went into his "work tone" immediately, his concern for Caterina evident.

"She's in more pain than she's ever been in after delivering a child. She's asking for medicine. You know how Caterina is about asking for help," Thomas groaned.

"Overnight me a sample of her blood and I'll have it analyzed as soon as possible," Gregorius said before hanging up so he could get back to work.

Thomas took a few deep breaths to calm himself before plastering a smile back onto his face and heading back into the room to be with his family.

Caterina's phone rang, waking both her and Vittoria from their post-nursing nap. It was 4:30 in the afternoon—she hadn't needed this much rest since becoming immortal. Her body wasn't healing the way it should have. She looked at the screen and her breath hitched when she saw Gregorius's name.

"Hi Gregorius," she tried to sound cheerful, but her voice sounded flat even in her own ears.

"Hello Caterina. Feeling any better?" Gregorius asked.

"I suppose a little. But not as healthy as I should at this point. It's been a full week, and I still have to take a few naps to get through the day."

"Well my people have analyzed the blood and there's nothing wrong with you. No signs of disease or anemia. No infections. All the cell counts match the levels in my blood. Of course, it's not in line with what doctors usually see, so they had to do a comparison with mine—but everything points to perfect health. I don't have any idea of why your body is taking so long to repair itself. But I'm glad there's nothing to report on our end," she could hear the hopefulness in his voice.

"Thank you for taking time out of your research and resources to do that for me. I hope you know how much we appreciate you," she said gratefully.

Vittoria started making her "I'm about to start crying" face before Caterina could say more.

"Sorry Gregorius, Vittoria is getting fussy. I have to let you go."

"No problem. I'll talk to you soon," he hung up.

Thomas and Lissie came into the room together to check on her and the baby, and she reported the good news while she changed Vittoria's diaper.

"I don't have any idea what's different this time, my dear," Thomas looked dejected. She knew he was happy with the report from Gregorius, but he hated not knowing the source of the problem.

"I know I'll be okay. Women have been giving birth for thousands of years without the benefit of healing quickly. I think we must give my body a few weeks to recover," she rested her hand on Thomas's cheek and he pulled her into a tight hug.

"I know. I just need you healthy again," he kissed her forehead and tried to change the subject. "I was thinking of taking Vittoria on her first tour of the grounds today. What do you think?"

SEVENTY-ONE

New York City, Three weeks later

MATTIA AND LISSIE walked into their apartment, completely exhausted from the past four weeks. Mattia was relieved that his mother was finally back to her normal self, but Lissie had exhausted herself taking care of Vittoria and Caterina during the month they had been at San Romolo. Lissie wouldn't let Caterina exert any unnecessary energy while her body was recovering, so she had overextended herself a little in the process. Lissie fell face down onto the couch as soon as she was in range.

"I'm going to sleep for the next week. Please order me some Thai—yellow curry. With an extra order of sticky rice. No, two extra orders. No... I don't need that much rice. Just one," Lissie's speech was slightly slurred from the sleep deprivation. She hadn't managed to sleep on the flight home either. "No, I want two," she called out as soon as he started placing the order from their favorite little place down the street.

"I already have three in the cart. If you decide you don't want both of yours, I'll eat the extra," he replied as she nodded her head. *She'll be asleep before it gets here.*

Mattia looked at the kitchen counter and realized there were dirty dishes still sitting out from the day they left for Italy. He stalked over to them, holding his breath as he plugged the sink and filled it with soap and piping hot water and submerged the mold-covered dishes. Lissie started snoring loudly as he got the cleaner from under the sink and started dousing every surface in the stuff. The whole apartment smelled like rotting food. He was afraid to open the trash can to throw away their expired food, but he powered through. By the time the buzzer rang with the food delivery, the kitchen smelled clean—or at least like cleaning spray—which was far better than the alternative.

Once the Thai food was in his hands, he noticed a small box on the floor next to the couch.

"Lissie, wake up. Food's here," he helped her sit up and handed her the sticky rice first.

"You're spoiling me. Don't you know dessert comes after dinner?" She eyed him with a knowing glance as she took a big bite and chewed slowly, enjoying every moment.

"I wish everyone could enjoy food as much as you do," Mattia said as he grabbed the little box from the floor. "What is this?"

"That's the box I had to fight that courier for the morning we left. I completely forgot about that!" The mystery of the small box brought her out of her sleepy state as she watched him cut the tape and peel open the cardboard flaps. There was an envelope resting on top of a small electronic device inside.

"What is it?" Lissie asked raptly.

"I have no idea," Mattia picked up the device and turned it over in his hands. He'd never seen anything like it—it was custom built for sure. He put it down gently in case it was meant to do some kind of harm. A warning prickled at the back of his neck as he opened the envelope, hoping there would be an explanation. As soon as he saw the handwriting, his heart dropped.

"It's from Samuel," he breathed as Lissie put her food down and moved to his side to read the note with him.

Mattia,

I left this at my safety deposit box with instructions for it to be delivered if they had not received any news from me for more than six months. So I have either forgotten to check in or I am on a long assignment or... well you get the general idea. I have been

working on this little device for the past few months. I want to see

if you can figure it out. But I'm not giving you any hints on what it

does or how you should proceed. I hope you stay stumped for at

least a few minutes. Ha! Thank you again for the private lessons—

I am truly honored you took the time to help out your favorite uncle.

Samuel

Mattia put the note down and picked up the electronic device once more, studying each side, hoping for some hint from the build. But it was a bizarre little thing. He didn't even know where to start.

"What do you think it is?" Lissie's eyes were lit with fascination.

"I have no idea. But we're going to find out."

SEVENTY-TWO

"I'VE TRIED EVERYTHING!" Lissie heard Mattia yell from the bedroom. He had barely slept for the past week, focusing only on the small electronic device from Samuel. "I think he's playing one final practical joke on me. That has to be it."

"Have you tried turning it on with an external power source?" Lissie asked, hoping to spark something in his mind that would finally be the key to unlocking the puzzle.

"Of course. And I've tried connecting it with exposed wires. And nothing works," he groaned, becoming increasingly frustrated. He skulked into the living room and plopped down next to her on the couch. "There's a camera lens right here, but it doesn't seem to be recording anything. There isn't a place for any power input or ports for transferring information. If I pry it open, I'll break it—but maybe he knew that's what I would end up doing. Should I just pry it open?"

"There's a camera?" Lissie narrowed her eyes as her mind began forming a hypothesis.

"Yeah, right here," he held it out and showed her.

"Could that be, like, scanning for something? Is it possible that it's something like face recognition?" she wondered aloud.

"I thought about that, but I've had my face shoved in it for a week, and nothing. I tried finger prints, voice commands, hand signals we did on missions, everything. Here, you try," he handed it over, but nothing happened. She set it on the coffee table and stared at it until a thought entered her mind. She started to pull Mattia's shirt off.

"I mean, this will obviously help my mood, but how did we get from there to here?" he began helping her take off his shirt and pulled her into a kiss. She pushed him away, ignoring his flirting entirely, and held the camera up to his tattoo. It was the only thing she could think of that they hadn't tried yet. The device did nothing and she set it back down, disappointed.

"Great idea. I hadn't thought of that, but I think I might have to break it open," Mattia sighed as his phone beeped with a new text message. He glanced at it and then his eyes connected with Lissie's excitedly. He began to read.

"Congratulations. I knew you would figure that out. Here are some coordinates to your next puzzle. Take the device along. It may come in handy. - Samuel"

"Ohhh!" Lissie's voice squeaked as she grabbed the phone to read the message for herself. "This is so exciting!"

Mattia's face was a mix of emotions, and Lissie gave him a small squeeze.

"I knew Samuel was fun from all the stories you told me, but this is amazing. Even now, he's making our lives more exciting," she kissed his cheek.

"Exciting. all right. Let's see where we're heading."

Three days later, they were in Southern California driving to a bank located just north of the Mexican border. Samuel hadn't provided any details about what they were supposed to do once they arrived at the coordinates, and Mattia didn't know if he should be walking through the front door or hacking into the bank's security system. Samuel had planned the little scavenger hunt—and Mattia felt like his uncle had taken great joy in preparing clues that would leave Mattia squirming in his seat.

Lissie had given Mattia three hours to survey the area around the bank and check the security cameras inside. She announced they had waited long enough to walk into the building by opening the car door and marching toward the bank's front doors. Mattia only took a few seconds to recover from the shock, and he was by her side by the time her hand began to reach for the door. She glanced sideways at him as he swatted her hand away from the door and opened it for her. She smiled widely, stepping inside, and he took one deep breath before following behind her.

Mattia glanced around the bank and found a woman smiling up at him from one of the desks in the "Personal Banking" area of the branch. Mattia flashed her a dazzling smile as he grabbed Lissie's hand and walked over to the woman.

"What can I do for you today, Mr...." the banker whose name tag said "Vicki" waited for him to give her his last name.

"Trapani," he thrust out his hand, unsure of why he had pulled out that particular surname in the moment. It was the one he had used during his time with Anamaria—and he hadn't used the name since. *Weird,* he shook his head a little, trying to focus on the present problem. What should he say to Vicki?

"We're having a bit of a bizarre problem, Vicki," Lissie spoke up as she plopped down into one of the chairs across from Vicki. "My fiancé's uncle sent us here to get something without an account number or safety deposit box key or even the name his account is under. We really don't know what to do."

"Hmm. That sounds like a problem I can't fix," Vicki worried. "Let me grab our branch manager and see if he has any ideas," she stood and headed toward the office with a wary look on her face.

"I don't see how this is going to get us anywhere," Mattia whispered in frustration. He wasn't accustomed to lacking a solid plan.

"I agree. But we have to start somewhere." Lissie ran her hands through his hair, and he felt his heart rate calm a little.

"Hello, Mr. Trapani," the branch manager said as he approached. "I'm Joseph Gonzales. It sounds like you're in a tricky situation. Do you want to come with me into my office?"

Mattia and Lissie followed the man back to his office. He was a short man, probably in his late sixties, with a healthy physique. Though it was nearly imperceptible, there was a hint of a Spanish accent peppered into his pronunciation of certain vowels. He kept glancing at Mattia and Lissie with suspicion clearly showing in his eyes, and Mattia wondered whether the man might call the cops to arrest him and Lissie.

Mr. Gonzales closed the door to his office as soon as they were inside the room, turning toward them with an odd expression on his face.

"Your uncle's name?" he asked, his brows scrunched together.

"Samuel," Mattia answered, not sure of what other information to give to the man. The manager stared down at his desk and traced a finger along the edge of the top drawer.

"Is he dead?" Mr. Gonzales asked quietly.

Lissie squeezed Mattia's hand as a jolt of excitement ran up Mattia's spine. He sat up straighter and leaned toward Mr. Gonzales.

"He is," Mattia answered, scrutinizing the pained expression that flashed over Mr. Gonzales's face.

"Did you bring the box with you?" the man asked after a short pause.

"Yes, I have it," Lissie answered, pulling the box from her purse and setting it on the desk.

"I'm sorry," Mattia's curiosity was peaked. "How did you know my uncle?"

"I've been his investment banker for a number of years. I am sorry we won't get to continue our work together."

Mattia thought Mr. Gonzales's choice of words was odd, but he was more interested in what Mr. Gonzales would do with the box.

Mr. Gonzales unlocked a drawer and dug around for a moment before pulling out a flat, square piece of plastic the same size as the base of the box. Mattia watched in fascination as the man set the box on top of the plastic with the camera facing Mattia.

"Use your key to activate it," Mr. Gonzales prompted him. Mattia pulled his shirt up and aligned his tattoo with the camera. The box began to click open, and as it unfurled on the table, Mattia saw a note and a key secured to the inside walls of the box. He grabbed the note and began to read.

Congratulations! You've reached the next step in this little game. I have a feeling this one was a bit frustrating. I'm laughing just thinking about you trying to decide if you were supposed to walk into the bank or hack the security system or look for tunnels underneath. Ha! This is rather fun for me—I'm not ashamed to admit it. Use the key to get into my safety deposit box. There will be more instructions inside. And take care of the box. You'll need it soon.

Samuel

"It's not here," Mr. Gonzales spoke up. "His safety deposit box is in Portland. He thought it was best to keep the box at one of the branches closer to his home."

"His home?" Mattia wondered over the man's words. Samuel hadn't owned a home on the west coast. The closest home he could remember Samuel owning was in Mexico City—but he had sold it in the 1960s and moved back to Europe.

"I thought you knew," Mr. Gonzales's expression was one of surprise and confusion. "Perhaps it's part of his game."

"I suppose that's possible," Mattia muttered more to himself than to the man sitting across the desk from him. *A home in Oregon? When would he have purchased that? Maybe it's not really a home.*

"Here's the address of the bank and a note from me about the situation. I put my office number here in case the branch needs verification. Samuel used the last name 'Clark' on his paperwork for the bank up there. Feel free to call if you have questions once you've reached your destination. And I'm sorry for your loss. Samuel was a great man," Mr. Gonzales held out his hand and Mattia shook it, thanking him for his help while his thoughts swirled over the various unknowns that had presented themselves in the past half hour. Had Samuel maintained a life Mattia had not known about?

SEVENTY-THREE

San Diego, California

LISSIE FELT Mattia toss and turn in bed next to her. Her own mind was restless from the implication that Samuel had lived a life not even Mattia knew about, and it was clear Mattia would not find sleep any time soon.

She reached over and turned the lamp on, illuminating the guest room of one of Mattia's cousin's apartments—though she couldn't remember which cousin. The proximity to the San Diego airport was the only real benefit to staying there. The constant noise of the planes taking off and landing was adding to the sleeplessness. After leaving the bank, they had booked seats on the next available flight to Portland—which left at 6:00 the next morning. They would have to be at the airport in a few hours, so the sleep wouldn't be quality even if they managed to get in an hour or so.

She sat up and began running her fingers through Mattia's hair. He looked up at her, his eyes half-shut as they adjusted to the light.

"I don't know what to think, Lissie. He told me everything. He was my best friend. I can't believe he would hide a home from me. And did you catch the way Mr. Gonzales said they worked together? It didn't sound like he meant investment banking. It all feels wrong," he rubbed his eyes roughly.

Lissie pulled him closer and held him tightly. She didn't know what to say—her thoughts mirrored Mattia's exactly. She stared at Mattia's dark brown, wavy hair as her fingers brushed the thick locks to the side.

"What is that?" she mumbled, leaning down to look more closely at something strange in Mattia's hair.

"What is what?" Mattia glanced up at her.

She grabbed the lamp off the side table and pulled Mattia's head closer to the light.

"Oww! What are you doing Lissie?" Mattia yelped.

"Hush and hold still," she commanded as she pushed a few pieces of his hair aside, searching for the odd strand she had seen before. "There you are." She yanked the short piece from Mattia's head as he recoiled from her with an angry glare.

"What the hell, Liss?" he rubbed his head where she had yanked out the thick hair.

She inspected it closely, confirming what she thought she'd seen before.

"This is white. You have a white hair."

He slid closer and grabbed the hair from her fingers, inspecting as she watched the confusion in his eyes grow more pronounced.

"This is a white hair from my head," he muttered with a tone that matched the look in his eyes. He grabbed his phone and called his brother. A few short seconds later, Antonio's face popped up on the screen.

"What are you two lovebirds doing? And where are you right now? That doesn't look like your flat," Antonio asked. Mattia didn't bother answering the questions before diving into his reason for the call.

"Were you serious about that wrinkle on your forehead?" Mattia asked, his voice lacking the normal humor it held when he spoke about Antonio's phantom wrinkle.

"Yeah of course. Look right here," Antonio held the phone up to his forehead and pointed—despite the fact that Lissie and Mattia had seen the aforementioned wrinkle in person a few weeks earlier. "Why?"

"Can you see this?" Mattia held up the white hair to the camera.

"Not really. What is it?" Antonio leaned in and squinted at the screen.

"Lissie just found it in my hair. It's white," Mattia said with a scowl on his face.

Antonio's expression transformed into horror, then he took off toward his bathroom. The phone ended up on the counter, the camera pointed upward as ran his hands through his hair, searching for the white invaders.

Lissie held back a giggle at Antonio's distress. He picked up the phone and pointed it at his temple.

"Two on the left side and three on the right. Oh my god. I have white hair!" Antonio moaned. "Did you find more?"

"I only have the one for now. Will you call Marcus and find out if he's noticed the same?"

"Yeah, I'll call you back in a few minutes," Antonio agreed as the call ended.

Mattia looked up at Lissie with a bewildered expression.

"What does that mean?" Lissie's mind started to spin as Mattia stared off at nothing-in-particular for a long moment. He grabbed his phone, shot a quick text to Gregorius, and put his phone down, resuming his silent stare into nothingness. A few seconds later his phone rang.

"Hello uncle. I hope I didn't wake you, but I need to know if you did any tests on your blood before Priest died?"

Lissie wanted to hear whatever Gregorius was saying. She reached over and hit the "speaker" button while Mattia tried to listen.

"I only started testing the differences after your mother's long recovery from the birth. I hadn't thought to test the blood from before Priest's death. I was testing Caterina's blood against my own—and of course the results were the same. But fortunately I had a few vials of blood preserved from before the trial. It's incredible really. The red blood cells from before instantly began repairing themselves if any damage was inflicted. The red blood cells I've been testing since then don't repair themselves—they simply die like any other person's blood cells. All the antibodies in my blood are still there—my resistance to disease and infection is exactly the same. But it seems my rate of healing—aside from being immune to infection—is exactly the same as a normal person's now. Did you encounter something similar?" Gregorius queried.

"Yes. A white hair on my head. Antonio has a new wrinkle on his forehead and a few white hairs on his temples. Does this mean what I think it means?" Mattia asked.

"Yes. Biologically speaking, all the evidence lends itself to the conclusion that we are no longer immortal," Gregorius's voice sounded more intrigued than anything else. "I was going to do some more tests to be sure before I told everyone, but what I've seen so far is enough for me to believe the change is real." The phone lit with an incoming call.

"Thank you, uncle. Antonio is calling me. I'll talk to you soon," Mattia switched over to Antonio's call.

"Yeah?" Mattia looked pale, and Lissie couldn't imagine the thoughts and feelings running through his mind. She couldn't process any of it—she was in complete shock. Antonio was rubbing his eyes, almost as if he'd been crying, and his voice sounded completely dejected.

"Marcus doesn't have any white hairs or new wrinkles. But I talked to Claudius, and he got a paper cut two days ago and it still hasn't healed," Antonio's stress was palpable.

"Well I just got off the phone with Gregorius. He's been doing tests on his blood from before the trial and after. It's completely different, Antonio. Gregorius believes we're no longer immortal."

"Oh my god," Antonio breathed. "I have to wrap my head around this. I'll talk to you later," the call ended.

Mattia stared down at his phone saying nothing until Lissie couldn't stand the silence any more.

"Mattia. Are you okay?" She didn't know what to do for him—how to comfort him. He looked completely shaken.

"I'm aging. My whole family is aging. We're not... we're not immortal anymore."

SEVENTY-FOUR

THE NEARLY THREE-HOUR flight to Portland was hell for Mattia. Lissie slept the entire time, but Mattia's brain was still in overdrive with the news Gregorius had given him a few hours earlier. He had barely slept in the past forty-eight hours, and his body didn't seem to be dealing with it as well as it had before.

Mortal. He turned the word over and over again in his head. It wasn't that the idea of mortality was disgusting or unwelcome or really negative in any way. Mortality was simply… an impossibility. The idea of dying from old age had never been an idea he had entertained.

He looked at Lissie as she slept, using his shoulder as a pillow, and imagined growing old with her. He had put off thinking about how she would die someday, but it had always been there in the back of his mind. Now, the image of the two of them in the twilight of their lives, holding hands and walking through the streets of New York together burned its way into his mind. It was the image of joy. Contentment. His mood lifted as he thought of how happy he would be going through all the future stages of life with Lissie by his side.

Lissie sat up and stretched, groaning at the stiffness from the awkward way she had slept. When she saw his expression, she immediately perked up.

"What is that look? Did you get news about something while I was asleep?" she asked.

"No," he took her gorgeous face in his hands and brushed his thumbs over her cheeks. "I just realized I get to grow old with you, and the realization was intoxicating." He leaned down and pulled her into a kiss that was probably too intense for a public place, but he didn't care.

"Oh," Lissie breathed, her cheeks flushed from the kiss. "I was thinking about that. We should probably set a date for our wedding."

Mattia searched her face for any hint she was joking, but he found none. She hadn't even wanted to agree to the engagement but had said yes when he proposed (though he suspected she had only agreed to not hurt his feelings).

"You didn't want to get married before though," he didn't know why his mortality would change anything.

"No. It wasn't that I didn't want to get married. I just… I don't know how to explain it. I wanted to pretend you and I were too young to think about getting married. I wanted to ignore the fact that I would get old and die and that you would go on as a widower living with that loss. It was more avoidance of an inevitable future than me not wanting to be married. But now I don't really have any excuse." She kissed him once and pulled back. "And if you want kids, you just have to tell me. I would happily have kids if you wanted to be a dad."

"Honestly, I really want to be selfish with you. Only you. I'll let you know if I change my mind—and of course the same goes for you. But I can't imagine sharing you with anyone," he leaned into another kiss, and Lissie's smile when she pulled away from the kiss and gazed up at him was a vision he would remember forever.

Lissie and Mattia walked into the bank, and she felt her stomach flip with anticipation of what they would find in the safety deposit box. There was little hassle to get into the box—only a quick phone call to Joseph Gonzales at the San Diego branch—and they were inserting the key to see what was inside. Mattia pulled the door open and found a large metal box inside with the label "Trovato Casa" on the side.

"It means 'found house'," Mattia told her as he pulled the box out and shut and locked the door to the safety deposit box. He thanked the man who had helped them, and then Lissie found herself nearly running to keep up with Mattia as they walked toward the nearest hotel. Mattia purchased a night in the hotel, and they immediately went to their room and set the box on the table. Lissie watched as he opened the top and looked inside. There was a note on top with Mattia's name written on the envelope. Lissie read it over Mattia's shoulder.

Mattia,

I'm sorry I never shared this part of my life with you. I always planned to tell you about it, but the timing was never right. Or maybe it was, and I was too afraid father would find out. But if I'm gone, I need you to handle everything for me. Thank you for always being the one person I could rely on no matter what. I can't seem to find any of my usual levity in this moment. Promise me you'll take care of everything. But of course, I know you will.

Samuel

Lissie and Mattia looked at each other, their eyes both glossy. Mattia pulled the first document from the box—it was the paperwork for a trust fund set up for something called the Trovato Casa. The second set of papers were numerous documents from bank accounts for which he had co-signed—Lissie counted at least fifty different accounts.

"What is all this?" Lissie breathed, flipping through the papers to see if there were any similarities in names. There weren't.

"I have no idea," Mattia spread everything out on the ground around him. "But I found a deed for land that was purchased in 1863—right after Oregon joined the US. It's huge piece of land, too. Most of this has been developed. If Samuel did all this development, he could easily have billions sitting in a bank somewhere," Mattia marveled at the map attached to the deed.

"We need to visit the Trovato Casa. Is the address on the trust documentation?" Lissie grabbed the paper and copied the address. "I'm renting a car so we can go out there. We should bring all this stuff with us in case we need it," she helped Mattia put everything back in the box, but it was like he was in a haze.

"It's too much information, Lissie. This is all too much," he muttered as he robotically picked up the box and headed down to the lobby beside Lissie. She knew he would be all right, but finding out your best friend has lived a secret life right beneath your nose and finding out you're no long immortal within a span of a few hours would probably take a while to process.

A few hours later, she was sitting quietly as Mattia drove to the Trovato Casa on the outskirts of Portland. She kept glancing discretely at her bewildered fiancé, but neither of them could find anything to say. When they pulled up to the security gate where the address directed them, she couldn't see anything but land and trees beyond the fence.

A guard who looked like he could have been ex-military exited the small guard house and approached the car.

"Name?" he asked, looking down at a clipboard.

"Mattia and Lissie," she said when Mattia didn't speak up. The man's face shifted to disappointment.

"Do you have the device?" the guard asked, seeming a bit distressed.

Lissie pulled the small electronic box out of her purse and held it out to the guard. He took it and turned it over a few times in his hand before giving it back to her.

"You can follow me," he opened the gate and they followed the guard as he drove a golf cart down a winding road that cut through a thick forest. About ten minutes later, the trees cleared and they were looking at a housing development with homes built in every different size and style. There was a massive ranch-style home that looked like it had been built during the 1800s right in the middle of the development. There was a two-story brick home to the left of it and an Italian-style villa to the right. A few hundred meters to the left there was a modern-style home with windows on every side instead of walls. And up on a little hill even further away was a log cabin. In the other direction, there was a playground, a lane pool, tennis and basketball courts, and a large brick building that resembled a school.

"What is this place?" Lissie whispered, and Mattia shrugged, just as confused as she was.

When they pulled to the front of the oldest home, no less than fifty people rushed out from the various buildings and headed down to greet them. There were children ranging from three years old to adults no younger than eighty. An old woman with olive skin and salt and pepper hair smiled at the guard.

They got out of the car and Mattia grabbed Lissie's hand more tightly than usual.

"Who are our visitors today, Eli?" the old woman asked, her eyes flitting between the guard and her and Mattia.

"This is Mattia and Lissie," he revealed quietly as a hush fell over the whole group. "And they brought the device," Eli's head hung as he let out a sigh. A few children started crying as those closest tried to comfort them. Lissie had no idea what to think.

"Please. *Someone* explain to us what is going on here," Mattia pleaded, unable to remain quiet any longer.

"Of course, Mattia. Come on in and let me tell you about your uncle's project," the woman nodded, her eyes filled with pain, as she led them inside the ranch-style home and into a beautiful sitting room. The walls were covered with photographs of Samuel with different groups of children and adults—and some looked like they could be from the early 1900s.

"My name is Elizabeth," she said, taking a seat and motioning for Lissie and Mattia to do the same.

"I guess I'll start with the history of this place," she glanced around at the photographs on the walls, and Lissie could see the memories behind her eyes.

"Samuel happened upon my great great grandmother—Maria—in Mexico City in 1862. She had just lost her father during the battle with the French, and her mother had died in labor along with the baby when Maria was only four years old. When Samuel found her, she was huddled in a street corner with nothing to eat. He picked her up off the ground, bought her food, found a family willing to take care of her, and paid for all the related expenses. Two years later, he returned to the family to find Maria wasn't being cared for to his standards. So he thanked the family and brought Maria here. Samuel built this house as a sort of refuge. He hired both American and Mexican nannies to care for Maria, and over a few short years, he found dozens of other orphans from all corners of the world who needed a loving home. Each time a new child came from a different county, he hired a new nanny who spoke the child's language. Most of us here speak at least five languages fluently. There are teachers and tutors hired for every age group, with extra tutors brought in for special subjects that anyone expresses interest in. Right now we have all standard classes along with teachers coming in a few times a week to teach ceramics, dance, book binding, comedy and improv. And soon we'll have a new class for advanced sciences—two of the students want to go into medical fields. I'm in charge of arranging all the specialty classes," she told them.

"So where do the kids go when they grow up?" Mattia spoke up, looking around at all the children in the photos.

"Most of them head off to new lives. Samuel requires that every child goes on after their basic schooling to some form of higher education—though that definition is rather broad. He doesn't define higher education only as university. We had three go to beautician school; many of the kids have gone to technical or vocational schools. And many choose to do continuing studies in whatever their chosen field is by doing an internship. I think it was fifteen or twenty years ago now, but we had a boy who did an internship with a watchmaker. How Samuel knew a watchmaker to set that up, I'll never know. But he knows everyone. Or knew, I suppose I should say," her posture sunk noticeably with those words.

"So everyone here was an orphan?" Lissie felt the emotion in her chest trying to escape.

"No, of course not. Those who wanted to stay and teach or tutor the new children were allowed to stay. With so many children coming into the home, many of us found love amongst the others. It's easy to connect with someone who comes from a similar background. There are private family homes all over this property. Many of the parents here send their children to the school on the property but work in town. It's probably the best school in Portland," Elizabeth beamed. "There are somewhere around thirty houses scattered outside of the main grouping here. The gates keep hikers out of the property, but anyone who wants to head out into the world is free to leave any time."

Lissie and Mattia absorbed the information in silence for a few minutes as they looked around at various photographs and handmade trinkets around the room. The room was a little museum to the life Samuel had lived in private, and Lissie could see Mattia was doing his best to hold himself together.

"We have the documents from the safety deposit box," Lissie set the box on the table in front of Elizabeth. "Do you need us to leave these here for you?"

"We'll have our lawyer look over everything, Samuel managed the finances with Joseph down in San Diego. He grew up here too."

Lissie could not find words as she looked around at the photos on the walls. There were famous musicians and politicians in a few of the photos. Samuel had given these children opportunities they could never have had before. Lissie wiped away tears as she looked back at Elizabeth.

"Samuel's accounts will all be transferred to Mattia's name now," Elizabeth announced. "It was in the plan in case something ever happened to him. He knew you would continue his work here. Of course, there's really not much you need to do. Just a few signatures every once in a while. He set up a bank account for every child that comes through here so they have a way to begin their lives once they finish their education. That's what these are for," she held up the co-signed bank account papers they had found in the safety deposit box earlier. "He took himself off the accounts when the children turned eighteen. After that, it was each individual's responsibility to manage their money. He always knew how to make us feel valuable." Her expression was wistful. "If you're willing to continue his work, we should probably introduce you to everyone here."

Mattia met dozens of his uncle's adopted children throughout the day. Some of them approached him immediately for hugs or to ask questions, while others hung back a little and observed. Nearly everyone shed tears for the death of the man who had given them a home.

He could not wrap his head around the idea that Samuel had kept this place a secret from the entire family. *All these years, I thought Samuel was alone. But he had his real family right here.* The people living at Trovato Casa loved and respected Samuel—idolized him even—in a way that none of his actual blood relations had ever done.

By the time he and Lissie left that evening, they had heard dozens of stories of the impact Samuel had made on the lives of the orphans living there.

Once Mattia and Lissie were back in their hotel room that night, he finally began to process what he had seen. "We have to continue his work," he whispered, fighting back the emotion he felt.

"Of course we do. That place is incredible," Lissie's eyes were lit with excitement. "I kept looking for ways to improve the property or education or financial setup, but I honestly could not find a single flaw. I think we just have to keep looking for children who need a good home. That's what Samuel would have wanted."

Mattia nodded his head, a new path for his and Lissie's future forming in his mind.

"Should we tell the rest of the family?" he wondered.

"I was thinking about that earlier. I think Samuel was only concerned about keeping Priest away from this. And now that Priest is gone, I can't see any reason to keep your family in the dark. I know that your mom and dad and brothers would love to visit. They might even have ideas for new classes. Maybe they would be interested in teaching a few in-depth history courses for students who want to go into those fields," Lissie's joy over the possibility of offering something new to the children was palpable.

"I think that's a great idea," Mattia smiled back at her. "Let's call everyone to see who wants to come to Portland to meet Samuel's family."

SEVENTY-FIVE

Castello San Romolo, Two years later

THE FAMILY SAT around the dining table of the great hall, talking cheerfully as they waited for Mattia to call everyone's attention for a toast. They had had to rent extra tables for the occasion, flying everyone from Lissie's family and Samuel's family into Italy to join in the festivities.

Mattia sat next to Lissie at the front of the room and he found difficulty tearing his eyes away from his beautiful wife. *Wife.* He said the word in his mind a few times, trying to get used to the sound of it.

Lissie's brother and parents sat to her left, and Mattia's parents and brothers sat to his right—though Lissie's family was under the impression that Thomas and Caterina were his third brother and sister-in-law. Mattia glanced around the room and felt a sense of completeness amongst those gathered.

He tapped his champagne flute to get everyone's attention and cleared his throat.

"I want to start by thanking you all for coming today. The wedding would not have been the same without each and every one of you joining us for this beautiful occasion. I wasn't sure if Lissie would ever agree to marry me," a murmur of agreement rumbled through the room, "so I'm feeling particularly fortunate today. Lissie, my perfect match, I have never loved you more than I do today. And I must admit, I almost passed out when you walked through the chapel doors in that gown. You have filled a part of my life that I was convinced could never be complete. Before you, my heart was broken and scarred by wounds so old and deep, I was certain it could never be mended. But one "I love you" and you made me whole again. I can't wait to go on more adventures with you. And I cannot wait to grow old with you by my side," he cleared his throat, and more than one tear was shed at the sentiment. "I want everyone to raise a glass to my beautiful bride and our wonderful families who came all this way to celebrate our wedding. Cheers!"

Glasses clanked all over the room, and Lissie and Mattia made their way around the room to greet all their guests.

Lissie sat, watching both her family and Mattia's interact for the first time. She had not realized how much joy she would receive from watching her brother and parents finally meet Mattia's family. She had made excuses to her family for so long, they hadn't truly believed Mattia existed. But after he became mortal, all the barriers to a relationship between them were immediately removed. The first time she took Mattia to meet her parents and brother, the three were enamored.

She glanced at Caterina, who was holding a soundly sleeping Vittoria in her arms, and marveled at how fortunate she was to enter into a family with so much kindness and openness. Mattia wouldn't be the man he was without his incredible family. Her eyes connected with Caterina's, and the smile her mother-in-law flashed was enough to bring her to tears.

"Love you," Caterina mouthed, wiping a tear away as she smiled her pleasure. And Lissie knew there was no other family she would rather be a part of.

Mattia pulled her up from her seat and wrapped his arms around her tightly.

"Hey there, gorgeous," he whispered, his eyes content as they moved over her eyes and lips.

"Hi, husband," she beamed and kissed him deeply.

"I think we're due for our next adventure," he smirked, repeating words he had spoken once before. "Imagine all the places in the world you have ever wanted to visit, and tell me where you would like to go," he tucked a lock of her hair behind her ear.

"Anywhere in the world?" she asked dramatically.

"Anywhere you want."

THE END

A NOTE FROM THE AUTHOR

THIS SERIES has been an absolute joy for me to write. But I feel like now that I've finished writing—and you've finished reading—I can finally share some tidbits about the story that I've been holding onto.

Each part of this series is based on real historical events. I want to challenge you to get online and search any of the people who were assassinated throughout the books—nearly every victim is a real historical figure or related in some way to a real historical figure. Take a look at the places and events surrounding the timeline of the books. Look up the political unrest that was rampant throughout the time frames of each story. You'll find a lot of fascinating articles that might make you wonder if the Family really does exist in our world.

I don't know for sure if I'll ever re-visit the Family. I feel at peace with where I've left them, and I hope you feel closure with each of the men and women you've come to know over the past three books. There *are* more adventures from the Family's past, present, and future, but I think some stories are best left to the imagination.

I have started working on a few new series. I can't make any promises on when they'll be available, but I can assure you, new stories (and new worlds) are in the works!

ACKNOWLEDGEMENTS

FIRST, a massive thank you to my fabulous readers who have waited entirely too long for this book. You are all incredible, and I'm grateful you stuck with me!

Second, thank you always to my husband, Caleb. You're my heart. And you've made this book so much better than it would have been without your help. Thank you for reading every little thing I write... even if you've already read it ten times. You're the best.

Melissa. You're the greatest editor of all editors. Your part in this series has been invaluable, and there's no way I could ever properly thank you for everything you've done.

Traci—I can't thank you enough for proofreading these books for me. Your thoroughness as a proofreader is unmatched. I'm grateful to have you as a part of this process.

Finally, thank you to everyone in my life who has asked time and time again when this book would finally be released. Your insistence kept me focused. And each of you played a role in getting this book released!

KARI NICHOLS

is a romance, historical fiction, and fantasy author. She was inspired to write after moving from Arkansas to the colorful and energetic city of New York. She and her husband now live in France and spend as much time as possible traveling across Europe. Kari's passion for creating art was developed from the time she was a child. Her artistic endeavors have ranged from music composition to photography to fashion design, but writing novels is far and away her favorite artistic outlet. She can often be found wrapped up in her favorite blanket, writing her next novel with a cup of hot tea or coffee in hand.

You can visit her online at

WWW.KARINICHOLS.COM

or on Twitter (@TheKariNichols)

www.ingramcontent.com/pod-product-compliance
Lightning Source LLC
Chambersburg PA
CBHW051332250626
47155CB00007B/2565